CW00402684

To The Victor

Steven Glazer

Published by Steven Glazer, 2023.

TO THE VICTOR

First edition. September 20, 2023.

ISBN: 979-8223839231

Written by Steven Glazer.

Also by Steven Glazer

The Tenth Seat: A Novel
To The Victor

Table of Contents

For my daughter Jordan, her husband Zach,

and my grandsons Kingston and Mason

TABLE OF FIGURES

If you set up the false for the true, if you attempt to blind the eyes of a mighty nation, and to say the Senate of the United States and the House of Representatives of the United States shall put upon their journals as a perpetual memorial to all generations that which they know to be false, and command all to bow down and worship it, your edict will be vain; because history will judge and will know the truth.

—*U.S. Representative George A. Jenks (D – Pennsylvania), speaking to the Electoral Commission as a Congressional objector to the Louisiana electoral vote, February 12, 1877*

* * *

They see nothing wrong in the rule that to the victor belong the spoils of the enemy.

—*Senator William Learned Marcy (D—New York), in an 1832 speech to Congress, referring to his fellow Jacksonian Democrats*

--

PART ONE – THE FOG AFTER WAR

Chapter One—Amid the Ruins

BY EARLY APRIL 1865, after five years of bitter civil war, the southern United States of America lay in ruins. U.S. General Ulysses S. Grant accepted Confederate General Robert E. Lee's surrender of the Army of Northern Virginia at Appomattox Courthouse and allowed Lee's men to return to their homes with their side arms and pack animals. A week later, U.S. General William T. Sherman ran down General Joseph E. Johnston and the tattered remains of the Confederate Army of Tennessee, who surrendered the rest of the Confederate Armies to Sherman on a small farm in Bennett Place, North Carolina. Finally, on June 19, 1865, U.S. Major General Gordon Granger landed Federal troops on the Gulf Coast shore of Galveston Island and declared the quarter-million slaves of Texas to be free.

This end launched a new beginning in the American South – the federal military occupation of the Old Confederacy. Every former Confederate state was placed in one of five Military Districts, each under the control of a Union General and occupied by the Union Army. Union soldiers governed every city and town in each of the eleven secessionist states. The daily lives of Southerners were now brought under the control of Edwin Stanton in Washington, D.C., the Secretary of War in President Abraham Lincoln's cabinet.

With Lincoln's shocking assassination by rebel sympathizer John Wilkes Booth only one week after Lee's surrender, the office of President fell on the shoulders of Vice-President Andrew Johnson, a pro-Union Democrat and former U.S. Senator from Tennessee. True to his roots if not to his oath of office, President Johnson professed sympathy for the South. It was not long before a pitched battle for control of federal reconstruction policy in that region raged between the President and acolytes of Abe Lincoln, led by Secretary Stanton.

The Nation found itself in an unanticipated quandary, almost (but not wholly) as if the South had won the Civil War. The remaining members of the U.S. Congress after the southern senators had left, comprising the so-called "Radical" wing of the Republican Party, were determined to punish all Confederates and establish civil rights for former slaves that were equal in all aspects to the rights of their former masters. President Johnson felt exactly the opposite way. He believed that Lincoln's statement in his second inaugural address, "with malice toward none; with charity for all," set the tone for Union policy toward the South and favored leniency for the former secessionists as well as a slower pace of liberation for African-Americans.

The Thirteenth Amendment to the U.S. Constitution proclaimed that "[n]either slavery nor involuntary servitude, except as a punishment for crime whereof the party shall have been duly convicted, shall exist within the United States, or any place subject to their jurisdiction." It was passed by Congress while Lincoln was alive, and ratified by the then-admitted states of the Union in the first year of President Johnson's term and with his support. Thereafter, Congress passed a Civil Rights bill to enforce the Amendment, but President Johnson vetoed it. The Radical Republicans in Congress overrode the veto, and the bill became law without Johnson's signature in 1866.

The Civil Rights Act of 1866 accorded black Americans citizenship and equal protection under the law. It listed as their civil rights the same rights as white persons "to make and enforce contracts, to sue, be parties and give evidence, to inherit, purchase, lease, sell, hold, and convey real and personal property, and to full and equal benefit of all laws and proceedings for the security of person and property." But it did not include their right to vote, which the framers of the law deemed to be a matter for the states to decide.

President Johnson and others questioned the constitutionality of the Civil Rights Act of 1866. Even with the enactment of the Thirteenth Amendment's abolition of slavery, the Act's conferral of citizenship and "privileges and immunities" on black persons to the same extent as white persons was considered by some to be many steps beyond merely releasing them from bondage. To eliminate this anomaly, the Radical Republican Congress passed the Fourteenth Amendment and sent it to the states for ratification. As a proposed amendment to the Constitution, President Johnson's signature was not required. The necessary number of states ratified it by 1868. Subsequently, the Civil Rights Act was re-enacted in 1870 under the newly-established authority of this Amendment and signed into law by President Johnson's successor, President Ulysses Grant.

With the election of President Grant in 1868, Radical Republicans in Congress saw the need to incorporate African-Americans into the voting electorate in order to insure their continuing power. The Fifteenth Amendment passed Congress in 1869 and was ratified by the states by 1870, prohibiting the denial or abridgment of the right of any citizen to vote "on account of race, color, or previous condition of servitude." Congress accorded itself the power "to enforce this article by appropriate legislation," which entitled (but did not require) the Federal Government to override state efforts to deprive blacks of the franchise.

Upon this new legal landscape, much transpired in the ruined South. "Reconstruction" began in earnest under the supervision and protection of the Union Army. The Census of 1870 now counted each African-American citizen as a "whole person" for the purpose of Congressional apportionment, not as merely "three-fifths of a person" as was the case under slavery. This change enlarged the Congressional representation of former slave states of the South in relation to the non-slave Northern states – again, another sign that maybe the South had won the War after all. Now, the millions of newly-enfranchised black citizens in the South began forming state and local governments of their own under the auspices and protection of the officers of the Military Districts. Newly-elected black Republicans became Governors of southern states and members of southern state legislatures. They also appeared in Washington as members of the U.S. House of Representatives.

Radical Republicans were delighted with these developments, but former Confederate whites were appalled and repelled. To them, the Union was imposing a military dictatorship on the South that upended their way of life. Soon, the South plunged into mayhem as white gangs battled blacks in the streets of Southern cities and towns. By 1898, race rioting had resulted in horrendous massacres. In Wilmington, North Carolina, a mob of two thousand white vigilantes murdered supporters of the biracial city government and succeeded in overthrowing it. Upwards of 300 black people were killed (the number is uncertain), about 50 were run out of town, and scores of black businesses and the city's black newspaper building were set on fire. The same occurred in Atlanta in 1906. Eventually, the carnage organized itself with the rise of the Ku Klux Klan.

Figure 1: "The Lynchings in the United States: Massacre of Negroes in Atlanta." Cover of "Le Petit Journal", 7 October 1906, by unknown author – Bibliothèque Nationale de France (PD)

Chapter Two – The Politics of Collapse

SUCH WAS THE STATE OF HUMANITY in the United States within the first decade after the end of the Civil War. The Confederacy was dead; the Armies had left the fields; but the War dragged on in the People's hearts and minds. The struggles moved from the battlefields to the South's city and village streets, and to the smoke-filled meeting rooms of its political cabals.

At first, under military occupation, Southern life almost returned to its pre-war norms. African-Americans remained repressed and white plantation owners got former slaves to work at their plantations for little or no wages. Military enforcement of the Thirteenth Amendment was spotty; each governing general of a Military District would create his own rules for the governance of society, and the "Black Codes" that had restricted the rights and privileges of both free and enslaved African-Americans before the War's end remained and were even expanded.

Andrew Johnson had no problem with this situation. The Radical Republicans in Congress, however, objected strenuously to the Southerners' failure to enfranchise Blacks, the return of Confederates to local government, and the return of rebel senators and congressmen to Washington to reclaim their seats in the U.S. Capitol. So the Radical Republicans passed four "Reconstruction Acts" over President Johnson's veto with the objective of reorienting the trajectory of the Southern society.

The Reconstruction Acts set preconditions for the re-admission of each rebel state into the Union. They established the five Military Districts under the command of Union generals. They required each former Confederate state to call a constitutional convention and draft a new state constitution, which was to be forwarded to

Congress for approval. They obligated each rebel state to ratify the Fourteenth Amendment to the U.S. Constitution, abolish the Black Codes, and bestow the vote upon every male African-American citizen.

Louisiana, substantially under Union occupation by 1862, was far enough along in its reform to rejoin the Union in that year. After ratifying the Fourteenth Amendment, President Johnson's home state of Tennessee rejoined in 1866, before the Reconstruction Acts were passed. The remaining rebel states followed rapidly: Alabama, Arkansas, Florida, North Carolina, and South Carolina in 1868; Georgia in 1869; Mississippi, Texas, and Virginia in 1870.

Most of the Union occupiers left after the states were re-admitted, and the Military Districts were disbanded. However, mayhem in politics and race relations persisted in some areas, and the troops remained where local Reconstructionist Republican leaders, attempting to form bi-racial governing structures in the face of virulent white opposition, asked them to stay. The white opposition coalesced under the banner of the Democratic Party, and the battles continued in the streets, in the town councils and state legislatures, and at the ballot box.

* * *

Two former rebel states – Florida and Louisiana – posed particular problems.

Florida was one of the least populous states in the Union before the Civil War started. Most of the settled population lived along the northern border with Georgia, Alabama, Mississippi, and Louisiana, whereas Seminole Indians maintained control over the Everglades of the southern peninsula. Plantations covered that northern end, taking advantage of the warm, humid climate that favored cotton fields and orange groves.

The small population of Florida's northern end was about evenly divided between white plantation owners, ranchers, farmers, and tradesmen on the one hand, and black slaves on the other. Florida had been admitted to the Union in 1845 as a slave state, and fifteen years later joined the Confederacy. There were very few military actions in Florida during the Civil War.

Throughout the War, the Confederate government of Florida was led by Governor John Milton. At the end of the war he committed suicide, leaving as his last message to his people that the leaders of the Union Army "have developed a character so odious that death would be preferable to reunion with them."[1] He was succeeded by another Confederate for a month and a half.[2] Then, following the onset of occupation by Union forces, President Johnson appointed a provisional governor for the rest of the year 1865.[3] Thereafter, the newly-formed Military District permitted an election for a governor. But blacks could not vote in that election.

The elected governor served for two and one-half years until Florida was readmitted to the Union in 1868.[4] By then Blacks could vote, and they ensured the next election for governor to Harrison Reed, a Republican, by an overwhelming majority.[5]

Figure 2: Governor Harrison Reed of Florida (PD)

But Governor Reed's single term from mid-1868 until January 1873 was not a peaceful one. His Democratic opponent in the election did not concede for a month, until the Military District commander recognized the new state constitution and the state was re-admitted to the Union. Republicans in the state legislature harassed Governor Reed as much as Democrats. They impeached him twice.

Given his tenuous political position, Governor Reed asked the Union forces to remain in Florida after the date of the state's re-admission to the Union, even though they were supposed to leave by that date. They remained in Florida for eight more years.[6] The entire period was one of political chaos and tumult between the races. Civil control had not yet been re-established.

In 1868, Florida did not conduct a popular vote for President because of its unsettled civil condition. Instead, the Reconstructionist State Legislature, then under Republican control that included black freedmen as delegates, awarded Florida's three electoral votes to General Ulysses S. Grant, the Republican candidate.[7] In 1872, the 33,190 voters of the state overwhelmingly chose President Grant over Horace Greeley by an eight-point margin. Black freedmen voted in overwhelming numbers for Grant, who won what had become all four of the state's electoral votes.[8]

* * *

In contrast to sparsely-populated, rural Florida, the State of Louisiana had a population of 113,418 voters in 1868. New Orleans was the most important port city in the South.[9] Like Florida, however, nearly half of Louisiana's total population of over 700,000 had formerly been enslaved.

Figure 3: Stereotype of Downtown New Orleans, Louisiana, in the 1880s (PD)

Louisiana differed from the rest of the South in that it had a large mixed-race population of *gens de couleur libre*, or "free people of color" in the French language spoken by most persons of that state. It also gained the dubious distinction in 1862 of being the first major Southern city to be conquered by the U.S. Navy and succumbing to Union occupation early in the Civil War.[10] Once occupied, the portion of Louisiana under federal control was admitted to the Union as a state and sent a delegation to Congress.[11]

The Reconstruction Acts combined Louisiana with Texas into the Fifth Military District. In 1868, the Union forces required Louisiana to adopt a new constitution, ratify the Fourteenth Amendment, abolish the Black Codes, and enfranchise freedmen. African-Americans and free people of color began to prosper and become educated in that state.

In the Presidential election of 1868, black people and free people of color could not yet vote. The white voters of Louisiana overwhelmingly chose Democrat Horatio Seymour over Ulysses Grant.[12]By the election of 1872, once the Fourteenth Amendment was in place and blacks and free people of color were enfranchised, the state reversed itself and voted for Grant by an overwhelming margin.[13]

* * *

The neighboring states of Florida and Louisiana, with their large formerly-enslaved populations that nearly equaled the populations of whites, were the epicenter of the post-war turmoil that engulfed the South. Where Reconstructionist Republicans held power, they would pass "loyalty oaths" that required people to swear that they had never aided or even supported the Confederacy; if they did not so swear, they were barred from practicing as lawyers, clergymen or teachers. Where Southern Democrats held power, they would pass laws that segregated railway cars and white vigilantes formed Ku Klux Klan rings to terrorize black citizens. It was in this atmosphere of recrimination and terror that the United States, on the 100th anniversary of its founding, held the Presidential election of 1876 between Republican Rutherford Birchard Hayes and Democrat Samuel Jones Tilden.

Chapter Three – Two State Governors

GOVERNOR RUTHERFORD BIRCHARD HAYES AND GOVERNOR SAMUEL JONES TILDEN were equally distinguished men. Both were governors of populous, industrialized Northern states, Ohio and New York. Both were successful lawyers and strongly supported the abolition of slavery before and during the Civil War. "Rud" Hayes (his childhood nickname rhymed with "mud") was married to Lucy Webb; they lived in Cincinnati and had three children.[14]

Figure 4: Governor Rutherford B. Hayes circa 1870-1880 (PD)

Tilden was eight years older than Hayes. He lived in New York City and was a lifelong bachelor.[15] By the outbreak of the Civil War, Tilden was already forty-seven years old; Hayes was only thirty-eight. Tilden played no military role in the war.

Figure 5: Governor Samuel J. Tilden, circa 1860-1886 (PD)

Hayes enlisted in the Union Army, took part in many battles, was wounded in action several times, and rose through the ranks of the 23rd Ohio Infantry, Kanawha Division, to brevet brigadier general.[16] Of his bravery in battle, Grant later wrote of Hayes that "[h]is conduct on the field was marked by conspicuous gallantry as well as the display of qualities of a higher order than that of mere personal daring."[17]

Tilden grew rich as a railroad lawyer. He got involved in New York state politics, becoming a State Assemblyman in 1845. He became part of the political faction known as the "Barnburners," who sought to preclude slavery from entering the territories won from the war with Mexico in 1848. In that year Tilden helped organize the "Free Soil" Convention, which nominated Martin Van Buren for President. Van Buren lost the election to the Whig candidate, Zachary Taylor.

Tilden opposed the election of Abraham Lincoln in 1860, fearful that his ascent to the Presidency would precipitate a Civil War. He proved to be correct. During the war, Tilden worked for the Democratic nomination and election of Horatio Seymour as governor of New York in 1862, and for the Democratic nomination of General George B. McClellan to run for the Presidency against Lincoln in 1864.

After the Civil War, Tilden broke with William Marcy Tweed of the Tammany Hall machine that controlled Democratic Party politics in New York City. In 1871, he ran for State Assemblyman from New York City's 18th District on a ticket of anti-Tammany Democrats and won election. Immediately thereafter, Tweed was indicted on 120 counts of fraud and other crimes. He left New York, but was found abroad and returned to the state for trial, where he died in prison in 1878.

Assemblyman Tilden's victory against "Boss" Tweed propelled him into the governorship of New York in 1874. He continued to fight corruption, breaking up the "Canal Ring" of politicians who had profited illegally from contracts for the maintenance of the Erie Canal. Tilden's role as a corruption fighter garnered national attention at a time when President Grant's administration was beset by it.

As the Presidential election of 1876 approached, neither Hayes nor Tilden won the nomination of his party on the first ballot. Hayes was chosen by the Republicans on the seventh ballot, overcoming the powerful Senator James G. Blaine of the State of Maine. Tilden won a majority of delegates on the first ballot of the Democratic convention, but fell short of the two-thirds of all delegates required to win the nomination. He won on the second ballot.

So the stage was set for the Presidential election of 1876, the centennial year of the United States, to be a contest between a Civil War hero and a crusading corruption fighter. The Thirteenth, Fourteenth, and Fifteenth Amendments to the Constitution were now the supreme law of the land, according universal suffrage to all adult males of all races and creeds. But the South remained wracked by violence between whites and blacks and occupation by federal troops. The electoral process across the country was not, charitably speaking, a model of honesty and propriety. If the election results turned out to be close, the aftermath would be fraught with denial and controversy.

And so it was.

PART TWO – THE STAGE IS SET

Chapter Four – Boys Become Men

I AM ABRAM STEVENS HEWITT. I was born in 1822 in Haverstraw, a town in upstate New York just north of New York City.[18] I attended Columbia College on a scholarship and graduated from there in 1842.[19] People tell me that I am a real "go-getter."

Figure 6: Abram S. Hewitt, circa 1888 (PD)

After I graduated from Columbia, I studied for and passed the New York Bar exam and became a lawyer.[20] After graduation, though, the grammar school of Columbia College offered me a teaching position. I was made the principal of the mathematics department.[21] I also tutored students and gained a good reputation in that vocation.

One of my tutoring students was a young man named Edward Cooper, who had been one of my classmates at Columbia.[22] Edward is the son of Peter Cooper, the world-famous, wealthy industrialist who founded and built Cooper Union, the free university in the City of New York.[23] I tutored Edward at the Coopers' family home.[24] Edward and I became good friends.

Figure 7: Edward Cooper, date unknown (PD)

After pursuing all of my rigorous work and study in the fall and winter of 1842, I felt utterly worn out. In the spring my eyesight failed from the constant strain of studying and tutoring by candlelight. My doctor suggested that I needed a good rest from all of this activity. Edward offered to take a vacation to Europe with me which he thought would do me a lot of good.[25] I had about one thousand dollars saved up by that time, so we arranged to take a ten-month trip to the Continent.[26]

Being the financial worrier that I am, I didn't trust my finances to be sufficient to carry me through a ten-month trip to Europe. So, to aid me financially in making the trip, I traveled down to Washington City from New York to see if I could land a job with the State Department taking diplomatic dispatches abroad. I arranged lots of letters of recommendation for the purpose. A professor friend of mine recommended me to President John Tyler, and an Episcopal minister I knew, who had officiated at the wedding of Daniel Webster, agreed to write to the President about me.[27] Another acquaintance of mine, a young New York lawyer by the name of Samuel J. Tilden, wrote a letter of recommendation for me to Senator Silas Wright.[28]

Alas, all these efforts were in vain. Getting a job in Washington is not an easy task, even with impeccable recommendations and demonstrated abilities. Nevertheless, I managed to land work as a European correspondent for a New York newspaper, the *New York Democrat*.[29] With gainful employment thus firmly in hand, Edward and I set sail on March 6, 1844.[30]

We had a delightful voyage to Liverpool, England. After landing, Edward and I visited my ancestral home of Penkridge in the midlands of Staffordshire.[31] I looked up some relatives at my father's request. Thereafter, Edward and I traveled to London.[32]

London fascinated me. Edward and I were well-entertained by hosts who had received our letters of introduction. We toured the famous edifices, sat in on the debates in Parliament, and scored occasional sightings of the Queen as we roamed the streets. Unfortunately, however, both Edward and I were struck by the abject squalor of the poor in that city.[33]

In late April 1844, Edward and I departed England for Paris.[34] We viewed the palaces, shops, cafes and museums. At this juncture I paused to write an article for the *Democrat* on "English affairs," which was well-received.[35] We traveled on to Germany, but our funds started to run low despite my savings and correspondent's fee. But we were favored there with good fortune – at the casino of the spa of Baden-Baden, Edward and I enjoyed winning streaks gambling with what meager resources we had left. They extended our journey handsomely.[36]

When summer came, we topped off our trip with a tour of Italy. We visited Venice, Florence, and Rome.[37] From there we booked passage for home on the four-masted schooner *Alabaman*, a ship bound for New York carrying a load of Tuscan marble and other goods.[38] Once on board for home, however, Edward and I nearly met a tragic end.

By October 29, 1844, the *Alabaman* had sailed past Gibraltar on its way from the Mediterranean to the Atlantic. Near the Azores, the ship sailed into a terrible storm. It survived the two-day gale thanks to the excellent seamanship of our captain, but the ship was badly damaged and started taking on water.[39] We barely made it across the ocean almost to the Delaware Bay, but hit another frightening storm just to the east of it. The Captain ordered crew and passengers to man the life-boats and abandon the slowly sinking ship. He joined us in our life-boat and managed to steer it safely through the storm and into the Bay.[40] The other life-boat carrying passengers and crew from the *Alabaman* made it to the Bay as well, and all of us were rescued by a passing ship.[41] The foundering *Alabaman*, along with its cargo and our baggage, was never seen again.

On our trans-Atlantic journey, Edward I saw much and experienced everything – the glories of Europe, the destitution of its poverty, our great good luck at gambling, and our near-disaster at sea. We arrived back in America nearly penniless, but that trip transformed us from boys into men. I had gained new survival skills and a respect for life. Since then, I have often told acquaintances of the faith that I gained on that voyage that my life had been given to me by God in trust and that it was to be employed not for my own pleasure or gain, but for the good of others.[42]

* * *

Thus imbued with a new sense of purpose, the "go-getter" in me dove into new pursuits. I am not one to spend my time idly. Through Edward, who now felt like a brother to me, I grew close to his family, that of the wealthy and famous industrialist and educator, Peter Cooper.

Peter Cooper was an inventor almost from his birth in 1791. He had no formal education; all of his prodigious knowledge of mechanics was self-taught.[43] From a small factory in Hempstead, Long Island, where he made machines for shearing off the rough surface, or "nap," of woolen cloth in order to create a smooth surface on the fabric,[44] Peter made good money from the boom in textile manufacturing that arose in New York and New England during the War of 1812 as a result of the embargo of foreign materials.[45] He married Sarah Bedell of Hempstead in 1813, bought a home there, and patented numerous inventions, including a self-rocking cradle for his first son that even played lullaby music.[46]

Figure 8: Peter Cooper, date unknown (PD)

After the end of the War of 1812 dashed the textile businesses of Cooper and others, he moved his family to New York City, which at the time was growing inexorably northward up Manhattan Island.[47] There he established a grocery store with his father-in-law, but shortly afterward acquired a failing glue factory at Fourth Avenue and Thirty-third Street for a small sum. Through tireless effort, he upgraded the factory's manufacturing process and acquired patents for his glue-making improvements. Cooper then developed a method for making isinglass (a collagenous substance from fish swim bladders that is used in the cooking of gelatins). Now firmly established in the lucrative glue-making and gelatin trade, Peter Cooper became wealthy.[48]

Cooper became even wealthier when he next entered the emerging business of railroading. He built a steam locomotive, the *Tom*

Thumb, and demonstrated it to the builders of the Baltimore & Ohio Railroad at a time when they purchased only British locomotives.[49] Although he failed to convince the railroad owners to buy his steam engine, Cooper went on to build an iron foundry in Manhattan for the manufacture of iron rails and wire.[50]

By the 1840s, when I became his son Edward's tutor and friend, Cooper was wealthy, famous, and endlessly busy.[51] Once Edward and I arrived back in New York from our voyage to Europe, Cooper insisted that his son become engaged in his business and proposed transferring his iron mill in Trenton, New Jersey to Edward. Edward insisted to his father that I be made his partner in the enterprise.[52] Thus began my lucrative career in the iron business.

Figure 9: Typical Iron Foundry, circa 1885 (PD-1996)

It was not long after that I fell in love with Edward's beautiful young sister, Amelia. She attracted many suitors, but warmed most to me as a near member of her family. After a long courtship, we married on April 6, 1855.[53]

By this time, Edward and I had become wealthy men in the iron business. In 1863, Edward married Cornelia Redmond and raised two children.[54] They, being Coopers, mingled with high society in New York, known to all as "The Four Hundred."[55] Amelia and I raised six children and our family lived both in the Cooper home on Lexington Avenue as well as the summer mansion that we built in Ringwood, New Jersey.[56] Both families were happy and prosperous.

Chapter Five – Men Become Statesmen

EDWARD AND I, "GO-GETTERS" THAT WE WERE, soon became engrossed in politics. As our iron business grew, public policy intruded upon it.

Both of us were Democrats, almost by default.[57] The Democratic Party, founded by Thomas Jefferson and named originally the "Democratic-Republican Party," was the party of most young men of the Jacksonian age.[58] Edward and I favored westward expansion, and we were friendly with prominent New York Democrats like Samuel Tilden.[59] As iron businessmen, we favored our country's "Manifest Destiny" – to settle the West – because it meant more railroads, hence more rails and more business for us.

Nonetheless, I voted for the Whig candidate, Zachary Taylor, in the 1848 Presidential election because the Democrats had passed the Walker Tariff two years earlier. That bill lowered from 100 percent to 30 percent the tariff on imported rolled bar-iron that had been paid by our mainly-British competitors.[60] This was a Congressional sop to the railroad interests who bankrolled Democratic politicians, at an enormous cost to our fledgling American iron industry.

Figure 10: Whig Candidates Zachary Taylor and Millard Fillmore, circa 1848 (PD)

One day in the late fall of 1850, Edward and I placed our lunch boxes on a table in our office in the mill and took our lunch break. While we ate, I said to Edward, "We must do whatever we can to restore the iron tariff! The British are killing us in the sale of iron rails to the railroads."

"They are," Edward agreed with me as he munched on his sandwich. "We are creating an essential industry in this country that allows America to sustain itself without needing help from any other country in the world," he added.

I railed on as we spooned our bowls of soup. "That's absolutely right! We create jobs for Americans! We feed, clothe, and house our people! And yet here is our own Congress, taking all that away from their own voters and giving it to the British for almost nothing!

"It is depressing how crassly the Democrats cave in to the bankers of Wall Street and their railroad clients!" I went on. "Not only do their British manipulators monopolize the sale of locomotives, like your father found out to his detriment, but they monopolize trade in the very rails that make up the roads themselves! *That* is why I voted for Zach Taylor and Millard Fillmore instead of Pierce and all the Democrats who were cheering for him."

"I heartily agree with you about the British and the way that the Democrats coddle them, Abram," Edward replied after taking another bite of his sandwich. "But I'm afraid that your lobbying for the Whigs will not bear you much fruit. Your champions, Zach Taylor and Millard Fillmore, have done absolutely nothing to stop the Democrats from holding down tariffs.

"The Democrats use an argument against your Whigs that wins every time," Edward continued. "When we raise iron tariffs on the British, we slow their imports down, but American ironworks then raise their prices to match the British price plus the tariff. We ironworkers just take home as profit what the British pay our government. The only loser is the American consumer.

"The banks and the railroad men have the Whigs in thrall even more than the Democrats," Edward went on. "They want to build railroads as cheaply as possible. What's more, the British can sell their iron below our cost at the drop of a hat. The cotton men in the South, who want to please their British customers as well, are only too happy to support the Democrats in this scheme.

"Look, Abram, it's the Democrats who control the House, and it's highly likely that a Democrat will win the White House in '52," said Edward. "Why, with this gold rush going on in California, the country is desperate to build railroads across the continent and it's begging for England's help. The rich bankers on Wall Street don't give a damn about the ordinary working man."

Edward leaned forward toward me on the table. "You have to look at this thing pragmatically, Abram. Whatever you think of the tariff, come back to the Democrats. Fight the fight from the inside, not the outside. If we side with the Democrats, if we offer them our money and the votes of our workers, they will listen to us eventually. The Whigs are weakening and collapsing anyway. No one knows what they even stand for anymore, except to say 'No!' to every good idea."

"I suppose you're right, Edward," I sighed. "I will think about that."

* * *

Not long after our talk, I had a change of heart and returned to the Democratic fold. I thereafter did my utmost in the Party to organize leaders in the iron industry to lobby Congress to raise the tariff.[61] We banded together, hired a lobbyist, and sent him to Washington. I visited Washington many times myself to talk to political leaders.

They leveled with me, just as Edward had done. They told me that we needed more money, more lobbyists, and newspaper pressure to bring political strength to our cause and influence the politicians to help us.

I implored my fellow ironmasters to contribute funds to the effort. "The politicians must be paid," I exhorted them. "Then they will listen to us."

But by 1852, we had lost the fight. The railroad men and the banks maintained a firm chokehold on the Democrats. In that year, they paid what it took to elect a new Democratic President, Franklin Pierce.

I had all but lost confidence in the direction of the greedy Democratic Party. The Whigs were a washout. I toyed with the idea of joining up with the new Republican Party in 1856. It favored higher tariffs and was more business-oriented. However, its stand on preventing slavery from entering the western territories frightened me and many other Northern industrialists. They were concerned for the destruction of the great slave asset that financially bolstered Southern plantations.

Figure 11: Franklin Pierce, circa 1852 (PD)

John C. Frémont, the Republican candidate for President in 1856, was quite an abolitionist extremist. I was convinced that if he became President, the South would secede from the Union. Despite my compunctions about my own party, I was relieved when James Buchanan emerged victorious and led the Democrats once more to the White House in that election year, forestalling a national catastrophe.[62]

* * *

What followed was a brief but intense burst of business activity that was unparalleled in my young career up to that time.

It was not long before I decided to join the railroad interests rather than beat them over tariffs. I decided to merge the fortunes of my ironworks with those of the railroads. For that purpose, my failed experiences with lobbying in Washington proved to be a valuable lesson in how to go about things properly.

Through my connections with Peter Cooper, I grew close to William H. Osborn, who in 1855 had become President of the Illinois Central Railroad.[63] My ironworks began selling iron rails to the Illinois Central in exchange for its construction bonds. I sold the bonds on the European markets for a tidy profit.[64] Soon I was all-in on the financing of the Dubuque & Pacific Railroad, crossing the huge new state of Iowa as an extension of the Illinois Central.[65]

Politicians now smiled on me in my new capacity as a railroad capitalist. I plunged into letter-writing and visitations to influential men in Congress. They favored my colleagues and me with land grants of over one million acres for the completion of the Dubuque & Pacific line across Iowa. In addition to that, my letters convinced the Illinois and Iowa legislatures to authorize the construction of a bridge over the Mississippi River at Dubuque for the road.[66] Millions in stocks and bonds for construction were readied for flotation on the London markets.[67]

All this railroad activity was matched by even more effort on behalf of my father-in-law for his role in that great international enterprise, the Atlantic Telegraph Cable. Peter Cooper was one of the principal American capitalists supporting the project, which was undertaken by Cyrus W. Field and his brother, lawyer David Dudley Field, with the aid of the great electrician and inventor, Samuel F.B. Morse. A consortium with British financiers also funded the enterprise, which at great cost laid an undersea cable beneath an ocean two miles deep from Ireland to Newfoundland.

I again bombarded politicians in Washington with letters and visits for the funding of a U.S. Navy ship to aid the Atlantic crossing, together with a British Naval vessel. The project was completed in 1858 with an exchange of telegraph messages across the Atlantic between President Buchanan and Queen Victoria.[68]

Alas, after only two months in operation, the telegraph line at the bottom of the ocean went dead. Even before that, my ambitious railroad plans came crashing to an end in the Panic of 1857. And thereafter, our nation plunged headlong into a bloody and devastating Civil War.

Chapter Six – Into the Crucible

TRENTON IRON COMPANY BARELY SURVIVED the brief but terrifying Panic of 1857, but many of our vendors and customers did not. There was simply no money to be had at a reasonable rate of interest from any bank. We paired our workforce to the bone, but managed to hold on to most of our married workmen with wives and children, albeit at reduced wages in order to spread funds more broadly. Pennsylvania iron mills were particularly hard hit.[69]

Mercifully, by the spring of 1858, the Panic was over. Money began to flow again and construction revived. Our capital was depleted but intact. We had a year without profits, but we managed to pay every bill.[70] The Company's reputation was greater and the loyalty of our workmen was stronger for the harrowing experience.

Throughout the financial crisis, I maintained my interest in politics. By the advent of the Democratic National Convention of 1856 that took place in Cincinnati, I had become a close advisor to the winning Democratic candidate for President, James Buchanan. He consulted with me on Cabinet picks. One of my recommendations, Howell Cobb, became Buchanan's Secretary of the Treasury. Subsequently, Cobb graciously consigned government contracts for structural iron to my ironworks.[71]

Alas, in the election of 1860, the Democratic Party was rent between North and South. The Republican Party was ascending and Abraham Lincoln was elected President. South Carolina seceded from the Union and other Southern States quickly followed. The "Confederate States of America" were formed.

I pleaded with Southern customers and vendors to forestall secession. "Secession" was a fantasy, I told them. Our Constitution does not provide for such a thing. Failing that, I advocated for a peaceful separation, or for maintaining the Union and negotiating our differences.

It was no use. The Southerners were adamant that the country must be split in two. Business came to a halt. Debts went unpaid; contracts were broken. Then the Confederates fired on Fort Sumter in Charleston harbor, and the War came.

To my managers at the Trenton ironworks, I wrote the following in a letter:

> *If you have a flag, hoist it over the works, and let it fly there until this contest is ended. If you have no flag, get one, and let it float in the breeze as soon as you can. If you cannot fly a flag ready-made, you can do as some of my people are doing,* make one.[72]

* * *

On January 23, 1862, I received an urgent telegram from General J.W. Ripley of the U.S. Army Ordinance Bureau. "Need thirty mortar-beds to be delivered as quickly as possible to General Grant at Cairo, Illinois. Necessary for imminent movement on Confederate forts."

A telegram from President Lincoln followed quickly thereafter:

> *I am told that you can do things which other men declare to be impossible. General Grant is at Cairo, ready to start on his movement to capture Fort Henry and Fort Donelson. He has the necessary troops and equipment,*

including thirty mortars, but the mortar-beds are lacking. The Chief of Ordinance informs me that nine months will be required to build the mortar-beds, which must be very heavy in order to carry 13-inch mortars now used for the first time. I appeal to you to have these mortar-beds built within thirty days, because otherwise the waters will fall and the expedition cannot proceed. Telegraph what you can do.

A. Lincoln[73]

Mortar-beds are gun carriages for mortars, short wide-mouthed cannons that are useful in fortress sieges for their delivery of large, heavy projectiles to great heights, often up to 45 degrees, at close range. Cannon are poor substitutes for mortars in this situation because they only fire directly ahead.

Mortars were essential for General Grant to take Fort Henry on the Tennessee River and Fort Donelson on the Cumberland River. The two rivers at this point were only eleven miles apart. If the fortresses were taken, the two rivers would serve as water highways into the heart of the Confederacy. General Albert Sidney Johnston's Confederate troops held the forts and were prepared to defend them to the last man.[74]

Figure 12: 13-inch Mortar Mounted on Typical Mortar-bed, circa 1864 (PD)

Mortar-beds are difficult to build. The recoil from a 13-inch mortar at a high angle has a devastating effect – it can shatter ordinary earthworks and concrete foundations, break through the deck of an ordinary vessel, or even sink a ship.[75] The mortar-bed has to be made of several tons of interlacing iron and wood, with roller-rings, recoil-buffers, and slide-frames capable of absorbing the terrific shock of the recoil before it reaches the foundation.[76]

I went to work at once. I ordered the Army's model mortar-bed to be shipped immediately to New York for transport to Trenton. I had templates of its parts made and distributed to four shops for the manufacture of thirty sets. I telegraphed the President to commandeer the chassis rails from Phoenix Iron Works in Pennsylvania to deliver in one week what the owner had said would take four weeks to make. He did so.[77]

The day after we first got the order, I telegraphed General Ripley:

The arrangements for building the mortar-beds will be completed today. One bed per day can be turned out after two weeks required for getting the materials in hand.[78]

I declined all compensation or profit for this business, I told Ripley by letter, "being glad that our knowledge and position can in any way be turned to account in the present crisis of our national existence."[79]

The War Department urged even more speed. A special messenger arrived from Washington on January 28, directing me on behalf of the President to alert the mills "that every human agency shall be employed on the mortar-beds, as the safety of one of our great expeditions may depend upon a delay of even one day."[80]

On February 7, I telegraphed the War Department that "We will ship four mortar-beds tomorrow and four a day afterwards."[81] On February 8, the first trainload with four mortar-beds went west to General Grant. Four more beds each day went on the 10th, 11th, and 12th. Five were shipped on the 14th, and the remaining followed quickly thereafter.[82] We finished the order in three weeks, one week earlier than the War Department had expected.

I heard on February 17th, three days after the last mortar-beds were ready to ship, that Fort Donelson had surrendered to General Grant the previous day with nearly all of its garrison. Fort Henry had fallen ten days earlier.[83] None of our mortar-beds were needed for the victories, but shortly thereafter they proved their worth in the capture of Island No. 10, opening the whole Mississippi as far as Vicksburg.[84]

We had advanced $21,000 for the costs of this project, and on February 14 I wrote to General Ripley for reimbursement. A fortnight passed without payment. Shortly after I had sent that letter, our office was visited by a gentleman who stated that he had heard that we had filed our claim. He offered, for a small fee, to "expedite" it.[85]

I was indignant. Obviously, someone in the War Department was delaying the payment of bills on purpose in order to assist such corruption. In March I wrote to General Ripley; after receiving no answer, I boarded a train to Washington.[86]

I arrived at 1600 Pennsylvania Avenue, N.W., and knocked on the front door. A servant answered. I presented my card. "One moment, sir," he responded.

I had to wait only five minutes. The servant returned. "Come with me, Mr. Hewitt."

We walked to the east side of the mansion, to a stairway to the second floor. A row of gentlemen waited on the steps to see the President. The servant and I climbed the stairs right past them.

Figure 13: East Stairs of White House circa 1892 (Library of Congress)

"Come right in, Mr. Hewitt! Come right in!" said President Lincoln as the servant led me to the office door. Inside the office with the President was the Secretary of War, Edwin Stanton.

President Lincoln paused for a moment and stared at me up and down. He asked me, "Why, you're not such a big fellow after all," he remarked with a Kentucky twang.

I was puzzled. "What did you expect to see, Mr. President?"

"Why, from what they told, me I expected to see a man at least six feet tall!"[87]

"I'm sorry to disappoint you, Mr. President."

"No, no! That's not what I meant," said Mr. Lincoln apologetically. "I am astonished that so small a man could do so great a work in so short a time."[88]

"Why, the same can be said of the late Emperor Napoleon!" I replied. The President and Secretary Stanton laughed heartily.

"What can I do for you, Mr. Hewitt?" the President asked me.

I explained to him about the delay in payment for the mortar-beds and the difficult financial straits in which my company found itself as a result.

Mr. Lincoln's eyebrows lowered and he frowned. "Why, I'm very surprised by that, Mr. Hewitt. Sometimes the Auditor of the Treasury takes a very long time to go over a requisition because of all the corruption that went on with war contracts let by Secretary of War Cameron, before Mr. Stanton here took over. Had you charged any profit in your bill?"

"No, Mr. President. The bill we presented was for costs only."

"In that case, I am truly outraged to learn of this!" Lincoln bellowed. "Speculators make enormous profits from their government contracts and are paid instantly whilst honest men, performing services at cost, have to wait!"

Lincoln turned to Secretary Stanton. "Ed," he said, "Do you suppose that if I should write on Mr. Hewitt's bill, 'Pay this bill now,' the Treasury would make settlement?"

Stanton simply shrugged his shoulders. "I can make some inquiries," he said.

Lincoln called in his secretary and asked for the warrant for my bill. Upon receiving it, the President wrote on the bottom of it, "Pay this bill now. A. Lincoln."

"Now, Mr. Stanton, he said to the Secretary of War, "I want you to do me a service. I am going to trouble you to go to the Treasury Department with Mr. Hewitt and see to it that this bill is sent through the proper channels for immediate payment."[89]

"Of course, Mr. President," the Secretary of War smiled and bowed slightly. "Mr. Hewitt," Stanton then said, turning to me, "would you be so kind as to come along with me?"

We walked together to the Treasury Building, which, conveniently, is right next door to the White House. We spoke to certain officials who labored daily within those "proper channels," and within the next month a Treasury check for $21,000, payable to me, was in my hands.[90]

* * *

The War dragged on for three more arduous years. Men died on the battlefields by the tens of thousands. The Union Army invaded the South at many points, sowing immense destruction every step of the way. Finally, in early 1865, the Confederate capital of Richmond fell and the Confederate government collapsed.

By the end of the Civil War, Cooper, Hewitt & Company's Trenton Iron Works had served the country, not only in the manufacture of mortar-beds, but also in the fabrication of gun metal for arms manufacturers.[91] Thanks to ceaseless efforts by

Edward, my employees, and myself, we led the field of iron and steel production, which was now developing rapidly throughout the world. In the United States, the burgeoning growth of railroads across the West assured the iron and steel industry a bright future. In a speech in 1876 that I gave as the then-President of the American Institute of Mining Engineers, I predicted that "the beginning of the twentieth century, which some among you may hope to see, will witness an annual production of over 40 million tons" of iron. Indeed, by 1900, annual production in the United States, Great Britain, and Germany alone reached 50 million tons.[92]

Figure 14: Trenton Iron Company Just After the Civil War[93]

* * *

By the early 1870s, competition for the manufacture of steel rails rose to great heights. Railroad construction slowed down, and the

Panic of 1873 set in. But the enterprise that Edward and I had built was by this time well-established and capable of withstanding any financial calamity.

I found myself working harder at managing Peter Cooper's many enterprises as Cooper aged and could no longer manage them himself. I was enlisted to run Cooper Union (now a thriving, tuition-free university) and to supervise the New York glue factory that garnered for Peter his original fortune.

As the War ended and our industry started to re-orient itself to peacetime production, I began to feel a personal need for a change of direction. Politics once again peaked my interest. The advent of the administration of then-President Ulysses S. Grant in 1869 brought to Washington a host of new players whose sole interest was not patriotism, but self-aggrandizement. The so-called "Reconstruction Era" of renewal of the Southern economy brought to the Grant Administration sordid excesses following the Civil War. The wrath of indictments and investigations into corrupt activities breathed new life into the Democratic Party. I decided that it was time for me to play a direct role in the upcoming Presidential election of 1876.

PART THREE – THE RACE IS ON!

Chapter Seven – A Call from a Candidate

AS IS WELL-KNOWN, CANDIDATES DO NOT CAMPAIGN publicly for the position of President of the United States. Instead, they appoint supporters to canvass the country in search of votes and campaign funds. The new Governor of the State of New York, my old friend Samuel J. Tilden, called upon me to lead his campaign for President in the election of 1876.

Two years prior, I was elected to Congress in the same election that swept Tilden into the Governor's Mansion. I was chosen to represent the Tenth District of Manhattan, a diverse East-Side district that included both the tony townhouses of Gramercy Park and the run-down tenements of the Lower East Side. Although I was one with the denizens of the wealthy northern part of the district, the far more populous locales of Delancey and Rivington Streets at the southern end furnished me with the most votes. Thanks in part to the frequent misspelling of my first name of "Abram" to "Abraham" on political flyers and newspaper articles, many Lower East Siders thought I was a Jew like themselves![94]

Across the nation, the voters had had quite enough with the corrupt dealings permeating the two terms of the Republican Grant Administration. There was the rank nepotism of Grant's choice of his brother-in-law to run the New Orleans Custom House and collect all bribes and gratuities incident thereto. There was the "spoils system" run by political bosses Roscoe Conkling and Simon Cameron. In the Crédit Mobilier scandal, Union Pacific executives managing Crédit Mobilier of America, the construction company building the Transcontinental Railroad, overbilled the line by $44 million in construction costs that they then pocketed personally and used to bribe politicians for favors.

There were also the crooked dealings of the "Whiskey Ring," in which government agents, politicians, whiskey distillers and distributors conspired to divert tax revenues to bribe Treasury officials to increase profits and evade taxes.[95] After eight years of thievery, voters were open to sweeping the Democrats back into power in the mid-term elections of 1874.

Sam Tilden ran a triumphant campaign for Governor of New York State that year. Although he is personally a quiet, secretive man, he is a master organizer and strategist. He had fought hard in the New York State Assembly against the Tweed Ring, amassing

CALLING IN FRAUDS.
"Step up, Gentlemen. (?) Don't be Bashful!"

Figure 15: Cartoon Lampooning the Corrupt Grant Administration (Bettman/Getty Images)

the evidence that proved essential to sending Tweed and his henchmen to jail. Thereafter, a grateful (not to mention raucous) Democratic State Convention in Syracuse named him their "reform" candidate for the top job in the state.

Across the nation, the election of 1874 was a Democratic landslide. The party swept the U.S. House of Representatives. Including myself, we captured 178 seats nationally to the Republicans' 106. Tilden won the governorship handily.

I called upon him at his Gramercy Park home (now within my Congressional district) the next day. Sam was sitting in an easy chair in his library, surrounded by telegraph tape, files, newspapers, and maps. He was pouring over a chart filled with numbers.

"Well, the tally is not in yet, Sam, but it looks like you took the state by storm," I said to him as I entered his study.

"Oh, my party workers have already reported to me from across the state," he replied. "Guess how much of a majority I won."

"Oh, I'd take anything, Sam!" I laughed.

"How about fifteen thousand?" he said, smiling.

"Quite enough!" I replied.

"Really! How about twenty-five thousand?"

I was incredulous. "Still better," I grinned, shrugging my shoulders and trying to sound blasé.

"The majority will be a little in excess of fifty thousand!" he shouted with joy.

Sure enough, by the official tally a day later, Sam had won by a whopping 50,317 votes.[96]

I'm very glad you stopped in, by the way," Sam said to me as he sat back down in his chair. "I'm sure you've already heard the talk at Tammany Hall. I'm the most likely pick for the run for President in '76."

"That's certainly the scuttlebutt," I replied.

Sam put his hand on my shoulder. "Abram, I need you to be my campaign manager. I can't think of anyone better to do it. It is going to take enormous organizational ability to pull together votes from every state in the Union, and from what I saw of the way you managed to get those enormous mortar-beds built and sent to General Grant for the Fort Henry and Donelson battles, I'm convinced that you have that ability in spades."

"Why, I'm flattered and honored, Sam!" I said. Indeed, I was stunned. I had been out of politics for quite a while, and was only now getting back into it. My election to Congress was surely the product of the tidal wave of reform votes that swept all Democrats into office across the country, not merely that of my genius in politics.

"Then you'll do it? Great!" Sam said, happily assuming that I had said yes. "There's absolutely no need to announce anything to the press now. There is plenty of time to worry about that later. The national convention is still a year and a half away. Just before that, I'll see to it that you're elected Democratic National Committee Chairman. That'll put you in charge.

"'Til then," Sam said, "we must both settle into our present new roles."

"True that," I replied.

Sam turned to the maps and tables lying at his feet on the floor. "We're in great shape in the reconstructed Southern States, and we've even made significant inroads into the Republican strongholds of Wisconsin, Ohio, Pennsylvania, and Massachusetts," he said. "Even if Ohio votes Republican, I'm convinced we'll give them a run for their money there."

"Yes," I said, "and what's also good for you is that, thanks to the repeal of the Three-Fifths Rule, the South will *gain* electoral votes over the North in '76." I was referring to the now-defunct

"Three-Fifths" Rule of the 1789 Constitution, which counted each slave as only three-fifths of a person in the pre-war decennial censuses of the U.S. Now freed by the Thirteenth Amendment, each former slave counted as a *whole* person in the 1870 census. This increase in the population count in the Southern States assured them more Representatives in Congress than they had before, and thus more electors in the Electoral College compared to the North.

"Why, that's right, Abram!" Sam pinched his lower lip calculatingly.

"What's more, Sam," I continued, "Reconstruction governments in the Southern States have assured former slaves that they can vote, so it's a given that none of them are being *deprived* by their states of the right to vote. Hence, no Southern State will have its Congressional seats reduced under the Fourteenth Amendment. So their electoral college votes will remain high. That will undoubtedly favor the Democratic Party in those states, even if most of the blacks in each of those states vote Republican."

By this comment I was referring to Section 2 of the new Fourteenth Amendment, which provided that whenever any male citizen over the age of 21 who inhabited a state was denied the right to vote, "except for participation in rebellion, or other crime," that state's apportionment of seats in the House of Representatives was to be reduced by the proportion that such persons bore to all of the state's male citizens over the age of 21.[97] Since the Democratic Party had the majority of the popular vote in every Southern State, all of the electoral votes of such states was assured to be Democratic. Hence, Democratic politicians surely would not vote for reapportioning Southern Congressional seats even if Black citizens *were* being denied the right to vote there.

"Impressive strategic thinking!" Sam said in a flattering tone. "That's what I like about you, Abram! The lawyer in you understands these Constitutional nuances. That makes you ever more valuable to me in planning for this campaign. We shall make a fine team!"

"Thank you, Sam," I said. "I look forward to helping you, both in Albany and in your eventual conquest of Washington!"

* * *

Figure 16: The Cooper-Hewitt Mansion at 9 Lexington Avenue, New York City, circa 1870 [98]

That afternoon, I returned to my family's home at 9 Lexington Avenue, which my family shared with the Coopers.

As I hung up my hat and coat, I spied Peter in the study that opens to the entry foyer. "Father! I'm glad you're here. I have some wonderful news to share with you!" I said to him.

"Good to see you too, my boy!" Peter replied. "I've got some good news for you too!"

"Oh, really?" I said. "Well, you're the patriarch in this household, Father. You go first."

"The Executive Committee of the National Independent Party has assured me," said Peter," that I am their first choice to be nominated as their candidate for President in '76!"

I was speechless. "You ... you are running for President?" I stammered. "For the Greenbackers?" I said, using the popular name for this newly-formed party.

"Why, yes, my boy! And they are the party of the future!" He said. "The Executive Committee is preparing a declaration of principles with the intent to call a formal founding convention within the year!"

As I stood there silently, Peter went on. "Abram, this war has meant more to the country than just the freeing of the slaves. It has formed an entirely new economy! Gold is no longer the only form of legal tender. Greenbacks replace them!"

"Father," I asked, "What earthly good are little pieces of green paper?"

"We now know, Abram," he said, "that one does not need some kind of rock to bestow value to money. Money can be printed on paper and circulated among the populace, and the only value to it is the "full faith and credit" of the United States Government.

"That is enough for a grocer to sell me bread if I give him a greenback, or for a wheelwright to fix my carriage, or for a lawyer to write my will!" Peter said excitedly. "And the reason why it is good enough for them is that they can then turn around and use the greenback to buy goods and services for themselves!

"But Father," I said back, "if you give a wheelwright a one-dollar greenback note instead of a one-dollar banknote redeemable in gold, he will raise the price on you immediately."

"Yes, of course, Abram," Peter said somewhat testily, "but all that means is that a one-dollar banknote redeemable in gold will buy what one dollar and fifty cents in greenbacks will buy. There is merely a rate of exchange between the two, and it is not that much. Both will buy goods and services; that's all that matters!"

"Father, both Republicans and Democrats don't like greenbacks," I said. "Banknotes are tied to the supply of gold in the market. On can only issue as many banknotes as a bank has gold in sufficient quantities to redeem such notes in gold on any given day. Greenbacks are not subject to such a limit; the Government can issue as many greenbacks as it wants. Pretty soon, runaway inflation sets in and the economy is ruined!"

Peter suddenly straightened up and stared at me. It dawned on him that I was up to something. "What news were you going to give me?" he asked warily.

"That Samuel Tilden has asked me confidentially to be his campaign manager for his own run for the presidency in '76."

"So that's it. Well, so much for *my* asking you to support *me*." Peter turned back to his chair and slumped down in dejection.

"Father," I pulled up a free chair and sat down next to him. "I think that it is admirable of you to help farmers and workingmen in this way. I don't question your desire to see that farm prices are made higher and wages are increased so that those families don't starve this winter. Inflation helps debtors over creditors, I get that. And anyone who is a debtor now would be only too happy to repay his current debts with cheaper money. But if the value of money is not stable, then the banks will simply stop lending altogether. Then what will farmers do?"

"That is the economic fallacy that the Wall Street bankers are telling you, Abram!" Peter said to me, shaking his head. "Bankers can take care of that problem by raising interest rates to make up for the exchange rate between greenbacks and banknotes. They will not stop lending! That's poppycock! Scare talk! They will no more stop lending than cows will stop giving milk! That's the only way that banks make money!"

He certainly had a valid point, I surmised. "Well, Father," I said sadly, "I can tell that you are gung-ho to run for President for the Greenbackers, and so be it. I must be true to myself, and what I have learned in building a successful business is that one must have bankers as friends, not foes. Banks can only give and take hard money, and they must think not only of the Western territories, but also of markets in Europe. They cannot do business in Europe without gold."

Peter stood up slowly from his easy chair, looked sadly at me, rested his hand on my shoulder and said, "Abram, I certainly don't love you any less as a son-in-law, and I applaud how well you have provided for the family. Sam Tilden is wise to snare you for his team." He smiled. "We shall simply have to be careful what we say to one another over the dinner table, eh?"

"I suppose so," I smiled.

Chapter Eight – Strategy

AS AN OUTGROWTH OF THE DEMOCRATIC CONGRESSIONAL VICTORY, I was anointed the Chairman of the Democratic National Committee.[99] It was now my job to steer our party and nominee to victory in the Presidential election of 1876.

My first task was to speak to William Pelton, Sam Tilden's nephew. My objective was to place him in charge of the printing house that we would set up for the publication of Tilden campaign propaganda. I also had to set up suitable campaign headquarters.

On the train trip from St. Louis back to New York, I had ample time to write down the outline of an idea I had while at the New York Convention. We should prepare a "textbook," I thought, to detail everything we wanted to accomplish in the campaign. It would contain the talking points that our speakers would use to spread the Tilden message across the country. It would detail all of the Grant Administration's scandals, Tilden's views on them, and Tilden's record of reform against corruption. It would summarize all of the testimony and findings of all of the investigations conducted in Congress and elsewhere on these scandals.[100] We would distribute the textbook for free to party workers, and send copies to the press to aid in publishing their pro-Tilden editorials.[101]

"I want you to talk to my nephew, Bill Pelton," Sam said. "Bill was a colonel in the Union Army. He was on my team for the Governor's race, and he's a whiz at organizing. We need to set up a print shop that will pump out campaign literature by the hundreds of thousands. Every eligible voter and every newspaper in the country should receive this literature absolutely free. Bill can handle that."

"Great. I'll talk to him," I said. "We also need to educate the campaign workers about our platform and the corruption of the Republicans. I want to put out a textbook on how to do it and distribute it to them."

"That's a good idea," Sam said.

I met with Bill Pelton and columnist A.M. Gibson of the New York *Sun*, a pro-Democratic newspaper, in the study of my home.

"I've found a location at 59 Liberty Street that is ideal for setting up a publishing house and a print shop," Bill told me. "We must rent it, and we must acquire a printing press for our pamphlet operation. But the Governor has not given me any funds to do it."

"No funds? Hm. Strange," I said. "Have you talked to my friend Edward Cooper, the Democratic National Committee Treasurer?"

"Yes. And the Governor hasn't given him any funds either. We're a bit stuck for money."

I could not understand how this could be. Samuel Tilden was one of the richest attorneys in New York. He was up in Albany right now, taking care of state business. But surely, he would have advanced the initial "seed" funds necessary for him to win the election, and I am sure that he had received funds from donors already. Why would Edward not have received them?

"I see," I said. "Well, it doesn't matter. He's good for the money, that I know. I'll advance you the funds for the Liberty Street shop and printing press out of my own pocket until the Committee is up and running and has adequate revenue from contributions to handle all of its expenses."

"That will be fine," Bill replied.

"Now, then," I said, turning to Gibson. "I have a special project for you. Here is the outline I came up with for the creation of a campaign textbook to deliver to our speakers and party workers across the country." I handed him the outline.

"What I'm thinking," I continued, "is to create a book that details all of Sam Tilden's views and accomplishments to date. It is also to document in detail all of the scandals and failings of the Grant Administration with reference to the findings of all of the investigations of all of the shady characters in it. I think you are perfect for the job, Mr. Gibson, because you work for the *Sun* and it is known for its investigative journalism work.

"We should unearth every sordid detail," I told Gibson. "Examine all of the transcripts of all the Committee hearings investigating the Grant scandals. I am sure that they will provide a great deal of ammunition for our speakers and our printing press to give to the voters and the newspapers."

"Sounds like a great plan, Abram," Gibson said. "I'll get right to it. One thing, though; I'll need funds too, and quickly. Acquiring the volumes of material and enlisting readers and writers will be costly."

"All right," I said. "I'll advance funds myself for you too. Both of you gentlemen should prepare budgets and give them to me. I'll forward you what you need."

"Agreed," both said.

Chapter Nine – A Conclave In Another Corner of the Ring

A FEW DAYS LATER, AT DELMONICO'S RESTAURANT on Beaver and South William Streets, yet another conclave gathered for a chat.

Figure 17: Delmonico's Restaurant, circa 1893 (PD)

These were the leaders of the Republican "Stalwarts," as the adherents of "Grantism" were by now being called. It was a small affair. It consisted of Zachariah Chandler, the Senator from Michigan and newly anointed Republican National Committee Chairman; James G. Blaine, Speaker of the U.S. House of

Representatives; Roscoe Conkling, the Senator from New York; and Chester A. Arthur, the Grant-appointed U.S. Customs Collector of the Port of New York.

Delmonico's famous steaks were ordered by each gentleman, courtesy of the Republican Party. Cigars and French wine passed freely around the table. Amid the

Figure 18:Senator Zachariah Chandler (PD-US)

congenial noise and cigar smoke of the crowded restaurant, no one but the participants could see or hear the conversation at this table.

"Grant's thinking of not running for a third term," said Zach Chandler in a low voice. He served as Chairman of the Republican National Committee as well as a Senator.

"Well, that's a relief," muttered Roscoe Conkling. "He's got to take the fall for this mess even if he is clean as a whistle."

Figure 19: Senator Roscoe Conkling (PD)

"Aah, look, I'm not worried," replied Chandler. "We've got great organization in all the states. We've got great speakers to send on the hustings. Best of all, we've got money. Tons of it. If we find the right guy to run, we can make everyone forget about the Grant Administration."

"I am worried about the Southern vote." Thus spoke the mellifluous voice of James Blaine, the most likely front-runner to capture the Republican nomination in lieu of Grant. "We need the Blacks to vote in large numbers, and if the Klan succeeds in scaring them away from the polls, then we can't count on an electoral majority."

"I intend to make that vote happen, Jim," said Chandler. "Black votes do not cost a heck of a lot. If we have to, we can induce county clerks in Reconstructionist local governments to certify Republican votes and electors. The Democrats are strong among the Whites down there, but they are still a disorganized mob of former Confederates who are powerless to turn around those states as long as the Army stays there. Blacks feel safe if armed Union soldiers are standing around the ballot box."

Figure 20: U.S. Customs Commissioner Chester A. Arthur (PD)

"They have to stay in South Carolina, Florida, and Louisiana," said Chet Arthur. "That's 19 electoral votes that we simply cannot give up. That's five percent of the total vote, and with New York in Tilden's camp instead of our own, the rest of the country is pretty evenly split."

"The keys to this election, I believe," said Chandler, "are, first, to make the North forget about the Panic of last year and all the Grant scandals. Without Grant in the picture, that should be much easier. Next, it is to point the finger at the Ku Klux Klan for all the atrocities that it has visited upon the Negro in the South.

"No matter what scandals there were under Grant," Zach said, "we are still the party of Lincoln! The Emancipation Proclamation that Northern boys fought and died for! There is a great deal of sympathy among Northern newspapers and voters for that kind of reasoning. The Democrats are still viewed as a cabal of Copperhead Confederate sympathizers.

"And even with Tilden's reform background, we can tout our stars too. Jim Blaine here supported black suffrage and lowered tariffs as Speaker. He put hard-earned dollars in the pockets of every American."

Blaine smiled, beaming with pride.

"Governor Hayes is a wounded war hero and a paragon of honesty," Chandler lauded the promising Governor of Ohio who was not in the room. "I think that we stand a good chance of convincing the American people that Republicans who had nothing to do with the Grant Administration are upstanding people who will do a good job."

Arthur and Blaine looked down at their feet. Both knew that there were embarrassing skeletons in each other's closet that had not come out yet. They were both worried that those bones might yet haunt the party.

"The most important key," said Conkling, the master of political strategy, "is to demolish Tilden. If he is the Democratic candidate, and that's looking pretty certain right now, I think that we can go after his business dealings. I hear that during the War, they were pretty shady. We have an excellent weapon to use now, especially with Grant still in the White House – the Civil War Income Tax.

We should get Tilden's wartime tax returns from Grant and examine them very closely. I think the public would be very interested in knowing whether he paid his fair share of the financial burden."

"That's an excellent idea, Roscoe," Chandler said. "I'll get somebody on that right away."

* * *

A few days later, Zachariah Chandler met with Governor Hayes and his campaign staffers in the Governor's office in Columbus, Ohio. They, too, were already hard at work preparing for what looked then like Rud's long-shot bid for the Presidency.

"Taxes!" Zachariah said, pounding the table with his fist. "We must look into Tilden's taxes! I am certain that he hasn't paid a dime of his wartime income tax obligation."

"I've already got a *New York Times* reporter looking into it, Secretary Chandler," John Marshall Harlan responded. Harlan was by now an ardent supporter and worker for Rutherford Hayes. "Rumor has it that at some point during the war, Tilden lied about the size of his income on a tax return. We should have no problem tracking down his wartime tax returns from the Commissioner of Internal Revenue and having the *Times* compare it to what else we know about his income and wealth."

"Excellent," Zachariah said. "If Tilden didn't pull his weight on his tax bill, Northern voters will be mighty angry. It'll be further evidence that he didn't support the war effort, just like the rest of his Copperhead cohorts. It will set the entire Union Army against him!

"And Wall Street!" Chandler went on. "Tilden is a notorious stock manipulator. He's financially ruined railroads that Western farmers relied upon to get their produce to Eastern markets!

"John, there's a New York cop that I want you to talk to," Chandler turned to Harlan. "He seems to have a lot of juicy information about Tilden's railroad dealings."

"I'll do that, Mr. Chandler," Harlan replied.

"Goodness!" Governor Hayes spoke up from behind his Governor's desk, apparently perplexed. "I had no idea that Governor Tilden was such a bad man!"

Chandler softened a bit. "Well, Rud," he said, "this is politics. It's war. It's 'no holds barred.' Whatever we can make of the facts as they are, then we must make it. If there are no facts, then we must offer suggestions and reasonable inferences. Tilden is not the direct target of this fight, he's merely an effigy of the Democrats and all that they stand for.

"We must paint the Democrats as slavers, as treasonous Copperheads, as oppressors of Negroes, as apologists for the Confederacy. Tilden has been nominated as their representative to the voters, and damn it, we must tell the voters what that stands for!"

"Won't Tilden respond in kind to these charges?" Hayes asked Chandler.

"That's an interesting question, Governor," said Chandler, as he pulled a cigar out of his vest pocket, cut it and lit it. "Sam Tilden is slow to burn. He doesn't react quickly to attacks on him. He's demonstrated this already in his gubernatorial campaign. So if we make some point about him, whether we've verified it yet or not, he will probably delay his response for much too long. If he does that, he will make himself appear to be guilty as charged. And that's good enough if it arises before the election."

"My goodness!" Rud replied, as if shocked. "You are probably right, Zachariah, but I must say that you charge at this like a bull in a rodeo."

Chandler blew a smoke ring the size of his head from his cigar. "Governor, this is not my first rodeo."

Chapter Ten – And In Yet Another Corner . . .

WHILE THESE CONVERSATIONS WERE GOING ON, a group of distinguished Republican gentlemen were convening a somewhat larger gathering at the posh Fifth Avenue Hotel.

FIFTH AVE. HOTEL. 5ᵀᴴ AVE. COR 23ᴿᴰ ST

Figure 21: Fifth Avenue Hotel, circa 1879 (PD)

The Hotel occupies an entire city block between 23rd and 24th Streets, across the Avenue from the southwest corner of Madison Square. The brick and white-marble structure, opened in 1859, comprises a ground floor of shops and restaurants and five stories of rooms above.

The Hotel's list of guests over the years have included the elite of national and world affairs, including General George B. McClellan and the Prince of Wales. It boasts the first passenger elevator ever built in a hotel in the United States – a "vertical screw railway," powered by a steam engine in the basement, which drives a revolving screw that passes right through the center of the passenger cab to move it up and down in the elevator shaft.[102]

On this day, the meeting's roster was no less stellar. Six *Brahmins* of Liberal Republicanism gathered in one of the Hotel's ornate private dining rooms. The meeting was convened by Henry Adams, a professor of history at Harvard. Carl Schurz, the recently defeated Republican Senator from Missouri, was present. The other attendees

Figure 22: Professor Henry Adams (PD)

were William Cullen Bryant of the *New York Evening Post*; Theodore Dwight Woolsey, the President of Yale; Alexander H. Bullock, the former governor of Massachusetts; and Horace White, editor of the *Chicago Tribune*.[103]

Four years before, these men were part of a vanguard within the Republican Party that called itself the "Liberal Republicans," who sought to defeat President Grant's re-election in 1872 and prevent his corrupt administration from returning to the White House. Senator Schurz founded the Liberal Republican Party in Missouri in 1870.

In addition to the group's disgust with corruption in the federal government (which so far had not implicated Grant himself), Schurz and his supporters felt that slavery was now dead, Reconstruction had completed its work, and Confederate rebels had been successfully driven out of government. It was time, they felt, to restore the

Figure 23: Senator Carl Schurz of Missouri (Boston Public Library)

southern United States to local control and to put an end to the excessive federal hegemony that maintained a large army to prop up unscrupulous carpetbag regimes.

They were also eager to initiate reform of the federal civil service, replacing the "spoils system" of filling federal jobs with political cronies that had lingered on since the Jacksonian era. The Liberal Republicans believed in states' rights, albeit new in form, without involuntary servitude and with universal male suffrage.[104]

Schurz led the Liberal Republicans to an upset election victory over Missouri's corrupt Reconstructionist Republican governor in 1870. By 1872, the Party had grown into a national movement and in that year took on President Grant. Schurz would have been an obvious contender for the party's Presidential nomination, but his birth in Germany prevented him from running for the office that was Constitutionally reserved for "natural-born" citizens. In his place, the party chose Horace Greeley, the editor of the *New York Times*, to run against Grant. The Democrats, equally disgusted with corruption in the Grant administration but too politically weak to defeat Grant at that time, backed the Liberal Republican ticket.[105]

Figure 24: Thomas Nast Cartoon of the 1872 Cincinnati Liberal Republican Convention Listening to Address by Horace Greeley (PD)

Greeley was soundly defeated by Grant. Grant won 352 electoral votes; Greeley only 66. Shortly after the 1872 election, Horace Greeley died.[106]

By 1876, the Liberal Republican Party was only a memory. Most of its associates had returned to the Republican fold, but many of them were determined not to allow the depravities of the Grant administration to go on any longer. They wanted reform, and the success of the reform movement in New York, particularly with the breakup of the Tweed Ring, inspired them to fight within the GOP for new, honest leadership.

* * *

After Professor Henry Adams, the youngest of the group, opened the meeting by thanking all for attending, Senator Schurz spoke first.

"Let me just get a show of hands first," he said. "Who here thinks that it is necessary to get rid of the Grant Administration?"

The hands of all six men rose up.

"I expected as much," Schurz then said. "We cannot let the Republican Party fall victim to corruption and vengefulness again. Corruption now bleeds this country. Vengefulness against our Southern brethren prolongs the violence of the late war."

"I agree, Senator," said William Cullen Bryant, the noted poet and editor of the *Evening Post*. "The Republican Party represents many of the soundest ideas that have been expressed in the last 20 years. Abolition, universal suffrage, sound money and reconciliation with the South are essential to it.

Figure 25: William Cullen Briant, circa 1876 (PD)

"It is what Abraham Lincoln wanted of us when he urged us to 'bind up the nation's wounds,'" Bryant continued. "But with Grant, the worst hucksters in the country have descended on the South and on Washington to feed on the carrion of the war. We must put a stop to it, and change the entire makeup of the Party's current leadership."

"That is true, Mr. Bryant," said Horace White, the editor of the *Chicago Tribune*. "I was a good friend of President Lincoln's, as far back as when I covered him for the *Tribune* in his debates with Stephen Douglas in Illinois. Lincoln was by no means naive, but he would have never stood by and done nothing while these men robbed the public blind."

Figure 26: Horace White (PD)

Turning then to Schurz, White then said, "And Lincoln certainly would not have exacted so much revenge on Confederate soldiers and sympathizers as we now see in many states, including yours, Carl, I am sorry to say."

Schurz showed no emotion. "I am in agreement with you, Horace," Schurz replied. "These demagogues in the Missouri legislature today do not stand for what I stood for when I was campaigning against the Governor. They were demanding oaths of past loyalty to the Union from former Confederates. It was absurd! Of course they could not give it! And for failing to give such oaths, these demagogues barred them from becoming lawyers or teachers or even clergymen! It was unconscionable!"

"I have a different concern about Grant," said Governor Bullock. "I've spent many years fighting slavery. Now that the fight is won, Black men and White men must learn to get along with one another and live in peace. They must both exercise the vote, and vote freely. But the vote cannot be free if the Union Army casts its shadow over the ballot box and intimidates Southerners from voting for candidates that they support. The Army must be removed from the South entirely."

Figure 27: Alexander H. Bullock (PD)

Dean Woolsey of Yale spoke last. "I am no economist, gentlemen," he said, "but I am very concerned about the soundness of the dollar. Yale manages a considerable endowment, as you all well know. But the controversy over the basis for our currency in recent years has caused great consternation with our faculty and alumni. They simply can't figure out what a contribution to the University is worth. This country must give up paper money based on nothing of value and go back to the gold standard."

Figure 28: Theodore Dwight Woolsey (PD)

"Gentlemen," Henry Adams spoke up, "thank you very much for all your thoughts. I want to poll all of you on one more point – whether you view Samuel Tilden to be the man to accomplish the reform that the country needs."

All the men, almost in unison, said "no," shook their heads, or chuckled derisively.

"Don't get me wrong, Henry," Schurz said apologetically. "Samuel Tilden is a good man, and a perfect gentleman," he continued. "He has done great things in New York. He favors hard money. He's against Greenbacks.

"But," Schurz said, leaning forward in his chair, "just because the Democrats backed Greeley in '72 does not mean that we must return the favor and back Tilden in '76. Tilden is not as honest and forthright as Horace Greeley was. He is too much of a wire puller and machine politician.[107]

"Tilden will defer too much to Tammany Hall Democrats," Schurz went on. "Democrats are having a hard time shaking off slavery and are prone to corrupt activities, like their Tweed Ring was. We should stand on our own this time and avoid endorsing him."

"All right," Adams interjected. "It's settled, then. I have a proposal to make to you.

"I propose that we meet again in the spring of '76, before the Republican and Democratic party conventions, to invite to a conference all of the Liberal Republicans who attended the Cincinnati Convention of '72. We can hold it right here in the Hotel. We should decide at that conference which declared candidate we will back for the 1876 election who satisfies our liberal reform goals.

"We certainly erred in 1872 by nominating Horace Greeley, even if the Democrats did join us in that choice," Adams continued. "Greeley put many of them off. As a consequence, many Democrats defected and Grant was re-elected in a landslide. We must avoid letting that happen again. This time, we should examine all the viable candidates out there before we decide which one to favor as the candidate of reform. That way, we can influence the choices of the Democrats or the Republicans without our going a third way and suffering the inevitable result."

"That is a capital idea," said Schurz enthusiastically. "I will be happy to help put such a conference together. I've been thinking about doing this myself for some time, and I'm glad to see that you are interested in doing it, Professor Adams.

"Frankly, to me," Schurz continued, "this reform movement should not have as its aim the mere selection of a favored candidate. Rather, it should be to consider what can be done to prevent the national election in the centennial year of our country from becoming a mere choice of the lesser of two evils."[108]

The others all agreed with Adams and Schurz, and all agreed to help assemble the future conference.

Chapter Eleven – A New Civil War

AS EACH OF THESE DISPARATE GROUPS of politicians and businessmen plotted their moves to capture the White House in 1876 and divert the flow of capitalism down their own gutters, a whole new Civil War was exploding in the South. It had nothing whatsoever to do with what those groups of men were talking about in their posh hotel rooms and over their succulent steaks. This new War was no longer between white slave-owner and white abolitionist; it was now between *former* white master and *former* black slave.

On Christmas Eve in 1865, six former Confederate soldiers got together in Pulaski, Tennessee to form a "social club."[109] The fraternity adopted some rituals of the "Independent Order of the Sons of Malta," a set of fraternal lodges throughout the South that had formed in the mid-1850s among local businessmen and had died out by 1860.[110] A manual of rituals was printed, hooded costumes were adopted, and secret initiation rites were established.[111] It came to be known as the "Kuklux Clan."[112]

This seemingly innocent fraternal order soon morphed into something more sinister, as its "Klaverns" spread throughout the beleaguered South. The Klan originally attracted Confederate veterans, which casts some light on its violent behavior. Eventually, though, the Klan attracted any White man who held some kind of grudge against society:

> a chaotic multitude of anti-Black vigilante groups, disgruntled poor white farmers, wartime guerrilla bands, displaced Democratic politicians, illegal whiskey distillers, coercive moral reformers, sadists, rapists, white

workmen fearful of Black competition, employers trying
to enforce labor discipline, common thieves, neighbors
with decades-old grudges, and even a few freedmen and
white Republicans who allied with Democratic whites
or had criminal agendas of their own.[113]

Murders, burnings, assassinations, lynchings and other havoc soon
spread throughout the South at the hands of Ku Klux Klan
vigilantes. They would target leaders among the freedmen and their
allies – Black activists, White Northern supporters,

Figure 29: Ku Klux Klan in North Carolina, circa 1870 (PD)

Reconstructionist politicians, and others. White supremacy and
the return of government to White control was their objective – at
least, their *stated* one.

And there was vehement resistance, too.

* * *

The Fourth of July of 1876 marked the centennial of the nation's birth. Most of America's focus this holiday was focused on the Centennial Exhibition in Philadelphia, Pennsylvania. On this day, 200,000 visitors toured the Exhibition. The main event was held in Independence Square, before the building in which the Declaration of Independence had been signed. The populace was treated to speeches, concerts, parades, food, drinks, and fireworks.[114]

Almost 700 miles southwest of Philadelphia, in Hamburg, South Carolina, a Fourth of July celebration was also being planned. It was a predominantly Black community across the Savannah River from Augusta, Georgia. Its militia commander was A.L. "Doc" Adams. His chief aide, A.T. Attaway, was a former member of the South Carolina State Legislature during Reconstruction who had advocated the forced removal of the entire white population of the state. The town marshal, James Cook, was known to fine white visitors for various petty offenses, from unauthorized use of the public water fountain to failing to yield the right of way.[115]

On this Fourth of July, the town militia was conducting a close-order drill on the main street. Two White farmers, Thomas Butler and Henry Getzen, passed through the street on their buggy on the way to their homes in Edgefield County. An altercation arose between the farmers who demanded that the drilling militia let them pass through the street, and the militiamen who surrounded the buggy and shouted menacingly at the riders. After some harsh words were exchanged, the militia let the farmers pass.[116]

The next day, Butler's father came to Hamburg to swear out a complaint against Doc Adams for obstructing a public thoroughfare. The town trial judge summoned Adams for questioning, who lost his temper and threatened the judge with bodily harm. He was charged with contempt of court and a hearing was set for the following Saturday.[117]

The Butlers hired former Confederate general Matthew Calbraith Butler (no relation to the plaintiffs) as their attorney for the hearing. A legendary Confederate cavalry hero and state politician, Butler entered Hamburg on the day of the trial accompanied by a White armed escort. Adams, seeing this posse entering into town, holed up with his colleagues in the town armory and refused to appear in court.[118]

Butler, after having waited for Adams to appear in court, crossed the river into Augusta and summoned a band of several hundred Georgians, warning the white populace that "a collision between the whites and blacks was imminent." They joined Butler's other forces and surrounded the Hamburg armory.Soon, gunfire erupted.[119]

More Whites crossed the river from Augusta into Hamburg with a large-caliber cannon. They fired on the armory. Adams and his men attempted to escape out the back. Marshal Cook was shot and killed and several other Hamburg militia members were wounded. Twenty-seven militia members were captured by the White force, and a number of them were shot and killed "while attempting to escape," according to the Whites.[120] Doc Adams managed to escape and attorney Butler left the scene before the murders occurred. One month later, a grand jury indicted seven white men for murder in connection with these deaths, but no one was ever convicted.[121]

The "Hamburg Massacre," as it came to be known, led to the creation of so-called "rifle clubs" throughout South Carolina, whose members wore bright red "bloody shirts" to unify themselves into a paramilitary force.[122] Supportive South Carolina Democrats nominated Wade Hampton for governor. The sitting Reconstructionist governor called upon President Grant to send troops to quell the violence, which Grant did not do. Hampton was unimpressed with Samuel Tilden as the presumptive Democratic candidate for President. "It is not Tilden we are working for," he said. He was working instead for "relief from the rule of the robbers here at home."[123]

* * *

In January 1870, the U.S. Senate convened a committee investigation into Ku Klux Klan atrocities in the South. Fifty-two witnesses were heard and twelve thick volumes of testimony were amassed. Senator Benjamin Franklin Butler wrote and Congress passed the Civil Rights Act of 1871, known as the "Ku Klux Klan Act." President Grant, who signed the bill into law, sent federal troops to nine South Carolina counties where the Klan was refusing to disband. KKK members were rounded up and tried for insurrection in federal court in Columbia, South Carolina. The defendants were fined and incarcerated. Black freedmen served as jurors.[124]

* * *

So was the stage set for the Presidential Election of 1876. In the wake of the carnage of the Civil War, the corruption of the two terms of President Ulysses Grant, the mayhem burning through the South, the Panic of 1873, and calls for government reform at all levels, all adult men of the "re-" United States prepared to go to the polls as free citizens to select electors for the Chief Magistrate of the Union. It is difficult to imagine how a nation so rent by conflict could hold a free and fair election for the highest official in the land.

It didn't.

PART FOUR – GLADIATORS ENTER THE ARENA

Chapter Twelve – The Dance of the Republicans

ON MONDAY, MAY 15, 1876, ONE MONTH before the Republican National Convention got underway in Cincinnati on June 14, Henry Adams' Conference of Liberal Republicans was held at the Fifth Avenue Hotel.[125] Filling the ballroom were over 200 gentlemen, far more than had been invited, but all of whom had attended the Liberal Republican Convention of 1872 that had spurned the renomination of Grant and had unsuccessfully backed the late Horace Greeley for President in that year.

Henry Cabot Lodge, the *ad hoc* secretary of the Conference, read to the gathering the stellar role of invitees who were present.[126] Governor Bullock, the temporary Chairman, appointed a committee of three to report on the organization of the meeting. They presented a report in short order appointing Theodore Woolsey as Conference President, together with several "Vice-Presidents" and "secretaries."[127] President Woolsey then assumed the podium and made a short opening speech.

The podium was then turned over to one of the primary motivators of the group, Carl Schurz, to make a welcoming speech. After a brief word of thanks, the ex-Senator said that he "had not for some time acted with any political party," which he attributed to "his idea [that] the first requisite the man should make of the party he was to act with is that it should be good."[128]

The invitations to this Conference, Schurz continued, were sent to "patriotic men—or men who had the good of the country at heart—men who were willing earnestly to work for its good, without being overridden by party."[129] He called for the adoption of "some definite plan of action" to accomplish this goal. He made a motion to form a five-man committee to make one. President Woolsey, to general consent that he personally should name the committee, then chose Schurz, Parke Godwin, Judge L.F.S. Foster, Dr. John W. Hoyt, and Martin Brimmer.[130]

While that committee deliberated for an hour, other speakers addressed the Conference. The most notable was the speech of Dr. Leonard Bacon, who set the theme for the Liberal Republicans – a return to hard money. Dr. Bacon said, *inter alia:*

> When a party had outlived the issues which were the only justifiable reason for its existence, the tendency to corruption was irresistible. There is an issue before the country today – there was one twenty years ago. They tried to compromise upon it then, because it would hurt the party to go to the country upon it; and they compromised and compromised till the crisis came and one party was swept away. There is a crisis today.
>
> * * *
>
> There is an issue – a moral issue. Shall the country pay its debts? The country is demoralized by bad faith on the part of the Government. [Uncle Sam] has thousands of protested notes all over the country; each note is a lie; it is an intentional fraud, a promise which he has not fulfilled, a pledge which remains unredeemed.
>
> * * *

This must be the question for us: Shall Uncle Sam pay his debts, and if he cannot pay them at once, shall he ask an extension of time, like any other honest man?[131]

Although the plurality of intellectuals at this Conference seemed to congregate around the question of hard money versus soft money rather than the pressing issue of violence that was wracking the South, the real problem that was being tackled by the five-man committee during its hour of deliberation was to find a suitable Presidential candidate to carry the "reform" banner – in reality, the "hard money" banner of the banking interests – to the Republican Convention. They tried to enlist Benjamin Bristow, then President Grant's Secretary of the Treasury and a staunch reformer, but he was interested in the Republican nomination without the "reform" endorsement.[132] Charles Francis Adams, Sr.'s name was brought up, as it unsuccessfully had been in 1872. But he was considered too old and senile to run by now.[133] In the end, the five-member committee failed to name a candidate or, for that matter, even come up with any "plan of action."[134]

The Fifth Avenue Conference of Liberal Republicans was, in short, a bust. Even though it was not his original idea, ex-Senator Schurz took most of the heat in the press for its failure. The *New York Times* complained that in Schurz's "own skill and discretion in the task to which he has been assigned, or has assigned himself, we have no very great degree of confidence."[135] As for the ability of the Liberal Republicans to impart on the Republican Convention their ideas and objectives, or instead to "embarrass those who are seeking them through the aid of the regular Republican organization," that capability "remains to be seen."[136]

* * *

After the Fifth Avenue Conference, the Republican National
Convention convened on Wednesday, June 14, 1876, in the
Cincinnati Exposition Hall, an immense tin-roofed wooden
coliseum. At the end of the year 1875, the House of
Representatives passed by an overwhelming majority a resolution
declaring that the tradition of a two-term presidency begun by
George Washington was important to the country to prevent
dictatorship. Bowing to that pressure, President Grant took
himself out of the running for a third term.[137]

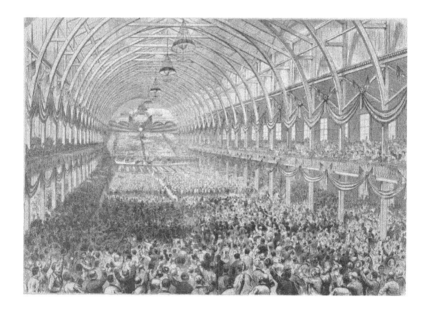

*Figure 30: Republican National Convention of 1876, Cincinnati
Exposition Hall (Courtesy Cornell University Library)*

With Grant now out of the picture, the field was wide open and
seven men stepped into the ring: James G. Blaine, Representative

from Maine and former Speaker of the House; Governor
Rutherford B. Hayes of Ohio; Benjamin Bristow of Kentucky,
Grant's Secretary of the Treasury; Senator Oliver P. Morton of
Indiana; Senator Roscoe Conkling of New York; Governor John F.
Hartranft of Pennsylvania; and U.S. Postmaster General Marshall
Jewell of Connecticut.[138]

Figure 31: James G. Blaine of Maine, circa 1870 (PD)

The clear frontrunner was James Blaine. His support going into
the Convention was more than twice the number of delegates for
the second most-favored candidate, Ben Bristow. The "Blainiacs,"
as they called themselves, adored the man for his debonair style and
charisma.

Blaine possessed a deep voice and a winning way with words; he was a gifted performer. He took care to step gingerly around the pitfalls of the Grant Administration, sometimes supporting the President, sometimes criticizing him. Even Democrats deemed him to be the most effective speaker since Henry Clay.[139]

Carl Schurz and the Liberal Republicans hated Blaine. He had made a great mistake of alienating them, and like-minded reform Democrats, when in January 1876 he viciously attacked a bill before the House from Congressman Samuel J. Randall, a Democrat from Pennsylvania. Congressman Randall's bill sought to grant amnesty to all former Confederates still subject to legal restrictions for insurrection. Blaine offered an amendment to the bill to except Jefferson Davis from the amnesty.[140]

In his speech in favor of his amendment, Blaine went to great lengths to offend House members from the South. He accused the Southerners of wanton abuse of Union prisoners of war. He declared that "Mr. Davis was the author, knowingly, deliberately, guiltily, and willfully, of the gigantic murder and crime at Andersonville," the notorious Confederate prison camp in Georgia. Blaine fumed that "neither the deeds of the Duke of Alva in the Low Countries, nor the massacre of St. Bartholomew's Day, nor the thumb-screws and engines of torture of the Spanish Inquisition, begin to compare in atrocity with the hideous crime of Andersonville."[141] By contrast, Blaine blustered, the Union Army's treatment of its Southern prisoners of war was marked by "an imperishable record of liberality, and large-mindedness, and magnanimity, and mercy."[142]

Furious recriminations followed on the House floor. Body counts from Union and Confederate prison camps were reported and compared; refused prisoner exchanges were recalled; Reconstruction was assailed. Northern newspapers responded to the debate with more venom toward the South. Not surprisingly, Congressman Randall's amnesty bill went down to an ignominious defeat.[143]

This incident preceded the start of the Democratic majority's launch of investigations into the many scandals of the Grant Administration, which occupied much of the time of the First Session of the 44th Congress. In April 1876, a long-simmering scandal implicating Blaine himself broke in the newspapers.

Back in 1871, then-House Speaker Blaine was under financial pressure to support his exorbitant lifestyle. To deal with it, he sold 75 bonds of the Little Rock & Fort Smith Railroad to the Union Pacific Railroad for $64,000 in cash. The bonds, however, were nearly worthless. The transaction was presumed to be a disguised bribe that Union Pacific paid to Blaine for political favors, and that charge was vouched for by the testimony of a government director of the Union Pacific. A packet of letters between Blaine and Little Rock associates were also brought to light that exposed details of the scheme.[144]

Although Blaine came into the convention at Cincinnati as the leading candidate for President, his reputation was badly besmirched by the Little Rock bribery scandal. His ham-handed attempts to prevent disclosure of the packet of incriminating letters before they came out further ruined his chances. The Fifth Avenue Conference took place in the midst of the publicity about this scandal, which fueled further the flames of reform.

* * *

At the end of the first ballot for the nomination for President, James Blaine polled 285 votes, 93 short of the number needed to win. There were nine names still in the race, with Ben Bristow close behind Blaine.[145]

"Ninety-three votes short!" Carl Schurz shouted over the din of the crowded Exposition Hall to Henry Adams, whom he heartily hugged. "And Bristow came in with one-hundred thirteen! Ben holds all the cards!" Schurz gushed.

"It certainly looks that way," Henry Adams happily shouted back. "We must do whatever we can to pull votes away from the others and turn them over to Ben!"

Schurz and Adams were well-provisioned with funds donated by the Fifth Avenue Conference attendees to accomplish this purpose. The Liberal Republicans, although professing "reform," were not above using the tried-and-true tactics of 19th Century politics to accomplish their goals.

Schurz and Adams ran all over the convention hall, hunting down potential delegates for Bristow. When another ballot was taken, it was sure to fail with such a large field of contestants still in play.

Adams found one more delegate for Bristow on the second ballot, a drunk who confessed to Adams, "I'll vote for Blaine before I will vote for a Democrat, but I hate like hell to vote for a man whose shirt tail is covered with shit."[146] He charged Adams $25 in cash for his vote. Regardless of Adam's efforts, however, Blaine picked up eleven more votes in the second round.[147]

"Have you noticed how many locals are milling about outside the Hall with "Hayes for President" buttons on their lapels?" Schurz remarked to Adams after the second ballot.

"Well, this *is* Governor Hayes' state, after all," Adams replied.

"Yes, but Ben Bristow is from just over the Ohio River in Kentucky, and there aren't nearly as many of his supporters as there are Hayes supporters out there," said Schurz.

"I wouldn't be too concerned," Adams said. "Hayes is far behind four other candidates, and holds only Ohio and a handful of delegates in other split states."

"Hm," Schurz replied. "He's an interesting candidate, but not a winner."

On the third ballot, Schurz and Adams picked up seven more votes for Bristow for another $300, and Blaine lost three. Blaine was still eighty-five votes short of the nomination. "It's turning for Bristow!" Adams shouted to a gleeful Schurz.

Meanwhile, Governor Hayes, who had started with 61 votes in the first ballot, had picked up three more in the second and three more in the third. He was now behind five candidates, but was holding Ohio and gaining a handful of delegates each time from around the country.

* * *

Rud Hayes spent the Convention at his Governor's desk in Columbus.[148] Informants from the Convention would come and go continuously with telegraph messages to and from him to Ohio delegates on the Convention floor. It would have been unseemly for any candidate to attend his party's convention.

Hayes had always been a quietly studious overachiever. He entered Kenyon College at the age of sixteen and graduated just three years later, with honors. His wealthy uncle helped him go to Harvard

Law School, after which he opened a practice in Cincinnati. Lucy Webb, Rud's fiancée from his home town of Delaware, Ohio, was attending Wesleyan Female College in Cincinnati at the time.[149]

At the outbreak of the war, Rud joined the local militia unit and secured a commission as a major in the 23rd Ohio Infantry Regiment. He greatly enjoyed army life. Hayes and the 23rd Ohio, under the command of Colonel William S. Rosecrans, a West Point graduate and Mexican War veteran, saw many fierce battles during the war, including Antietam and South Mountain.

Rud was seriously wounded four times during his four-year tour of duty. Promoted to Colonel, he took part in the brutal battles of the Shenandoah Valley campaign of 1864. At Cedar Creek, Hayes helped Major General Phil Sheridan conquer Jubal Early's Confederates, had his horse shot from under him, and took a bullet wound in the head while still maintaining control of his troops.[150]

During his time in the service, Rud's Republican friends back in Cincinnati nominated him for the U.S. House of Representatives. He refused to leave his command to campaign for election; he was elected anyway. In December 1864, Rud was promoted to brigadier general "for gallant and meritorious services in the battles of Opequan, Fisher's Hill, and Cedar Creek."[151]

After the war, Congressman Hayes supported the "radical Republican" policies of Congressman Thaddeus Stevens of Pennsylvania.[152] Following Stevens' lead, Rud adopted even more extreme positions on race and Reconstruction than many of his own constituents held. Stevens hated the South. He opposed re-admitting the Southern States to the Union, commenting: "I do not wish to sit side by side with men whose garments smell of the blood of my kindred."[153]

Figure 32: Congressman Thaddeus Stevens of Pennsylvania (PD)

Rud won re-election to Congress in the Republican landslide of 1866.[154] He continued as a Radical Republican in the Stevens camp. He supported Stevens' harsh Reconstruction Act of 1867, which repudiated the new Southern State governments and replaced them with military districts. Under the Act, the Confederates were disenfranchised, the Southern States were required to draft new constitutions, and had to ratify the Fourteenth Amendment before being re-admitted to the Union.[155]

The Radicals nominated Rud for Governor of Ohio in 1867. He was elected by a razor-thin margin.[156] But a Democratic Legislature had also been elected, and Rud had to moderate his Radicalism in order to get along better with it. He was renominated in 1869, and won along with the election of a Republican Legislature this time.[157]

After his term was up in 1872, Rud withdrew from politics and spent a few years renovating the country estate of Spiegel Grove that he inherited from his wealthy uncle. But the politicians, appreciating his vote-getting prowess, pressured Rud to run for a third term for Governor. The Ohio race of 1875 was tainted by decidedly anti-Catholic Republican rants. Although Rud did not do the same, the prejudice benefitted him among Ohio's large Protestant German population.[158]

Governor Hayes immediately became a favorite among Ohio newspapers for a run for the Presidency. He liked the idea. In January 1876, Ohio Senator John Sherman, brother of Civil War General William Tecumseh Sherman, published an open letter in the press heartily endorsing Hayes for President, saying: "I believe the nomination of Governor Hayes would give us more strength, taking the country at large, than any other man. In General Hayes we will have a candidate for President who can combine greater popular strength and greater assurance of success than any other candidate." With that, the Ohio Republican convention met that March and endorsed Hayes for the nomination.[159]

* * *

"You seem to be everybody's choice for second place," Edward F. Noyes, Rud's campaign manager, telegraphed from the

Convention's telegraph room to Hayes in Columbus. The third ballot had just been cast, still without a winner, in the early afternoon of the Convention's third day.

Rud was not amused. One side of him was the courtly Ohio teetotaler of his wife's class; the other side was the gruff, gutsy brigadier general charging sword-branding rebel soldiers on his horse. His martial side came out in this reply telegram: "HAVE ALREADY TOLD LEADER OF OHIO DELEGATION THAT NO LONGER INTERESTED – IF EVER HAD BEEN – IN VICE PRESIDENTIAL NOMINATION."

Figure 33: Edward F. Noyes of Ohio (Ohio Historical Society)

"Rud is certainly being courted by the big shots, including your boy," Ed said to Stanley Matthews, Bristow's manager, who was in the same room manning the telegraphs.

"We all know, Ed, that Rud can deliver Ohio," Stanley replied, tapping a cigar ash into a tray. "That's a big deal. And Rud is free of scandal and financial taint, thanks to his rich uncle. We all need someone like that on the second line of the ballot. Especially Blaine."

Noyes had welcomed the delegates in a speech on the first day of the Convention. In it, he took a not-too-veiled whack at Blaine: "Give us a man of great purity of private life and an unexceptionable public record, and count on Ohio next November."[160] Even though Noyes did not mention Hayes by name, who but Hayes filled these criteria, one was left to wonder?

"Have you heard Conkling's pitch to Hayes?" Ed said laughingly. "He hired a vaudeville troupe to launch a campaign song with the lyrics, "Conkling and Hayes/Is the ticket that pays!"[161]

"Yeah," Stanley chortled back. "Roscoe is desperate. He's way behind and sinking fast. Although he's ahead of Rutherford right now."

"Stan, come with me to the back room behind the telegraphs. I want to talk to you about something." Ed wheeled his wheelchair (his left leg had been amputated after being wounded in the war) to the back room, and Stanley followed."

Once inside the room, Ed lit a cigar and said, "Stan, I don't mean any offense, but I think you know that Ben Bristow is not going to win the nomination, even with a vote count as big as he has right now. He's nowhere near Blaine. There are plenty of delegates here who owe their livelihoods to Grant, and the ones who support Blaine know that he is the most likely candidate to preserve their positions in life. The Fifth Avenue Conference already cast Bristow aside a month ago. Even if Henry Adams and Carl Schurz manage to pick off a delegate or two with Wall Street money, Ben still won't have the votes to beat Blaine."

"I can't argue with you, Ed," Stanley admitted. "I want Ben to win of course, and so do the Liberal Republicans since they've came up with no alternative. They're not doing enough for Ben. Having Schurz and Adams run around the floor trying to buy delegates is childish, to say the least. I'm afraid it doesn't look good for Ben right now."

"Stan, I'll give it to you straight," Ed said. "If there's anybody who can stop Blaine, it's Rud."

"Ed, stop kidding yourself," Stanley replied. "Morton and Conkling are ahead of Hayes. Morton is ahead of him by a large margin!"

"Morton is a hothead, a dictator, a soft-money man, a stroke victim, and he's riddled with guilt by association with the worst crooks in the Grant Administration," Ed replied. "And Conkling, well, Conkling is Conkling. He's a corrupt and greedy New York boss, as crooked as the Mississippi River. If our party puts up Blaine, Morton, or Conkling, it will go down to a hideous defeat across the entire country. I'm no fan of Sam Tilden, of course, but the chance of one of those mobsters beating Tilden is slim to none."

"Well, what if Hayes goes in the second slot?" said Stanley.

"Hayes can't help any of them there. It's the Presidential candidate that everybody votes for, not the Vice-Presidential candidate," said Ed. "Sure, if Bristow could win the Presidential nomination, then adding Hayes to that ticket afterwards might be a winner against Tilden. But Bristow can't win the Presidential nomination — Blaine has a lock on it right now. So, the way the game is played, we can never get to that dream ticket. At this point, only Hayes as the nominee for President has any chance of stopping Blaine and winning against Tilden in November."

Stanley pondered Ed's rationale for a few seconds. "Ed, I'll tell you what. You make some good points. Why don't we see if we can bring Morton's boys in on this conversation? If all three of us act in concert and test each other's chances for another ballot or two, we'll see which way the wind is blowing and then decide on which one we should all back to take down Blaine."

"Agreed. Let's do that right now," said Ed eagerly.

Within minutes, Ed and Stanley hunted down the Morton handlers on the Convention floor. Stanley's aide-de-camp for the Bristow movement, a young man named John Marshall Harlan, joined them in the same room behind the telegraphs.

All agreed that none of them wanted Blaine at the top of the ticket. Abasing Jeff Davis and having a hand in the railroad briberies were sure to get Blaine pilloried in a series of devastating Thomas Nast cartoons. It was also assumed that Conkling would stay in the race as long as he could stop Blaine and Morton's chances of winning, because he intensely disliked both of them.[162]

They all decided that they would endure another ballot or two in order to test each candidate's individual strengths. If the results stayed the same, then the Morton and Bristow camps would throw their votes to Hayes. It was true that he was the cleanest candidate of all of them, and thus had the best chance of beating Tilden. These votes for Hayes still would not be enough to secure the nomination, but they figured that it just might convince the remaining delegates in that hot, stuffy Exposition Hall to admit that enough was enough and the best path was to rally around Rud.

"John," Ed said to John Harlan, "I hear that you are a heck of a good lawyer. You were even a partner of Ben Bristow's for a little while, I heard. Help us nominate Hayes, and if he wins, I'll see to it that there's a job for you in the new Administration – maybe even a seat on the Supreme Court!"

"That would be wonderful, Mr. Noyes," Harlan said. "I would be honored!"

* * *

The fourth ballot was taken, and everything stayed pretty much the same. Hayes picked up a delegate; Blaine lost one. Bristow picked up four Morton delegates from Texas, and one New York delegate broke from Conkling to join the Bristow camp. Morton and Conkling continued their steady decline. Hartranft of Pennsylvania picked up three delegates from each of the split states of Nevada, Mississippi, and Florida. Washburne stole two Bristow delegates, one from Illinois and one from Georgia.[163]

It looked like Ed and Stanley's deal might just come about.

On the fifth ballot, divided Michigan and North Carolina staged a revolution in the mid-section of the alphabetical state roll-call vote. They united their delegations behind Hayes. Michigan's delegation chairman, casting the state's votes, proclaimed from the floor:

> There is a man in this section of the country who has beaten in succession three Democratic candidates for President in his own state, and we want to give him a chance to beat another Democratic candidate for the presidency in the broader field of the United States. Michigan therefore casts her twenty-two votes for Rutherford B. Hayes of Ohio![164]

North Carolina followed shortly after in the alphabetical order. It switched its nine votes from Blaine to Hayes. Then two Pennsylvania delegates switched from Hartranft to Hayes.[165] Blaine netted six lost votes on the fifth ballot.

The applause throughout the Exposition Hall was deafening. Blaine was going down! The Hayes Train was gathering steam!

Carl Schurz and Henry Adams stood dumbfounded on the floor. Could Hayes be the one to carry the Liberal Republican banner to the White House? "I have to admit," Schurz shouted to Adams against the uproar, "If it will not be Bristow, it might as well be Hayes!"

Simon Cameron of Pennsylvania, facing a revolt in Governor Hartranft's favorite-son camp, ran up to Blaine's managers on the floor. "You can avoid this split in my delegation and get all my state's votes for Blaine if you promise me one thing. Put one of my fellow Pennsylvanians in Blaine's Cabinet."[166]

The Blaine managers scoffed. "Michigan's breaking from Bristow," they told Cameron. "That just means that the lesser candidates are collapsing. Blaine is still 172 votes ahead of Bristow, the largest one of them! Blaine is not going to lose, and he doesn't need Pennsylvania badly enough to promise a Cabinet post to one of your men."

"Oh, hell, suit yourself!" Cameron stuffed his cigar in his mouth and stomped off. Just like that, 53 Pennsylvania votes that might have galvanized the Blaine delegates were laid to waste by Blaine's clueless henchmen.

The sixth ballot was taken. Hayes and Blaine both gained. Now the managers in the two camps lobbied delegates furiously as coalitions among the other candidates fell apart.

Everyone in the Hall knew that the seventh ballot would be decisive. The stomping and yelling and waving of hats shook the floor and moved the fetid air. In alphabetical order, Alabama, Arkansas, Florida, Georgia, and Illinois firmed up the splits in their twenty-four total votes and gave them to Blaine. At the start of the ballot, it looked like Blaine would be coronated. But then the chairman of the Indiana delegation mounted the stage and announced that Oliver Morton had withdrawn his name from consideration, and that Indiana would cast twenty-five votes for Hayes and five for Bristow. With Morton gone, there could now be only one direction, and everyone knew it. The crowd was hushed as the roll-call continued.

Kentucky was next, and John Harlan, its chairman, elated by the prospect of his future Supreme Court nomination, mounted the stage. He announced that Ben Bristow had withdrawn his name from consideration and that all of Kentucky's twenty-four votes would go to Hayes. Pandemonium erupted on the floor and in the rafters from 7,000 spectators.

New York abandoned Conkling, casting 61 votes for Hayes and nine for Blaine. Pennsylvania, miffed by Cameron's brush-off from the Blaine camp, split thirty for Blaine and twenty-eight for Hayes. If Cameron's offer to Blaine had been accepted, the entire Pennsylvania bloc vote would have handed the nomination to Blaine.

At the end of the seventh ballot, Hayes had won the Republican nomination for President by five votes.[167]

* * *

Up in Columbus, the telegraph announced the nomination around 6 p.m. Well-wishers jammed into the Governor's Office to shake Rud's hand. Halfway through the meet-and-greet, Rud turned to his son Webb and said, "My hand is sore with shaking hands."[168]

Figure 34: Congressman William A. Wheeler of New York (PD)

Meanwhile, down in Cincinnati, the Convention wound up its work with a unanimous vote for Congressman William A. Wheeler of New York for the Republican nomination for Vice-President.[169] As the name rattled off the telegraph, Rud turned to Lucy and said, "I'm ashamed to say, who is *Wheeler*?"[170]

Figure 35: Lucy Webb Hayes (PD)

Chapter Thirteen – The Annunciation of the Democrats

"*NOW* WE MUST GET STARTED, ABRAM," said Governor Tilden to me from his easy chair in the study of his Gramercy Park home.

"I am ready, Sam," I replied enthusiastically.

It was a snowy evening in the moderately snowy February of 1876. Hansom cabs trod slowly through two inches of snow on the gas-lit cobblestone streets as more snow kept falling.[171]

The Democratic National Convention had just been scheduled to convene for three days in late June. St. Louis, Missouri was chosen by the Democratic National Committee as the venue. It was a momentous choice, for it would be the first national party convention ever to be held west of the Mississippi River.[172] It would take place nine days after the three-day Republican National Convention in Cincinnati, Ohio.[173]

"Abram, when I vacate the Governor's Mansion to go to the White House, I want you to replace me there."

I did not like that idea, which I had already heard being bandied about at Tammany Hall. I liked being in Congress, and I was intrigued by the thought of securing a Cabinet position in Washington, or maybe even the Speakership of the House of Representatives. Albany would have sidelined me from my national ambitions.

"I will have to think about that, Sam," I replied. " I think that there are some excellent candidates besides me who can fill your shoes in the Governor's Mansion. Bill Dorsheimer of Buffalo is new to this game, but he is a good man and would make an excellent candidate."

"Well, think about it, Abram," said Sam. "Talk to your father-in-law Peter about it, and your friend Edward. Talk to your wife about it. See what they think. The Governorship is a fine stepping stone to high office in Washington, believe me."

"I will definitely let you know, Sam," I said.

* * *

At the Merchants Exchange Building on Third Street between Chestnut and Pine in St. Louis, Missouri, the Democratic National Convention of 1876 got underway on June 27.[174] Five thousand delegates and spectators jammed inside the immense building, the largest indoor structure built in the United States to date.[175] We Democrats felt exultingly confident that, for the first time in 20 years, we would recapture the White House.

Figure 36: 1876 Democratic National Convention, Merchants Exchange Building, St. Louis, Missouri (Cornell University Library)

There were six candidates in the running for the Democratic nomination for President. All but two were present or former governors.[176] There were 738 delegates, of which a vote of two-thirds was required to win the nomination. Of the 492 delegates needed to win, Sam Tilden walked into the Convention with over 400 in his camp.[177]

Figure 37:"Honest" John Kelly of Tammany Hall (PD)

As Tilden's hand-picked manager, I knew that only one person stood in the way of Tilden's nomination – John Kelly, the boss of Tammany Hall. "Honest John," as he was facetiously known, disliked Tilden intensely. He had helped Tilden dispose of William Marcy Tweed, the former boss of Tammany, and then replaced him as boss. But Sam and he had a falling-out afterwards. Now, Kelly stood in the way of my securing the 92 extra delegates necessary for Sam to be the nominee.

I had called upon Kelly before leaving New York for St. Louis to discuss the nomination, and I met him again in St. Louis. We sat down for a conference with several other campaign assistants at a St. Louis hotel conference room on the eve of the Convention.

"Hello, John!" I attempted to greet Boss Kelly cheerfully.

"Abram," was all Kelly said while shaking my hand. There was no smile on his face.

We both sat down at the conference table. I said, "Mr. Kelly, I am sure you know that Governor Tilden has the overwhelming majority of delegates committed to him for the Presidential nomination."

"Yes," was Kelly's curt reply.

"I feel confident that we will pick up the split states of Missouri and North Carolina after Tilden comes out on top of the first ballot," I continued. "I am also confident that the few delegates in the South who are pledged to Governors Hancock and Bayard will switch to Tilden after the first vote. So the second ballot should put Governor Tilden over the top."

"Honest John" did not respond.

"So," I continued, "although I understand that you expect New Jersey, Pennsylvania, and the Midwestern states to hold out for Hendricks and their favorite son candidates, that will not prevent Tilden from taking the nomination on the second ballot. And since Tilden is already assured in New York, your own base is in his camp. So there is no reason for Tammany to hold out against him any longer."

"That depends," Kelly said, "on what Tilden can assure Tammany if and when he becomes President.

"Many people will descend on Washington to meet him and secure federal jobs and other favors," he continued. "Tammany has always been a required endorsement for any such person to obtain jobs and favors from New York governors. Governor Tilden has experienced that himself already.

"This is a new ball game," Kelly said. "The federal bureaucracy is filled with Republicans. Many of them showed up at the Republican Convention and will be campaigning hard for Hayes in order to keep their jobs. When Tilden becomes President, he will have to toss every one of them out. Hundreds of jobs will open up."

Kelly cut and lit a cigar. He offered me one, but I don't smoke. "It will be essential to put loyal Democrats in those jobs in order to make sure that they work for Democratic Presidential nominees in the future, and picking such people is what Tammany does best," he said, leaning into the cigar smoke.

"So, if you want Tammany's endorsement, I'm expecting you and the Governor to listen to me when it comes to federal appointments," Kelly concluded.

"Of course we want Tammany's endorsement, John," I replied. "But when Sam Tilden becomes President, things are going to work differently in Washington. First of all, Sam is committed to a civil service based on merit, not politics. So even if we don't get civil service reform through Congress immediately, we will still examine every candidate for every federal job competitively and on the basis of merit, not on the basis of the endorsement of a political boss. So I can't promise you anything there, John."

Kelly dropped some cigar ashes in a tray. "Abram," he said, "I can assure you that that will not work. When the first Senator walks into Sam's office that he needs to pass a bill on some pet project, you can bet that the Senator will expect some favors, and they usually have a list of candidates that they want the President to put in charge of various customs houses at the ports. It's a business, Abram, and as you and Sam well know from your own personal experience, business works on personal relationships. Money is not always the deciding factor."

"John, I will tell Sam what you told me," I replied. "I will leave it to him to decide about it. But for now, I can tell you that the nomination for President is not in Tammany's control, and I cannot promise you the access you request in return for Tammany's endorsement."

"Then Tammany will remain silent rather than give Tilden an endorsement," Kelly replied, stuck his cigar in his mouth, and stood up, extending his hand.

"It was good talking to you, John," I said as I also stood and shook his hand.

"Honest John" walked out of the room, saying nothing more to me.

* * *

Honest John was not finished with Tilden.

After Senator Francis Kernan took the stage and placed Tilden's name in the running, a deafening cheer erupted from the enormous crowd. While the roar went on, and before Tilden's seconding delegate could reach the stage, Honest John Kelly rushed to the podium.

"Gentlemen!" Kelly roared. "I urge this Convention to nominate Governor Thomas A. Hendricks of Indiana! We cannot win this election from coast to coast by relying on Samuel Tilden! Samuel Tilden will not even carry New York!"

The rousing cheers turned into a chorus of boos. "Three cheers for Tilden!" came from the crowd and "Hip! Hip! Hoorays!" followed. Honest John skulked off the stage.[178]

Unlike the Republican Convention, this crowd made swift work of its choice. On the first ballot, as expected, Tilden garnered 403½ delegate votes. After some shifts of position, the tally was 410½ votes. The closest follower was Hendricks with 140½ votes. Only 81½ votes were left for Tilden to go.[179]

On the second ballot, as I expected, three split states firmed up behind Tilden, one state switched from Hendricks to Tilden, one state switched from Bayard to Tilden, and some states that already had Tilden majorities grew into bigger Tilden majorities. The final count was 534 votes for Tilden, well over the two-thirds majority needed to win.[180] A final vote of 738 made the nomination of Tilden unanimous.[181]

Thomas Hendricks, who had come closest to Tilden in the six-man race, was the only contender and unanimous choice of the Convention for Vice-President.[182] Honest John had at least some consolation to take back to Tammany Hall.

I telegraphed the good news to Governor Tilden. He telegraphed back: COME HOME IMMEDIATELY. NEED YOU HERE TO START THE REAL WORK. It was a characteristic response for a man whose nose is always on the grindstone.

PART FIVE – SPRINT TO THE BALLOT BOX

Chapter Fourteen – Skirmishes

HALF A MONTH AFTER THE DEMOCRATIC CONVENTION, I was present in New York for the opening of the "Samuel J. Tilden for President National Campaign Headquarters" at Everett House, the posh hotel on Union Square in Manhattan.

Figure 38: Stereotype of Everett House Hotel, Union Square, 1860 (Library of Congress)

Shortly thereafter, we opened the "Literary Bureau" at 59 Liberty Street, further downtown. Bill Pelton was placed in charge. A massive printing press was installed in the basement of the building, and the office space was occupied by campaign volunteers (many of whom were New York City and New York State employees on "furlough" for the purpose of helping Governor Tilden) who researched records of Congressional Committee investigations into the Grant Administration.[183]

I returned to Washington on the train to attend the remainder of the session of Congress, which would recess in August. I traveled back up to New York every weekend, however, to supervise efforts at Everett House and the Literary Bureau.[184]

Pelton and his minions at Liberty Street were furiously churning out speeches, newsletters, handbills, and cartoons to be delivered to headquarters staff for distribution to party regulars across the country. Misdoings in the Grant Administration were the most fruitful sources of cannon fodder to fire at the Republicans.

There was the misconduct of our Ambassador to the Court of St. James, Robert Schenck, who was caught hawking bonds in England for the long-defunct Emma Silver Mine; the appointment of John W. Forney to represent the President's Centennial Commission abroad, a lobbyist who had defrauded the Pacific Mail Company; the money-lending wrongdoing of our Ambassador to Peru; the complicity of Grant's private secretary, Orville E. Babcock, in the Whiskey Ring thefts; and Secretary of War William W. Belknap's acceptance of bribes for years from a New York contractor to allow a friend of his wife to share in the profits of an Indian-post tradership.[185]

And that wasn't all. There were also the shady dealings of Grant's brother, Orville, with Indian-post traderships; the Freedmen's Savings Bank failure, whose white officials defrauded black freedmen of their life savings; attempts by Attorney General Pierrepont to influence western district attorneys not to grant immunity from prosecution for informers against the Whiskey Ring; election fraud in New York City; fraud in the New Orleans Custom House; and, of course, James G. Blaine's notorious incident involving his sale of worthless Little Rock & Fort Smith Railroad bonds.[186]

The "Tilden Campaign Textbook" turned out to be 750 pages long.[187] Gibson had taken my brief outline and turned it into a treatise of Grant Administration scandals that was even more extensive than any report of any Congressional Committee investigating them. The documentation was voluminous and exhaustive. Gibson didn't consult Tilden on the preparation of the textbook, nor did he have to. Sam was no expert on the peccadillos of the Grant Administration, and he offered Gibson no advice.[188]

* * *

One of the post-convention duties of each party's Presidential nominee was to write a letter of acceptance to the national committee of the party. As the candidates traditionally did not actively campaign or make speeches, their acceptance letters were the main vehicles of communication to the voters of their philosophies and programs.

Governor Hayes issued his acceptance letter promptly, on July 8. He had the difficult task of embracing reform while distancing himself from the misdeeds and misfeasance of the Grant Administration. He also had to address the distressed South, which was suffering under the pressure of riot and Reconstruction.[189]

In his letter, Hayes endorsed civil service reform and a sound currency, which went over very well in the press.[190] Surprisingly, he promised not to seek a second term as President if elected, which limited his potential governing mandate, to the consternation of many Republican supporters seeking spoils system jobs.[191] Concerning the South, Hayes said nothing about the recent racial incident in Hamburg, South Carolina. He offered only vague generalities about "an intelligent and honest administration of government, which will protect all classes of citizens in their official and private rights," without many specifics. He also signaled a weariness with Reconstruction that was felt by Republican voters in the North as well as Democrats in the South. These words deeply disappointed Reconstructionist Republican Whites working with Blacks in the South to fend off the violence being meted out by the ex-Confederate White vigilantes of the Ku Klux Klan.[192]

Governor Tilden's letter of acceptance was late in coming. Being characteristically a cautious man, he issued his on August 4, almost a month after Hayes' letter.[193] Sam had good cause in his personal life for the delay, however. He had serious health issues for quite some time. He had suffered a stroke in February 1875 that had left him partially paralyzed.[194] He was also mourning the recent passing of his older brother, whose estate had left him with legal and financial burdens.[195] Sam, like Governor Hayes, also had to maneuver through treacherous political territory in his own party, justifying his hard-money position to Democratic farm voters displaying inflationary Greenback fervor.[196]

Tilden wrote a rather pedantic letter on the money problem, offering a treatise on financial history that most voters found too long to read and somewhat over their heads.[197] He offered lukewarm support for federal civil service reform and excoriated the excesses of the Grant Administration.[198] On the South, Sam was particularly equivocal. Anxious not to invite criticism from Republicans about Northern Democratic sentiments purportedly favoring the Confederate cause, he decried Reconstructionist "systematic and insupportable misgovernment imposed on the states of the South," and tied violent conditions there to the general "distress in business" that affected the country as a whole.[199] Like Hayes, Sam said nothing about Hamburg. Instead, he dwelled on an appeal to "the moral influence of every good citizen to establish a cordial fraternity and good-will among citizens, whatever their race or color," and pledged to enforce the laws and protect "every political and personal right" of all citizens.[200]

The Northern press savaged Tilden's 4,400-word letter. In *Harper's Weekly*, Thomas Nast portrayed Tilden over a pile of Black bodies from Hamburg against a wall of racist posters, with Tilden standing in front looking apologetic and stating, "It is not I, but the idea of reform which I represent."[201]

THE HAMBURG RIOT, JULY, 1876

Figure 39: Thomas Nast Cartoon Blaming Tilden for the Hamburg Massacre (PD)

* * *

When I returned to New York following the August Congressional recess, I was faced with a conundrum – New York Democrats were calling for me to run for Governor to succeed Tilden.[202] They were impressed with the job I was doing for the Tilden campaign. The New York *World* and the labor unions were endorsing the idea.[203] Tilden had asked me to consider it back when he won the governor's race. I had too much to do to even devote time to thinking about it.

By the end of August, however, I sent a letter to Sam bowing out of the governor's race in favor of another Democratic candidate:

> I have been very much concerned at the suggestion of my name for Governor, because on the one hand I do not wish the nomination, and on the other I am so anxious to do the best thing to secure the election that I fear to refuse to do what your friends desire and deem best. ... While therefore I have been and am willing to make any necessary sacrifice of personal feeling to ensure success, I do not feel this sacrifice is either necessary or advantageous.[204]

With that bullet safely dodged, I got down to campaign business with my staff at Everett House, lining up speakers to stump the country for Sam. We enlisted a stellar cast: Senator Thomas F. Bayard; Senator Allen G. Thurman; author Charles Francis Adams, Jr.; abolitionist and Ambassador to Russia Cassius M. Clay; Vice-Presidential nominee Thomas A. Hendricks; and many other Democratic luminaries. We had German speakers to send to the Middle West and Negro speakers to send to southern Illinois and

Indiana. We had Swedish, Bohemian, and French campaigners.[205]

Everett House became a beehive of excitement and activity among New York Democrats. Leaders from upstate and downstate congregated there to discuss campaign strategy, socialize, and even bet on the race. Everyone was enthusiastic, predicting a "Tilden wave" across the country.[206]

Curiously, one person whom we didn't see much of at the outset was Sam Tilden himself. He remained in Albany, busying himself with official state business, or so he said. Those who were able to worm their way into his office for an interview usually came out unimpressed. He seemed to many to be tardy, vacillating, and excessively conservative.[207]

We were gratified to hear, however, that Governor Hayes was not scoring more favorable points. *The Nation* reported:

> No ingenuity of interviewers was sufficient to extract from [Hayes] any expressions of opinion on any topic having the remotest bearing on the Presidential contest. He recognized nothing, and neither authorized nor repudiated anybody. According to the newspaper accounts he would hardly go further in political discussion than to accede to the proposition that there was a republican form of government and that this was the hundredth year of the national government.[208]

What we missed most from Sam Tilden's lack of presence at Everett House and Liberty Street was not his advice and counsel – it was his money. Ed Cooper, the Treasurer of the National Committee, came to see me on August 26 while I was handling ten things at once in that frenetic month.

"I have bad news, Abram," Ed said. "At the present time, the National Committee has only $150,000 to disburse for the expenses of the campaign."

"Oh, my God," I replied. "I have already tapped a good deal of my personal funds to cover expenses for printing, train tickets and hotel bills for speakers from all over the country. I'm ashamed to say that I have even dunned your father for money, even though he's an opposing Presidential candidate!"

"You needn't concern yourself with that," Ed said. "My father's attitude is that he would be a Democrat if he were not campaigning for the Greenbacks, and he is not so foolish as to think that the Greenbacks can actually beat the Republicans and the Democrats. He is more than happy to ensure his influence in the future Tilden Administration by donating to the Tilden campaign."

"Yes, well," I said grumpily, "he may very well want to donate some money to the Hayes campaign as well, for at this rate our presses will stop and our speakers will be kicked off trains and out of hotels if Sam doesn't fork over some of his millions toward his own election!"

"I couldn't agree more," Ed replied. "One thing about Sam is really troubling me, Abram. It's my understanding that many campaign donations have been handed to Sam directly. *He has not turned over those funds to me.* Isn't it his responsibility to do so?"

"I would think so, Ed," I said. I was becoming alarmed. Could it be that Samuel Tilden, a millionaire in his own right and the purported "great reformer," was corruptly pocketing large sums from donors that were legitimately supposed to be given to the campaign to defray its expenses?

"Well, we must confront him at the first opportunity when he comes down here from Albany next," Ed said. "I think he owes us an explanation, as well as cash."

"You're right, Ed. I'm with you on that."

"Mr. Hewitt?" said a young campaign staffer who walked up to me.

I turned to him. "Yes?"

"I'm afraid I have some bad news, sir," he said to me. Oh, great, I thought; more bad news! He handed me that day's edition of the *New York Times* and pointed to the headline of the lead story at the top of the leftmost column of the first page:[209]

TILDEN BECOME ODIOUS.

DETESTATION OF HIM IN ALBANY.

THE IMPRESSION MADE BY HIM CONTRASTED

WITH THAT MADE BY GOV. MORGAN

WHILE AT THE CAPITAL – THE DIFFER-

ENCE BETWEEN A MAN OF HONOR AND

SINCERITY AND ONE DESTITUTE OF THEM

– TILDEN'S TREACHERY TO HIS DEMO-

CRATIC FRIENDS.

"Oh. My. God," Ed and I said in unison.

"I'm afraid it gets worse, sir," the staffer said with a frown. He opened the paper to page five, and pointed to the principal story in the leftmost column of that page:[210]

MR. TILDEN'S FALSE OATH.

FACTS WHICH HE CANNOT EXPLAIN.

HIS INCOME-TAX FRAUD – TEXT OF THE

OATHS HE MADE ON DIFFERENT OC-

CASIONS – HIS GUILT FULLY ESTAB-

LISHED BY THE OFFICIAL RECORDS –

CUMULATIVE EVIDENCE AGAINST HIM.

"Oh. My. God," Ed and I simultaneously said again.

Chapter Fifteen – Damage Control

ED AND I CAUGHT THE 6:30 P.M. NEW YORK CENTRAL train to Albany out of the Grand Central Depot on 42nd Street. We arrived in the New York State Capital around midnight. We rode a wagon into town and booked rooms for the night at a hotel near the State Capitol Building.

Figure 40: New York State Capitol in 1876 (PD)

The next morning, we proceeded without invitations to the Governor's Office in the State Capitol Building. We announced ourselves to Governor Tilden's secretary, who ushered us into his office immediately. Sam was sitting at his desk, pouring over some documents. He looked up.

"Gentlemen!" Sam greeted us brightly. "How good to see you! What brings you here?"

"Good morning, Governor," I replied. "Ed Cooper and I have a few matters to discuss with you of the greatest urgency, which is why we took the liberty of travelling up from New York City to see you on no notice today. Indeed, we had no notice of the matters ourselves until yesterday."

"This is about the articles in the *New York Times*, isn't it?" he asked as his smile faded.

"Yes, in part," I said. "But before we get to that, there is the matter of the National Committee's perilous lack of funding on your part. The National Committee has $150,000 left in the bank to devote to your campaign. Three more months are left to go. We are now funding numerous speakers all over the United States to bring your message to the people. Along with that, we have printed thousands of copies of speeches and pamphlets to distribute to our volunteers, workers and voters.

"To date, I have personally donated thousands of dollars of my own money to defray the expenses of the campaign," I told Sam. "Even my father-in-law, Peter Cooper, has donated funds to your campaign despite the fact that he is one of your opponents in the race. He is hoping to stay in your good graces in the likelihood that you will be the one who wins the election.

"I am also aware," I continued, "that considerable sums have been donated to you personally for your campaign. Those funds are needed urgently by the National Committee. Surely you do not need those funds yourself. We need you to account to us for those amounts, and to ask you to contribute what we need to defray the expenses of the campaign as soon as practicable."

Tilden stood up from his desk and walked over to the fireplace behind him. He stared out the window for a half-minute. Then he turned back to Ed and me.

"I was unaware that the funds that I have received directly from donors have been so urgently needed by the Committee," he said. "From what I could tell from here, the Committee was doing a superlative job of getting up to speed and canvassing all state Democratic chairmen to identify all the voters in their states. I found that to be essential when we won the Governorship. Are you telling me that there are not enough funds in the party Treasury to continue the fight for the next three months?"

"There are not, Governor," Ed, the Treasurer, replied. "The National Committee expended enormous sums to hold the National Convention, and so it started the campaign very low on funds. I believe that everyone assumed that you would designate a large amount of your own personal wealth to this campaign, since you are the one to gain the most from it."

"Oh, I beg to differ, Mr. Cooper," Sam replied, somewhat testily. "This is not a campaign for myself alone. This is a campaign for the people, who demand reform in Washington! It is they, not I, who must support this campaign with the funds it needs to continue. If they are unwilling to do it, or if the Party is unwilling to raise the funds necessary to do so, then there is no campaign at all!"

Ed and I sat there, speechless. We had before us one of the wealthiest men in America, justifying to us why his parsimoniousness was in the best interest of his own political campaign!

"Governor," I said at last, adopting a less confrontational tone, "I understand fully how you feel about devoting personal funds to a campaign that is meant for the good of the people. It is an enormous personal responsibility on your part. You are certainly right that if the people want the reform that you are prepared to give, then they must be the ones to support the campaign to make that happen.

"But the fact of the matter is that one cannot win a political campaign without spending money himself. I have realized that myself, and I have freely advanced funds out of my own pocket to the campaign because it needs money immediately to continue, and I believe in you and in your message.

"Let us start with the donor funds that you have received personally," I continued, somewhat pleadingly. "Can you provide us with those funds as soon as possible so that we may defray outstanding expenses and expenses that are yet to come? I am sure that that money will go a long way to make the campaign a success well before we have to ask you to advance funds out of your own pocket."

Sam looked down at his shoes and thought for a few seconds more. He then looked at me. "Abram, I appreciate everything you have said and I am deeply persuaded by it. Allow me to prepare an accounting of the funds that have been donated to me. I will get that to you by messenger within the week. You may then use that accounting to prepare a budget of the expenses that you foresee for the remainder of the campaign, and I will disburse these funds over that time period as you require."

Ed broke in at this point. "That is acceptable to me, Governor. We can accept funding on a rolling basis in accordance with a budget that we send to you and you have approved."

"I'm glad that we have had this conversation, Governor," I said. "Now I'd like to turn to the other matters that have prompted us to travel up to Albany. As you know, the two *New York Times* articles in yesterday's paper are very unflattering toward you. One is somewhat superfluous and petty, I think. It proclaims that you are unpopular among the people of the Albany area and have maintained an aloof and unfriendly attitude toward them during your time here."

"That is rubbish!" Sam shot back. "Allow me to explain the situation to you. Here in the Upper Hudson Valley, there is an upper class of old families, direct descendants of the Dutch settlers of New Netherland and the early English settlers after the Duke of York conquered the colony. They own immense homes on large estates overlooking the Hudson River on both sides. The views of the Valley from these homes are stunning.

"When I moved up here to occupy the Governors' Mansion in town," Sam continued, "I found that it was not to my liking. I felt that it was not suitable for the social gatherings and political events that I was accustomed to holding in my home in Manhattan, and certainly not suitable for the social and political gatherings that must be conducted by the Governor of this state. I decided, therefore, to live elsewhere.

"I found a mansion in Albany that I felt was suitable for my needs. I rented it for the sum of $10,000 per year. I made it publicly clear that I would accept from the state no more for the rental of the mansion than was provided to Governor Dix in the past, and that I would make up the extra difference in rent out of my own funds.

"Now, despite the fact that I have indeed used this mansion for the purposes I publicly announced, there are certain 'notables' in this part of the Valley who feel that they have been excluded from my social attentions," Sam said. "They are miffed that I do not host special events for them as often as they would like. They are upset that I do not grant them exclusive access to me or grant them any special favors. They take my bachelorhood as a topic for their vicious gossip and presumptiveness."

Sam started pacing back and forth, his hands clasped behind his back. I could tell that his temper was rising at the thought of the contempt that had been shown toward him by the snobbish crowd of Knickerbockers whose prejudices are well known throughout the state.

"It is clear to me, Abram," Sam continued, his voice louder than before, "that this *Times* reporter has done nothing more than sit down with a number of dowdy old hags who inhabit these estates and transcribed every falsehood and calumny that they could concoct for his benefit. Despite what he says about the 'similar' sentiments of more common people, I seriously doubt that he interviewed a single one of them. I have never felt any hint of animosity from the shopkeepers, or farmers, or laborers whom I have had the pleasure to deal with in my time here that this defamatory article suggests is present.

"I will happily write a scathing reply to this article at my earliest opportunity and have it published in the *Times*," he concluded.

"Very good, Sam," I said. "Now I would like to turn to this other article. It asserts that you did not pay your fair share of the Federal Income Tax for the year 1862. It claims that the *Times* has documentation showing that you made far more in income than you claimed in your return for that year. You claimed under oath on that return that in that year, your income 'from all sources' totaled $7,118 and it was on that sum that you paid your tax. Yet when the Federal District Court here examined your handling of the stock of the Terre Haute, Alton and St. Louis Railroad, you testified under oath that you were paid $20,000 for your services as Trustee of that railroad in that year of 1862. The article further alleges that you earned attorneys' fees from other companies in that year that enlarged your income even more. So the *Times* asserts that you lied under oath on your income tax return for 1862 and significantly underpaid your income tax."

"Again, complete rubbish!" Sam exclaimed, now highly agitated. "When I saw that statement in the *Times*, I went straight to my files and hunted for every scrap of paper that contains evidence of what I made in income fourteen years ago. Needless to say, it is not something that simply pops up in my files after all these years! I distinctly remember, however, that in that year I suffered some significant losses that offset my income considerably. I promise you; I will locate those papers and respond to this falsehood accordingly."

"I am very glad for that, Sam," I responded. "I have it on good authority that the *Times* is not going to let go of this issue, and plans to print more articles on the subject in the future. So, if you can research this matter thoroughly and reply accordingly, it will be a great help. We will also see to it that our speakers on your behalf echo your defenses vigorously on the campaign circuit."

Sam started to calm down. "Excellent. Thank you both, gentlemen, for taking the time to come all this way and alert me about these developments. I will prepare my responses and send them to you right away."

* * *

On the train home, Ed and I talked over what we had just seen and heard.

"What do you think, Abram? Is he being truthful with us?"

"Ed, to be perfectly honest with you, I don't really know. I have always considered Sam Tilden to be a close friend. He is a financial genius and a shrewd businessman and financier. He has made a fortune in the stock market on railroads. The press has long harassed him for allegedly 'wrecking' railroads that he's traded. Anything can happen in a career like that, and it is surely impossible for Sam to remember every detail that a newspaper may dig up."

"I can tell you, Abram," Ed said, "that from the moment that the Federal Government started collecting income taxes in 1862 to defray the costs of the war, it has been nothing but a source of financial controversy. Even if Sam did cheat on his tax return, he was not alone in that. Hardly anyone keeps track of how much income they make in any given year. No one keeps careful records. Everybody just guesses what amount it is and pays the tax on that guess. Most people had some idea of what amount they felt they owed for the conduct of the war, and paid that amount regardless of their true income. I can't say with confidence that Republicans who felt strongly about the war paid more tax than Democrats who leaned Copperhead."

"I'm sure that's right," I replied. "You know what's more, Ed? I remember learning in law school about a provision in the Constitution that says that no direct tax shall be imposed except in proportion to the census. I've never been quite sure what that meant, but I'll tell you this – a tax on incomes that costs one man far more per dollar of earnings than another man, like this tax law does, cannot possibly be "in proportion to the Census." It's *only* 'in proportion to' a person's income. So everyone is treated differently. I don't think it would pass muster under the 'Equal Protection' clause of the Fourteenth Amendment if it were ever brought to court."

"I don't think anybody in this country would object to the Revenue Act of 1862 being declared unconstitutional, Abram, especially now that the war is over and the tax is still being imposed," said Ed.

"What did you think of Sam's comments about the local Albany *hoi polloi*?" I asked Ed.

Ed laughed. "As my wife and I are considered Manhattan socialites in our own rights, I would say that he was entirely correct. That article was written about, by, and for the snobs! And that reporter surely doesn't know what the local butcher thinks of Tilden!"

* * *

"George," Rud Hayes asked George William Curtis one day in early September, after the Tilden tax scandal broke, "What is there to the charge that Tilden swindled the government out of its income tax? If the charge is false, then it ought to be dropped."

"The *New York Times* has Tilden dead to rights," the New York Republican Reform Club member and friend of Rud replied. "He falsified his return under oath."

"Hm," was Rud's only reply, with a perplexed look on his face.

Curtis was instantly suspicious. "Why? Do you have the same problem?"

"Oh, no," replied Rud. "After hearing about Tilden's taxes, I went over my file of tax statements from the past few years. I keep good records, you know. Well ... it appears that in 1868 and 1869, I made no return at all."

"You failed to file *any* tax return?" Curtis' eyes went wide.

"That's correct."

* * *

As the Tilden tax scandal unfolded, I decided to look into Governor Hayes' taxes as well. I thought that Ed was right that tax returns were fudged by practically everybody, maybe even Hayes.

I wrote to the Treasury Department requesting copies of Hayes' annual tax statements going back to 1862, when the income tax started. I received no answer from the Grant Administration. On September 6, the *Chicago Times*, which favored Tilden, published an article vaguely alluding to Hayes' failure to file some tax returns, but with little factual support. No Republican-leaning newspaper picked up on the story. I determined that there was little to go by, and dropped looking further into the matter.

Throughout the rest of September, I worked with Sam's former law clerk, James P. Sinnott, now a judge, to locate relevant records and prepare a response to the charges in the *New York Times* against Governor Tilden. While we were doing so, the Republican newspapers savaged him. He was accused of "wrecking" a Pennsylvania railroad for his own gain and other supposed financial misdeeds.[211] A spurious Republican pamphlet denounced Tilden as "the farmer's foe, a perfidious attorney, a sycophant of corporations, a corrupter of the press, a dangerous demagogue, an enemy of state schools and the Erie Canal, a traitor to the Democratic party, a disgrace to the state of New York and a menace to the United States."[212]Obviously it was the work of another gossipy old Knickerbocker from the stuffy side of Albany.

At last, before September ended, Tilden issued his refutation of the charges. He explained that most of his income-producing property in 1862 consisted of railroad stocks and bonds on which taxes had already been paid outside of the income tax return for that year. Sam had also owned a drug company in his hometown of New Lebanon, New York, which incurred large business losses in that year that offset a great deal of his income.[213]

The Democratic newspapers across the country proclaimed Tilden totally vindicated of the charge. Even the Republican-leaning *Chicago Daily News* deemed the response "complete and satisfactory."[214]

I have never been able to shake off my suspicion that the Republicans' ready acceptance of Tilden's refutation was designed to deflect attention away from as-yet undisclosed tax misdeeds on Hayes' part.

Chapter Sixteen – Election Day Dawns

ALL I KNOW ABOUT THE MONTH OF OCTOBER 1876 is that I managed to survive it.

All the while that I was feverishly working on the business of the National Committee and the press shop at Liberty Street, I was receiving letters from men in the iron business whom I was sadly neglecting at this time. I was able to devote about 30 seconds to one important decision about the ironworks that I made in the midst of my political work that month.[215] I intended to travel to the Philadelphia Centennial Exhibition in October, where my company was awarded a medal, but I had to give up the journey due to the press of political business.[216]

Sam Tilden, by contrast, was seldom seen around Everett House or Liberty Street. He seldom conferred with me. He was always too busy in Albany to visit us in Manhattan. None of the propaganda that we were pumping out was written by him, although his approval of it was never withheld. Sam continued to be parsimonious with cash contributions, and all we ever heard back from him were his complaints about the level of our expenses.[217]

We worked assiduously to insure the largest possible voter registration of Democrats in New York City. We even sent out letters to Democrats urging them to arrange their visits to the Philadelphia Centennial Exposition with an eye toward being home on Election Day.[218] Not surprisingly, Republicans cried "Fraud!" at our efforts and carped that we were taking unfair advantage of the political leanings of "illegal aliens."[219]

We did our best to beat back the savage attacks from the *New York Times* and other Republican-leaning newspapers intended to smear Governor Tilden's good name. The New York *Tribune* charged that Tilden "postpones too much and waits too long." A leading political historian wrote, "In the larger field of action [Tilden] had displayed a timid, vacillating character."[220] The *Times*, continuing its attack on Sam's tax returns and his alleged false oath thereon, published a screed in September headlined, "TILDEN'S FALSE SWEARING. What His Brother Lawyers Paid in Income Taxes When the 'Reform' Governor Was Cheating the Government."[221]

I responded to members of the press, "I defy any gentleman to lay his hand upon a dishonest dollar in the possession of Mr. Tilden." I came to regret that statement. *Harper's Weekly* ran with a front-page Thomas Nast cartoon of Tilden and incarcerated ex-Tammany Boss William Marcy Tweed embracing one another while Tilden passes funds to Tweed. My statement was used and misused in the background.

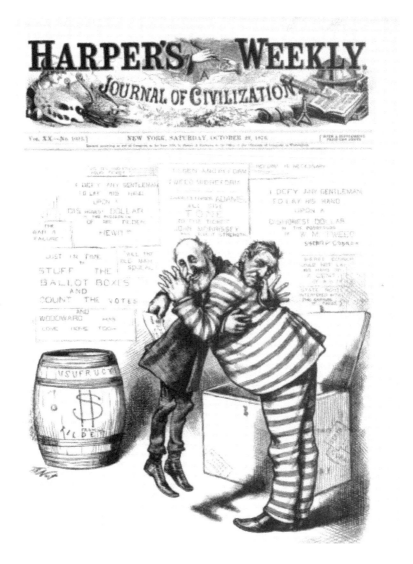

Figure 41: Alleged "Friendship" Between Sam Tilden and Jailed ex-Boss Tweed, Harper's Weekly, *October 28, 1876 (PD)*

Those of us at Everett House responded in kind to all of these charges. Governor Tilden, by contrast and characteristically, said nothing.

Zachariah Chandler and his Republican stooges fed red meat on Tilden to the newspapers, but they managed to preserve Governor Hayes' "sterling" reputation. Chandler assured the public that Hayes was "every day and all day quietly and steadily attending to his duties as governor of Ohio."[222] He was reputed in the Republican press to possess "stainless character and his church-relationship," overlooking the fact that Hayes did not belong to any church and considered himself an agnostic.[223]

In late September, the Republicans riled up a convention of Union veterans in Indianapolis. Speaking for Hayes at the convention, the orator Robert G. Ingersoll, known to all as "The Great Agnostic," bellowed, "Every state that seceded from the United States was a Democratic state. "Every ordinance of secession that was drawn was drawn by a Democrat. Every man that endeavored to tear the old flag from the heaven that it enriches was a Democrat," and so on.[224]Ingersoll even had the gall to say to the veterans that "every scar you have on your heroic bodies was given you by a Democrat."[225]

Figure 42: Robert G. Ingersoll, "The Great Agnostic" (PD)

Republicans ran hard after their Negro base as well. One Florida Republican, "Boss" Dennis of Alachua County, advised Negroes in his county to carry guns when they went to the polls on Election Day. Another pol, William Hicks, urged Blacks to vote "early and often," or else the Democrats would return them to slavery once they took power.[226]

Republican speakers went after Tilden not only for his policies, but personally. Ingersoll called him "a little, dried-up old bachelor who courted men because women cannot vote."[227] More than once, Republican speakers accused Tilden of being a homosexual, contrasting him with their "manly" candidate with his wife and five well-raised children.[228] Thomas Nast cartoons often caricatured

Tilden as wearing a dress.[229]Sam ignored these jibes – he had heard them throughout his career and lifelong bachelorhood – but we didn't ignore them. Everett House floated a rumor that Tilden was planning to marry shortly after entering the White House. That diverted the gullible social reporters of the press toward vying for the right guess as to which beautiful young Manhattan socialite the potential bride might be.[230]

Importantly, we were without sufficient funds from Tilden or Democratic donors to devote enough attention to the situation unfolding in the South. The states of Louisiana, South Carolina, and Florida were shamefully neglected.[231] A Florida Democratic committeeman contacted me for help in his teetering state; "For ten thousand dollars," he wrote me, "I will *insure* Florida for Tilden."[232] To my later regret, I had to turn him down.

Short on funds as they were, Southern Democrats resorted to other means to insure votes for Tilden. Economic persuasion worked well. Democratic landowners and merchants warned Black sharecroppers that their credit would be adversely affected by a vote for Hayes. Those suspected of voting Republican were charged a 25 percent surtax by local landlords, shopkeepers, doctors, and lawyers. The Florida Central Railroad Company handed out numbered ballots to its employees to use on election day.

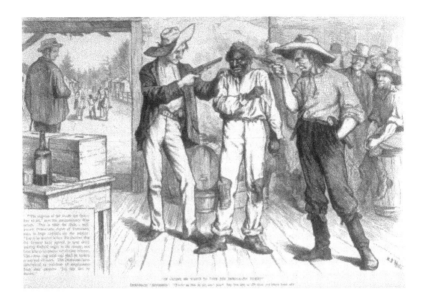

Figure 43: "Of Course He Wants to Vote the Democratic Ticket"—Harper's Weekly *Cartoon, October 1876 (Indiana University Bloomington)*

Violence also seemed to work. In Columbia County, Florida, armed White vigilantes captured several Black men, wrapped nooses around their necks, and set about calmly considering the options that were most efficient to hang them. Eventually, they released their frightened captives in return for their promise to quit the Republican Party.[233]

* * *

By dawn on Election Day, Tuesday, November 7, 1876, I awoke with the feeling that Tilden had a measurable lead over Hayes going to the ballot boxes. Tilden had drawn bigger crowds at the Centennial Exposition when he visited it on September 21 than

Hayes did when he visited it on October 26.[234] We took this to be a favorable sign at Everett House.

On that day, eight and one-half million Americans went to the polls to vote, more than had voted in the election of 1872.[235]

The candidates' actions for that day could not have been more different and more characteristic of each man. Hayes thought that it would be unseemly to vote for himself, so he stayed home in Columbus. Tilden wore a bright red carnation as he entered the polling station early in New York City, then spent hours at Everett House greeting well-wishers, thereafter shaking hands with another crowd of celebrants at his home in Gramercy Park. After dinner Sam returned to Everett House to await the early returns.[236]

Figure 44: Secret Voting Booths in Massachusetts, circa 1891
(www.familytree.com)

At about this same time, an incident took place in a swampy rural county in Florida that I can only think of as the final act of the Civil War.

.

PART SIX – TROUBLE

Chapter Seventeen – Tilden Elected!

I WAS EXHAUSTED FROM SIX MONTHS OF DRIVING MYSELF through my first Congressional session in Washington, the Convention in St. Louis, and the campaign in New York City. I could not bear the thought of boarding another train for another 1,000 miles of travel. On Election Day, after I voted, I spent the day and much of the night at Everett House in front of the wire that ran there from the special telegraph receiving Democratic returns at Irving Hall.[237]

The early returns from the East Coast cities portended a Tilden landslide. The headquarters, filled with Democratic politicians, let up a rousing cheer. As the night wore on, the returns from the Midwest evened things out to a closer race.[238]

A staffer climbed the stepladder in front of the chalk-board showing the tallies in each state. At about 8 o'clock New York time, he wrote out the tally from New York State – a sweep for Tilden! At around 10 o'clock, he climbed again to chalk up the tallies for Indiana, New Jersey and Connecticut – we carried them as well![239] Sixty-five electoral votes for Tilden![240] But as more reports came over the wire, we learned of our loss of the rest of New England, Pennsylvania, Ohio, Michigan, Illinois and Wisconsin – 127 electoral votes for Hayes.[241]

The South started reporting in, and the tally again looked like a landslide for Tilden – Delaware, Maryland, Virginia, West Virginia, Kentucky, North Carolina, Tennessee, Georgia, Alabama, Mississippi, Arkansas, and Missouri all went to Tilden, raising him to 176 electoral votes.Iowa and Minnesota raised Hayes to 143.[242]

South Carolina, Florida, and Louisiana did not yet report. Sam was nine electoral votes away from becoming President of the United States! Hayes was trailing!

Around 1 a.m., the Plains states began to report in. I watched as the staffer climbed the stepladder and chalked Texas' eight electoral votes for Tilden. But the eleven electoral votes of Kansas, Nebraska, and the new State of Colorado went to Hayes.[243]

The count now was 184 for Tilden against 154 for Hayes. There was a lusty roar from the crowd in Everett House – Sam Tilden was one electoral vote away from victory! We anxiously awaited the much later results that would be telegraphed in from the West Coast.

At about 3 a.m., California and Nevada reported in – nine electoral votes for Hayes. At dawn, the electoral vote count stood at 184 for Tilden and 163 for Hayes. Oregon did not yet report. Only 22 electoral votes hung in the balance – those of Florida, South Carolina, Louisiana, and Oregon. Ominously, the telegraph wires from them were silent. [244]

Staggering from exhaustion, thick cigar smoke and beer, the staff and I were ecstatic. We had done it! Florida, South Carolina, and Louisiana were sure bets for Tilden, and would accord him a victory of 203 electoral votes. Oregon's three votes, likely to go to Hayes, didn't even matter! As far as we were concerned, Sam Tilden was the President-elect!

* * *

In Columbus, Governor Rutherford B. Hayes went to bed certain that he had been defeated.[245] He woke the next morning, he later said, "contented and cheerful" despite his loss.[246]

As the sun rose on the eighth of November, I made my way to the street to hail a hansom cab. A newsboy came up with copies of the New York *Tribune*.[247] I bought one with a headline that read:

TILDEN ELECTED

HIS ELECTORAL MAJORITY SMALL

"Those Republicans," I thought confidently to myself of the Republican-leaning *Tribune* editors. "They can never accept it when they lose!"

Chapter Eighteen – A Miscount in Baker County, Florida

BAKER COUNTY, JUST WEST OF JACKSONVILLE in northeastern Florida, is for all intents and purposes a swamp. In 1870, it had a population of 1,325 people that, at that time, was about 80 percent White and 20 percent Black.[248] The only major battle of the Civil War that was fought in Florida, the Battle of Olustee, took place in Baker County in 1864.[249]

The county is covered with pine flatwoods and cypress swamps. Its main industry is lumber-making, with several sawmills along the St. Mary's River that forms the boundaries of both Baker County and the State of Florida with the State of Georgia.[250]

At the time of the 1876 election, Florida's counties were divided into polling precincts. The votes of those precincts were returned to the county clerk at each county seat.[251] In Baker County's case, the county seat was MacClenny, a hamlet of about 300 people.[252]

The State Election Law required the county clerk to count the votes and certify the result to the Florida Board of Canvassers in the state capital of Tallahassee. The county

Figure 45: MacClenny, Florida, circa 1908 (PD)

clerk was to be aided in that endeavor by the county judge and a justice of the peace. In case either the judge or the clerk was absent or could not attend, the sheriff of the county could be enlisted to help.[253]

There were four precincts in Baker County in 1876, and the Presidential election returns from the four precincts were all collected by the county clerk in three days, well before the deadline of November 13. On November 10, the county clerk requested the county judge, Judge Dreiggers, to join him in canvassing the votes, but the judge refused. The clerk then asked the sheriff, David Tickson, who also refused.[254]

The clerk then called upon a justice of the peace to help him canvass the votes. They conducted an accurate canvass of the returns of all four precincts. But on that same day, Judge Dreiggers issued a notice to the county clerk and to another justice of the peace to come before him at the courthouse on November 13 for the purpose of counting the votes.[255]

When the county clerk and the summoned justice of the peace showed up at the courthouse on November 13, Judge Dreiggers was absent. The clerk sent word to the Judge at his home that both he and the justice of the peace were present in his courtroom and were prepared to conduct the canvass, but Judge Dreiggers declined to attend. Sheriff Tickson was then called upon, but he refused to attend as well.[256]

So, at the courtroom that day, the clerk and the as-summoned justice of the peace conducted yet another canvass of the returns of all four precincts, which came out the same as the earlier canvass. The clerk then certified the result to the State Canvassing Board on that day, the deadline date of November 13, stating in their certificate why neither the judge nor the sheriff was present for the count or to sign the certification. He placed it in an official envelope and dropped it in the courthouse mailbox to be sent to Tallahassee.[257]

Why had both the county judge and the county sheriff been so uncooperative? Were they trying to avoid having anything to do with the county clerk's tally of votes or to avoid having their signatures appear on the county certification? Were they trying by their lack of cooperation to have the vote disqualified? Or were the reasons far simpler, like family problems or illnesses? The facts and consequences would soon unfold.

* * *

With the canvassing done and the results mailed out, the county clerk closed his office for the day, leaving the returns from the precincts in his desk drawer.

That evening, Sheriff Tickson received a note from Judge Dreiggers. The Judge asked the Sheriff to assist him in making the canvass of the Baker County votes. Judge Dreiggers asked Sheriff Tickson to meet him and a Justice of the Peace named Green at the County Clerk's Office in MacClenny between four and five o'clock.

All three men were Reconstructionist Republicans who owed their jobs to the Reconstructionist Republican Governor, Marcellus Stearns. Mr. Green had just received

Figure 46: Governor Marcellus Stearns of Florida (PD)

his commission to be a Justice of the Peace from Governor Stearns on November 10. He had never acted in that capacity before.

Judge Dreiggers greeted the two men at the front door of the building where the Clerk's Office was located. It was now about six o'clock. The Clerk's Office was closed and the clerk was gone.

"Thanks for coming, gentlemen. Now let's have a look at those ballots, shall we?" The Judge pulled out a key from his pocket, unlocked the door, and entered with the other two.

The men lit candles throughout the office and began searching for the ballots. Judge Dreiggers found them in the clerk's unlocked desk drawer.

Figure 47: George F. Drew, Democratic Gubernatorial Candidate (PD)

The first thing the three men did was to count all the votes from all four of the precincts of Baker County. There was a total of 381 ballots. Of these, 238 were Democratic and 143 were Republican. That meant that the Tilden electors had won Baker County and Governor Stearns' Democratic rival, George F. Drew, had won the county race for Governor, both by 95 votes.

"Lemme see, here," Judge Dreiggers said, picking up the papers with the tally and examining them. "This can't be right.

"OK," the Judge said, "here's the ballots for the Johnsville Precinct." Johnsville was a majority Democratic precinct. "Now I heard that one of the niggers who went to vote at the polling station in Johnsville was harassed by a bunch of rowdies wielding guns. We can't allow that to happen, now, can we?"

"No, sir," said Sheriff Tickson and Justice Green in unison.

"All right, then," said the Judge, "the law allows me to remedy the harassment by throwing out the votes of the Johnsville Precinct." He put all of the Johnsville votes in a separate pile on the clerk's desk.

Sheriff Tickson and Justice Green gaped at the Judge but said nothing. They were not in the habit of questioning judges.

"Now," said the Judge, "here's the Darbyville Precinct." Darbyville was also mostly Democratic. "I heard a rumor that seven voters there illegally voted twice. Have you heard that?"

"No, Your Honor," said Sheriff Tickson in a low voice.

"No, sir," said Justice Green.

"Well, *I've* heard it. We can't abide that!" The Judge placed all of the Darbyville ballots on the separate pile with the Johnsville ballots.

"All right, then," said the Judge. "Let's re-count the remaining votes." The votes from the remaining two Baker County precincts were counted and gave the election to Governor Stearns and the Hayes electors.

"All right then, gentlemen," Judge Dreiggers said. "The Republicans have won. Let's get this certification signed and sent to Tallahassee." He pulled a forms book down from the clerk's library shelf and found the proper form for a canvass return to the State Board of Canvassers. He copied it onto a piece of paper, filled in the blanks, signed it along with the other two men, and placed it in an envelope addressed to the State Board.

"I'll put it in the mailbox as soon as I leave here," he said. The men gathered up all the ballots and put them back in the drawer of the clerk's desk where they had found them. They then walked out the door and re-locked it.[258]

* * *

When the three members of the State Board of Canvassers – two Republicans and one Democrat – received the two conflicting certificates from Baker County – one signed by the county clerk and a justice of the peace showing that Tilden and Drew had won; the other signed by the county judge, the county sheriff, and another justice of the peace showing that Hayes and Stearns had won – they could find no reason written down in the second set as to why it did not match the first set. They decided to accept the first set from the county clerk as the correct one. However, in what could only be justified as an inexplicably odd attempt on their part to resolve the anomaly, the Board of State Canvassers eliminated from the returns of certain other counties a number of votes that were equal to the votes in the clerk's accurate Baker County tally that the judge, sheriff, and their justice of the peace had thrown out of their own tally.

These machinations were enough to award all of Florida's four electors to Hayes, whereas using all accurately-canvassed votes from all of the counties, including Baker, would have awarded them all to Tilden.[259]

Out of an approximate total of 48,700 votes cast in Florida, Tilden had won the popular vote in that state (taking *all* the votes into consideration) by *only about 87 votes*.[260]

In the conduct of U.S. Presidential elections in most states, the winner of the majority of the popular vote in a particular state wins all of the electoral votes of that state – a custom known as "Winner-Takes-All." In this case, despite the razor-thin margin favoring Tilden and Drew, Governor Stearns announced that he himself had won the governor's race and that Hayes had won all of the Florida Presidential electors. He certified this result on December 6, 1876 to the U.S. Senate in Washington.[261]

Figure 48: Florida Attorney-General William A. Cocke (PD)

The only Democrat on the three-member Board of State Canvassers – William A. Cocke, the State Attorney-General – objected to these actions. He prepared a certification of electors of his own that was based on the correct count from Baker County that the county clerk had submitted, together with the complete votes of all the other counties, without nullifying any vote. This certification awarded all four electoral votes to Tilden. Cocke signed the certification all by himself on December 6, 1877 and forwarded it to the Clerk of the U.S. Senate in Washington, D.C.[262]

The Board's elimination of the votes of the other counties affected the Florida gubernatorial election as well as its Presidential election. George Drew challenged the legality of the Board's action as to that election and won a judgment in the State Supreme Court that it was the Board's purely ministerial duty to count the votes as properly returned, which gave them no right to eliminate votes for Governor from any county.[263]

So the Board duly declared Drew to be the winner of the gubernatorial race. But the Court had said nothing about the *electoral vote*. Consequently, the Board took the inaccurate Baker County tally of Judge Dreiggers, Sheriff Tickson, and Justice Green that now-ex-Governor Stearns had certified to be the electoral vote tally, restored all the electoral vote tallies of all the other counties, *but again declared the Hayes electors to be the winners.*[264]

Things only got worse. As a result of the Board's perverse actions on the electoral vote, the newly-elected State Legislature irately passed a law that *declared* Tilden to be the winner of all of Florida's four electoral votes and *ordered* newly-elected Governor Drew to certify the same to the U.S. Senate. So yet a *third* certificate, this one signed by Governor Drew on January 26, 1877, made its way to Washington.[265]

Chapter Nineteen – Corruption and Chaos in Louisiana and South Carolina

MEANWHILE, IN BATON ROUGE, LOUISIANA, the State Board of Elections had before it a statewide count of 83,723 votes for Sam Tilden.[266] Tilden's lead over Hayes was anywhere from 6,300 to 8,957 votes.[267] However, Louisiana's reputation for corrupt and disputed elections is legendary.

The all-Reconstructionist Republican Board of Elections reduced Tilden's count down to 70,508 votes, more than a 13,000-vote drop. This drop was enough to hand all eight of Louisiana's electoral votes to Governor Hayes instead of Governor Tilden.[268] Again, it was a case of "winner takes all."

The Board's reason for throwing out approximately 10,000 of these Tilden votes was its alleged receipt of a certificate in accordance with a Louisiana statute that authorizes the Board to throw out votes "whenever, from any poll or voting-place, there should be received the statement of any supervisor of registration or commissioner of election, in form as required by section 26 of this act, on affidavit of three or more citizens, of any riot, tumult, acts of violence, intimidation, armed disturbance, bribery, or corrupt influences, which prevented or tended to prevent, a fair, free, and peaceable vote of all qualified electors entitled to vote at such poll or voting-place."[269]

As it turned out, the "certificate" that the Board allegedly received against the purported "intimidation" against Hayes voters by Tilden supporters was fabricated, and the four required signatures forged, *by direction of the Board itself*, according to lawyers for the Democratic Party.[270]

On top of that, of the eight Republican electors so certified by Louisiana, two at the time of the election held "offices of profit" under the United States. One was the U.S. Surveyor General for the District of Louisiana, and the other was a Commissioner of the United States Circuit Court for that District. This violated Article II, Section 1 of the United States Constitution, which states "that no Senator or Representative, *or person holding an office of trust or profit under the United States*, shall be appointed an elector."[271]

* * *

Likewise, Election Day in South Carolina was utter chaos. This state was new to the choice of Presidential electors by popular vote. From the state's beginning through the pre-Civil War Presidential campaign that took place there in 1860, the State Legislature had chosen its electors rather than the people, which is permitted by the U.S. Constitution.[272] Following the Civil War, South Carolina held its first popular vote for Presidential electors in 1868.

Figure 49: Democratic Gubernatorial Candidate Wade Hampton III (PD)

On Election Day 1876, one thousand Federal troops, under orders from the Justice Department, occupied every polling station in the state.[273] The race for Governor was far more heated than the race for President. Democrat Wade Hampton III, formerly a Confederate lieutenant general, one of the state's largest slaveholders, a State Legislator before the war, and the devastatingly handsome heart-throb of every Southern belle, beat out Reconstructionist Republican Daniel H. Chamberlain by a 1,134-vote lead.

Figure 50: Republican Gubernatorial Candidate Daniel Henry Chamberlain (PD)

Suspiciously, however, Republican electors for Hayes led Democratic electors for Tilden by a narrow margin – only 889 votes, less than a one-half of one percent margin of victory.[274] *And somehow, the total vote count exceeded the number of eligible voters.*[275]

There were multiple reports of soldiers intimidating voters.[276] These reports were contested by the Army.[277] It was also reported that approximately 150 Black Republicans were murdered.[278]

The gubernatorial vote was handed over to the South Carolina State Legislature to decide, which had a one-vote Democratic majority. The Republicans hotly contested its choice of Hampton for Governor.[279] After a battle in the State Supreme Court, Hampton was declared the winner.[280]

Meanwhile, however, the Election Board awarded all of the state's seven electors to Hayes, resolving all protests in his favor, despite the overwhelming vote in favor of the Democratic candidate for Governor.[281]

Chapter Twenty – An Ineligible Elector in Oregon

NOT ALL OF THE QUESTIONABLE ELECTORAL VOTES occurred in the South. In Oregon, Hayes won the popular vote over Tilden, and therefore was awarded all three of that state's electoral votes. But one of those electors, John Watts, had been a

Figure 51: Governor LaFayette Grover of Oregon (PD)

U.S. Postmaster during the election, and therefore held "an office of trust or profit under the United States" that under the Constitution rendered him ineligible for service as an elector.[282]

Governor LaFayette Grover of Oregon, a Democrat, declared Mr. Watts ineligible to serve as an elector and substituted a member of the slate of Democratic electors in his place, one C.A. Cronin. Oregon therefore had two Republican electoral votes and one Democratic electoral vote.[283] As Tilden's overall electoral count was only one vote short of victory, this decision should have made Tilden the winner.

The two Republican electors, however, did not take kindly to Governor Grover's interference and declared vacant the office of elector formerly occupied by Mr. Watts. Mr. Watts then resigned his position as Postmaster and, now as a private citizen, resumed his electoral office. All three electors, now solidly Republican once again, awarded all of the state's electoral votes to Hayes.[284] To make it official, the three electors' certification for Hayes was signed by the Oregon Secretary of State, whereas the certification presented by Mr. Cronin of two electors for Hayes and one for Tilden was signed by Governor Grover.[285] And matters were left at that.

Chapter Twenty-one – An Offer

BY LATE NOVEMBER, WE HAD CLOSED DOWN the printing press on Liberty Street. Everett House was gradually emptying out of politicians, job seekers and staffers. Ed Cooper, Bill Pelton and I continued to maintain offices at Everett House for a short period after the election in order to wind up the affairs of the Democratic National Committee.

"Mr. Hewitt," a staffer said to me one day upon entering my office, "A gentleman named John T. Pickett is here to see you. He says that he represents James Madison Wells, the chairman of the Louisiana Board of Elections."

I was instantly suspicious. There were rampant rumors of bribery coming out of that state for the purpose of throwing the Presidential election one way or the other. Wells was the head of that Board, the most unabashedly corrupt Board of Elections in the country.

Another reason for my suspicion was that John T. Pickett was a notorious lobbyist. He is a peddler of influence in Washington. He goes from Congressman to Congressman and Senator to Senator buying and selling the favors and needs sought from the federal government by this or that mogul or institution. He collects handsome fees for his work, ambling from office to office in a nice suit and fine shoes. He rarely carries a briefcase or even papers. Everything he knows is in his head. He is a modern version of the itinerant peddler who roamed the West from town to town, carrying pots, pans, washboards, girdles, and all other sorts of accessories on his back to sell or trade.

Figure 51: James Madison Wells of Louisiana (PD)

"Show him in," I replied guardedly, looking up from the newspaper I was reading that detailed all the sordid activities going on in Florida, Louisiana, South Carolina, and Oregon.

"Mister Hewitt," Pickett said with only a slight Southern drawl as he offered his hand to shake mine. "I am very pleased to make your acquaintance. I have heard a great deal about your heroic efforts on behalf of Governor Tilden."

Mr. Pickett was a tall, very good-looking, well-dressed man. I knew of him as a former die-hard Confederate who had graduated from West Point.[286]

"The pleasure is all mine, Mr. Pickett," I lied, shaking his hand and offering him a seat in front of my desk. I sat back down in my chair.

"Mister Hewitt, I am here on a mission for James Madison Wells, the Chairman of the Board of Elections of the State of Louisiana. As I'm sure you know, the Board is struggling with this intractable issue of which slate of electors it should choose to represent our state. It appears that Governor Tilden has won the majority of votes for electors, but the Republicans are raising a massive fuss about it.

"Now, Chairman Wells is committed to resolving this controversy as equitably as possible. However, such controversies are not resolved in Louisiana without reasonable compensation to the Board members for their assent."

"I see. How much 'compensation' is required for their 'assent?'" I asked.

"Well," Pickett replied, "Chairman Wells has given this matter a lot of thought. He believes that for one million dollars, he can offer you his personal assurance that the Board's choice will be the slate of electors for Governor Tilden."

"I see," I replied. "I presume that the other Board members would require similar compensation for their assent. How much would each of them require?"

"Our Board has five seats," Pickett explained. "The Republicans are currently occupying their four seats, but the Democrat resigned from his seat two years ago. The remaining members have been unable to agree on a successor, who must be a Democrat. So, as you can see, it will be costly to insure that they will choose the Democratic slate of electors as the public election has urged the Board to do."

"Insure that they will choose Democrats," I thought to myself. "How generous of this Board to abide by the popular vote!"

"I believe," Pickett continued, "that each of the remaining three Board members can be compensated this way: One hundred thousand dollars for Thomas Anderson, the remaining white man on the Board, and twenty-five thousand dollars apiece for the two Negroes on the Board. That'll do it, sir."

I glared at him. "Mr. Pickett," I said evenly. "is bribery a crime in Louisiana like it is here in New York?"

Pickett reeled back somewhat, as if surprised that I would even raise the issue. "Why, yes, I believe it is," he said. "But that law is not applied that stringently at the political level in my state. Indeed, as I understand the law of New York, it isn't here either. In fact," Pickett oozed flatteringly, "it is only through the courageous efforts of Governor Tilden to incarcerate Boss Tweed and his assistants that the bribery law has ever been enforced here at all."

He certainly had a point there. "That is true, Mr. Pickett," I replied icily. "And that is the very reason why the Democratic National Committee cannot possibly accept Mr. Wells' offer."

Pickett showed no emotion, obviously expecting this answer. "I fully understand your point, Mister Hewitt," he replied. "Mister Wells authorized me to reduce his compensation request if you found it to be unacceptable. He would accept a reduction to ..." He pulled out a small notebook and perused it for a moment. "Two hundred thousand dollars. How is that?"

"No more acceptable than the first offer, Mr. Pickett," I said as I rose from my chair and extended my hand; even though I found the offer odious, I did not want to throw Mr. Pickett out on unfriendly terms in case we needed him at some time in the future.

"The Democratic Party is the party of reform," I said to him. "Governor Tilden is committed to reform. Governor Tilden has fought corruption in New York, and he will fight it in Louisiana as President. I must bid you good day, Mr. Pickett."

Pickett did not take my hand to shake. "Well, sir, that is very unfortunate. Governor Tilden is one electoral vote short of becoming President, and it is very unlikely at this juncture that he will get that vote from Louisiana. Good day, Mister Hewitt." Pickett turned and left.

* * *

The next day, I talked with Bill Pelton about Pickett's visit over coffee and doughnuts at the Everett House coffee shop. Short of talking to Governor Tilden himself, who was back in Albany working on state affairs, his nephew was the man best able to inform me of what Sam's take on the matter would be.

"Abram, I'm sure that your reaction to Pickett would have been the same initial opinion that Sam would have had," Bill said to me. "But I don't think that Uncle would have responded to Pickett immediately. He's a very cautious man. He probably would have told Pickett that he would think over the offer and let him know. Then he would wait for some time. Not to think it over, mind you, but to see if Pickett would come back with a much lower offer, both for Wells and the other Board members."

"Really?" I said, somewhat astonished. "You don't think that Sam would have rejected it outright, like I did?"

"Frankly, no, Abram," Bill replied. "Sam would have calculated the costs and the benefits of accepting or rejecting the offer, I think. If the offer were large enough to convince the Board members to decide his way, but small enough to avoid detection by the Republican press, then he might just have reached into his own pocket and made the payments. He wouldn't take DNC money for the task; he'd use his own cash. He's only one vote short of winning, but he would have figured that he doesn't know where the extra vote is going to come from. Therefore, he must insure a vote in his favor in at least one disputed state, and would take his chances with the rest, I think. That way, he's assured of winning no matter what the other disputed states end up doing."

"Hm. You're probably right," I replied. "But we can be sure that Pickett has not only approached me. He is undoubtedly going to Chandler too, to see if the Republicans will buy the Board. If we both buy the Board, they would just vote for the highest bidder and keep the money from both parties, right?"

"Maybe, Abram, and then again, maybe not," said Bill. "And Sam would figure that out too, which makes taking such an offer such a no-win situation. Maybe Sam would be able to extract a promise from the Board not to solicit payments from the Republicans. But that certainly would not be an enforceable promise."

"But of course," I said, "you'd be paying thieves, whose promises you can't trust. So what good is such a promise? Would Sam realize that too?"

"Again, Sam is a realist. He would think it over very carefully. He would evaluate just how dumb the Board members are, and whether he could leverage them in some fashion. He might negotiate a "deposit" if you will, with full payment after they vote in his favor. Or he might even arrange a set-up, in which he offers to pay them after the vote is taken, and then arranges a meeting allegedly to make payment but in reality, to have them arrested for soliciting bribes. Sam thinks of all sorts of options like that."

"Which is why he's such a good politician, I guess," I said. "I suppose the best way to handle this is to take whatever path will insure the longest delay in the certification of the Louisiana electoral vote as possible. Even if we do not get the Louisiana vote, and it is disqualified altogether, that leaves us three other states to win over, hopefully. We only need one damn vote."

"That sounds right to me," Bill replied as he dunked a vanilla-creme doughnut into his cup of coffee and bit into it.

* * *

In early December, the Louisiana Board of Elections announced its decision. After a lengthy and intense hearing accompanied by heavy lobbying by distinguished Republican politicians who came down from Washington, opposed by an equally hefty set of distinguished Democrats, the Board, in secret session, threw out all the votes of two parishes and sixty-nine partial votes from twenty-two more parishes. The Board disallowed over 13,000 votes for Tilden and over 2,400 for Hayes (which didn't matter because he failed to carry those parishes anyway), thus awarding all seven Louisiana electors, to my horror and regret for my hubris in declining Mr. Pickett's offer, to Hayes.[287]

PART SEVEN – DEBATE

Chapter Twenty-two – The Eve of Battle

AT THE END OF NOVEMBER 1876, AS I PREPARED to return to Washington for the lame-duck session of the 44th Congress beginning on Thursday, December 7, the following was where matters stood in the country.

Samuel Tilden had won the majority of the "raw" popular votes cast for President – 4,286,808, equaling 50.92 percent of the total votes cast. Rutherford Hayes had won 4,032,142 popular votes, equaling 47.92 percent of the total.[288] The remaining 1.16 percent, amounting to approximately 96,500 votes nationwide, splintered among various unaffiliated write-in candidates.

Sam Tilden had received 184 uncontested electoral votes. He was one electoral vote short of the majority of such votes necessary to become President of the United States.

Rud Hayes had received 165 uncontested electoral votes. He was twenty electoral votes short of winning the Presidency.

Twenty electoral votes were in dispute from the States of Florida (four electoral votes), Louisiana (eight electoral votes), Oregon (one electoral vote), and South Carolina (seven electoral votes).

On December 6, the electors met in their various state capitols to vote formally for President and Vice-President. In the three disputed Southern states, the Democratic and Republican slates of electors met separately from each other and cast votes contrary to one another. In Oregon, the purported Democratic elector and the purported Republican elector cast opposing ballots to one another while the remaining electors voted for Hayes.[289]

Thereafter, along with the uncontested electoral vote certifications of the other states, each of the disputed states submitted to Congress at least two opposing certifications – one of electors for Tilden and one of electors for Hayes. Each was formally certified by different state officials; some governors, some secretaries of state, and some other officials.[290]

This weirdness was matched only by the fateful setup of the 44th Congress itself. The 45th Congress, which would convene in 1877, was much the same. Democrats controlled the House; Republicans controlled the Senate. Grant's Vice-President, Henry Wilson, had died on November 22, 1875; thus, the office of Vice-President was currently vacant. Consequently, the office of President of the Senate was vacant, and was occupied temporarily for the remainder of Grant's term by a President *pro tempore*, who was Senator Thomas W. Ferry of Michigan, a Republican.[291]

Figure 52: Senator Thomas W. Ferry of Michigan (PD)

The Twelfth Amendment to the U.S. Constitution, ratified in 1804 and untested up to this point, governs the manner in which Congress counts electors and determines who are the new President and Vice-President. After the President of the Senate receives the certifications of electors from the states, a joint session of both houses of Congress convenes to open the certificates and count the votes. "The person having the greatest number of votes for President, shall be the President, if such number be a majority of the whole number of Electors appointed," the Twelfth Amendment provides. However, "if no person have such majority, then from the persons having the highest numbers not exceeding three on the list of those voted for as President, the House of Representatives shall choose immediately, by ballot, the President."

Some interpreted this provision to be applicable to the election of Tilden and Hayes. Neither had a "majority of the whole number of Electors appointed." Tilden was short by one and Hayes was short by twenty. In that case, the choice of President would be up to the Democratic-controlled House of Representatives. By the same token, the choice of Vice-President would be up to the Republican-controlled Senate.

There was yet one more wrinkle in the Twelfth Amendment's manner of choosing a President by the House of Representatives: "[I]n choosing the President, the votes shall be taken by states, the representation from each state having one vote; a quorum for this purpose shall consist of a member or members from two-thirds of the states, and a majority of all the states shall be necessary to a choice." In the Senate, by contrast, the choice of Vice-President was to be decided by a majority of the whole number of Senators.

In the 44th Congress, which would count the electoral votes during its lame-duck session, the majority of delegations of Representatives from each of the 38 states in the Union was Democratic; the majority of all Senators in the Senate was Republican. Therefore, if the Twelfth Amendment were followed, Tilden would be most likely chosen President and Hayes' Vice-Presidential running mate, William A. Wheeler, would be most likely chosen Vice-President.

* * *

Shortly after Congress reconvened in early December, I attended a dinner with Governor Tilden, who had traveled by overnight train down to Washington for the occasion, and several of my fellow Democratic Congressmen. We dined at the Ebbitt House at 14th and F Streets, NW, near the U.S. Treasury Building.

Ebbitt House is an elegantly-appointed hotel in the middle of the city, recently renovated by its new owner, with a beautiful Mansard Roof in the French Empire style and 300 rooms. The dining room is known as "The Crystal Room" for its enormous chandeliers, and occupies two stories with floor-to-ceiling windows, a white marble floor, and a frescoed ceiling.[292]

The topic of discussion, of course, was the election.

"I understand that there is a theory developing among the Republicans," I said, "about the Twelfth Amendment's provision that, in the joint session of Congress to count the electoral votes, the President of the Senate opens all the certificates and the votes are counted.

Figure 53: Congressman Henry B. Payne of Ohio (PD)

"They theorize that this provision makes the President of the Senate, as the joint session's presiding official, the final arbiter of competing certificates. That means that President Pro Tem Ferry, being Republican, would undoubtedly accept the Hayes electors and reject the Tilden electors. That would make Hayes President."[293]

"I have heard that theory too, Abram, and it's pure bunk," said Henry Payne, a congressman from Ohio. "The Twelfth Amendment says nothing more about the power of the President of the Senate than that he opens all the certificates in the presence of the House and Senate and 'the votes shall then be counted.' It does not say that he *counts the votes*; it says that the votes *shall then be counted*, which does not specify who is to conduct the count. In past Presidential elections, a team of tellers, two from the House and one from the Senate, always counted the votes and resolved any dispute amongst themselves."[294]

"I propose a different approach," Payne continued. "The only electoral certificates that count are the *uncontested* ones, and neither Tilden nor Hayes has been given the majority of those votes. The contested ones should simply be thrown out as invalid, like the Louisiana electoral votes were thrown out in 1872. Thus, according to the Twelfth Amendment, the House would choose the President and the Senate would choose the Vice-President from the highest recipients of electoral votes for each office. For choosing a President, each state delegation in the House has only one vote, which that delegation determines. Since we Democrats control the majority of delegations, Tilden will win."

Figure 54: Congressman Eppa Hunton of Virginia (PD)

"But Wheeler will win in the Senate because it is controlled by the Republicans," Congressman Eppa Hunton interjected. "So we'll have a Democratic President and a Republican Vice-President. That hasn't happened since Adams and Jefferson, and that outcome wasn't pleasant. It's what led to the Twelfth Amendment in the first place."

"But this problem has been solved already!" Congressman William Springer interjected. "The Twenty-second Joint Rule of both houses of Congress provides that no electoral vote objected to by either house should be counted except by the concurrent vote of both chambers.[295] It was used to resolve disputed electoral votes in the election of Lincoln in 1864 and both elections of Grant in 1868 and 1872. It supported the elections

Figure 55: Congressman William M. Springer of Illinois (PD)

of those Presidents in those years because the Republicans controlled both the Senate and the House. But now, Democrats control the House. If the House throws out Republican electoral votes, then Senate Republicans cannot reverse it. If the thrown-out electoral votes result in no majority for either candidate, the Presidential election would then be thrown into the House by the Twelfth Amendment and Tilden would be chosen."[296]

"One problem there, Bill," I replied. "The Republicans managed to get that Rule for joint sessions of Congress eliminated a year ago. Rules only apply for one Congress, and if they are not renewed by joint action of both houses, they are gone. So Joint Rule 22 is now gone, and the Republican Senate won't agree to renew it. Certainly not now."

By now, I was thoroughly exasperated. "Gentlemen," I said, "I have been forced to watch helplessly as depredations of every kind were perpetrated by the Republicans for the purpose of defrauding the voters. It is unimaginable to me that Governor Tilden can be defeated in this election by one electoral vote, and that none of the candidates for that one vote was honestly earned by the Republican Party.

"Every one of the twenty disputed votes were procured by the Republicans through outright fraud," I went on. "All four states in which this has happened corruptly threw out legitimate votes for Governor Tilden and handed the state over to Hayes. I have personally received a full report on the Louisiana Board's handling of Tilden votes, and they were thrown out dishonestly and secretly.

"I propose that we put this question directly to the voters of this land," I said, pounding the table with my index finger at every word I spoke. "We should call mass meetings of the people to denounce this outrage!"[297]

"Mass meetings, Abram?" Governor Tilden asked, puzzledly. "What do you mean?"

"I mean, Governor," I said pointedly, "that on January 8, 1877, the date when Congress convenes in joint session in Washington to count the electoral votes, all who love this country should assemble in every city, town and hamlet in this land, and in Washington as well, to consider the dangers of the situation, and by calm, firm, and temperate resolutions, to enlighten their representatives in Congress as to their duties in this great crisis of our institutions, which we are bound by every consideration of duty and by every impulse of patriotism to transmit unimpaired to our children!"[298]

I must admit that, by the time I reached this point in the dinner, I was quite exhausted and anxious from a year of constant turmoil and controversy resulting from my hectic role in the campaign. It should come as no surprise that I spoke so extremely. Both Edward and I had devoted hundreds of hours, days and nights pursuing our goal of electing our friend Sam to the highest office in the land. We had both lost touch with our wives and children, foregone our businesses, and traveled thousands of miles by train all over the country to supervise the amassing of votes. We were both substantially in debt as well, from fronting all the expenses of the campaign which, by this point in time, Governor Tilden had still not yet reimbursed us.

So if I sounded strident at this dinner, literally proposing a mass uprising across the country to convince Congress that the Republicans had stolen this election from our candidate, I am not ashamed. At this point, given the thorny and complicated twists and turns of constitutional law and procedure that were blockading our path to victory, I could envision nothing less than a massive appeal to the people to fill the streets and protest this robbery of their democracy!

"Abram," Sam said calmly and quietly after I had finished my diatribe, which the others at the table had listened to do with silent stares, "I understand fully how you feel. No one can be more outraged and disappointed in this state of affairs than I.

"As I see it, gentlemen," Sam continued, "there are three options to take here: We can fight; we can back down; or we can arbitrate. It will not do to fight. We have just emerged from one Civil War, and it will never do to engage in another Civil War; it would end in the destruction of free government. We cannot back down. We can, therefore, only arbitrate.[299]

"Gentlemen," Sam said, turning to the others, "for the good of the country, let us work with the Republicans to find some other way."

* * *

Zachariah Chandler, Rud Hayes, Carl Schurz, James Blaine, and a few other Republican leaders sat around a large table in a conference room of the Office of the Governor in Columbus, Ohio. The haze of cigar smoke hung like a storm cloud over the table.

The topic of discussion, of course, was the election.

"Zachary," Rud asked puzzledly, "there is one thing that I fail to understand. As to Florida, there is only one certificate of electoral votes now before Congress that is signed by the Governor who was sitting when the popular vote was taken, and signed by the Secretary of State who was sitting at the same time. That is what the state law requires the certificate to have. Another certificate is signed by the Attorney General, which means nothing. And yet another is signed by the new Governor who was inaugurated this year, long after the popular election; and by the new Secretary of State, who was also inaugurated this year, long after the election. The first certificate chooses our slate of Republican electors.

"What possible ground for overturning this official electoral count could the Democrats have?"

"Rud, it is a total mystery to me," Zachary answered. "Undoubtedly, there were irregularities in the Florida popular vote. There are irregularities in the popular votes of every state in the

Union, North and South. But the ultimate choice of *electors*, based on the popular vote as a state's Board of Elections counts it, is up to that Board. That is the law in every state, as far as I can tell.

"Who's to say that there weren't irregularities in New York?" Zach asked, regarding Tilden's win in his home state.

"That is precisely it, Zachary," Schurz replied. "As I understand it, the Democrats are basing their argument about Florida on the deposition of a single sheriff in one rural county who says that the ballots of two out of four precincts in the county were thrown out on suspicion of intimidation, or something like that. So, to prove vote fraud, they are relying on the testimony of the fraudster himself! That doesn't sound very reliable to me.

"But even more puzzling is that this sort of thing happens everywhere!" Schurz continued. "Tilden votes are defiled just as often as Hayes votes are! The only reason that I can discern for the Democrats' focus on this one small Florida county is because changing its count to add the two ignored precincts will give Tilden that one electoral vote that he needs to win the election."

"It wasn't just Tilden voters whose ballots were thrown out," added Blaine. "The ballots of Hayes voters were undoubtedly thrown out too."

"Well, gentlemen," said Zachary, "in any event, there is no point to conceding the election to Governor Tilden unless and until he wins one more electoral vote, and right now four states remain uncertain. Twenty electoral votes are in play, and if Rud and Bill win them all, then Rud becomes President and Bill becomes Vice-President. So there is nothing to concede."

"The Democrats could file writs of *quo warranto* in the courts of the disputed states," Schurz pointed out. "One is already pending in Florida. Those writs require the courts to examine the titles of the electors to their offices and determine which of them has valid title."

"Yes," Blaine replied, "but the courts would take forever to act, and they would be appealed, which would also take forever. It is not even clear whether the decisions of the Supreme Courts of the affected states could be appealed thereafter to the U.S. Supreme Court. The President must be inaugurated by March 4. There is not enough time to wait."

Rud shook his head in exasperation. "Well, the people are getting antsy, gentlemen," Rud said. "There is talk of violence in the streets of this country if the matter is not resolved. The electoral votes must be counted by a joint session of Congress on February first, and there must be electoral votes from every state to count. So we must find some way to determine these votes quickly. We cannot extend President Grant's term, and we cannot have a vacant Presidency and Vice-Presidency!"

* * *

Another way *was* found.

During Christmas week, equally confounded Republicans agreed with us Democrats in both houses of Congress to form special committees in each chamber to establish a process to resolve the dispute. In the House, a bipartisan committee of seven Congressmen, including myself, was formed; a bipartisan committee of seven was formed as well in the Senate.[300]

Our committees jointly reached an agreement that the Constitutional term "shall be counted" did not specify *who* was to perform the count, and therefore left the decision to Congress on how to proceed. So, we agreed to form a bipartisan commission of Representatives, Senators, and Supreme Court Justices that would count the questionable electoral votes and resolve all disputes. The plan provided that both houses of Congress would have to reject the Commission's decision on a case in order to render it invalid.

Although I heard that Governor Hayes was displeased with this approach and considered it to be unconstitutional, neither Republicans nor Democrats on the committees believed that the issue would be taken up by the Supreme Court. We believed that, as a "political question," the Court would likely deem it best to be left to Congress.

Republicans objected to the plan at first, favoring the notion that the President of the Senate should be the one to resolve all disputes by himself. But most of the other Republicans in the two chambers agreed that such an approach would place the entire burden of the resolution upon Senator Ferry, the Senate President Pro Tem, who would be presiding over the joint session of Congress. It would potentially expose him to disrepute irrespective of his decision, and even put his life in danger from the violence that was beginning to roil many sections of the country over this dispute.

In response to these concerns, I wrote a passage into the proposed bill that was being circulated to the effect that the bipartisan commission would count the votes and declare the winner, "whose authority none can question and whose decision all will accept."[301] I felt that this passage would prove that the House of Representatives, controlled by Democrats largely from the South, wanted a peaceful result if possible, and would give effect to Governor Tilden's desire to arbitrate the controversy.[302]

The Electoral Commission Act, which set up this body, was passed by both Houses of Congress on January 25 and 26, 1877 by sizable majorities. President Grant signed the bill into law on January 29, 1877.[303]

Chapter Twenty-three – The Electoral Commission Is Organized

THE ELECTORAL COMMISSION THAT WAS ESTABLISHED by the Act comprised 15 members – eight Republicans and seven Democrats. There were five Senators, five Congressmen, and five Supreme Court Justices. None were from the disputed states, and only one, from Virginia, was a Southerner.

The Republican Senators chosen for the Commission were George F. Edmunds of Vermont, Frederick T. Frelinghuysen of New Jersey, and Oliver H. P. Morton of Indiana. The two Democratic Senators were Thomas F. Bayard of Delaware and Allen G. Thurman of Ohio.

The partisan split was reversed for the House members. The two Republican Representatives were James A. Garfield of Ohio and George F. Hoar of Massachusetts. The three Democratic Representatives were Josiah G. Abbott of Massachusetts, Eppa Hunton II of Virginia, and Henry B. Payne of Ohio.

Of the five members from the Supreme Court, the two Republicans were Samuel F. Miller of Iowa and William Strong of Pennsylvania. The two Democrats were Stephen J. Field of California and Nathan Clifford of Maine.[304] The President of the Commission was the senior-most member of the Supreme Court, Justice Clifford.

The fifth Supreme Court Justice to be placed on the Commission, David Davis of Illinois, was an independent.[305] The portly Justice Davis had transformed himself over his political career from being a Whig to a Republican (he was Abraham Lincoln's

223

Figure 56: Supreme Court Justice David Davis of Illinois (PD)

campaign manager during the election of 1860), then for two years to a Liberal Republican, then after the 1872 election to an independent. He was considered to be the crucial "swing vote" of the Commission.[306]

But it did not turn out that way. On January 26, 1877, the day that the Electoral Commission bill passed the House and went to President Grant for his signature, word came that the Illinois Legislature had just elected Judge Davis to serve in the United States Senate.[307]

The carefully concocted plan that those of us on the House and Senate committees had hammered out and incorporated into the Electoral Commission Act suddenly went awry. Illinois Senator

John A. Logan's term in the Senate was to end on March 3, and the Illinois Legislature convened on January 10 to either re-elect him or choose his successor. Republicans and Democrats in the Legislature were nearly evenly divided, and five Independents held the balance of power. The Republicans put forward the re-election of Logan by 98 votes; the Democrats voted for John M. Palmer by 88 votes; and the Independents nominated Justice Davis by 8 votes.[308]

There were more than 30 ballots taken by the deadlocked Legislature. Davis was not at all favored. Suddenly, on January 24, most of the Democrats and a few Republicans broke ranks and joined the Independents. The vote for Davis went from 8 to 98 by the 37th ballot. By the last ballot on January 25, Davis was elected Senator by 101 votes.[309]

Immediately upon learning of his election, Justice Davis came to my office at the U.S. Capitol and informed me that he would no longer be available for appointment to the Electoral Commission.

I was taken entirely by surprise at this development. Why would the Illinois Democrats do such a thing to Sam Tilden, their man for the Presidency, at this critical juncture? They knew that Davis held the key to the Presidency by his independent vote on the Commission. He would be the critical eighth vote that, in a straight party-line split, would throw the result either way by a vote of 8-7.

Some said that Democrats in the Illinois Legislature thought that awarding Davis the Senate seat would ingratiate him to the Tilden side. Others surmised that it was a Republican plot to tip the balance on the Commission to Hayes. Personally, I attributed the move to sheer stupidity.

"But why refuse to serve, Your Honor?" I said to Davis after he had submitted his Supreme Court resignation to the Chief Justice. "Your election to the Senate in no way disqualifies you from sitting on the Commission. I specifically vouched for you with my fellow Democrats in the House committee on the assumption that you would be the sole independent voice that we could count on to decide the questions before the Commission without prejudice or party feeling."

"I am sorry, Congressman," Davis said, "but with this Senate seat now in hand, I have a shot at winning the Presidency in the future that I have long sought. I cannot accept a position on the Commission that would almost certainly render me ineligible to be a Presidential candidate down the road. I'm afraid that I see this matter as a conflict of interest that I cannot allow myself to entertain."

I certainly did not see any conflict of interest for Justice Davis, but given his apparent personal lust for Presidential office, I was relieved to some degree that Governor Tilden's fate would not rest in Justice Davis's shifty hands.

* * *

It was now necessary to find a suitable Justice to take Davis's place. The remaining Justices who were available to serve were Noah Haynes Swayne of Ohio, Ward Hunt of New York, and Joseph Philo Bradley of New Jersey. Swayne was a non-starter because he was from Rutherford Hayes' state. That left Hunt and Bradley. Hunt, being from Tilden's state, might be deemed unacceptable to the Republicans for the same reason that Swayne was unacceptable to Democrats. That left Bradley.

Figure 57: Supreme Court Associate Justice Joseph P. Bradley of New Jersey (PD)

Would Bradley be acceptable to all? I needed an independent opinion other than my own. I decided to consult with Senator Roscoe Conkling of New York, even though he was a Republican. Despite that fact, I knew that he had a reputation in our mutual home state for being a "kingmaker" of sorts on local, state and federal positions. If anyone could give me an informed answer, it would be him.

"Hewitt!" Conkling greeted me as I was ushered into his U.S. Capitol office. "Good to see you! What's on your mind?"

"Roscoe, I need your advice," I replied. "I realize that it's a bit unusual for a Democrat to seek the advice of a leader of the Republicans, but in this instance, I think we can be discreet about what I need to ask you. It concerns choosing the fifth Justice for the Electoral Commission."

"We certainly can be discreet, Abram," Roscoe said. "I have already informed my Republican colleagues that I think that Tilden won the election and ought to be seated. So I'm only too happy to give you advice."

"I appreciate that greatly, Roscoe," I said. "As you know, it looks like the selection for the fifth justice is coming down to Bradley. I've known him for many years as a very able lawyer in New Jersey, and I believe he is a man of the highest integrity. Governor Tilden shares my esteem for him. I also asked a mutual friend of Bradley and myself to confer with him to see whether he felt that he could decide the issues before the Electoral Commission without prejudice or party feeling, and my friend's report back was entirely satisfactory.

"What's your view?" I asked Roscoe.

"Well, I'm certainly flattered that you would ask me, Abram," Roscoe replied. "I also think the Democrats' only reasonable choice is Bradley. Hunt is from New York, so certainly my side would look askance at him just as your side will view Swayne. I think that the Democrats should avoid Hunt altogether. He and I are very good friends, and he knows my opinion that Tilden won the election. He might bend over backwards to *avoid* choosing Tilden just to keep clear of giving his party colleagues the impression that I twisted his arm."

I also consulted with Justice Stephen Johnson Field, one of the Democrats who had been selected for the Commission. I explained the situation to him.

Figure 58: Supreme Court Associate Justice Stephen J. Field (PD)

"Oh, I think we can be quite sure that Justice Bradley will be fair," Justice Field told me. "Indeed, it is absurd to worry that any Justice of the Supreme Court would be governed by partisan feeling or influence, and I think Congress and the people know that to be true."

To myself, I reserved judgment on Justice Field's view about the partisanship of Supreme Court Justices in general, having seen how the judicial confirmation process works in the Senate. But Justice Field's support for Bradley reassured me that we were on the right track to choose Justice Bradley. Bradley was not decidedly partisan in his judicial opinions, which was comforting. Therefore, we

Democrats agreed with the Republicans to allow Bradley to fill the fifth judicial seat on the Commission.

It would prove to be a horrific mistake.

Chapter Twenty-four – Florida Confounds Congress

ON THURSDAY, FEBRUARY 1, 1877, I ATTENDED the joint session of Congress that is mandated by the Constitution for counting the electoral votes for President and Vice-President of the United States.[310]

The Chamber of the House of Representatives was packed with a distinguished crowd. President Pro Tem Ferry, leading the joint session, took the chair usually occupied by the Speaker of the House, and the Speaker, Samuel J. Randall of Pennsylvania, sat in a chair to Ferry's left.[311] From their view, the members of the House of Representatives occupied benches on their left, while members of the Senate occupied benches on their right.[312]

The galleries and added seats on the floor of the House were occupied by foreign ministers, politicians, generals, and other distinguished observers.[313] Senator Ferry banged the gavel for the session to come to order.

After making a few opening remarks, Senator Ferry said, "The Clerks will now call the roll of the states and the electoral votes of each state."

In front of the podium was a polished mahogany box containing the official electoral certificates from all thirty-eight states. There was one Teller appointed by the Senate and two Tellers appointed by the House. The Teller of the Senate called out the names of the states in succession; one of the two House Tellers would alternately locate that state's certificate in the box and hand it to Senator Ferry; Senator Ferry would then break open the state seal on the envelope containing the certificate and hand the certificate back to the Teller to declare and list that state's electoral vote.[314]

"Alabama!" declared the Senate Teller. One of the House Tellers reached into the box, pulled out the enveloped enclosed by the wax seal of the State of Alabama, and handed it up to Ferry. Ferry then ran his envelope opener under the seal to break it off, opened the envelope and peered at its contents, then handed it down to the other House Teller to read and announce.

"Alabama casts 10 electoral votes respectively for Samuel J. Tilden for President and Thomas A. Hendricks for Vice-President," the House Teller announced.

"Arkansas!"

"Arkansas casts 6 electoral votes respectively for Samuel J. Tilden for President and Thomas A. Hendricks for Vice-President."

"California!"

"California casts 6 electoral votes respectively for Rutherford B. Hayes for President and William A. Wheeler for Vice-President."

"Connecticut!"

"Connecticut casts 6 electoral votes respectively for Samuel J. Tilden for President and Thomas A. Hendricks for Vice-President."

"Delaware!"

"Delaware casts 3 electoral votes respectively for Samuel J. Tilden for President and Thomas A. Hendricks for Vice-President."

"Florida!"

The chamber, previously a hubbub of mumbled conversation, fell silent. The first House Teller handed to Senator Ferry the three sealed envelopes that had been sent from Florida.

Senator Ferry broke open the wax seals on all the envelopes. "I have three certificates from Florida," he said to the hushed chamber. "The first one is in regular form and was signed on December 6, 1876 by Marcellus Stearns, the Governor at the time of the election, and the then-Secretary of State, Samuel B. McLin.

"The second certificate is in irregular form and was signed on December 6, 1876 by Florida Attorney-General William A. Cocke.

"The third certificate is in regular form and was signed on January 26, 1877 by the current Governor of Florida, George F. Drew, and the current Secretary of State, William D. Bloxham." Appended to the third certificate was a copy of an act of the Florida Legislature dated January 17, 1877; the certificate of the state canvassers who recanvassed the vote under that act; and a reference, in the governor's certificate, to a judgment of the circuit court in the *quo warranto* proceeding that was affirmed by the Supreme Court of the State of Florida.

Senator Ferry handed the opened envelopes to the second House Teller. The Teller said, "the first certificate states that Florida casts 4 electoral votes respectively for Rutherford B. Hayes for President and William A. Wheeler for Vice-President. The second certificate states that Florida casts 4 electoral votes respectively for Samuel J. Tilden for President and Thomas A. Hendricks for Vice-President. The third certificate states that Florida casts 4 electoral votes respectively for Samuel J. Tilden for President and Thomas A. Hendricks for Vice-President."[315]

Objections were heard and seconded by House and Senate members of the joint session to each one of the certificates.[316] The Democrats injected an additional objection to the reception of the vote of Hayes elector F. C. Humphreys on the ground that he was a federal office-holder at the time that he cast his electoral vote, and was therefore constitutionally ineligible to be an elector.[317]

"There being a dispute as to which of the three certificates is true and correct, the electoral vote of the State of Florida will be referred to the Electoral Commission for resolution," Senator Ferry intoned, rapping his gavel. A motion for adjournment of the Joint Session of Congress pending the decision of the Electoral Commission on the Florida electoral vote was accepted, and the chamber emptied out.[318]

Chapter Twenty-five – The Electoral Commission, Round One

THE FIRST SESSION OF THE COMMISSION WAS CALLED for three o'clock that afternoon for the purpose of taking care of some housekeeping matters.[319]

Figure 59: Justice Nathan Clifford, President of the Commission (PD)

To allow the testifying parties time to prepare, however, the Commission President, Justice Clifford, adjourned the session until 10:30 a.m. the following day, Friday, February 2.[320]

* * *

The Supreme Court Chamber of the U.S. Capitol was formerly the chamber of the U.S. Senate until 1860, when it was turned over to the Supreme Court to serve as its courtroom.[321] The Chamber is inadequate in size to accommodate the enormous crowd of lawyers and luminaries who filled it on Friday, the first day of oral argument before the Electoral Commission.

I attended the Commission on Friday, February 2, 1877, the date of its first working session, with my wife Amelia. She was one of very few distinguished and well-known women who occupied the chamber on that day. She insisted on attending with me because of the history that we both knew would be made.

Figure 60: The Electoral Commission of 1877 Meets in the Supreme Court Chamber of the U.S. Capitol (PD)

On the first day of arguments concerning the three Florida certificates, the Commission President, Justice Clifford, established the rules of the proceeding: two Congressional objectors on each side would speak to each certificate. Each side was allotted two hours to make its arguments.[322] After the Congressional objectors made their arguments against each certificate, the lawyers for each side would be heard.[323]

The first to rise for the Democratic objectors was Representative David Dudley Field of New York.[324] He had been chosen by the New York Legislature to fill out the last three months of the unexpired term of Representative Smith Ely, who had resigned his House seat to serve as Mayor of New York City. Perhaps not wholly guilelessly, the

Figure 61: Congressman David Dudley Field of New York (PD)

Democrats' choice of their leadoff batter was the brother of Justice Stephen J. Field, who sat before him on the Commission bench as he spoke.[325] No objections were raised.

As David Field rose to speak, his brother Stephen could not help suppressing a broad grin from the bench, to which David returned a quick wink in Stephen's direction. After greeting the Commission in the traditional manner, Representative Field stated that he would "endeavor ...to set forth with as much conciseness as I may the facts that we expect to prove and the propositions of law which we hope to establish."[326]

Field began by offering the Commission a recitation of the facts of the Florida case as they appeared in the record of state court *quo warranto* proceedings that were conducted after the election. He described the initial canvass of the Baker County clerk and the justice of the peace; the second canvass by that clerk and a second justice of the peace in the courtroom of the then-absent county judge; and the evening intrusion of the county judge, the sheriff, and yet a third justice of the peace into the clerk's closed office, whereupon they surreptitiously removed the ballots of two precincts and certified the remainder (that is, the false third canvass) to the State Board of Canvassers for compilation.[327]

Field went on to recite the State Canvassing Board's subsequent amendment of the certified returns to include all ballots from the Baker County clerk's first two accurate identical counts. Field explained how the board then excluded from other county canvasses a number of ballots equal to the two precinct counts that the Baker County judge had removed. Thus, Field said, the board accomplished the same purpose as the false Baker County canvass of appointing electors favoring Hayes, which he called "Return No.

1."[328] This was the return on which the Hayes supporters pinned their hopes.

Field then described the result of the *quo warranto* circuit court proceeding brought by the defeated Tilden electors against the Hayes electors, which invalidated this falsified count. The resulting re-canvass of all votes, including the removed votes, favored the Tilden electors. On the strength of the court's order, the State Attorney- General certified the count himself to Congress. This certification Field called "Return No. 2."[329] This was the first of the two certificates that the Tilden supporters vouched for.

Finally, Field described the actions of the Supreme Court of Florida and the Florida Legislature to back up Return No. 2 with affirmative legislation and a certificate from the new Governor confirming the appointment of the Tilden electors. This certificate Field called "Return No. 3."[330] This was the second pro-Tilden certificate.

Field then offered the Commission his argument – that the Commission was empowered to "go behind" Return No. 1, the only Return signed by the Governor in office at the time of the election – to decide if it should be rejected as fraudulent.

"We are told," said Field, "that the certificate of Governor Stearns ... annexed to the lists of votes of the Hayes electors countervails all this evidence, and that no matter what amount of testimony we may offer, ... we can never invalidate the signature of Marcellus L. Stearns ...."[331]

"It is putting the question in an erroneous form," Field continued, "to put it thus, 'You cannot go behind the certificate.' The form should be reversed. *Can the certificate go before the truth and conceal it?*"[332]

Field continued his point. "I venture to say that it is the universal rule, and there is no court of general jurisdiction known to American or Anglo-Saxon law in which it is not a fundamental principle that whenever a court can inquire into facts necessary to its judgment, it may take all the pertinent evidence, that is to say all evidence that tends to prove the fact, unless it is restricted by some positive law."[333]

Amelia asked me, in the quietest of whispers that one could manage there, "Is Field implying that the Commission may not accept the Tilden evidence? I thought they had to take *all* the evidence."

"This has been heavily discussed on both sides," I replied, also in the quietest of whispers. "Much of this debate is going to turn on exactly *what* evidence the Commission will consider."

"Shush!" Senator Blaine, who sat in front of us, turned an icy Republican glare in our Democratic direction.

"My apologies, Senator," I said contritely. Blaine, obviously still smarting from his humiliating defeat at the Republican Convention, disgruntledly turned back around.

Field rhetorically asked the Commission, "Show me a positive law that makes the certificate of Stearns evidence against the truth! Where is it? In what book? It is not in the Constitution. It is not in the laws of Florida. Is it in any law of Congress? The only act of Congress applicable is that which provides that the executive of the State shall deliver to the electors a certificate that they are such electors, but that act does not declare that this certificate shall be conclusive – neither declares it, nor implies it."[334]

"The Constitution," Field went on, "declares that the person having the highest number of votes shall be the President, *not that the person declared to have the highest number of votes, but 'the person having the highest number.'* No certificate can be manufactured to take that away."[335]

Field then raised the specter of fraud and the potential for tyranny. "I submit to the Commission that there is another rule of law which necessarily leads us to answer affirmatively the question whether the truth can be given in evidence notwithstanding the certificate; and that is that fraud vitiates all transactions and can always be inquired into in every case .... Is it a true proposition of law that you cannot inquire whether [the Governor] has acted fraudulently? If it be true that the certificate of the governor is conclusive evidence that these persons were elected, *then it follows that the certificate would be sufficient if there were no election at all.*"[336]

This time, Amelia had pencil and paper in hand for me to read. She wrote, "Could a governor 'certify' that an election had occurred when it really did not?"

I shrugged at first, but then nodded in agreement. Her eyebrows rose in astonishment.

Once finished, Field yielded to the second pro-Tilden Congressional objector, Representative John Randolph Tucker of Virginia. Tucker spoke more of fraud and demanded that the Commission find a way to prevent it. "Is there any power in the Constitution under which we live," he asked, "by which a fraudulent and illegal title to the office of President can be prevented? Must a man that everybody knows to be a usurper be pronounced by the two Houses of Congress or by this tribunal in their stead to have a valid title to the office when all the world knows he has not?"[337]

Tucker sternly informed the commissioners that "If the Board of Canvassers, either contrary to law, or transcending their legal authority, or under their legal authority, fraudulently counted in as elected those who were not elected by the people, their act was void."[338] He pointed to the decision of the Supreme Court of Florida to that effect,

Figure 62: Congressman John R. Tucker of Virginia (PD)

emphasizing that it "settles the question of the power of this Board, that their duty was merely ministerial, that they had no right to throw out votes, that they had a right merely to enumerate the votes as they were sent up from the counties, but that they had no right to reject on the idea that there was fraud or intimidation, or on such loose evidence as my friend read this morning, that they had heard somewhere the air was full of rumors of bull-dozing and intimidation, and therefore we throw out any amount of votes."[339]

Tucker concluded with a further reference to the pro-Tilden ruling of the Florida Supreme Court: "The question is, are the Hayes electors *appointed*, not are they returned by the trio [of Canvassing Board members] or by [Governor] Stearns, but are they *appointed by the people of Florida*; not who gave them [their] commission but *who gave them title to speak for Florida?*[340]

"The title comes from the body of the people," Tucker emphasized. "The commission may come from the ... Board and Governor. Have *they* the legal right to say it? The judgment of the court answers no. Did they fraudulently make the return? The court answers they did. Now shall this tribunal, in the teeth of this ultimate State determinant power, give title to any such commission or give title under the voice of the people? Shall you hold the commission which the state court of Florida has declared to be invalid, to be valid in order to stifle the elective power of the people and give power to the determinant functions of the oligarchy? That is the question."[341]

Tucker returned to his seat, and the Commission adjourned at noon for a three-hour lunch break.

* * *

Justice-Commission President Nathan Clifford ambled over to the U.S. Capitol Cafeteria for lunch. As he picked up a tray and entered the line for his meal, he found Justice-Commissioner Samuel F. Miller holding a tray right behind him.

Figure 63: Supreme Court Justice Samuel Freeman Miller (PD)

The two Associate Justices were close in age – Clifford was a few years older than Miller – and Clifford was elevated to the Supreme Court in 1858, four years before Miller in 1862. They were well-acquainted with each other, even though Clifford was a Democrat and Miller a Republican.

"Well, Brother Sam! Glad to see this is where the elite meet to eat!" Nathan joked.

"Without question, Brother Nate! The Senate Bean Soup just can't be beat!" Sam reposted.

As they paid the cashier, Nate asked Sam if he would join him for lunch. "I'd be delighted, Nate," Sam replied.

Once they found a small table next to the wall and began their meal, Sam said, "Nate, may I talk to you about a procedural matter concerning the Commission?"

"Why, certainly, Sam," Nate replied. "Although I can't say that there's any 'procedure' to this brand-new creature that I'm aware of, other than that I have to ask everyone on it for consent to everything I do."

"Well, you *are* the "President" of this Commission, *and* you're a Justice, *and* you have a career practicing law that goes a long way back. So I can't think of anyone more knowledgeable than you to answer a procedural question that I have.

"What is that?" Nate asked.

"I know from everything that I've read and heard so far that the lawyers for Tilden intend to introduce evidence of what happened at the polls in Baker County, Florida," said Sam. "This will include tallies and certifications of the raw votes from the precincts that were compiled by volunteer pollsters and low-level officials of the State Canvassing Board. There will probably be evidence and testimony that were introduced in the state court *quo warranto* proceeding. Should we really listen to all that? Shouldn't we only decide on the basis of what the certifications that were sent to the President of the Senate say?"

"You mean should we go behind the certificates themselves and hear evidence about voter fraud at the polls themselves?" Nate asked Sam.

"Precisely," Sam replied. "We are not a court of law. We have not been constituted as one. We are not created under Article III of the Constitution. We've only been formed to advise Congress on what it should do about the disputed states. In one sense we're a factfinding committee, but in another sense we are only an advisory board. And the fact that we are made up of all three of the deliberative bodies of the federal government – the Senate, the House, and the Court – nothing in the Electoral Commission Act requires that the procedures followed by any one of those bodies is supposed to prevail in our deliberations."

"That makes sense," said Nate.

"So," Sam continued, "if we're supposed to merely advise and find facts regarding Congress' duty to count electoral votes and declare a winner for President and Vice-President, is it really our Commission's place to initiate an investigation into the way that the popular votes were counted in Florida? Isn't that Florida's duty to do? Isn't it a duty of *every* state in the Union to ensure that votes were properly amassed? I don't know of anything that leaves that duty in the hands of the fgovernment."

"That's true, Sam," said Nate.

"Then why take any evidence of fraud at the polls at all?" Sam asked.

Nate pondered that a moment as he sipped his Senate Bean Soup. "Well, there's precedent for doing it. The Senate did it in the 1872 Presidential election. They threw out all of Louisiana's votes because of all the fraud there. Once the Senate did that under the rules of the Joint Session as they existed then, that was it. The House couldn't revive them without the Senate's consent. Of course," Nate said, "it didn't matter because Grant won that election in a landslide. So Louisiana's electoral votes didn't matter.

"Now here," Nate continued, "Florida's electoral votes *do* matter. One elector is all Tilden needs to become President. And there's three different certifications. How are we going to pick the right one without going into the votes that support each one of them?"

"I don't think it's a question of *fact*, Nate," Sam said. "I think it's a question of *law*. Florida's election law. It's *that* law that states which certificate is the legitimate one. We're not a court, so we can't render a decision about what the law means. We can only follow what the law *is*. So the raw facts – who threw out this poll, who lied on that poll – are really irrelevant to us. Why take evidence on it?"

Nate lowered his soup spoon and pinched his lower lip. "I get your point, Brother. We're only advisory. We have no more power than Congress does on this matter. And the only power Congress has is to count electoral votes and declare the winner. *Amassing* the electoral votes are purely state matters. The states can initiate *quo warranto* proceedings to determine who is a legitimate elector. The federal government certainly can't do that.

"But Florida conducted a *quo warranto* proceeding," Nate continued. "It decided that there was fraud at the polls."

"The *quo warranto* proceeding decided only the *governor's* race, Nate," Sam replied. "It didn't rule on the Presidential election. All there is about the Presidential election in that case are raw evidence of voter tallies, and it's merely *assumed* that since a Democrat won the governor's race, Democratic electors must have won the electoral race as well. The State of Florida did not formally declare that until long after the fact, by a new Democratic administration that did not itself conduct the election.

"Is it the intention of the Tilden lawyers to simply put the raw *quo warranto* evidence in front of us and say, "Commission, you decide?" Sam asked Nate. "Are *we* authorized to say what the *people of Florida* want? I don't think even Congress is empowered to do that! That's a state power, not a federal one."

Nate stared at Sam. His Senate Bean Soup was cold by now. "Sam, I understand your point. I am sure that seven other commissioners will agree with you. I will ask the lawyers tomorrow whether they intend to make *offers* of proof before we hear their arguments. That will lock them into presenting their evidence if we then decide to take it. If we decide not to, then at least we will not have wasted their time lodging evidence that we decide to discard. Of course, this must be discussed and voted upon by the Commission as a whole. Will you accept that approach?"

"I will live with that, Nate."

* * *

Amelia and I caught a hansom cab over to the Ebbitt House restaurant on 14th and F Streets Northwest. Pennsylvania Avenue, as usual, was teeming with horses, cabs, trolleys and carts. But our driver adeptly finessed all obstacles, knowing that our time for lunch was short.

Figure 64: Ebbitt House, circa 1903 (PD)

"Field and Tucker are interesting men," Amelia remarked over our open-faced hot roast beef sandwiches.

"Oh, they're very different from one another," I remarked. "You know Field, of course. A classic New York attorney. Tucker, on the other hand, is a dyed-in-the-wool Southern aristocrat from Virginia. He was attorney general of the Commonwealth during the Civil War, and received a pardon from Andrew Johnson. He's been in Congress about two years."

"So now we're going to hear from two Congressmen who support Hayes, right?" Amelia asked.

"Right," I said. "John Kasson and George McCrary, both from Iowa. They will buck up the first certificate that Governor Stearns certified for Hayes, which is based on the faulty Baker County canvass. That would be the official certificate of Florida electors if only fraud were not involved. The second certificate was signed by William Cocke, the Florida Attorney-General, who was on the State Canvassing Board and believed that Tilden had been elected by the accurate canvass. He took it upon himself to certify the vote of the Tilden electors, which was taken on the same official day as the vote of the Hayes electors. He then sent the second certificate up to Washington.

"The third certificate is quite a story," I continued. "Governor Stearns was defeated by George Drew in the same election as the Presidential one. Stearns was the Republican and Drew was the Democrat. After the Tilden electors and Attorney-General Cocke sued the Hayes electors in the Florida state courts to oust them, and won in the State Supreme Court, Governor Drew had the new Legislature pass a law declaring Tilden to be the winner of the election. He then certified the vote of the Tilden electors and sent that third certificate up to Washington."

"So this Commission of eight Republicans and seven Democrats has to decide which certificate, the one signed by a Republican Governor or one of the the two signed by a Democratic Attorney-General and a new Democratic Governor, is the right certificate?" Amelia asked.

Figure 65: Amelia Cooper Hewitt (PD)

"That's right, Dear," I replied, looking down at my plate, for I knew what her next observation would be.

"Sounds like a no-brainer to me," she smirked. "Sam will lose by a vote of eight to seven."

"I guess it sure looks that way, doesn't it, Dear?" I admitted.

After dessert, we flagged down a hansom cab, galloped back to the Capitol, and squeezed into our seats for Round Two.

Chapter Twenty-six – The Electoral Commission, Round Two

THE COMMISSION RE-ASSEMBLED AT THREE O'CLOCK in the afternoon. Justice-Commission President Clifford (no one had as yet figured out what his true title on the Commission was), said, "One of the objectors to the second certificate will now be heard on the same rules and conditions prescribed in respect to the objectors to the first."[342] Representative John A. Kasson, Republican from Iowa, stood up to speak.

Kasson lunged at the second certificate that supported the Tilden electors. "There is a second so-called certificate opened in the joint meeting of the two Houses of Congress in which the persons signing the same preface their own certificate by one signed by an officer not recognized by the laws of the United States nor by the statutes of Florida as a certifying officer, being the Attorney-General of the State of Florida. He certifies that there is no provision of the law of Florida 'whereby the result of said return can be certified to the executive of

Figure 66: Congressman John A. Kasson of Iowa (PD)

said State,' admitting by that certificate, if it has any force at all, that his action is without the law and without any sanction of the statutes of the State."

Exuding contempt, Kasson continued: "Next, the self-styled electors certify to their own election and their own qualifications, and that they themselves notified the governor of their own election." It is, he said, "a certificate of unauthorized persons and uncertified persons in the view of the laws, state and national, and that was presented and opened in pursuance of the recent act of Congress for what it is worth."[343]

Kasson next belittled Certificate No. 3, the new Democratic Governor's certification of the Tilden electors. "There is a third certificate still more extraordinary, still more wanting in all the legal elements of electoral verification, and which asks for itself consideration," he said to the commissioners. "It is a certificate which is thoroughly *ex post facto*, certified by an officer not in existence until the functions of the office had been exhausted ...." Kasson pointed out that the court proceedings that underlie Certificate No. 3 all happened after the date fixed by the Constitution for the nationwide voting day for the electors. The Certificate, he charged, is of a type "which has never been sent to the Congress of the United States or to the President of the Senate for their consideration in the one hundred years in which we have been a Republic."[344]

Expressing more contempt, Kasson then said, "I ought, perhaps, to say to the honorable Commission that it is fortunate they did not grant the request of our objectors for an adjournment till tomorrow. The next mail might have brought to you Certificate No. 4 or 5, reciting to you new proceedings, a new action before the courts, and no end would come to the papers that might be presented in party or personal interest as establishing a retroactive right to exercise an electoral function in the State of Florida!"[345]

Having thus trashed the credibility of Certificate Nos. 2 and 3, at least in his own mind, Congressman Kasson turned to exalting the credibility of Certificate No. 1. To the Democrats' claim that local state officials committed fraud in collecting ballots, Kasson said that "if you go into that question in Baker County ... we should inevitably ask that you go into Jackson County, where, under other political domination, they rejected 271 votes actually cast for the Hayes electors. We should ask you to go into Alachua County and find at one precinct a railroad train of non-resident passengers getting off on their passage through and voting the ticket which was supported by the objector [Congressman Field] who made the allegation against Baker County. We should invoke your attention to Waldo Precinct of the same county to find that they had vitiated that poll also by what is called stuffing the ballot-box. And so on with other counties passed upon by the state board.

"We answer, then, the allegation that their charges of fraud have not been denied by us," he said, "by stating that if they are ever reached in the exercise of your jurisdiction, we propose to show, and shall show in that contingency, that there was such a case of fraud in the incipiency of that vote which they claim should elect their candidate as would astonish not only this Commission, but the whole country by its presentation.... I do not believe that this Commission by the Constitution or laws was ever intended, or has the power, to go to the extent that would be required if they attempted to probe these mutual allegations of fraudulent voting and fraudulent canvassing to the bottom by judicial investigation and judicial decision."[346]

So, as we all expected on the Democratic side, the Republicans defended their acts by pointing the finger at us and saying that we were just as corrupt. Two "wrongs," they contended, made a "right." Kasson made no effort, however, to identify his evidence of our "wrong."

Kasson then made a statement that confounded us all. He claimed that the recount ordered by the Florida Courts at the behest of the Tilden electors and the Attorney General *favored the Hayes electors by some 200 votes, not the Tilden electors.* "These electors appear to have run two or three hundred votes ahead of the state ticket, and the recanvass left them still some two hundred majority. That appeared on the record," Kasson claimed.

Kasson clouded in mystery the proof of his assertion of what came out in the Florida *quo warranto* case. "It does not appear on the printed document which has been submitted on the other side here, I suppose, because the court ruled that they intended their order to only apply to state officers; and therefore they struck out, after it had once gone in the record, the result as to the electors; but it was originally a part of the proceedings under order of the court, which, if gone into, will show the fact that not only canvass number one showed the election of the Hayes electors, but canvass number two had, under the order and in accordance with the ruling of the Supreme Court, showed both the election of the Democratic state ticket and the election of the Hayes electors."[347]

"Where does he get that??" Amelia couldn't help whispering to me, "Is he claiming that the Hayes electors won the count that supports the second and third certificates, not the Tilden electors?" Senator Blaine turned again to shoot another testy glance our way. We ignored him this time.

"He's saying it," I whispered back, "but the court proceedings officially concerned only the gubernatorial election, not the Presidential election, so the court order doesn't mention who won the vote for Presidential electors. We say that Tilden won that vote, not Hayes. There's been a lot of mud slung between the parties over that controversy."

Congressman Field rose in protest to reiterate that the State Canvassing Board had persisted in juggling the votes for the second count as well as the first. "Please to state that in the recanvass this Canvassing Board put back Baker County so as to include only two precincts."

Congressman Kasson shot back, "That is only to say that the gentlemen on the other side want to take just so much of that action under order of the court as suits their case and reject all the rest."[348] Although he had no evidence to prove it, Kasson maintained that the Florida court that decided the *quo warranto* decision actually had before it a state-wide canvass that supported the Hayes electors, not the Tilden electors. To him, Baker County was only one example of the juggling that went on in *all* counties, by Democrats as well as Republicans.

Wrapping up, Kasson asked one more rhetorical question of the commissioners: "I ask this Commission if there be a *prima facie* presumption of fraud, whether it exists against those officers elected before fraud could have been contemplated, against a Board that acted at the time required by the state law, against a Board that acted at the time provided by congressional law, against a Board that acted in ignorance of the electoral vote in other states, as it was contemplated by our fathers they should do? Or," he said, pointing a finger at the Democratic objectors, "does that presumption of fraud exist against the men who knew of the importance of a change of the result in Florida, against men who acted in full knowledge of the necessity of the action they took to accomplish their results, against men who organized a new tribunal and enacted a new law to accomplish that result ?"[349]

In Kasson's mind, *we* were the bad guys.

* * *

"The second objector will be heard on the same conditions and limitations," said the President, Justice Clifford. Representative George Washington McCrary, another Iowa Republican, rose from his crowded desk to speak.

Figure 67: Congressman George W. McCrary of Iowa (PD)

McCrary first apologized to the Commission for his lack of preparation for this presentation, having learned only at four o'clock the day before that the Congressional objectors would be required to speak before it.

McCrary called into question the reach of the Commission's authority to decide the election. "If one case can be made against one elector in the United States, requiring Congress or this tribunal to go down among the forty-five millions of people and decide how many votes were legally cast for this candidate or that, a case can be made against every one of the members of the electoral college of the United States. The result is ... that, unless the two Houses of Congress shall consent, the people of the United States can never again be allowed to choose a President and Vice-President."[350]

So this Congressman was predicting doomsday if Tilden was inaugurated like the people wanted him to be, I thought to myself.

McCrary picked up on Congressman Kasson's astonishing statement made earlier. "[I]t is a fact which will appear, if this commission shall go into the inquiry, that on three separate occasions, the first and regular canvass, the second canvass made under the mandamus proceedings and in relation to the office of governor, and on a third canvass made subsequently, this Board constituted by the laws of the State of Florida ascertained and declared that the gentlemen known as the Hayes electors had a majority of all the votes cast."[351]

McCrary countervailed the Democrats' argument that the *quo warranto* proceeding in the Florida State Courts to test the titles of the Hayes electors to their offices could retroactively invalidate their official act of voting. "It is claimed by counsel that this *quo warranto* proceeding, which went into judgment nearly two months after the casting of the vote of Florida for President and Vice-President by the electors, relates back to the date of the filing of the petition and vacates and vitiates everything that was done in the meantime. That I think is not the law.

"The writ of *quo warranto* is a proceeding to test the right of an incumbent of an office. It does not restrain him from acting from the time that the original summons may be served. It does not oust him from the office until there is a final judgment of ouster ...."[352]

The Congressman from Iowa then cited several American and British cases for the proposition that a court order ousting an officer acted only prospectively to invalidate the officer's actions after it was issued, not retroactively to invalidate his actions preceding ouster.[353]

Amelia silently passed a furiously-scribbled note to me. "Why does he question the validity of the court proceeding if he says there was evidence before it that vindicates Hayes? Why not just *offer that evidence?*" I scribbled back, "Smokescreen."

McCrary then explained correctly why all electors of all states were required by the Constitution to meet in their respective state capitals on the same day in order to cast their electoral votes. "[A]fter the time fixed by the law, after the result of the election in the whole Union has been ascertained, after it has been discovered that by changing the vote of a single state the result of the election in the whole nation may be changed, parties may institute their [*quo warranto* court cases], ... may proceed to try the case, and may determine that the electors who have discharged this duty on the day fixed by the Constitution and the laws were not the legal electors.[354]

"In one state," McCrary pointed out, "an inferior court having power to issue the writ of *quo warranto*, being attached to one side of the question, will entertain a petition of this character and will decide in favor of one set of electors, and send up to the President of the Senate the record of its proceedings declaring that the men who had voted on the day fixed by the law were not the electors. In another state, another judge will perhaps render a judgment in favor of a set belonging to the other side. And so we shall be called upon, instead of counting the votes provided for by the

Constitution of the United States and the laws of the land, to investigate the decisions of all these courts in all the states."[355]

After making a few more remarks against the second and third Certificates, Congressman McCrary thanked the Commission and sat down. That brought the presentations of the Congressional objectors to an end.

* * *

As the next session of the Commission would be devoted to arguments by legal counsel for each side, President Clifford took the opportunity to raise the issue he had discussed at lunch with Justice Miller:

> For the information of the Commission, I desire to inquire of the objectors to the first certificate whether they propose before the argument by counsel to offer evidence. I inquire of counsel for the information merely of the Commission, that we may know how to act in consultation, do you propose to offer evidence before proceeding to the argument?[356]

There followed a conversation among the commissioners and the lawyers about the submission of evidence. The lawyers for the Tilden side stated that they would present evidence. To that, Justice Miller declared:

> Before proceeding with that I wish to say, as one of the commissioners, that I do not understand that any evidence has yet been admitted in this case; and I suggest to the counsel who propose to offer evidence tomorrow morning, that they make a brief synopsis or

a brief statement of what it is they propose to offer altogether, instead of offering it in details and having objections raised to every particular piece of testimony.

This is a mere suggestion from myself.[357]

The lawyers for the Hayes side stated that they would only present rebuttal evidence if the Tilden side presented direct evidence that the Commission had chosen to accept.[358] With that, at a little after five p.m., President Clifford adjourned the Commission to 10:30 a.m. the next day, Saturday, February 3.

This brief housekeeping discussion would have enormous consequences later in the proceedings.

* * *

Amelia and I dined at Willard's Hotel at Fourteenth Street and Pennsylvania Avenue, N.W. The Hotel lobby was always a beehive of "lobbying" activity among Congressmen and the professional gentlemen who specialized in seeking favors from them for their clients across the nation.

After dinner, I spent the evening in the smoking lounge with fellow Democratic Congressmen discussing that day's events at the Electoral Commission. I later learned, however, that a gathering in the Tea Room of the Hotel that Amelia simultaneously sat in

Figure 68: Willard's Hotel during the Civil War (PD)

on, of female attendees present for that day's Commission hearings, was far more interesting than my own.

"Well, Justice Clifford is old and immensely fat, but certainly not as fat as Justice Davis!" said Sue Virginia Sweringen Field, Justice Stephen Field's wife, to hearty laughter all around. "That man would have occupied *two* seats in the Supreme Court Chamber if he had taken on the job, and we women would without a doubt have been deprived of our seats!"

Figure 69: Sue Virginia Sweringen Field (PD)

"Oh, there were plenty of gentlemen to gaze at besides Judge Clifford, Sue," said the beautiful and fashionable Kate Chase Sprague, daughter of the late Supreme Court Chief Justice Salmon P. Chase and wife of the immensely wealthy Senator William Sprague IV of Rhode Island.

Figure 70: Kate Chase Sprague (PD)

"We certainly noticed, Kate dear," laughed Lucretia Garfield, wife of Senator James Garfield (Republican and Democratic women in Washington mingled far more easily than the men). "I particularly took notice of Congressman McCrary! What a handsome, well-put-together fellow!"

"Do you think that Wade Hampton III will make an appearance?" asked Alva Vanderbilt, the daring socialite and suffragette from New York high society (although not at this time among "The Four Hundred," which was deemed by *New York Times* gossip columnist Ward McAllister to be the number of social elites who could fit into Caroline

Figure 71: Lucretia Garfield (PD)

Astor's drawing room).[359] "I just *adore* him! I would just love to have a go at him!" she sighed hungrily.

"I'm sure that he'd make an appearance here if he were to learn that *you're* here!" Sue giggled.

Figure 72: Alva Vanderbilt (PD)

"Ladies," Alva continued, "changing the subject for a minute, there's a serious question that I want to ask you. Do you think that this would be happening if women had the vote?"

The laughter stopped. It was a very serious – and volatile – question. All of their husbands had deeply-held views on the matter.

"I'll be frank with you, Alva," Amelia spoke up, "I have no doubt that the same thing would *not* have happened. Men seem to have a very protective view of politics. They seem to think that it's their exclusive province. They like to tell us that they incorporate their wives' and daughters' views in their election decisions. But we know that's not true. I do think, however, that the corruption and fraud would subside greatly if women had the vote."

"I agree," Lucretia said. It heartened the other women to hear a Republican say this to a primarily Democratic audience. "Think of it! Former slaves now vote. But fifty percent of the nation – made up of both freed slaves and whites – have no voice in how this country is run. And women are employed in many factories and shops, we are selling produce in the marketplaces, and we are raising and teaching our children. Men cannot say that they know even the half of what is going on right under their noses!"

"I do not think that women would have tolerated their men monkeying with the ballots the way they've done," said Sue. "If they had to answer to us as well as to their friends in the saloons, they would probably have exercised a bit more caution than they did in Florida."

"The polling stations are just extensions of the saloons, Sue," said Alva. "The behavior of the men is atrocious! I cannot help thinking of that Thomas Nast cartoon of the two cowboys pointing their pistols at the head of a black man trying to cast his vote. They would not do that if their wives were present!"

"I can only hope that this calamity will hasten the day when we can enter the polling stations ourselves and cast our votes too," Kate observed. "It will settle the men down and make them take this sacred duty seriously."

Chapter Twenty-seven – The Agony of Justice Joseph Philo Bradley

UNLIKE THE GAIETY OF THE LOBBY OF WILLARD'S HOTEL, all was somber and worrisome at the home of Supreme Court Associate Justice Joseph Philo Bradley.

Mr. Justice Bradley of New Jersey was deliberately chosen by a sundered Congress to be the "swing vote" of the Commission. Justice Davis was unquestionably an independent who would have fulfilled that role perfectly. Instead, Democrats shot themselves in the foot by awarding him the perquisite of being Senator from Illinois. The unintended consequence of their act was to prompt him to resign from the Supreme Court and dodge the thankless role of being the Electoral Commission's baby-splitter.

This event put Bradley in the hot seat as Davis's replacement. He was a staunch Republican, but he faced the Hobson's choice of enraging one half of the country or the other. He knew that, in the end, he would forever be either a pariah to Republicans or a fiend to Democrats.

Joseph was a fair man and a devout member of the Dutch Reformed Church.[360] He favored federal over state power in constitutional matters involving the Interstate Commerce Clause, which pleased Republican business and railroad interests. Nevertheless, in the *Slaughter-House Cases* of 1872, he sided with the four dissenters against the majority's opinion in favor of the state-sanctioned monopoly known as the Slaughter-House Trust of New Orleans. Joseph wrote in his own dissent that "a law which prohibits a large class of citizens from adopting a lawful employment, or from following a lawful employment previously adopted, does deprive them of liberty as well as property, without due process of law."[361]

This was a broad reading of the new Fourteenth Amendment, and it greatly pleased Democrats. These contrasting sentiments of Bradley's prompted both Republicans and Democrats in Congress to view him as an adequately neutral judicial replacement for Justice Davis.

Joseph became an insomniac after his appointment. He would stay up in his study until eleven o'clock at night and wake up at three in the morning, his mind anxiously racing about the Florida election. Late on the night after the Friday Commission hearing, he began to write out what he thought would be a suitable draft decision for the Florida case. He wrote the draft in favor of the Tilden side, just to see whether it seemed to be the stronger argument against his Republican predilections.

Joseph's wife of over 30 years, Mary Hornblower Bradley, worried about his anxiety, his insomnia, and his opinions. She was a religious woman and a devoted Republican.[362] To her, the thought of Southern Democrats, whom she considered to be no better than camoflagued Confederate traitors, swinging the election their way through subterfuge filled her with dread. She saw Joseph's draft and read it after he exhaustedly went to bed. It troubled her deeply.

Early the next morning, before Joseph left home to go to the Commission hearing, she quizzed him about it. "How can you find for Tilden?" she asked him indignantly.

"I have not yet decided one way or the other, Mary," Joseph replied. "I have always thought that states have the sole power of governing elections. Therefore, the state's manner of choosing Presidential electors should not be questioned by Congress."

"Then obviously the certification of a state's governor of what the vote was should be the end of the matter," Mary retorted. "Is Congress going to tell the states and the people whom their choice of President ought to be? Do you think that anyone will ever believe that the people choose the President ever again? Don't you realize that it will only affirm in their minds that the big shots in Washington dictate the choice? Are the only votes that count in choosing a President those of Cornelius Vanderbilt and Leland Stanford?"

Mary was well-schooled in debating her husband about his legal and political ideas.

"But there is something new at work here," Joseph replied. "I dissented in *Slaughter-House* over it, remember?[363] Under the new Fourteenth Amendment, a state cannot deprive a large class of citizens of liberty or property without due process of law. Their right of choice is a portion of their liberty. Therefore, the state cannot simply throw out votes. It deprives those citizens of the equal protection of the laws.

"Also, the Fifteenth Amendment prohibits the denial or abridgement of the right to vote on account of race, color, or having previously been a slave.

"Congress can enforce these Amendments. These developments change things. Florida cannot simply throw out legitimate votes like they're charged with doing."

Mary sighed and shook her head. "Joseph, what happened in Florida undoubtedly happened in *every* state," she replied. "How is

Congress supposed to decide who is President if it must look into every state process to see if it was fair and legal? Isn't that what the certificates of the governors are supposed to assure?"

"You're right, Dear," Joseph admitted. "Congressman Kasson made that very point at the hearing yesterday." Joseph despondently shook his head.

"I am truly torn, Mary."

"Well, it wouldn't surprise me, Joseph, if you started hearing from your Republican brethren very soon," she warned.

Chapter Twenty-eight – The Procession of the Lawyers

THE SATURDAY SESSION OF THE COMMISSION BEGAN at 10:30 a.m. Justice Clifford continued to push matters along at a rapid pace. The lawyers made ready to fill in the blank spaces of the pictures that the four Congressmen had painted with broad brush strokes on the previous day. Amelia and I again attended together. Blessedly, the Chamber was a bit less crowded on this day.

We Democrats had retained several of the most prominent attorneys to lead our case for Certificate Nos. 2 and 3: former Supreme Court Justice John Archibald Campbell, former Pennsylvania Supreme Court Chief Justice Jeremiah S. Black, and ex-prosecutor Charles O'Conor. We also engaged other distinguished members of the bar: Montgomery Blair, former Wisconsin Senator Matthew H. Carpenter, former Illinois Senator Lyman Trumbull, former New Jersey Circuit Judge Ashbel Green, George Hoadly, Richard Merrick, and William Whitney. The Republicans retained an equally stellar team of lawyers in favor of Certificate No. 1: former U.S. Attorney General William Maxwell Evarts, Stanley Matthews, former Ohio Congressman Samuel Shellabarger, and Edwin Wallace Stoughton.[364]

The Saturday session began with a continuation of the discussion that closed the Friday hearing, that of how evidence (if there was any) was to be submitted. The lawyers for the Tilden side stated that they intended to present evidence of wrongdoing at the Baker County polls and on the part of the State Canvassing Board.

However, President Clifford and Commissioner Miller, without any dissent from the other commissioners, told the lawyers that the Commission would not admit that evidence in advance, but would decide later, after its offer by the Tilden lawyers, whether it would be entered into the record. If it was decided not to be admitted, they said, then the Hayes lawyers would not be required to submit rebuttal evidence in response to it.[365]

This ruling caused a murmur among the Tilden lawyers. They passed notes to one another expressing concern.

"Are we being told that the canvassing evidence might not be taken into the record?" Judge Black wrote to Mr. Hoadly.

"Yes – that's news," Hoadly wrote back to Black. It was a disturbing sign that the Commission might not even *consider* the evidence of fraudulent acts by the canvassers in Baker County and at the Florida Canvassing Board. That was the factual support for their whole case!

"Something amiss here," Hoadly wrote to Black. "Republican conspiracy? Why is Clifford going along with it?" "No idea, but troubling," Black replied. "Maybe Clifford is insisting on the delay."

With the evidentiary debate concluded, Charles O'Conor stood up to make the first legal argument for the Democratic supporters of the second and third Certificates favoring Tilden.

Figure 73: Charles O'Conor (PD)

Mr. O'Conor had in his hand a document that he had hastily prepared the night before, which he intended to read to the Commission. It was a summary of the legal and factual propositions that the Tilden side sought to have the Commission adopt, as Commissioner Miller had suggested the day before. But first, O'Conor tried to pin down the Commission on the new question of whether it would even take the Tilden evidence.

"It would be *very* inconvenient," he said carefully to the commissioners, if any evidence outside of the certificates themselves were not admitted to the record, because it "makes the question whether any evidence outside of that record shall be received the whole question in controversy in this case."[366] The Hayes lawyers did not object to the evidence, he pointed out; "there is literally nothing which the supporters of the Hayes electors desire to say and desire to present to this Commission in any branch of this controversy" that contradicts any of it.[367]

"On the contrary," O'Conor added, "with great respect to the better judgment of my learned opponents, if they shall differ with me, or to any honorable member of this Commission who may have taken a different view of it, my conception of the matter is, that *all* the needful evidence should come in, subject to such questions as to its competency and its effect as may exist, for the reason that they necessarily incorporate themselves with the main question that you have finally to decide."[368]

He recommended that the Commission take the evidence subject to objections from the other side, but President Clifford cut him off. He was only interested in hearing what the legal arguments would be, not what the evidence would be. "Mr. O Conor," Clifford said, "I am obliged to ask you to submit your propositions."[369]

William Evarts, at the Hayes counsel table, rose and requested to be heard. "Shall we be heard on this preliminary inquiry or await the submission of the proposition?"

"I think you had better wait until you hear the proposition," Clifford replied, and Evarts sat back down.

O'Conor then read from his document. "First, on December 6, 1876, ... both the Tilden and the Hayes electors respectively met and cast their votes, and transmitted the same to the seat of Government." Each of the votes of the rival electors complied in all respects with the Constitution and relevant laws, he said, except that the certified lists required by law "were, as to the Tilden electors, certified by the attorney-general; and were, as to the Hayes electors, certified by Mr. Stearns, then governor."[370] All of this, O'Conor pointed out, was already in the record.

"Secondly," he continued to read, "a *quo warranto* was commenced against the Hayes electors in the proper court of Florida on the said 6th day of December, 1876, before they had cast their votes, which eventuated in a judgment against them on the 25th of January, 1877. It also determined that the Tilden electors were duly appointed." This matter, too, was already in the record, he stated.[371] With minor exceptions, O'Conor pointed out, the whole case of his side depends on this Court judgment.

"Thirdly," he further stated, the new Governor's legal action to back up the Tilden electors was consistent with the common law of Florida, as the decision of the Florida Supreme Court found.[372]

"Fourthly," the law passed by the Florida legislature after the electoral votes were cast on December 6, 1876 authorized "a new canvass of the electoral vote," and this new canvass and its transmission to Washington was "in perfect conformity to the Constitution and laws except that they were subsequent in point of time" to the date that the electoral votes were cast. This, too, O'Conor pointed out, was already a matter of record before the Commission.[373]

"Fifthly," O'Conor said, the only additional evidence that the Tilden electors sought to lay before the Commission was that "One, the Board of State Canvassers, acting on certain erroneous views when making their canvass, by which the Hayes electors appeared to be chosen, rejected wholly the returns from the county of Manatee and parts of returns from each of the following counties: Hamilton, Jackson, and Monroe;"[374] and "Two, that

Mr. Humphreys, a Hayes elector, held office under the United States," rendering him as ineligible to be a Hayes elector.[375]

"Sixthly," O'Conor said, "Judging from the objections taken by those supporting the Hayes electors and the opening argument offered in their behalf, the supporters of the Tilden electors are led to believe that no evidence is needed or intended to be offered by the supporters of the Hayes electors," except that appeals of the court cases were then pending and that Mr. Humphries had resigned his federal office before voting as a Hayes elector.[376]

"That's Tilden's whole case?" Amelia wrote in a note that she passed to me.

"That's it," I wrote in reply.

"Tilden will lose," she wrote back.

I didn't reply.

* * *

Judge Jeremiah Black stood up for the Tilden electors and requested permission to urge the Commission to admit the crucial evidence his side sought to introduce into the record.[377]

President Clifford interrupted him. "Mr. Black, I think we ought to give Mr. Evarts an opportunity to explain his views before we hear you." Turning away from Mr. Black, Clifford motioned for the Hayes side to make its case.

Figure 74: Judge Jeremiah S. Black (PD)

William Evarts, whose turn it now was to speak on behalf of the Hayes side, spoke up. "I waive my privilege to proceed." Judge Black, appreciative of Evart's deference, demurred and said that he was "perfectly willing that Mr. Evarts shall be heard."

President Clifford replied that "I have indicated to Mr. Evarts that he would be heard," but Evarts then waived "the privilege to precedence." Black urged Clifford to let him continue in light of Evart's deferral, but Clifford was adamant. "It is not the moment for argument now."

Black became testy. "It *is* the moment for suggesting the course of proceeding and our rights with reference to the evidence which is to be given. I insist upon it that the evidence is in, and that we are not bound to make any offer at all. ...[I]s it to be decided that this evidence is out or in now?"

"Not by the presiding officer," Clifford shot back, hiding behind his lack of authority to act without a Commission vote.

Justice Miller offered a suggestion to defuse the awkward situation. "Let me suggest that Mr. O'Conor has made a proposition to submit certain evidence. If counsel on the other side have no objection to it, there is no occasion for further argument. If counsel on the other side submit to have that evidence come in, it will come in, and we can go on."[378]

Evarts whispered to his co-counsel for advice, then proceeded to dodge the question in a stall for time. Miller pressed him: "If you want to object to this proposition for evidence, now is the time to object, certainly."

"That I understand, if the Commission please," Evarts replied, holding back whether he objected or not. He would get back to it presently.

Clifford, sensing Evart's predicament, then interjected, "I think Judge Black had better defer until we hear from Mr. Evarts. Otherwise there may be misunderstanding."[379]

Figure 75: William Maxwell Evarts (PD)

Mr. Evarts rose to speak for the Hayes side.

Evarts, like Black, encouraged the commissioners to first figure out the procedure for accepting evidence. Whether the certificates already received by the Congress from the states, or whether additional evidence may be introduced, "is no doubt a principal inquiry of law and of jurisdiction in this Commission, which, once settled upon principle and by your decision, will go to a certain extent in superseding or predetermining your action upon the merits."[380]

At that moment, Commissioner Hoar had an idea about what to do. "Mr. President, suppose Mr. O'Conor's offer of testimony be objected to by the other side, and then the Commission hears the argument of the case as it then stands, resembling more nearly than any other judicial proceeding that I can think of, an argument made on a demurrer to the plaintiff's evidence, the evidence not being considered as *in* evidence but only as *offered* in evidence."[381]

Clifford liked that idea so much that he adopted it as if he had thought of it himself. "That was the view of the Chair," he said."I shall regard the paper read by Mr. O'Conor as an offer of proof. Nothing, therefore, remains to the other side except to object or waive objections."[382]

Clifford then turned to Evarts. "Do you object to the offer of proof ?"

Evarts replied that as he understood it, the resolution of this procedural conundrum would be resolved "by provisional acceptance of the mass of proof, whatever it may be, to be discussed as to admissibility and pertinency and efficacy in the conclusions of the tribunal as a part of the final argument."[383]

But if that is the case, Evarts protested, then "it requires the inclusion of all the countervailing proof that we opposing their certificate or supporting ours have a right to present under some determination of this court as to that right. If you go beyond the evidence furnished from the hands of the President of the Senate into an inspection and scrutiny of the election in the state as if in a *quo warranto* hearing to try a right to an office, then we say that the tribunal that accepts that task and is to fulfill that duty is to receive evidence that will make the scrutiny judicial and complete from the primary deposit of the votes to the conclusion of the election.

"That," Evarts concluded, "is the difficulty in selecting a part of the evidence to be admitted provisionally as furnishing the ground and area of a final discussion, because it does not include the evidence upon both sides which under some *post hoc* determination of the court on the final argument may be properly introducible.

"Now," Evarts said at last before sitting down, "I object to the evidence now offered.[384]

Judge Black then rose. "Am I in order to say a word or two in reply to Mr. Evarts?" he asked the President.

"A brief explanation," Clifford replied. "I wish to get to the argument as soon as may be."

"We insist," Black said, "that the whole of the evidence, including that mentioned by Mr. O'Conor, in this paper of his, has been given already, and *is* a part of the record." This was a convenient suggestion – rather than fight over admitting the evidence or not, simply *assume* that it is already in.

The evidence was all received by the Congress before it set up this Commission and was turned over to the Commission President, Black explained. Congress told this Commission "to tell them what they ought to do and to make the decision which upon the evidence that was before them they ought to make." Black reminded the commissioners that the portion of the evidence that was taken by the committees of the House of Representatives "was laid before that House after a fierce struggle and the filibustering of half a night to keep it out."[385]

Black argued that objections to evidence offered into the record is a procedure known only in jury trials, not trials before judges and experts like this Commission. "You cannot safely adopt an artificial rule of the common law which prevails in a trial by jury, and where evidence is offered piece by piece to the court, and is there sifted and scrutinized before it is allowed to go to the jury." That rule, he said, is necessary in order to keep the jury "in utter ignorance of everything that is not material, lest their judgments might be misled." "In all other cases," Black continued, "the doctrine is, that whenever the evidence is offered it becomes a part of the record by the fact that it is put on the record."[386]

"I do not say that you are bound to believe whatever is here," Black explained, "but you are to sift it and scrutinize it and to separate the chaff from the wheat upon the final hearing of the cause, and it is impossible for you to proceed otherwise without a very great amount of trouble, without an expenditure of more time than you have got to expend upon this subject."[387]

"Mr. Black," Clifford said curtly, "Your time has expired."

"Has already expired ?" Black asked with surprise.

"Yes, sir," Clifford replied.

Justice Miller then moved that counsel for both sides should be allotted two hours to argue to the Commission "whether any other testimony will be considered by this Commission than that which was laid before the two Houses by the presiding officer of the Senate."[388] After some more wrangling among the commissioners as to the exact language to be used in the motion, President Clifford stated the motion as whether "counsel be now heard for two hours on each side on the effect of the matters laid before the two Houses by the President of the Senate and of the offer of testimony made by Mr. O'Conor and objected to by Mr. Evarts." The Commission agreed to the motion.[389] On further request of both sides, the time was extended to three hours on each side.

The Commission then took a half-hour recess to allow the parties to prepare for the argument.[390]

Chapter Twenty-nine – Consternation in the War Room

I ASKED AMELIA TO EXCUSE ME. I hurried over to the conference room outside of the Supreme Court Chamber that was being used by the Tilden attorneys as their "war room."

Cigars were already lit up and puffing smoke furiously. It was as if a forest fire had started in the room. Several of the lawyers had glasses of whiskey and bourbon in their hands to calm themselves down from the stress they were feeling.

"This is outrageous!" Judge Black was booming. "This is a plot by the Republicans. We are being railroaded!" He downed his shot of Tennessee whiskey in a single gulp.

"I cannot understand what Clifford is doing. He is one of us! Why is he bowing to everything that Sam Miller says?" O'Conor wondered in between cigar puffs.

"For a 'Commission President,' Nathan certainly is not driving the horses straight," Judge Campbell sneered. "He considers himself powerless to direct the Commission without a vote of all fifteen of them. He is old and addled!"

"What 'countervailing evidence' is Evarts talking about?" Black said, a fresh shot of whiskey already in his hand. "All the Republicans have offered so far is rumor and innuendo. There is not a shred of evidence in favor of Governor Stearns' ploy to get himself and Hayes elected!" One gulp, and the second shot was gone.

"Which means that in the end, the big question will be decided in favor of the Republicans by a vote of eight to seven, and justice be damned," Campbell replied in disgust.

"Forgive me for intruding into your legal strategizing, gentlemen," I interjected. "But as an observer who is not fighting in the pit with all of you, I do not understand why the commissioners are arguing over whether or not to hear evidence that Congress itself gathered in our House and Senate committees and gave to them to consider.

"We Congressmen were the ones who acquired that evidence from our investigators who went into the field to get it," I said. "We were the ones who found out about how the precincts in Baker County were ignored in the count. We were the ones who discovered how the state then manipulated the counts of other counties. The Florida Supreme Court itself was shocked by this evidence and ordered the Canvassing Board to choose the Tilden electors over the Hayes electors because so many votes were ignored. Even with that, the Canvassing Board *continued* to manipulate the votes! There is no more evidence for the Republicans to give against these facts!"

Someone handed me a cigar, already cut and lit. Although I am not a smoker, I was soon puffing away as furiously as everyone else.

"Why is the Commission bogging down over procedure?" I asked them. "Why are the Republicans entitled to 'object' to this evidence or not? Why is the Commission fighting with us over whether the evidence is 'in' the record or not? Of course it's 'in the record!' The Congress has already heard it! This evidence is what the controversy is all about!"

Now I found a shot of Tennessee whiskey shoved into my hand, and I downed that in one gulp too. I was as infuriated as the lawyers now.

"You are absolutely right, Abram," Judge Black said to me. "I've had to argue with Nathan Clifford over 'objections' and 'the record' until I'm hoarse, and whenever I point out that the evidence is already 'in the record' and therefore *has* to be considered, and that there is nothing to 'object' to, he hides behind his so-called 'lack of authority' to affirm that. That demented old codger is the problem, and he's a Democrat!"

O'Conor interjected to explain. "It seems, Abram," he said, "that Clifford and Miller have hit upon a well-known court procedure to block the intake of evidence that they don't want to hear. In non-jury trials, usually in courts of equity, only judges hear evidence and make decisions based on the facts in evidence and the law. In jury trials, however, a jury of laymen hear the facts and decide them, while the judge hears the law and decides that. Since the jurors are laymen, the court considers first whether evidence offered by one side that is objected to by the other side is suitable for admission into the record so that the jury sees only what is relevant and material and is kept in the dark about all the rest that is offered.

"What Clifford and Miller are suggesting is that, even though all fifteen men on the Commission are legal experts as much as any court judge, they should follow a procedure that is used in courts when the facts are to be presented to a jury. So, first we are supposed to make an "offer of proof" to them of what our evidence will show, then the other side may "object" to what we offer, and the Commission then decides whether to "admit" the evidence into the record or not. When there is no jury, by contrast, the evidence is just put in the record right away, along with any objections from the other side, and the judge simply decides whether the record as it stands convinces him one way or the other."

"Why are Clifford and Miller insisting on this cumbersome procedure when there is no jury and this is not a court?"

"You want my opinion?" Black cut in. "Clifford and Miller want to keep our evidence of ballot fraud out of the record. They want to bury these facts. Miller surely wants to bury them because he is a Republican and if these facts were in the record, they would doom them in the next election. Clifford's reason mystifies me. He's a Democrat. I think that the addled old man is just looking for a way to gum up the Commission so the whole issue gets thrown back into Congress and they are forced to decide who's President and Vice President, the way the Twelfth Amendment says they should do!"

"Well, it seems to me," I said, "that Clifford is getting ready to have the Republican majority exclude all of our most important evidence, the evidence that our House and Senate committees gathered about how the election in Florida was mismanaged. Governor Stearns certified fraud, and we have already found it! Fraud voids everything!"

"It seems to me," Black said, "that Clifford is being manipulated by Miller. I suspect that strings are being pulled by the Republicans here."

"Well, it doesn't really matter what type of kangaroo court Clifford and Miller are running here," O'Conor said. "All that matters in the end is the result, and that is a matter of simple arithmetic. The result will be eight to seven against Tilden unless Bradley has an open mind."

"It does not matter if we win Florida or not," Black continued. "We only have to win one of the four states in controversy in order to put Tilden over the top. He is only one electoral vote short of being President. Hayes needs all twenty votes that are at stake.

"What about Humphreys, the shipping commissioner?" O'Conor asked. "If he gets knocked out, and Florida just loses an electoral vote, then Hayes can't win even if he gets all of the other disputed votes. The Presidential contest would be thrown into the House and the Vice-Presidential one into the Senate. And we control the House, at least, so at least Tilden would win!"

"That is certainly the backup plan, Charles," Judge Black replied. "We might even find a back-door way to pull the needed elector over to Tilden and forgo all the rest of the disputes."

"But it still all comes down to Bradley," Campbell interjected. "Clifford is going to put everything down to a motion and a vote of all the commissioners. He will not rule on anything himself, even the slightest matter of procedure. He won't even brighten the gas lamps without a vote of all fifteen commissioners. If he decided something by executive fiat, then Democrats might have a chance. The way he's running things, every Democratic initiative is doomed. If Bradley is just a part of a Republican conspiracy, then we are lost. Is he truly neutral?"

"I think I know a way to find out," I told them. "I will endeavor to find out and let you know as quickly as I can."

"Gentlemen, the Commission is reassembling," a clerk entered the room to announce. We staunched our cigars and left our shot glasses on the table as we exited the cloudy room.

Chapter Thirty – A Portent of Good Luck

THE REST OF SATURDAY AFTERNOON AT THE COMMISSION was consumed with oral argument from Richard Merrick and Judge Black on the Tilden side, and Edwin Stoughton and William Evarts on the Hayes side, on the question, as put by President Clifford, of "whether any evidence will be considered by the Commission that was not submitted to the two Houses by the President of the Senate, and if so, what evidence can properly be considered; and also the question what is the evidence now before the commission." The Commission decided to devote three hours to the debate, with each side taking an hour and a half for each side to speak.[391]

The Commission managed to get through the oratory of the Tilden side, but stalled after Mr. Stoughton had consumed almost an hour of the Hayes side without getting to Mr. Evarts. Around three o'clock, the Commission adjourned until the following Monday, February 5.[392]

* * *

A friend of mine from Trenton, an attorney named John G. Stevens, was a mutual friend of Justice Bradley and myself from our days as New Jersey lawyers. He was staying with us at our Washington home while he transacted business in the city. After Amelia and I returned home on Saturday afternoon, he arrived from work in the early evening.

"Have you paid a visit to Justice Bradley while you're here?" I asked John when he arrived.

"Why, yes!" he replied. "I paid a visit to him at his house after the Commission hearing."

"What has he told you about it?"

"Oh, he's been in absolute agony over it, Abram," John replied. "He is clearly torn between his Republican loyalties and his Constitutional views. Are you familiar with the *Slaughter-House Cases*?"

"Yes," I replied. "He dissented."

"He did, and he is convinced that the Fourteenth and Fifteenth Amendments have changed the ball game when it comes to federal elections," John said. "He feels certain that the federal government must step in to monitor fairness and equality in the states' conduct of them. The states don't have *carte blanche* to do what they like anymore, he feels."

"Well," I said, "if he feels strongly enough about that, it would be very good news for Tilden. The Republicans are trying to keep the shenanigans at the Florida polls out of the record in the case."

"I think you Democrats may have a friend in Bradley," John said. "Joe showed me a draft opinion that he wrote. He finds for Tilden in it. He's in favor of counting the vote of the Democratic electors in Florida."

"He is?"

"Yes, indeed. He's trying very hard to reconcile the facts of the Commission's case with his views on the Constitution."

I did my utmost to retain my composure, despite the great news!

"I must admit to you, I certainly hope he manages to do that," I said, controlling my joy. "The whole problem in Florida is that the politicians in that state can do whatever they want to twist the vote any which way they want. Once they certify it, the Republicans claim, the contest is all over, even if the State Supreme Court decides otherwise."

"From what I saw of Bradley's draft, and from what he told me at dinner, he is very upset about that development. 'There must be some way to get them under control,' was exactly what he told me.

"Well, I'm bushed, Abram. I'm heading up to sleep. Good night."

"Good night, John," I said, pretending to read over the mail. Once John shut his bedroom door, I replaced my hat and bolted out the door to hail a cab to the Capitol.

* * *

It was nine o'clock at night. The Tilden lawyers were still in their war room.

I told them what John told me. "That certainly is good news." said Judge Black guardedly. "Of course, he could change his mind."

"Jeremiah, that fits exactly into what we are planning on tomorrow," Charles O'Conor jumped in and said to Black. "Even if the Commission adopts Certificate No. 1, the key to the case is still Humphreys. We have to hit him very hard."

"That's true, gentlemen," I said. "If you knock out Humphreys, the election goes into the House even if Hayes wins all the other disputed electoral votes. And the House belongs to us."

O'Conor added, "you know, at this point, I would not be the least bit surprised if the entire Commission would be just delighted to throw this whole mess back to Congress to let them battle it out. The nerve of Congress to pass the buck to these fifteen innocent people! Why should these commissioners take the heat for starting another Civil War by a vote of eight to seven? Leave it to the Congressmen."

"I cannot think of a more just result," Judge Black smiled as he lit another cigar.

Chapter Thirty-one – Meanwhile, In the Other Trench . . .

AT ABOUT THAT SAME TIME OF THE EVENING, SEVERAL CARRIAGES of visitors pulled up to Judge Bradley's Capitol Hill home. Two in particular were owned by Senator Frederick T. Frelinghuysen and Secretary of the Navy George M. Robeson, fellow

Figure 76: Senator Frederick T. Frelinghuysen of New Jersey (PD)

Figure 77: George M. Robeson, Secretary of the Navy (PD)

New Jersey lawyers who had practiced with Bradley. Frelinghuysen, of course, was a fellow Commission member with Bradley.[393]

"Gentlemen," Judge Bradley said, greeting them both at his door, "I am aware of why you are here." They all smiled at one another. "Please follow me into my study."

Once they were all in, Judge Bradley shut the double office doors and sat down in one of the three chairs that were arranged around a coffee table with a bottle of port. The Judge offered a glass to them both, but they declined. The Judge decided to forego a glass as well, at least for now.

"Mr. Justice Bradley," Senator Frelinghuysen began, "as you've gathered, we're here on behalf of our Party – your Party as well – to talk about your upcoming vote in the Electoral Commission. We are both commissioners, of course, so discussion between us should cause neither of us any concern. Secretary Robeson asked me to join us in the discussion on behalf of the Party."

"I understand fully, Senator," Judge Bradley answered, without any concern. "The Commission is not a Court; it is merely a Congressional factfinding committee. So there is no rule against having this discussion."

"Judge," Frelinghuysen continued, "when this Commission was formed, I knew from the start that I would be on it. You were a late-comer. So obviously, I have had a great deal more time to formulate my opinions on this matter than you have. I certainly appreciate that you are filling the position that was intended for an 'independent' commissioner, but things didn't work out that way.

"The rest of the Republican commissioners have had an opportunity to express their opinions to one another and arrive at a consensus on the facts and the law here. We have not heard from you, however. May I, as a fellow Republican, ask where you stand on whether Tilden or Hayes wins this fight?"

"I have not made up my mind, gentlemen," the Judge replied.

"May I ask why?" Secretary Robeson asked him.

"Since I wrote my dissent in the *Slaughter-house Cases*," the Judge replied, "I have come to understand the Fourteenth Amendment in a new light. That was a 5-4 decision of the Supreme Court, and the four of us dissenters perceived something new in that provision.

"I think Justice Field said it best in his dissent," the Judge continued, "when he remarked that the Fourteenth Amendment recognizes an 'equality of right among citizens in the pursuit of the ordinary avocations of life,' and that 'all grants of exclusive privileges, in contravention of this equality, are against common right, and void.'"[394] This is a major change in our understanding of the Constitution, gentlemen.

"We have heard at length in this matter that Congress has no power to go behind the Florida Governor's Certificate in order to determine if the popular vote supporting it was legitimate," the Judge said. "I think the Fourteenth Amendment *compels* the Commission to do so.

"Consider the clause of the Amendment that requires that if the right of qualified citizens to vote in a federal election is denied or abridged in any state, then the number of representatives of that state in the House shall be reduced proportionately. It also provides that Congress has the power to enforce this provision by appropriate legislation.

"To me, and I feel safe to say that the other three dissenters on the Court feel the same way, this means that the federal government is now the guarantor of free and fair federal elections. The states continue to set the procedures and the rules, of course, but the federal government makes certain that those procedures and rules treat citizens of the United States equally in federal votes.

"If all citizens are equal as voters, by federal law," Bradley continued, "then states cannot just arbitrarily and capriciously count some votes and throw out other votes. *All* votes must be counted. And it is up to Congress to see that that is done by 'appropriate legislation.'" By setting up this Electoral Commission, Congress has done exactly that.

"So," Bradley explained, "when the Tilden objectors point out that otherwise legitimate votes were thrown out in the Florida election, and that act caused the electors for Hayes to be certified instead of the electors for Tilden, then it is our Constitutional duty to correct this error."

The Senator and the Secretary exchanged glances at one another. Senator Frelinghuysen then leaned forward toward Bradley. "Joe," he said quietly, "we have been friends for a long time, from a long history as colleagues in the courts of New Jersey. And what I am about to say means no disrespect to you, or your dissenting opinion, or your distinguished fellow dissenters in any manner whatsoever. But Joe, what you and your fellow dissenters said in *Slaughter-house* was just that – *dissents*. They are not the law. The law was decided by the majority. And in his opinion for the majority, Justice Miller dealt specifically with the Fourteenth Amendment.

"Like the Thirteenth and Fifteenth Amendments," Frelinghuysen continued, "the Fourteenth was about the abolition of all ill effects and badges of slavery. It was directed at freeing the Negro race. And the protections that it afforded were limited to the privileges and immunities of citizens of the *United States*, not the privileges and immunities of citizens of *a single state*.

"So," said Frelinghuysen, "if a state attempts to reimpose slavery within its borders, the Thirteenth Amendment forbids it. But if a state exercises its police power toward its own citizens in other respects, it is free to do so without restraint from the Fourteenth Amendment.

"Consequently, when a state rejects the votes of a county in which there has been fraud or intimidation, it is asserting its police power correctly. And when a Governor certifies the electors of a state for the purpose of choosing a President and Vice-President of the United States, he asserts the state's police power correctly."

Bradley pursed his lips and stared out into space for a long time. Frelinghuysen and Robeson stared intently at him, saying nothing, giving him as much time as he needed to absorb Frelinghuysen's viewpoint.

At length, Bradley turned back to the Senator and said, "Fred, I understand what you are saying, and I do not dispute with you that what you've described is indeed the current law. I will consider your words very deeply and carefully and make up my mind as carefully and justly as I can possibly do."

"Joe," said Frelinghuysen, "I trust that you will. I have faith that you will see what the law requires and follow your experience and years of practice, not to mention your judicial wisdom." With that, glancing over to Robeson for approval, Frelinghuysen said, "I bid you good night."

After the two gentlemen left, Bradley returned to his study, sat at his desk, put his head in his hands and wept.

Mary, in her dressing gown, entered the study and wrapped an arm around his shoulder. "Dearest," she said to him, "let us pray."

Both of them got down on their knees, clasped each other's hands together, and prayed to the Almighty for guidance and forgiveness.

"In the name of the Father, the Son, and the Holy Ghost, Amen," both ended.

Mary held Joseph's hands and stood closely to him. "Are you all right now, Dearest?" she asked him.

"Thank you, my Love. I will stay up for a while longer and write some more of this draft. I will join you right afterward."

* * *

"Well?" Zachariah Chandler asked Frederick Frelinghuysen and George Robeson when they returned to the Willard Hotel lobby after midnight. The Hayes lawyers were also present, uncomfortably dressed in the same clothes they had worn before the Commission all that day.

"He was hung up on his dissenting rationale in the *Slaughter-house* case," Frelinghuysen reported. "I emphasized to him that he was a dissenter, not in the majority, and that his dissent is not the law. I think he accepted it. After I said it, he said nothing more about his dissenting rationale, and he said he would consider my words very carefully and deeply."

"Do you think it would be wise to offer Bradley a Cabinet position, or the ambassadorship to London or Paris?" Zach asked, ever weighing the pros and cons of political perquisites.

"I decidedly think not," Frelinghuysen retorted, fearing the danger of a disclosure and a newspaper firestorm. "The man is a dedicated Republican. I have known him all my legal career. Give him a chance to make up his own mind."

"I have never found that to be a good strategy," Zach responded, "but in deference to you and your friendship with him, I'll hold my fire."

PART EIGHT – RESOLUTION

Chapter Thirty-two – Backstage Maneuvers

MEANWHILE, WHAT WAS UP WITH THE TWO MEN that the controversy roiling Washington was all about? I mean, of course, Sam Tilden and Rud Hayes.

Since December, Sam put some researchers to work writing a huge tome that studied previous Presidential elections ponderously entitled, *The Presidential Counts: A Complete Official Record of the Proceedings of Congress at the Counting of the Electoral Votes in all the Elections of President and Vice-President of the United States, together with all Congressional Debates incident thereto or to Proposed Legislation upon that Subject; with an Analytical Introduction.*[395] He planned to place a copy on the desk of every U.S. senator and congressman.[396]

The Presidential Counts, as the tome came to be known, traced the Congressional procedure followed by each of the twenty-one Presidential elections preceding the 1876 contest. At the end of the piece, Sam appended citations from speeches and writings of prominent Washington officials supporting the propositions that "(1) the President of the Senate does not count the electoral vote under our Constitution; (2) the two Houses Congress, in joint session, count it; (3) the two Houses decide what are votes, and upon the legality of the votes; (4) the two Houses inspect the returns, each by its own chosen tellers; (5) the two Houses may go behind the returns; and (6) allowing the President of the Senate to count the vote might prove fatal to the public peace, might enable one man to disfranchise a state, and even elect himself."[397]

I thought that Sam had accomplished little of value by preparing this enormous work. It was absurd for the head of the Party to labor on it to the neglect of more vital tasks. What we needed from Tilden at this moment was a focused, carefully orchestrated plan to seat him in the White House. Instead, as the dispute wore on in Congress, Sam grew increasingly remote from our efforts on Capitol Hill.[398] He avoided us and remained in New York.

Several Democrats traveled up to New York from Washington to confer with Tilden in December, only to leave from meetings with him puzzled, frustrated, and angry at his unwillingness to act in his own behalf. "Oh, Tilden won't do anything; he's cold as a damn clam," one of our politicians told the *New York Tribune* after speaking with Tilden.[399]

Harper's Weekly   August 12, 1876   664

SLIPPERY SAM.

Figure 78: "Slippery Sam," Cartoon by Thomas Nast (PD)

One of Sam's greatest mistakes at this critical time was his alienation of Southern politicians who had supported him during his campaign. John B. Gordon, the Senator from Georgia and a rehabilitated former Confederate, traveled to New York to exhort him to act more forcefully with Congress. The Senator came away from his conversation convinced that "we were being robbed of our victory by our own supineness."Another former Confederate, Kentucky Congressman Henry Watterson, also tried to rouse Sam, also to little avail. Watterson's plan to call for a mass convention of 100,000 "peaceful citizens" in Washington to demand Tilden's inauguration was watered down by Tilden to a much smaller gathering at – of all places – Ford's Theater, site of Abraham Lincoln's assassination.[400]

I, too, renewed my call for mass demonstrations across the land for Tilden's inauguration as President. Tilden refused to have anything to do with it. Gatherings were held in some states, but without his support or attendance. In mid-December, I issued a statement as Democratic National Committee Chairman, declaring that Tilden had been elected President with a rightful claim to 203 electoral votes. I heard nothing about it from Sam, and the Republican newspapers laughed it off.[401]

I began to fear that Sam, prone to moodiness and depression as he was, had already given up.

* * *

By decided contrast, all was abuzz within the Hayes camp. They were beginning to sense that victory was at hand.

Congressman James A. Garfield of Ohio told Rud that "the Democrats are without a policy or a leader. They are full of passion and want to do something desperate but hardly know how to get at it."[402] Hearing this, Rud became convinced that if the election in the South had been conducted fairly, he would have won the popular and electoral votes by a sizable majority.[403]

Zachariah Chandler visited Rud at the Governor's Mansion in Columbus in late November. "I think that the Southerners are starting to see that their future is not bright if they continue to follow Tilden," Rud told him.

"I certainly think that there is an opening for us on that front, Governor," Zach replied, sipping his iced tea with lemon and sugar, the only beverage beside water served at the tee-totaling Hayes home.

"We should arrange meetings with Southern Democratic congressmen, Zach," Hayes said. "We need to find out just what it is that is enough to turn them over to our side."

"The answer to that is crystal clear, Rud," Zach replied. "Kick the Army out of the South."

"Well that's pretty much already the case everywhere down there, except in Florida, South Carolina and Louisiana," Rud said. "Why can't we give them back those three states too?"

"Reconstructionist Republicans now run those states," Zach replied. "They are hanging on for dear life down there. They and the Army are all that stands between the Negroes and the ex-rebels' ropes hanging around tree limbs."

"Well, surely we could extract some concessions from the Southerners to leave the Negroes alone and in peace," Rud surmised.

"If it gets you over the finish line, then it's worth a shot, Governor," said Zach.

The next day, Zach telegraphed Colonel William H. Roberts, the managing editor of the *New Orleans Times*. "GOV. HAYES WOULD BE PLEASED TO DISCUSS SOUTHERN INTERESTS WITH YOU AT YOUR EARLIEST CONVENIENCE," the telegram read.

On December 1, Colonel Roberts arrived in Columbus by train to pay a call on Governor Hayes. He was ushered into the Governor's Office and introduced to Rud and Zach.

"Very pleased to make your acquaintance, Governor. And you as well, Mr. Chandler," the Colonel said, with handshakes and a slight bow.

"The pleasure is all mine, Colonel!" Rud replied. "Can I interest you in a glass of iced tea or lemonade?"

"Well," said the Colonel, "I usually rely on stronger stuff, Governor. But I'll oblige you to pour me a glass of lemonade, sure."

Rud's secretary brought him a glass. "I am very interested in hearing about your views on the South, Governor," Roberts said. "I can tell you, by the way, that I say so not only for myself, but for several Southern Democrats who share my interests."

"Oh?" said Rud. "If you'll pardon my asking, whom might they be?"

"Governor Wade Hampton, Senator John Gordon, and Congressman Lucius Lamar, just to name a few," Roberts replied.[404]

Zach and Rud caught each other's eye. They were *very* impressed. These were *the* leading Southerners in the Democratic Party.

"I am open to helping the South in any way that I can," Rud said eagerly. "What do your people want that I can give?"

"Let me put it to you this way, Governor," Roberts replied. "All thinking Southerners are anxious to avoid any further conflict with the North. The War Between the States has devastated us and we want to rebuild and rejuvenate our land. To do so, we first and foremost must rid our states of the carpetbag Republican governments that have been foisted upon us by the Union Army and the Northern financial interests.

"We have stuck by the Democratic Party and Governor Tilden for President," Roberts continued, "primarily because the Republicans have always been adamantly opposed to our Southern way of life and our interests. The end of slavery has freed the Negro, but the slave represented an enormous economic asset to us. Losing that asset has ruined us financially. Republicans have treated our predicament with utter contempt.

"But, Governor, if we Southerners felt that you were at the very least friendly to us," he said, "we would not make the desperate personal fight to keep you out that we intend to make if you are not friendly."

"Colonel, I would like to have a word with Mr. Chandler in private before I give you an answer. Will you excuse us for a moment while we leave the room to talk briefly?"

"Why certainly, Governor," Roberts replied. "I'll just sit right here and sip my lemonade," he sat back and smiled.

Hayes and Chandler exited the office for a few minutes. They returned and resumed their seats.

The Governor spoke. "Colonel, I first want to say that I feel no ill will at all toward the South. I fought for the Union, and I was wounded in battle. But my lot in the War was no different from the lot of many other men on both sides of the war, and there were many, many heroes on both sides of the conflict.

"Now I agree with you that the carpetbag governments have not been successful," Rud said. "The complaints of the Southern people are justifiable.

"It is imperative on me," Rud continued, "to require absolute justice and fair play for the Negro. However, I am convinced that this could be achieved best and most surely by trusting honorable and influential Southern whites to accomplish these goals.

"How do you and your colleagues whom you represent feel about my following that approach in my administration?"

Colonel Roberts thought a moment before he gave Rud an answer. He was impressed that Rud had used the words "carpetbag governments," which was the pejorative term that all Southern whites used for them.

"Governor, I think that we would look very favorably on that approach, if it would mean that white Southerners could count on the support of the federal government to recover control of our state governments from the carpetbaggers and their Negro accomplices. First and foremost, we would expect you to withdraw the Union troops from Florida, Louisiana and South Carolina, which are the last Southern states in which they now remain."

"I would be happy to give that request a great deal of thought and consideration," Rud replied. "I am concerned, of course, that the troops are presently maintaining law and order in the impacted states where disorder is at its worst. So I would have to be very careful not to remove troops that are desperately needed in certain areas for that purpose. But as a general rule, I am not at all adverse to the idea."

"Well, gentlemen," the Colonel said, smiling, "this has been a very encouraging and fruitful meeting, even though it is a short one!

I trust that you have no problem, Governor, with my reporting this conversation to the Southern gentlemen whom I named earlier that I represent?"

"I would be delighted if you would do so!" Rud said.

"I would ask, though, Colonel," Zach interjected, "that this conversation be conveyed only to them, and with the understanding that they will keep it strictly confidential. I would also ask all of you not to disclose this conversation to the newspapers, which must include barring publication in *your* newspaper ... at least for now."

"I am certain that we can respect that," Roberts told Zach. "Gentlemen, I have accomplished all that I wished to accomplish today, and I won't trouble you any more for your valuable time."

They all rose to go. As Roberts shook the hands of Rud and Zach, he said to Rud, with each other's hands clasped firmly, "Governor, you will be President. We will make no trouble. We want peace."

"Thank you, Colonel," Rud said intently.

* * *

The next day, the *Cincinnati Enquirer* reported the details of the meeting, including Hayes' disavowal of the "carpetbag governments." A second story was printed two days later in the *New York Herald*. It included a "clarification" of Hayes' position, but did not disavow the *Enquirer*'s earlier report.[405]

I was very upset with this development. By late January, I was strenuously warning Sam of the danger of losing Southern support. "The Southerners helped us win our victory in the popular vote," I told him, "and if we fail to follow through on that, they will feel betrayed and make terms with Hayes. He is assuring them of some of the highest offices in the administration as a reward."

"Abram, we have agreed to arbitrate this dispute, and we must remain calm," Sam aloofly replied. "There are calls among some Democrats for 'Tilden or blood!' I am *not* interested in encouraging that sentiment with public demonstrations and volatile speeches."

"Well, then, Sam, it behooves you to meet with Southern Democrats and assure them that their best interests lie with us, not with the Republicans," I retorted.

Figure 79: "A Truce—Not a Compromise," Thomas Nast, Harper's Weekly, *February 17, 1877 (PD)*

"They *know* that!" Sam replied testily. "Look what our campaign has done for their candidates! Wade Hampton is now Governor of South Carolina! George Drew is now Governor of Florida!

Francis Nicholls will be Governor of Louisiana as soon as they can straighten out what their vote count is. They all beat Republican incumbents while hanging onto *my* coat-tails!"

"Well, you must do more to keep them in the fold," I told Sam. "They surely would like to have a fellow Democrat in the White House, but if they become convinced that Hayes is a man with whom they can do business, then they will lose interest in securing a favorable outcome for us from the Electoral Commission. We can't let Southern Democrats start thinking that no matter what horse loses, they win!"

Chapter Thirty-three – A Question of Relevant Evidence

ON MONDAY, FEBRUARY 5, 1877, THE HEARING of the Electoral Commission resumed.[406] Amelia and I were in attendance once again. It was now Mr. Evart's turn to make the case against the Tilden side's offer of "extrinsic" evidence of vote fraud. He had an hour and thirty-two minutes to speak.[407]

Evarts addressed three issues: (1) Whether under the powers possessed by the Commission any evidence beyond that disclosed in the three certificates from the State of Florida which were opened by the President of the Senate in the presence of the two Houses of Congress can be received; (2) If any can be received, what that evidence is; and (3) What evidence other than these certificates, if any, is already before the Commission.[408]

Evarts, a masterful litigator, proceeded in reverse order. The third issue was dispensed with quickly. Mr. Evarts noted that the evidence in question was said to have *already* been entered in evidence because it was appended to the objections that had been made to Certificate No. 1 during the joint session of the House and Senate.[409] But it is unheard of, Evarts argued, that documents enter the record of a court of law merely by being appended to the plaintiff's complaint.

The objections made in this proceeding, he said, merely started the proceeding. "They bind nobody. They are merely the action upon which the reference to this Commission arises. If there be no objection, the case provided for the exercise of your authority is not produced." If, on the other hand, the objection is made, Evarts

321

continued, it does not narrow or limit or provide the issue or affect the controversy that the Commission must hear. That, he said, "is a pure fabrication out of utterly unsubstantial and immaterial suggestions in the law."[410]

As for the second issue, Evarts considered it to be subordinate to the first one, so he turned at last to the first one.[411] As to whether any evidence beyond that disclosed in the three certificates could be considered by the Commission, Evarts argued that the only questions that the other side sought to be answered by any such evidence had been set forth in Mr. O'Conor's document that he read to the Commission at the last session: (1) that the Florida Board of State canvassers, acting on certain erroneous views when making their canvass, by which the Hayes electors appeared to be chosen, wholly rejected the returns from the county of Manatee and parts of returns from each of several other counties; (2) that in so doing the State Board acted without jurisdiction, as the Florida courts decided; and (3) that the Florida courts concluded that Mr. Drew had been elected Governor, that the Hayes electors were usurpers, and that the Tilden electors had been duly chosen. [412]

Evarts contested every one of these points. "It is proposed, therefore, ... not that the certificate of Governor Stearns falsifies the fact he was to certify; not that it falsifies the record that makes the basis of the fact which he was to certify to; but that the record at the time on which by law he was to base his certificate, departing from which his certificate would be false, is itself to be penetrated or surmounted by extraneous proof, showing that by matters of substance occurring in the progress of the election itself errors or frauds intervened."[413]

But the Governor's certificate is required by an act of Congress to certify only "as to the list of persons that have been appointed electors," Evarts said; it does not certify "that every stage and step of the process of the election has been honest and true and clear and lawful and effectual, and free from all exception of fraud. Unless you make that the fact to be certified by the Governor you lay no basis for introducing evidence of discord between the fact to be certified and the fact that has been certified."[414]

"So Congress should pay no attention to fraud because a corrupt governor paid no attention to fraud?" Amelia wrote to me angrily in another one of her notes. I closed my eyes and shook my head in sad affirmance.

Evarts droned on. What the Tilden side seeks to do, he argued, is to put the Commission "at the same stage of inquiry and with the same right to investigate the election itself to the bottom as a judicial court exercising the familiar jurisdiction of *quo warranto*."[415] In other words, the Commission would be expected to exercise the investigative powers of a court, which according to him it has not been given jurisdiction to do, nor does Congress have such jurisdiction out of its power to "count the votes."

"How can he argue out of one side of his mouth that these court proceedings are too late to stop a vote and out of the other side of his mouth that they are the only recourse?" Amelia wrote to me testily. I looked up at her sheepishly from reading her note.

Evarts then addressed the question of whether Mr. Humphreys was ineligible, as a federal official, to be appointed as an elector. This, he claimed, had already been determined by the State Canvassing

Board on the day that the votes of electors were taken, and Evarts read Humphrey's testimony to the Board on that date:

Examined by the CHAIRMAN:

Q: "Are you shipping commissioner for the port of Pensacola?"

A: "I am not."

Q: "Were you at one time?"

A: "I was."

Q: "At what time?"

A: "Previous to the 7th of November."

Q: "What time did you resign?"

A: "The acceptance of my resignation was received by me from Judge Woods about a week or ten days before the day of election, which I have on file in my office. I did not think of its being questioned, or I would have had it here. He stated in his letter to me that the collector of customs would perform the duties of the office, and the collector of customs has since done so."[416]

Evarts next discussed whether the joint session of Congress, when it opens and counts the electoral votes, has any legal power to intervene or take extraneous proof. "There is no act of Congress on the subject," he argued. "Our proposition is that at that stage of the transaction of the election the two Houses cannot entertain any subject of extraneous proof. The process of counting must go on. If a disqualified elector has passed the observation of the voters in the state, passed the observation of any sentinels or safeguards that may have been provided in the state law, that when these are all overpassed and the vote stands on the presentation and authentication of the Constitution that is upon the certificate of the electors themselves and of the Governor, it must stand unchallengeable and unimpeachable in the count."[417]

So, Evarts argued, "this Commission cannot receive evidence in addition to the certificates of the nature of that which is offered; that is, evidence that goes behind the state's record of its election, which has been certified by the Governor as resulting in the appointment of these electors."[418] That power belongs to a court in a matter of *quo warranto*, and since "*quo warranto* is a matter and an action of the common law, [i]t involves as matter of right the introduction of a jury into its methods of trial."[419]

But Evarts then belittled the idea of courts acting in *quo warranto* to stop and interfere with any step of an electoral process. He told the Commission of a case in his home state of New York, where "not very many years ago an attempt was made to obtain an injunction against inspectors canvassing votes ...because they had been sworn on the [Board rulebook] and not on the Bible. They had no right to discharge their function," Evarts described the complainants to have averred, "without taking an official oath. The court refused it necessarily. However much this irregularity might find play and place in a *quo warranto* investigation of the whole transaction, piecemeal inquiry cannot be made and no injunction of a court can intrude into the course of the political action of an election."[420]

* * *

After Mr. Evarts made a few more remarks, President Clifford turned the floor over to the Tilden side for rebuttal by Mr. O'Conor.

In answer to Mr. Evarts' claim that the Commission had no jurisdiction to go behind the Governor's certificate by presenting additional evidence, O'Conor answered that "we stand in direct conflict with the other side, and the issue formed between us is this: We maintain ... that this tribunal has full authority to investigate by all just and legitimate means of proof the very fact, and thereby to ascertain what was the electoral vote of Florida."[421]

O'Conor pointed out that the Commission possessed, by act of Congress, "the same powers, if any, now possessed for the purpose in hand by the two Houses acting separately or together."[422] He then explained what those powers were. When the Constitution provides for a count, said O'Conor, "we are not told that there shall be a count of all the certificates presented, or of the certificates, or of anything in the certificates, but that there shall be a count of 'the votes.' This, I humbly submit, introduces a necessary implication that somehow and by some authority there shall be made, if necessary, a selection of the *actual votes* from the mass of papers produced and physically present before the Houses."[423]

"This is a preliminary inquiry," O'Conor argued, "and whether you denominate it judicial or ministerial or executive, it is to be an *inquiry*, and the power to institute or carry it on" is not granted to the President of the Senate," but "is to be exercised by those who may have occasion to act officially on the result of the electoral vote" – the two Houses of Congress.[424] "[T]hose who have thus to act officially on the count," O'Conor pointed out, "are the persons who must do whatever may be needful for the purpose of enabling a count to be made. Those who are bound to act in the one direction or in the other as the case may require must possess the power of making any preliminary investigation that may become necessary."[425]

The powers of these Houses are broad, O'Conor pointed out. "The competency of each House to ascertain the truth is unquestionable. Each has complete powers of investigation; they can take proof through their committees or otherwise as to any matter on which they may be obliged to decide, and, either before or after the opening of all the votes, they can thus investigate, though not, it must be admitted, with the aid of a jury, nor in the precise forms of a judicial proceeding. They can investigate, as political and legislative bodies may, all the facts and circumstances that are necessary to be known in order to enlighten their judgment and guide them to a just and righteous decision. Our construction thus recognizes in those two bodies on such a contingency as is here presented full power to do whatever may be needful to the accomplishment of justice."[426]

As for Florida's vote, O'Conor pointed out that state law actually contemplates just this type of investigation by Congress when it gives the State Canvassing Board the authority to reject votes. The statute says:

> If any such returns shall be shown or shall appear to be so irregular, false, or fraudulent that the board shall be unable to determine the true vote for any such officer or member, *they shall so certify*, and shall not include such return in their determination and declaration; *and the secretary of state shall preserve and file in his office*

all such returns, together with such other documents and
papers as may have been received by him or by said board
of canvassers.[427]

One of the powers of Congress, O'Conor maintained, must be
to investigate the Canvassing Board's "certificate of their action
rejecting these returns. The law itself provides for and contemplates
an investigation of the action of the Board of State
Canvassers."[428] Thus, O'Conor argued, "We show it by their own
certificate which the law compelled them to file and place along
with the canvass which they made, and which, very short, brief ,
and simple, will demonstrate the monstrosity of the deed that we
seek to set aside."[429]

Mr. O'Conor made a few more remarks, then concluded his
presentation. Mr. Evarts then stood up and offered the
Commission a Congressional minority report published in the
Congressional Record which he said shows that the result of the
different computations that were made by the Florida courts and
Governor Drew after the electoral vote all resulted in favor of the
Hayes electors. Mr. O'Conor objected to its introduction as
evidence, but Mr. Evarts claimed that he was not offering the article
in evidence, but only "for your honors' information, and in answer
to the intimation of the learned counsel that every man, woman,
and child knew that, if the canvass was not so, then the Hayes
electors were not chosen."[430]

* * *

At this point, the Commission voted to recess for three-quarters
of an hour.[431] As all the commissioners entered the antechamber
behind the curtains of the bench, President Clifford remarked,

"Gentlemen, we've heard a full round of oral argument, including a rebuttal from the Tilden side. What say you to our retiring behind closed doors to deliberate on whether any, and what, evidence should be entered on the record with respect to Florida's electoral vote?"

There was no dissent. "How long should we take for this?" asked Commissioner Thurman.

"Let's just take whatever time it takes us and vote every now and then on whether to extend the time," said Commissioner Miller.

"Are there sufficient copies of the minority report for each of us to read, Judge Clifford?" asked Senator Morton.

"There are," Clifford replied. "I will distribute them to each of you."

On resuming the bench at 3:15 p.m., the Commission cleared the courtroom to deliberate behind closed doors.[432] We spectators left and the lawyers retreated to their respective war-rooms. Amelia and I stepped into the Tilden war-room. I introduced her to the lawyers, who were delighted to meet her after dealing with so *many* men for so *many* days.

* * *

"So are the Republicans now claiming that the Hayes electors *really did* win Florida, not the Tilden electors, despite what the Florida Supreme Court and the Florida Legislature said?" I asked Mr. O'Conor.

"That seems to be the case, Abram," O'Conor replied. "Their alleged 'proof' is nothing more than this House Republican Minority Report. We're reviewing it now."

I asked for and received a copy of the Report, which Amelia and I proceeded to read.

The report said:

> *As a summary of the various ways of estimating the vote of the State of Florida on the 7th of November, the minority submit the following:*
>
> *I. If the vote be reckoned by the face of the returns which were opened by the Board on the 28th of November, and unanimously declared (Attorney-General Cocke concurring,) under the rule of the Board, to be the regular returns, having all the legal formalities complied with, the majority for the Hayes electors is 43.*
>
> *II. If the vote be reckoned by the official statutory declaration of the Canvassing Board exercising its jurisdiction under the state statute, in accordance with the practice adopted without objection, and by the advice of the Democratic Attorney-General Cocke and never disputed until the result of this canvass was about to be determined, which declaration in the belief of the minority is final and irreversible, the majority for the Hayes electors is 925.*
>
> *III. If the vote be reckoned upon the principles laid down by the Supreme Court in their order to recanvass in the case of Drew vs. Governor Stearns, of not purging the polls of illegal votes and retaining the true vote, but of rejecting the whole county return when appearing or shown to be so irregular, false, or fraudulent that the true vote could not be ascertained, the result would be, according to the declaration of the board, a majority for the Hayes electors of 211.*

IV. If the board had thoroughly reconsidered, according to the decision of the Supreme Court, the various county returns for the purpose of throwing out in toto all that could be shown to be irregular, false, or fraudulent, instead of purging the returns of their illegalities and returning the true vote, there should be thrown out the returns from the following counties:

Counties	Tilden Electors	Hayes Electors
Baker............................	*238*	*143*
Clay...............................	*287*	*122*
Hamilton........................	*617*	*330*
Jackson..........................	*1,397*	*1,299*
Manatee.........................	*262*	*26*
Totals................	*2,801*	*1,920*

leaving a majority for the Hayes electors of 791.

V. If the vote of the State were to be estimated according to the honest and true vote of the people at the polls, without regard to precinct, county, or State canvassers, the result would be, according to the judgment of the minority, a larger majority for the Hayes electors than the declared majority of 925.[433]

When Amelia and I finished reading, we went back to Judge Black. "Well," I said to him, "if you read I. through IV., the minority report agrees with throwing out votes. The table shows that it throws out all of Baker County on both sides. That's the first time I've seen *this* result.

"Then if you read V.," I continued, "it doesn't say that votes were thrown out, but it *does* say that it only counts 'the honest and true vote of the people at the polls.' That's just a sneaky way of referring to votes that were *not* thrown out!"

"The report is a Republican subterfuge, Abram," Black replied. "Every point it makes contains an *admission* that votes were thrown out. There is absolutely no evidence that there was any intimidation or violence at the polls that would have justified throwing out votes. So *no* votes should have been thrown out. This report just says that 'black' is 'white.'"

"This minority report just proves that the Republicans are playing politics!" O'Conor interjected. "And Evarts didn't introduce the report into the record. He merely 'offered' it to the commissioners as 'information.' So my objection to it is for naught! And we haven't even gotten a chance to introduce *our* evidence yet! Evarts is just prejudicing them! Undoubtedly every commissioner will read it!"

"And certainly not as carefully as we just did,'" Black said sarcastically.

"Well, Bradley may still be on our side, and he's all that counts," I said hopefully.

Chapter Thirty-four – A Closed-Door Debate

THE COMMISSION CONTINUED TO DELIBERATE behind closed doors for another half-hour.

Figure 80: The Electoral Commission in Closed-door Session (PD)

The only light in the interior chamber where the Commission met behind closed-doors was a candle placed before each commissioner's place at the conference table.

"Mr. President," Justice Field addressed his fellow Democratic commissioner, Justice Clifford, "we cannot look at this minority report. We haven't seen the evidence to be presented by the Tilden side yet."

"Nonsense," retorted Justice Miller. "We haven't accepted any evidence at all yet! This was not moved into evidence at all! It is mere information."

"It is prejudicial information!" Field replied. "Mr. Evarts offered this report to support his argument that the Hayes electors won the Florida popular vote. The Tilden side is saying the exact opposite! Now that Evarts has prejudiced us, we *have* to admit all the extrinsic evidence into the record because he opened the door to it!"

"Gentlemen, please," said President Clifford. "We have already heard all the argument that we are going to receive from the lawyers on whether we should admit any evidence of the popular vote canvass in Florida. The Tilden electors have made an offer of proof. Let us discuss this tomorrow."

"I so move," said Commissioner Thurman.

The motion was seconded, and the Commission adjourned until the next day, Tuesday, February 6, at ten o'clock.[434]

* * *

On Tuesday, the commissioners deliberated behind closed doors from ten a.m. until eight p.m. The topic was whether "extrinsic" evidence of the events surrounding the Florida canvass of the popular electoral vote was going to be heard and admitted into the record.

The closed-door meeting was a welcome break for Amelia and me. We used the day to catch up on much-neglected personal affairs.

In the Commission committee room, Justice Field led off. "Gentlemen, it should be clear to all of us at this juncture that the real issue before us is not the certificates themselves, but the popular vote count. The certificates say what they say, and each of them constitutes an avowal by a state official of what he *thinks* the popular vote is. But Certificate No. 1 simply does not cite the same evidence that Certificate Nos. 2 and 3 cite. It is undisputed that two sets of popular votes count *all* submitted ballots, but the other set of popular votes *excludes* votes in counties where the canvassers purportedly surmised without any proof that 'intimidation' or 'violence' occurred at the polls. It is clearly our job to determine which one of these sets is the true one."

"I cannot disagree with you more, Justice Field," replied Justice Miller. "It is neither Congress' job nor our job to count raw popular votes. Neither body has any authority under the Constitution to do so. The Twelfth Amendment says in this regard only that '[t]he President of the Senate shall, in the presence of the Senate and House of Representatives, open all the *certificates* and the *votes* shall then be counted.' Congress is given only *certificates*, and the *certificates* only have *electoral votes* on them. That is all that Congress can 'count.'

"Remember, gentlemen," Miller said to all the commissioners, "the Tenth Amendment, part of our Bill of Rights, states that '[t]he powers not delegated to the United States by the Constitution, nor prohibited by it to the States, are reserved to the States respectively, or to the people.' The Constitution, therefore, delegates to Congress only the power to count *certified electoral votes*, and the *choice* of those electoral votes is a power 'reserved to the States respectively, or to the people.'"

"So," Miller concluded, "I wouldn't admit any of this popular vote evidence."

"I have to agree," said Congressman Garfield, a Republican Commissioner from Ohio. "And if we go behind these certificates to examine the Baker County and other affected county votes, don't we then have to examine *all* of Florida's popular vote? It is ludicrous to call upon us to canvass the state all over again. It is not within our authority, it is not a Congressional power, and it is not something that we even have the *time* to do. The inauguration is less than a month away!"

Congressman Henry Payne of Ohio spoke up to offer the pet solution that he offered to Sam Tilden and fellow Democrats when they dined at the Ebbitt House back in December. "Gentlemen, you are not viewing this correctly. In my view, the only electoral certificates that count are the *uncontested* ones. All three of the Florida certificates are contested. Why don't we simply throw Florida's certificates out altogether and rely only on the electoral votes of states that are not contested like this? That is what Congress did with Louisiana's contested electoral votes in 1872, and that is what we should do with Florida now."

"That would certainly send a message to the states," Congressman Hunton of Virginia, a Democratic Commissioner, interjected. "If you mess with your popular vote, you lose your place at the Electoral College table."

"I cannot abide by that logic," retorted Congressman Hoar of Massachusetts, a Republican Commissioner. "There are maybe two more disputed states coming our way, and by that reasoning we would simply throw out those electoral votes too. Sure, we did it with Louisiana in '72, but we had an incumbent Republican President and a Republican House and Senate. The result was a foregone conclusion, even without Louisiana.

"But if we do that now, then this whole question is thrown to a divided Congress, and we all know that with its current makeup, we would have a Democratic President and a Republican Vice-President. It didn't work with President Adams and Vice-President Jefferson in 1796; the Twelfth Amendment came out of that. We can't let that happen again."

So the debate went, on and on, for the rest of the day. Finally, at eight p.m., the exhausted commissioners moved to adjourn until ten o'clock tomorrow morning, Wednesday, February 7.[435]

* * *

On Wednesday, February 7, the Commission convened at ten o'clock, but after an hour it went back into closed-door session.[436] Amelia and I returned home.

In the committee room, the vigorous debate about extrinsic evidence continued. After some time, Justice Bradley cleared his voice to speak. Everyone else in the room suddenly hushed to hear what the all-important "eighth vote" had to say.

"Gentlemen, I have heard all the argument about admitting or excluding evidence. I have not yet decided my vote on the main question, but on this matter of procedure I have one request. Irrespective of what we decide on the matter of the Florida popular vote, I believe that we must take evidence on the issue of whether Mr. Humphreys, the Republican elector who was a federal shipping commissioner beforehand, was eligible to be an elector.

"I am mindful of my brother Miller's cogent argument of yesterday that the Constitution does not specify a role for Congress to play in counting the popular vote. But the Constitution *does* specify what are the qualifications to be an elector. It states in particular, at Article II, Section 1, Clause 2, that no 'Person holding an Office of Trust or Profit under the United States, shall be appointed an Elector.'

"This is an important provision," Bradley continued, "as Alexander Hamilton noted in *The Federalist* 68, because it excludes from the office of elector 'all those who from situation might be suspected of too great devotion to the President in office.' Thus, no paid sycophant of the current President can be made an elector for the purpose of re-electing the current President, or the current President's favorite candidate.

"I believe too," said Bradley, "that it is Congress which must enforce this rule, not the states. It is too easy for states to overlook this restriction, as they are prone to choose their favorites for the position of elector, and those most likely would be citizens of their states who work for the federal government. There is only one rule of eligibility in the Constitution, and that should be regulated from Washington, not from every state capital.

"And so, gentlemen," Bradley concluded, "I ask that our ruling on hearing extrinsic evidence in this case provide at least for taking evidence on the qualification of Mr. Humphreys to be an elector."

The commissioners all looked at one another and nodded in agreement. This might just be the one substantive point on which they were unanimous!

At three o'clock in the afternoon, Justice Miller made a motion to exclude the evidence of Florida's popular vote irregularities, but not the evidence of Mr. Humphreys' eligibility as an elector:

> *Ordered*, That no evidence will be received or considered
> by the Commission which was not submitted to the

joint convention of the two Houses by the President of the Senate with the different certificates, except such as relates to the eligibility of F. C. Humphreys, one of the electors.

The seven Democrats were obviously displeased with this motion, since it excluded all of the evidence that the Tilden side wished to present except for the ineligibility of Mr. Humphreys. They realized, however, that the Humphreys matter left open the possibility that if the evidence of his unfitness was convincing enough, Bradley might side with them as their "eighth vote," and thereby knock out one elector which would throw the whole election back into Congress.

When President Clifford called for a vote on the motion, the result was the first of what was to be many splits of eight Republicans versus seven Democrats.[437] Justice Bradley was pleased to vote for the motion.

Commissioner Abbott, a Democrat, now offered a second motion:

> *Ordered*, That in the case of Florida the Commission will receive evidence relating to the eligibility of Frederick C. Humphreys, one of the persons named in Certificate No. 1, as elector.

Another vote was taken. It was eight to seven in favor of the motion. All of the Democrats, including Bradley, voted "aye." All of the other Republicans voted "nay."[438] Commissioner Hoar, a Republican, moved that the day's closed-door proceedings and statements be read by the Secretary at the public session the following day. It was agreed to.[439]

Commissioner Thurman, a Democrat, moved to furnish copies of the day's orders immediately to counsel for both sides, and to let them know that the Commission would be ready at eleven o'clock the next morning to hear the rest of the Florida case. It was carried.[440]

The Commission adjourned for the day at a quarter to four p.m.[441]

Chapter Thirty-five – The Facts Narrow

WHEN I HEARD ABOUT THE VOTE, I HURRIED OVER TO THE TILDEN WAR-ROOM. The lawyers and I gathered after the orders and statements were read. We were stunned.

"Bradley caved!" I said, incredulously. And John Stevens seemed so certain after visiting Bradley that he was on our side! Undoubtedly, the Hayes side got to Bradley after Stevens had visited him. There were already reports of certain carriages carrying important personages away from Bradley's house in the early hours of Sunday morning.

"Certainly Bradley does not harbor any warm feelings for Tilden," Judge Black said, cutting and lighting a cigar. The room was soon filled with smoke.

Ashbel Green, our lawyer who was tasked with the Humphreys matter for our side, entered the war-room and removed his hat and coat. He opened his briefcase and placed several large stacks of documents from out of it onto the conference table.

Figure 81: Ashbel Green, Esq.

"Ashbel," O'Conor said to him, "What say you of the Humphreys affair?"

"I have two witnesses to present to the Commission," Ashbel said. "The first one is George P. Raney, of Florida. He is the Attorney-General of Florida. He can testify about the precise moment when the Hayes electors, including Humphreys, were served with process of the *quo warranto* proceeding challenging their title to the offices of electors.

"The *quo warranto* proceeding," Green said, "as you gentlemen well know, was filed in Florida circuit court on December 6, 1876, the same day that the Hayes electors and the Tilden electors met separately in Tallahassee to cast their electoral votes. We can show that they were served before the electoral vote session began, so they had not yet cast their votes when they were informed that their titles as electors were being challenged in court."

"We might have trouble with that one," Judge Black observed. "The Hayes lawyers will probably object that *quo warranto* evidence is out of the case now."

"I intend to argue vigorously against such an objection if it is offered," Green replied.

"My next witness is James E. Younge, Esquire, a lawyer from Pensacola. He was a Tilden elector. He transacted business with Mr. Humphreys as shipping commissioner up to August of 1876 at the latest. While Humphreys claims that he did not resign until October, it will at least close the door on any earlier date he may attempt to claim for resigning his federal job."

"If nothing else," O'Conor observed," it can show that it was well-known to the Republican National Committee after their Convention that Humphreys was a federal official, and shouldn't have been considered by them to be eligible to be an elector."

"That is all I have, gentlemen," Green said. "Humphreys has been summoned as a witness for the Hayes lawyers, and we must cross-examine him vigorously."

"Dick Merrick is assigned to do that," O'Conor said. "He gave a fine oral argument last Saturday. I'm sure he's up to the job."

Figure 82: Richard T. Merrick, Esq. (PD)

* * *

The Commission resumed its hearing in open-session on Thursday, February 8, at eleven o'clock in the morning.[442] I attended in the audience, but Amelia stayed home, at this point being rather bored and annoyed with the whole mess.

President Clifford reiterated the orders for the day: "one, that no evidence will be received except what was submitted to the two Houses by the President of the Senate; and the other, that in the case of Florida this Commission will receive evidence relating to the eligibility of one elector named."[443]

The witnesses for the Tilden side were admitted into the Chamber. First on the stand was George Raney. He was sworn, and Mr. Green began the direct examination.

Q: "Where do you reside?"

A: "I reside in Tallahassee, Florida."

Q: "What is your occupation or profession?"

A: "I am a lawyer by profession."

Q: "What official position do you hold, if any?"

A: "I am Attorney-General of the State of Florida."

Q: "Where were you on the 6th of December, 1876?"

A: "I was in the city of Tallahassee in the State of Florida."

Q: "Have you any knowledge as to the time of the service of the writ of *quo warranto*?"

Mr. Evarts stood up to object to the question. "One moment," he said. "That is not within the license, as we understand, of the order of the Commission."

Green replied, "I should like to hear the objection stated."

Evarts explained, "The objection is that it is not within the order of the Commission admitting evidence concerning the eligibility of Mr. Humphreys and excluding all other evidence."

Green turned to the commissioners to explain. "We propose to prove by this witness the simple fact as to the precise time when the writ of *quo warranto* was served upon Messrs. Humphreys and others, known as the Hayes electors. It is apprehended upon our side that the order which has been made by the Commission does not in its spirit exclude the consideration of the *quo warranto* proceedings which have been laid upon the table, and it is in aid of what may be perhaps considered a question as to the precise moment when the writ of *quo warranto* was served upon Humphreys and others that we desire to make this proof this morning."

President Clifford put the question to the Commission as a whole. "Gentlemen of the Commission, is the objection well taken?"

A vote was taken. Evarts' objection was sustained, again on the now-familiar eight-to-seven party-line vote. "The objection is sustained. Proceed with the examination of the witness," the President told Mr. Green.[444]

Green dejectedly told the President, "We can now dispense with this witness and will call James E. Yonge."

"This is all going to go rather quickly," O'Conor whispered to Black, who was gritting his teeth.

After Mr. Yonge was sworn and seated, Green approached him.

Q: "Where do you reside?"

A: "At Pensacola, Florida."

Q: "Do you know Frederick C. Humphreys?"

A: "I do."

Q: "Where does he reside?"

A: "At Pensacola, Florida."

Q: "How long have you known him?"

A: "I have known him for about ten years."

Q: "What is his business or occupation?"

A: "Agent for an express company, and has been United States shipping commissioner."

Q: "Have you known him to act in the capacity of United States shipping commissioner?"

A: "I have."

Evarts stood to object. "We submit that if an official position is to be proved as by the authority communicated from the Government, in the absence of some reason to the contrary, the official appointment should be given."

Green started fumbling through his briefcase. "Perhaps it is about to be produced," President Clifford observed.

Green turned to the Commission, a document in hand. "This is evidence of his use of the office."

Evarts was not satisfied with the document. "That is my objection, that use is not sufficient on a matter depending upon authority."

Green pulled another document from his briefcase. "I offer in evidence an order of the United States Circuit Court for the Northern District of Florida at the December term, 1872."

The document read:

> *United States Circuit Court, Northern District of Florida.*
> *December term, 1872.*

December 3, 1872.

IN THE MATTER OF THE APPOINTMENT OF

Frederick C. Humphreys, Shipping Commissioner

of the Port of Pensacola.

ORDERED by the court that Frederick C. Humphreys, of Pensacola, be, and he is hereby, appointed Shipping Commissioner for the Port of Pensacola.

Further ORDERED that said Commissioner may enter upon the duties of his said appointment upon taking and filing the oath prescribed by law.

And it is further ORDERED that the Clerk of this Court do furnish said Commissioner with a certified copy of this order.

***

I, J. E. Townsend, Clerk of the Circuit Court of the United States for the Northern District of Florida, do certify that the above and foregoing is a true copy of the original order as of record in this office.

[SEAL.] J. E. TOWNSEND, Clerk.

***

I do solemnly swear that I will support the Constitution of the United States; and that I will truly and faithfully discharge the duties of a Shipping Commissioner to the best of my ability and according to law.

F. C. HUMPHREYS

Sworn and subscribed before me this 9th day of December, A. D. 1872.

GEO. E. WENTWORTH, United States Commissioner for the United States Circuit Court, Northern District of Florida.

Filed December 9, 1872

***

M. P. DE RIOBOO, Clerk Northern District of Florida:

I, M P. De Rioboo, Clerk of the United States Circuit Court, in and for said District, at Pensacola, do hereby certify the foregoing to be a true copy as the same remains on file in my office. I further certify that no resignation of said office of Shipping Commissioner has been filed in my office by the said Frederick C. Humphreys.

Given under my hand and seal of said Court, at Pensacola, this January 24,1877.

[SEAL] M. P. DE RIOBOO, Clerk

Green turned again to Yonge.

Q: "Do you know Frederick C. Humphreys, one of the persons who was voted for as an elector for President and Vice-President of the United States at the election in November, 1876?"

A: "I do."

Q: "Is he, or is ho not, the same Frederick C. Humphreys of whom you have spoken as being United States shipping commissioner?"

A: "He is the same person."

Q: "Have you seen Mr. Frederick C. Humphreys in the exercise of any acts as United States shipping commissioner?"

A: "I have had transactions with him in that capacity."

Q: "How late and when?"

A: "I had transactions with him from time to time from the early part of 1873 up to the date of my leaving Pensacola, sometime between the middle and latter part of August of last year."

Q: "Describe the business you had with Mr. Humphreys as shipping commissioner."

A: "I frequently had occasion to communicate with him on the subject of the discharge of American seamen. His duties in the capacity of shipping commissioner related to such matters between American seamen and shipping masters."

Q: "Did you testify as to your occupation?"

A: "I did not."

Q: "What is your occupation?"

A: "I am a lawyer."

Q: "Engaged in the practice of your profession where?"

A: "In Pensacola."

Q: "And as a lawyer have you from time to time had transactions with Mr. Humphreys as United States shipping commissioner?"

A: "I have."

Q: "Have you appeared before him from time to time?"

A: "Yes, sir."

Q: "How late?"

A: "From time to time, as I answered before, up to the date of my leaving Pensacola, which was between the middle and latter part of August of last year, 1876."

Q: "Did Mr. Humphreys, as United States commissioner, take cognizance of any, and, if so, what, questions which may have been from time to time presented to him?"

A: "The ordinary questions of difference between seamen and masters of vessels; questions of the right to their discharge and the right to receive their wages."

Q: "Did he hold court there for that purpose?"

A: "It was a sort of informal court."

Q: "In which parties appeared before him?"

A: "Yes, sir."

Q: "Did he hear evidence?"

A: "He heard the testimony."

Q: "And arguments of counsel?"

A: "When arguments were presented. It was seldom that arguments were presented in such cases."

Green then told the Commission that all of his questions of the witness were finished. The Hayes lawyers announced that they had no cross-examination. Mr. Yonge was excused.[445]

Next, the Hayes lawyers called Mr. Humphreys to the witness stand. After he was sworn and seated, Mr. Stoughton from the Hayes side approached him.

Figure 83: Edwin Stoughton, Esq. (PD)

Q: "Where do you reside?"

A: "In Pensacola."

Q: "Were you a candidate for elector?"

A: "I was."

Q: "On the Republican ticket?"

A: "Yes, sir."

Q: "Had you prior to being such candidate held any office?"

A: "Yes, sir."

Q: "What?"

A: "I was United States shipping commissioner for the port of Pensacola."

Q: "When did you cease to act as such?"

A: "On the 5th day of October when acceptance of my resignation was received from Judge Woods."

Q: "Did you resign your office?"

A: "I did."

Q: "By resignation to whom?"

A: "By resignation through the mail."

Q: "To whom?"

A: "To Judge Woods."

Q: "Have you the acceptance of that resignation?"

A: "I have."

Q: "Have you that in your possession?"

A: "I have."

Q: "Be kind enough to let me see it?"

A: "[Producing a paper.] That is the paper."

Charles O'Conor leaned forward and whispered to Ashbel Green, "Ashbel, that document you produced this morning to prove Humphreys' appointment as shipping commissioner. Didn't the Clerk of the Circuit Court affirm in it that no resignation letter from Humphreys exists in the Court's records?"

"You're absolutely right, Charles," Ashbel whispered in reply. "I'll be bringing that up in oral argument."

Stoughton's direct examination of Humphreys was continuing:

Q: "Judge Woods is one of the circuit judges of the United States?"

After an objection to the paper from the Tilden lawyers was heard and reconciled, Stoughton then asked Humphreys:

Q: "You received from Judge Woods in reply to your resignation this paper?"

A: "Yes, sir."

Commissioner Miller asked that the reply be read. Stoughton read it out loud:

NEWARK, October, 1876.

DEAR SIR:

I enclose the acceptance of your resignation as shipping commissioner. The vacancy can only be filled by the circuit court, and until I can go to Pensacola to open court for that purpose the duties of the office will have to be discharged by the collector.

Respectfully, yours,

W. B. WOODS.

Major F. C. HUMPHREYS, Pensacola, Fla.

***

To F. C. HUMPHREYS, Esq.,

Pensacola, Fla. :

Your letter of the 24th of September, 1876, resigning your office of United States shipping commissioner for the port of Pensacola in the State of Florida, has been received, and your resignation of said office is hereby accepted.

Very respectfully, your obedient servant,

W. B. WOODS,

U.S. Circuit Judge.

OCT. 2, 1876.

Before Humphrey's testimony resumed, a Tilden lawyer rose and asked, "What place is it dated?" Stoughton responded, "Newark." Then Mr. Evarts asked, "What state?" To which Stoughton replied, "There is no state on it."

Stoughton brought forward another document, to which the Tilden lawyers objected as well. After the objection was resolved, it was read:

> *CUSTOM-HOUSE, PENSACOLA, FLORIDA, Collector's Office, October 5, 1876.*
>
> *F. C. HUMPHREYS, Esq.,*
>
> *Pensacola, Fla.:*
>
> *SIR : I am informed by Judge Woods that he has accepted your resignation as U.S. shipping commissioner and that it devolves upon me to assume the duties of the office until a regular appointment shall be made by the circuit court. I respectfully request, therefore, that you will turn over to me such public books, papers, records, &c., as may pertain to the business.*
>
> *I remain, very respectfully, your obedient servant,*
>
> *HIRAM POTTER, JR., Collector of Customs.*

Stoughton continued the direct examination of Humphreys:

Q: "Was he the Collector?"

A: "Yes, sir."

Q: "Did you cease to act in your office from the time of the receipt of the letter accepting your resignation?"

A: "I did."

Q: "Have you acted at all in that capacity since?"

A: "No, sir."

Q: "Has the Collector acted in your place?"

A: "Yes, sir."

Q: "Did you turn over to the Collector whatever you had of public papers or property connected with the office, if you had any?"

A: "I had none. The blanks were my personal property, bought and paid for with my own money."[446]

Once Stoughton finished, Mr. Hoadly cross-examined Humphreys for the Tilden side.

Q: "Have you a copy of your letter of resignation?"

A: "Yes, sir."

Q: "How did you convey it to Judge Woods?"

A: "Through the mail."

Q: "To what point did you address that?"

A: "To Newark, in the State of Ohio. He was there on a visit."

Q: "Judge Woods was on a visit to Newark, Ohio?"

A: "Yes, sir."

Q: "Has there been any open session of the Circuit Court of the United States for the Northern District of Florida since the date of that resignation?"

A: "No, sir."

Q: "When did you receive Judge Woods' reply to your letter?"

A: "On the 5th of October."

Hoadly's cross-examination was finished. President Clifford asked the Hayes side, "Is there anything further?" Stoughton replied, "Nothing further." He asked the Tilden side, "Anything in rebuttal?" Merrick said, "Nothing further."[447]

Chapter Thirty-six – The Law Is Debated

"THE TESTIMONY IS CLOSED," CLIFFORD THEN ANNOUNCED. He then pronounced the rule for the concluding oral arguments of the attorneys.

"Counsel, not exceeding two in number on each side, will be heard by the Commission on the merits of any case presented to it, not longer than two hours being allowed to each side, unless a longer time and additional counsel shall be specially authorized by the Commission."

Clifford then suggested the order of argument: "one counsel representing the objections to Certificate No. 1 should open, then two on the other side should reply, and then the other counsel having the affirmative should have the close."[448]

The Tilden lawyers requested that three of their lawyers speak instead of two, and that they have an extra hour. The Hayes lawyers did not object and did not ask for an equal extension. The Commission granted the Tilden lawyers' request.[449]

* * *

The Tilden lawyers decided to reverse the order of argument that President Clifford recommended, saving their weakened argument against Certificate No. 1 for last. George Hoadly rose for the Tilden side to speak on the still-pending Humphreys matter.

Figure 84: George Hoadly, Esq. (PD)

Hoadly's argument was simple: Judge Wood was not in his home court, the U.S. District Court for the Northern District of Florida, when he received and acted on Humphreys' resignation. He was in Newark, Ohio on personal business and his Court was not in session.[450]

"It has been established by the proof," Hoadly argued, "that Frederick C. Humphreys held the office of shipping commissioner by appointment from the Circuit Court of the United States in Florida. It has been established by the proof that before the November election he attempted to divest himself of this office by forwarding to the city of Newark, in the State of Ohio, a paper resignation of that office, and by receiving from the Judge, not the Court, acting not in Florida but in Ohio, an acceptance of that resignation.

"The powers of this office are derived from section 4501 of the Revised Statutes: 'The several circuit courts within the jurisdiction of which there is a port of entry, &c., shall appoint.'

"The resignation cannot be made except to the same authority that appointed. The resignation could not, therefore, be made by letter addressed to the judge in Ohio. The acceptance of the resignation could not emanate from the judge in Ohio. The court has not since held a session.

"The Court – which clothed the officer with the power – has not relieved him from the performance of the duty, and I respectfully submit that this proposition is within the cause recently decided in the Supreme Court of the United States, the opinion in which has just been placed in my hands, the case of *Badger and others v. The United States on the Relation of Bolton*, a copy of the decision in which will be furnished to your honors....

"Therefore," Hoadly continued, "considering that Frederick C. Humphreys had been duly appointed to this office, that by the laws of the United States it is shown to be an office of profit and trust, is by the Revised Statutes so made; considering that the Judge of the Circuit Court acting in Ohio was not the Circuit Court and was not the power that clothed him with the authority, and could not relieve him from the performance of the duty with which he had been entrusted by another power; considering that the Judge of the Circuit Court of the United States acting in chambers could not in Ohio release him from a trust which the Court not in chambers clothed him in Florida; considering these circumstances, we respectfully submit that he held an office of profit and trust on the day of the November election for electors of President and Vice-President, and that therefore the vote that he cast cannot be counted."[451]

Commissioner Thurman asked Hoadly whether the commission that Humphreys held "was an office a resignation of which must be accepted, or could the officer resign of his own motion at any time?"

Hoadly responded by reading the appointment statute in full, and then argued that "where the legislative body have created an office, and the judicial authority has, according to the law, clothed a person with the trusts of that office, public policy requires that it should not be held at his will and pleasure, it being an office of public convenience and necessity, for the performance of which bond is required to be given, and the filling of which may be at all times essential to the performance of public duty."[452]

There followed a lengthy discussion of the Constitutional provision disqualifying federal officials as electors, which reads: "But no person shall be appointed an elector who is a member of the Legislature of the United States, or who holds any office of profit or trust under the United States."

"The object of our fathers in introducing without dissent this provision," Hoadly contended, "was to prevent the federal power, the officers controlling federal agencies, from continuing their power through the influence of the offices of trust with which they were clothed for federal and state benefit.[453]

"It was not merely to protect the state in which the candidate might be elected from the intrusion of a federal office-holder into the electoral office," Hoadly maintained, "but it was to protect every other state, each state, all the states, and the people of each and every state by a mutual covenant in the form of a limitation of power that no state should appoint a disqualified person."[454]

Hoadly pointed out that a federal statute provides a remedy for a state when it is faced with the election of an elector who is ineligible to hold the position. Section 134 of the Revised Statutes, Hoadly said, states that "[w]henever any state has held an election for the purpose of choosing electors, and has failed to make a choice on the day prescribed by law, the electors may be appointed on a subsequent day in such a manner as the Legislature of such state may direct."[455]

By this statute, Hoadly argued, the Florida Legislature could have replaced Humphreys with a qualified elector once he was found to be unqualified, which they undoubtedly became aware of before Humphreys resigned. The Rhode Island Legislature did this very thing during this same election because of an elector who was found to be unqualified by reason of his position on a federal commission. But the Florida Legislature did not do the same with Humphreys.

Therefore, Hoadly argued, "if there be a provision of statute law of the United States contemplating the emergency and providing a remedy, and if the power of appointment be with the state and if the opportunity of remedy be with the state, then I submit that it must be shown that the state has taken advantage of this provision of the Revised Statutes, section 134, or the single vote is lost."[456]

Hoadly's argument was precisely the fallback position that the lawyers and I had discussed in the war-room a few days before. If the Commission accepted the idea that Humphreys' resignation as a federal shipping commissioner was ineffective, and that he was therefore still in office on Election Day, and therefore was ineligible to run for elector, then the Florida Legislature's failure to avail itself of the remedy of Section 134 of the Revised Statutes by replacing him rendered Humphreys' election a nullity. Consequently, Florida would lose that one electoral vote. In the absence of that vote, the Hayes-Tilden contest would be a tie and would be thrown into the House to choose a President and the Senate to choose a Vice-President.

* * *

Once Hoadly rested, Ashbel Green stood next to argue against the validity of Certificate No. 1 for the Tilden side.

First, however, Green made a few supplemental remarks about the Humphreys side of the case. He called into question the authenticity of the letter of resignation and Judge Woods' letter of acceptance of it: "that the so-called letter of resignation sent to Judge Woods, and for aught this Commission knows by him still retained, fails to perform the office sought to be imputed to it until it reaches the records of the court or receives some official recognition from the court itself. If that letter had been sent by mail, it could have no effect until it reached its destination. Had it been sent by messenger, no effect could have been given to it until it reached the archives of the court; and the mere fact of its reception by Judge Woods himself gives it no other or greater validity than if it had been in the pocket of the messenger or in the mail-bag."[457]

He then reminded the Commission of the affirmation of the Clerk of the Circuit Court in Florida: "Moreover I am desired to call the attention of the Commission to the certificate of the clerk of the circuit court read in evidence this morning. I have not the paper before me, and therefore may not state its date with accuracy; but my recollection of it is that it contains a certificate that up to a very recent period, certainly subsequent to the time when Humphreys acted as an elector, no resignation of his office had yet reached the archives of the court ...."[458]

Green searched the faces of the commissioners to see if there was any glimmer of curiosity in or recognition of this telling point. There was none. "and with these suggestions," he finally said, "I pass to the other branch of the case."

He summarized the contents of the three certificates: Certificate No. 1, based on the "false" canvass, duly signed by Governor Stearns in accordance with the federal electoral statute, naming the Hayes electors; Certificate No. 2, certified by Attorney-General Cocke, based on the "true" canvass, naming the Tilden electors; and Certificate No. 3, certified by newly-elected Governor Drew, naming the Tilden electors in accordance with the finding of the State Court *quo warranto* proceeding and the newly-passed Florida statute.[459]

Green admitted that the Florida statute and its underlying documents were not in evidence before the Commission. But, he noted, the decision by the Supreme Court of Florida, recognizing that the *quo warranto* proceeding determined that the Tilden electors were chosen by the popular vote, is a decision of the highest court of the state that the commissioners were duty-bound to recognize and give precedence.These documents, Green maintained, "clearly demonstrate that the action of the State Board of Canvassers in November last, by which the Hayes electors claimed to have been rightfully elected, has been solemnly pronounced by adjudication of the Supreme Court of that state to be unauthorized, illegal, and void."[460]

In Certificate No. 3 declaring the Tilden electors to be the winners, Green said, "we have practically all the branches of the government of the State of Florida speaking with unanimous and united voice to the same effect, and certifying to the same fact which is the question now before this tribunal for decision."[461]

Green argued that the state's delay in forwarding its statutory determination that the Tilden electors had won past the date for taking the votes of all electors nationwide was not fatal to it. "Delay in the transmission of the certificates within proper limits cannot produce any invalidity or work any legal consequences," he said.[462] "There is no express direction anywhere which requires that the electoral college, after it shall have met and cast its ballots, shall immediately proceed to make out the lists which are to be transmitted to the President of the Senate." Failure to do so immediately, Green maintained, does not mean that "their action shall be nugatory."[463]

Green maintained emphatically, "Now, taking all these statutory provisions together, they exhibit careful precautions that the votes shall be received before the count. That is the point to be arrived at, that the votes shall be received before the counting takes place. Whether they get there one day after the meeting of the electoral college or thirty days after the meeting of the electoral college is immaterial. The point to be arrived at is that they get to the seat of Government before the count."[464]

Green cited several cases to support his propositions. He then concluded his remarks with this plea to the commissioners: "in the name of the American people; in the name of that Constitution which we all have sworn to uphold and maintain; in the name of that Union to form and perpetuate [for] which the Constitution was framed, and of that liberty which is at once the origin and the result of that Union; not as a partisan; not as an advocate of Mr. Tilden or Mr. Hendricks; nor yet as an opponent of Mr. Hayes or Mr. Wheeler, but as an American citizen, speaking to American citizens, I demand your judgment for the right."[465]

* * *

"We will now hear the other side," President Clifford declared. Samuel Shellabarger rose for the Hayes electors.

Figure 85: Samuel Shellabarger, Esq. (PD)

Like the Tilden lawyers, the Hayes lawyers were somewhat taken aback by the Commission's vote not to hear witness Raney's testimony earlier that morning. Said Shellabarger, "Since I came into court and heard the decision of the Commission excluding the offer of testimony touching the date of the service of process in the *quo warranto* case, all that part of the case of Florida which I had proposed to discuss seems to me to be thoroughly disposed of and such discussion rendered unnecessary. It is only because on the other side discussion has been indulged in with regard to the effect of matters subsequent to the electoral vote that I venture to do

what I would not otherwise do, make some few remarks in regard
to the legal values of those matters that follow in point of time the
date of that vote."[466]

Shellabarger first argued that the *quo warranto* proceedings that
the Tilden lawyers relied on so heavily was *not* in evidence before
the Commission. He noted that the documentation that the
Commission had accepted – the three certificates themselves, but
none of the attachments to Certificate No. 3 – made only one
passing reference to the *quo warranto* proceeding. Thus, said
Shellabarger, "it will not be claimed, I think, even on the other
side, that there is any evidence in the record before this body that
any judgment in *quo warranto* was ever pronounced. The governor
cannot make you acquainted with the existence of the record in
that way.

"The action of the Commission in excluding that manuscript copy
of the record of such judgment tendered as evidence – in moreover
excluding all evidence about the date of service of process taken in
connection with all else which has transpired – makes it entirely
and utterly certain that we have reached a stage in the case where at
least that proceeding and judgment in *quo warranto* are excluded,"
said Shellabarger. "So too in regard to the certificates No. 2 and No.
3."Nevertheless," he said, since the Tilden side had brought it up,
he would make a few comments about "the legal effect upon the
electoral vote of transactions of the state functionaries occurring
after the date of such vote."[467]

"[T]his power, bestowed by the Constitution upon the state, of
appointing an electoral college for the election of a President and
Vice-President of the United States," Shellabarger argued, "is such,
in its very nature, and by the necessities of the case, that every
act of the state in accomplishing the appointment *must antedate*

the performance of that one single function which the appointee is competent to discharge under the Constitution.[468]

"If that proposition is sound," he maintained, "then of course all that the gentlemen say in regard to the effect of the decisions of the courts in determining the signification of their own statutes, all the decisions which have been referred to in regard to the obligation of all federal tribunals to follow the interpretation which the state courts put upon their own statutes, loses all significance in this case."[469]

When, after the electoral vote of a state has been cast, Shellabarger said, "the power of the states to manipulate that vote, their jurisdiction over it, has gone away from the states to the nation, then, of course, these acts of Florida done after the electoral vote, in the frantic effort to change the result of a national election, lose every semblance of legal significance."[470]

Over on the Tilden side, Green sneered in a whisper to Merrick: "How in the hell is a state supposed to do all of that in only one month between the general election and the electoral vote?"

Shellabarger argued that if it were true that states could alter electoral votes after they were cast, then it would be "competent for them through their courts, after the voting day has passed, to make interpretations of their own election laws which shall act backward, shall throw light on and bindingly decide the question who of rival claimants were the true functionaries of the state on that voting day, and thus competent for the states to settle the question which of the two rival bodies were really the lawful electors of the state.[471]

"That is, I think, about the substance of the strongest statement I have seen of this claim so zealously pressed by the other side," said Shellabarger, "alleging power in the state after the electoral vote is cast to destroy it, and to unseat a President though elected by electors who held in favor of their title every judgment, determination, and certificate which it was *possible* for the state to bestow under her existing laws, *before* the time when the electoral vote must be cast and sent off, under seal, to its federal custody."[472]

"Is it not plain, therefore," Shellabarger asked the Commission rhetorically, "that it was the design of the Constitution, is the express requirement of Constitution, that every act of the state being all appointment, and appointment only, shall antedate the vote?"[473]

Shellabarger belittled the proposition of the Tilden lawyers. "How would an act of a Legislature sound," he said, "which read: 'Be it enacted, That this State reserves to herself the power to try by *quo warranto* who were her federal electors after the time when they are compelled to cast the electoral vote.' Would not such an act be, on its very face, simply a monstrosity?"[474]

He offered an explanation why the Constitution set up the electoral college system in this way: "Everybody agrees – the Constitution's terms and its history both combine to make everybody agree – that the reasons why the Constitution held back from the states and kept within the nation the power to fix the day for counting the vote, also the requirement that the day shall be the same in all the states, also the requirement that the vote shall be by ballot and that it shall remain under seal from the moment of its casting until the day of its counting – those requirements are confessed all to be in the Constitution for the vital purpose of *rendering it impossible for the states to intrigue after they knew the votes of sister states for the changing of the result of the election.* They meant that no *post hoc* judgments, no political intrigues, no subsidized courts, should be enabled to destroy the votes of states and unseat a President after they had found out just how many votes must be destroyed ... in order to unseat a President elected and even inaugurated according to all the forms of law."[475]

"Which is just what the judge and sheriff of Baker County did when they threw out the popular vote for Tilden," Merrick whispered perplexedly to Green.

Shellabarger predicted an ominous future if the position of Tilden supporters was adopted: "Your honors, if I, in my own state, being an earnest partisan, after I have found out how my sister-states have voted and after I have learned that it only requires, say, nineteen votes to be destroyed in order to change the Presidential election, can go to ... my local ... court and get a judgment in *quo warranto*, ... that will unseat the electors of my state and unseat a President, then I have turned the Government into a farce and the Constitution into a sham." He defied opposing counsel to devise a reply to disprove that such "opportunities for mischief" will never come to pass, that states will never re-think "who were their electors ... after they have found out how the other states have voted." Indeed, he predicted, "It therefore puts it in the power of every individual who is disappointed, who is unhappy about results, or who is 'enterprising,' to attack and destroy the title to the greatest office of the world, and to precipitate the nation in revolution and unutterable disaster."[476]

"Such poppycock!" Green whispered indignantly to Merrick. "As if the ballot fraud in Baker County didn't do the very same thing!"

* * *

After a few more remarks, Shellabarger thanked the gentlemen of the Commission "for the very singular kindness with which I have been listened to" and sat down. Mr. Evarts then stood to make the case in favor of Mr. Humphreys' eligibility to be an elector.[477]

We Democrats were keenly aware, as our Republican counterparts no doubt were too, that the Humphreys issue posed an "easy out" for the commissioners to pass the buck back to the Congress and force them to break this political deadlock on their own, as the Constitution provides. We were not at all surprised that the Hayes lawyers chose Evarts to make this critical argument – we readily observed that he had so far made the best overall impression on the commissioners.

Evarts lunged at the weak link in our argument – that we had no solid proof of Humphreys' continuance as shipping commissioner from the preceding August of 1876 through Election Day in November of that year. "I except to the mode of proof as to its effect when it stops where it did," Evarts retorted, "that they used a commission of the date of 1872 and proved no occupation of the office later than August 1876. ... The danger of that proposition in a transaction of this nature can be at once discerned.

"Let whosoever take up the burden of proving," Evarts continued, "that on the 7th day of November, one of these certified electors having the warrant of the seal and authority of the state as having been elected, was disqualified for that election, *he must prove it down to and as of that day*." But when the proof stops short of the obligatory day on which qualification must be determined, Evarts contended, "you have *failed* to find that actual possession and use of the office, even presumptively, beyond the date ...." He pointed out that "no reason was given in the witness' evidence why his knowledge stopped there unless the action of the officer stopped there.... I submit that there is no claim, the proof there stopping, that it is to be regarded as a challenge which requires the fact that he was in office on the 7th of November to be presumed."[478]

Evarts next turned to Humphreys' counter-proof of his resignation letter and its acceptance in October 1876. "Now, this office," Evarts went on, "had no term whatever prescribed by statute; it had no enlargement by necessity or by prescription beyond the present will of resignation. The office itself was secured for the public by no clause requiring it to be occupied and exercised until a successor was qualified. There was no need of the office being refilled. The act took care of the service by prescribing that when there was no officer of this kind, the collector should discharge the duty of this act of Congress. ...

"[I]s it to be pretended for a moment that there was any power to hold an occupant of that office to the performance of its duties one moment beyond his will?" Evarts asked rhetorically. He further asked rhetorically, "now when Mr. Humphreys, to the knowledge of his neighbors in Pensacola and the community throughout the State of Florida, is out of his office and its constant duties are performed by another from and after the date in October, are they to lose the effect of their suffrage by the production of a certificate that in 1872 he held the office? I think not."[479]

Evarts quoted federal statutes to the effect that "[a] civil officer has the absolute right to resign his office at pleasure, and it is not within the power of the executive to compel him to remain in office."Another authority that Evarts presented stated: "It is only necessary that the resignation should be received to take effect;

and this does not depend upon the acceptance or rejection of the resignation by the President."[480]

Evarts turned next to whether any provision of law prescribed what should be done if an elector is found to be disqualified. "Congress has not undertaken to execute it; the states have not undertaken to execute any procedure by which votes for disqualified persons shall cause the failure of the vote of the state. They have provided no means; none have been exercised here, ... [Therefore,] you must hold that in this particular also, unless there be statutory provisions of the United States or of the state purging the lists, you must count the vote that the state sends forward and that its governor certifies ...."[481]

Turning then to the relative strengths and weaknesses of the three competing certificates, the first certificate, Evarts pointed out to the Commission, "is subject to no criticism. You have rejected all means whatever of questioning it by evidence as to what occurred before the vote was cast, before the vote was certified by the governor, or after either of those parts of the transaction up to the time of the counting.... This vote then is to be counted, not because it is the best that is seen, but by the absolute fullness of its title in complying with all the laws that have been imposed by Congress concerning the complete verification of a certificate. The fact certified is not gainsaid by proof, for it is excluded."[482]

Regarding the second certificate, Evarts argued, "this second certificate, so far from competing with the first or disparaging the first, confirms it in all respects; in the first place negatively, for it wants the certificate of the executive that is prescribed; in the second place, by an entirely superfluous and worthless paper, so far as the Constitution and laws of the United States are concerned and so far as the laws of Florida are concerned, of an attorney-general of that state, having no more power or authority to certify anything about the election than the commander of the militia of the state ...."[483]

As for the third certificate, he disparagingly maintained, "here we have a certificate of a governor who was not governor at that time!"[484]

"What becomes of the provision of the act of Congress, justified by the Constitution," Evarts asked, "that the elections or other methods of appointment that the state may use shall be on the same day? What does it mean? Does it mean anything? Did our fathers trifle upon questions of punctilio and order? No. If it means anything, it means that it must be done on one day, that it shall not be undone on any other day."[485]

Concluding his remarks, Evarts characterized the Commission's conclusions up to this point: "When you have determined that evidence shall not invade the regularity of the finished transaction of the state or defeat the regularity of the certification under the acts of Congress at the time when the votes are sealed up in their packages and transmitted, when you have determined that that shall not be invaded by extraneous evidence, you have determined as by a double decision that it shall not be invaded, disparaged, or exposed to any question by a mere certificate that is its own agent and author and volunteer in disturbance of the counting of the votes."[486]

* * *

The job finally fell to Richard Merrick to present the rebuttal on the part of the Tilden side. This not only meant that Merrick would be tasked with wrapping up the entire case for the Tilden electors; it also meant that Merrick would be fielding the last questions of the commissioners on all of the issues that they could ask before they cast their final votes on the Florida case.

His first duty was to counteract Evart's portrayal of his side's position. "[W]hile the learned counsel who has just closed has so eloquently called your attention to the painful condition that would be presented should we proceed to an election of a President of the United States subject to the delays that might be incident to the various judgments that might be rendered on *quo warrantos* instituted for the purpose of ascertaining the truth of the due election of electors," Merrick opened, "he omitted to call your attention to the counterpart of that picture, the condition of Government we should have with a President walking up to the Presidential chair along a pathway strewn with recognized frauds, perjuries, and crime, into which the people of this country are neither allowed to inquire through their representatives in the federal Congress nor through their representatives in the government of the states."[487]

Speaking of the Constitutional provision barring federal officers from being appointed as electors, said Merrick, "[y]ou will see from the phraseology of the article that it is a limitation upon the power of appointment rather than a designation of the disability of the appointee. A state has the power to appoint whom it pleases within certain limitations, and when it transcends those limitations, it does not execute a power which is given to it, but assumes to act beyond the given power, and the attempted appointment is necessarily absolutely null and void." Yet the other side would have the Commission believe, said Merrick, that if a state did appoint such a person, "we are not to enter into the inquiry, forsooth, but to accept as final and conclusive in a Presidential election the vote of one whom the Constitution of the United States has declared the state shall under no circumstances appoint."[488]

This limitation on state appointing power is different from the minimum age limitations for Representatives and Senators, argued Merrick, because while younger persons may run for these seats before they reach these ages, they may nevertheless be seated if they win and reach the age of eligibility before they assume the position. "But in the case of the state as to its electors," Merrick argued, "it is not a matter of time nor a personal disability that either the lapse of time or anything on earth can dispense with, for it is a limitation upon the power, and if the state exceeds the power granted the act is void from the very day it was attempted to be performed, and the individual who assumes to cast the ballot when appointed in excess of that power of appointment casts a piece of paper that might in every view of constitutional law and every ordinary view of power in the law be regarded as a blank."[489]

Merrick then examined the nature of the proof needed to show that Humphreys had resigned before becoming an elector. "The learned counsel on the other side require," he said, "that we should be limited to the strictest possible proof of the fact of his incumbency on the day of the appointment. I apprehend that as far as legal principles are known and recognized, when you have once proved the incumbency of an individual, the presumption of law follows and goes with you and the burden of proof is upon him to show that that incumbency has ceased to exist." So here, said Merrick, "[i]f we prove the commission under the broad seal by which he holds that office, and then superadd to that commission the fact that he has discharged the functions of that office at a period of time somewhat near in date to the period of his appointment, the presumption of law is that he acted under the commission from the date of his appointment and up to the present time, until that presumption is rebutted by evidence upon the other side."[490]

But that is not what has happened here, said Merrick. Here, "the learned counsel on the other side had the officer himself upon the stand; and if the resignation as proved by that officer is not a sufficient resignation, then, as a matter of course, he did not resign at all according to his own evidence, and was still in office on the day of his pretended appointment as elector.

"The resignation," Merrick pointed out, "was a private letter addressed to the judge of the Circuit Court, who was then in ... Newark, Ohio; and the receipt of a letter by him from the judge indicating his acceptance of that resignation. The statute of the United States requires that this appointment shall be made by the Circuit Court, and if any resignation is necessary at all, as we hold that it is, and the acceptance of a resignation, that resignation can only be made to the power that gave the appointment, and the power that gave the appointment is the only power capable of accepting that resignation and relieving the party from the incumbency of the official position.[491]

"The Circuit Court being the power that gave the appointment," said Merrick, "it was to the Circuit Court that his resignation should have been sent, and if an acceptance was necessary, it was the Circuit Court that should have given that acceptance, and the acceptance should have appeared upon the records of that Court if ever given, alongside of the commission, nullifying the commission by the same sanctity of record which the commission had in bestowing the office. But it is in proof before this honorable Commission that there is no record of that resignation; that the commission stands upon the records of the court today unimpeached and unimpaired by any recorded resignation of the officer that it clothed with official power; and I respectfully submit that, until that resignation is there recorded, until that resignation is accepted by the power which gave it and appears of record, this party still continues in office."[492]

"If I resign a position as of a certain date, must I be a slave until the employer finishes the paperwork?" Evarts leeringly whispered to Shellabarger on the Hayes side.

At this point, Merrick was peppered with the expected blizzard of last-minute questions from the bench. Seven commissioners – four Republicans and three Democrats – assailed him.

"Now if this gentleman had been elected a Senator or Representative of the United States, and the judge of the Circuit Court had refused to accept his resignation as shipping commissioner, do you hold that he never could have taken the office of Senator or Representative? If not, how do you distinguish the case from the present one?" asked Commissioner Hoar, a Republican.[493]

His election to the Senate would have constituted his discharge from the incompatible office of elector, Merrick answered.

Hoar then sprang a trap. "Then if taking upon himself the incompatible office be a sufficient discharge from the other one, in that case is not the taking upon himself the office of elector?"[494] In other words, Hoar's trap suggested that Humphrey's taking the position of elector *automatically* relieves him of the position of shipping commissioner.

Merrick dodged the trap. "If this were a personal disability it would have been. If it was a personal disqualification in the man, it would have effected that result. But where the difficulty in taking the office is not a personal disqualification in the individual, but a limitation upon the power that is to give the office, it does not have that effect."[495]

Commissioner Abbott, a Democrat, offered Merrick a helping hand: "I understand you to claim in this case that an acceptance is not necessary, but still the resignation must be to the party or court or person appointing."[496]

"It must be unquestionably," Merrick replied, figuratively grasping Abbott's hand. "[I]f he had resigned, whether accepted or not, the offer of the resignation is necessary, and that offer must be made to the power that gave the appointment."[497]

Now Commissioner Garfield jumped into the fray. "Do you hold that in case there should be a long vacation of the court, or the court should be abolished by law, or the judge should die and for a year or two no appointment be made in his place, this commissioner could never have resigned?"[498]

Merrick started becoming testy about these hypotheticals that were consuming his precious time. "I should refer that case to one of the returning boards of the South. I hardly know in such an extreme case what reply to make."[499]

Garfield persisted. "I understand your position to be that he cannot resign except when the court is in session."[500]

Merrick punched back, somewhat sarcastically: "He cannot resign except when the court is in session; but I presume that death and the abolition of an office and the extinction of a government and the wiping out of a country and the destruction of a whole people would make exceptions to all principles of law!"[501]

President Clifford sought to relieve Merrick of his time concern. "I shall not take these interruptions out of your time, Mr. Merrick," he said.[502]

Merrick indicated that he would now change to a different topic of the case. But at that point, Commissioner Miller interjected yet another query. "You say that the distinction between a man who accepts the office of Senator or Member of the House of Representatives, who is ineligible by holding another office, and the man who accepts and acts in the office of elector, being in the same situation, is that in one case the disability or inhibition goes to the power of the state and in the other it does not.

Now, if the language is precisely the same," Miller asked, "that no man shall be elected to the office of Senator unless he is thirty years old and no man shall be appointed to the office of elector who holds another office, where is the difference in the question of power in the state?"[503]

Merrick replied with a sigh, "I am not prepared to answer that the language quoted is the exact language."[504]

Commissioner Miller mused a bit. "I do not know that it is the exact language, for the text is not before me."[505]

Merrick, now assured that his time was not being eaten up, replied, "Allow me to look at the Constitution before I answer the question."[506] He thereupon took his revenge on the dilatory Republican commissioners by wasting some of the Commission's *own* time in flipping through pages of documents. Snickers could be heard throughout the room.

Miller tried to cut to the chase. "Are not both state officers in one sense, at least, both elected by the power of the state?" he asked.

Merrick found the relevant provisions of the Constitution. "'No person shall be a Representative who shall not have attained the age of twenty-five years.' 'No person shall be a Senator, who shall not have attained to the age of thirty years.'

"But in reference to the electors," Merrick noted, "it is that 'no person shall be appointed,' following a previous grant of power to appoint; and according to the rules of law, wherever there is a power given to do an act the donee of the power can only execute it according to the law, when he pursues strictly the limitations and the directions of the donor. You will perceive there is a marked difference in the two cases."[507]

Merrick moved to the next subject of his argument. He turned to the other side's suggestion that the Tilden side had waited to see how the election would turn out before complaining about perceived irregularities in the vote. "It was not, as the learned counsel on the other side have intimated, that we waited until after it was seen how the election had gone. There is no danger from this case whatever, as he would suggest, that hereafter, if the precedent of a favorable decision to [us] should be reached, that [a] door would be thrown open to fraud and to the bad passions of men, to the excitements of politics, and the acerbity of party hatreds, to interfere with the just result of popular expression; none whatever. On the contrary, what we seek and what we ask for is that those excitements should be suppressed by the calm voice of reason of this august tribunal and that men who would hereafter seek to perpetuate political power through the instrumentalities of fraud, deceit, and bad practices should find in the history of the Government recorded today the declaration that all such iniquitous proceedings, schemes, and designs will be utter failures and unavailing for the production of any result."[508]

Merrick turned on its head the argument that Democrats had lain in wait before acting, in order to point the finger back at the Republicans. Regarding Governor Stearns' refusal to certify the Tilden electors, Merrick said, "Instead of waiting to see how these elections had gone, as intimated by the counsel, ... the men who claimed to be elected as the so-called Tilden electors of Florida went to the governor, carrying with them a majority of the electors of that state, and asked the governor to give them the certificate which under the statute law of the United States they were entitled to receive. That governor, possibly influenced by some of those motives which the gentleman has so kindly ascribed as impelling the action of other people, declined to give that certificate, and they were left to look for the next best evidence they could find."[509]

Commissioner Thurman, a Democrat, asked Merrick: "Suppose that what you call the Tilden electors had never voted at all; ... is it competent, by subsequent state proceedings, to show that the men who did vote, the Hayes electors, had no title to vote?"[510]

Merrick replied, "Most unquestionably. The state cannot have her voice simulated. It happens that on this occasion the true voice of the state was spoken; but if it had not been, there could have been no more power and vigor in the simulated tones of her voice to reach the councils of the Federal Government than there is when those simulated tones come ringing along with the true sentiments of her people. The state is not to be deceived and cheated in that way."[511]

Merrick vouched for the primacy of Certificate No. 3: "Now it appears in Certificate No. 3 that the governor issued this certificate in obedience to the acts of the Legislature of Florida and in obedience to the decision of her courts, and this Certificate No. 3 is the only certificate before this tribunal that contains a canvass of the votes of Florida.

"The learned counsel spoke of the incoming of a new administration and the displacement of an old, of there being hostile political parties;" Merrick recalled, "but I apprehend that such a circumstance is a matter of very little importance in this inquiry, for the state as apolitical organization goes on forever and never dies, and whatever the governor who was governor at the time the electors voted could do after that event, his successor can do just as well. The change of the administration makes no difference whatever in the gubernatorial power."[512]

Following a final flurry of ending remarks, Merrick closed his argument: "May it please your honors, I have endeavored in the remarks I have made to present this case, as far as I possibly could, as I would any ordinary case at law, keeping far away from my heart and lips all feeling or expression of a partisan character. If, in the heat of the argument or in response to inquiries made of me, I should have broken in any particular the resolution I had formed in that regard, I can only beg pardon of the sacred traditions that cluster about this chamber of justice."[513]

With that final word, President Clifford closed the proceeding for the day. The Commission would resume for the final hearing on

the Florida case at 10 o'clock a.m. on the following day, Friday,
February 9.

* * *

At the end of this long Thursday, Sam Shellabarger and William
Evarts, two exhausted Republican lawyers, met at Ebbitt House for
a couple of good steaks and Tennessee whiskeys.

Figure 86: William Evarts (PD)

Bill Evarts, one of the name partners of the eminent New York law
firm of Evarts, Southmayd and Choate, was considered the finest
jury-trial litigator of his day. Charles Southmayd was a master of
case preparation, which his partners Evarts and Joseph H. Choate
were masters at presenting to a court.

Figure 87: Sam Shellabarger (PD)

Immediately prior to the Electoral Commission hearings, Evarts had concluded an infamous case in New York in which he represented the famed pastor Henry Ward Beecher in a suit for "unlawful conversation" (that is, illicit sexual intercourse) with the wife of plaintiff Theodore Tilton. Although the evidence seemed to be beyond dispute, Evarts managed to secure a hung jury in favor of the clergyman. Indeed, so convincing was Evarts that only three of the twelve jurors voted in favor of Tilton.[514]

Congressman Shellabarger had served a term in the Ohio House of Representatives and three separate terms for Ohio in the U.S. House. For eight months in 1869, he served under appointment by President Grant as Ambassador to Portugal. His fame emanated from his drafting of the anti-Ku Klux Klan bill that was passed by Congress as the Civil Rights Act of 1871.[515]

They ordered a private booth in the restaurant away from other diners, courtesy of the maître-d', to allow them to converse freely out of earshot of prying journalists.

"I am not entirely free from doubt," Bill told Sam over their whiskeys, "but I think it went very well."

The steaks were served. After the waiter left, Sam said, "I am quite confident of the outcome. I think that Bradley has come around to our side and the political divide will hold."

"Bradley clearly wanted to give Tilden one last clear chance to knock off Humphreys as a Hayes elector," said Bill.

"And throw the whole thing into the House? Not a chance," Sam retorted. "Bradley knows that that outcome would start another Civil War."

"I suppose that's right, Sam, but I can't help thinking that the Florida Canvassing Board's shenanigans might persuade him to leave the whole mess to the House to straighten out."

"The wisest thing they did was to bifurcate the proceeding into a preliminary phase about admitting evidence and a later phase of taking evidence if permitted by the first phase," said Sam. "Cutting all the canvassing evidence out of the case simplifies matters tremendously. It's not their job to be a Super Canvassing Board over all the states. That is clearly unconstitutional."

"I can't agree more with that, Sam," Bill replied, cutting into his steak. "Canvassing Boards all over the country are guilty of the same thing. If the Tilden side wins, then no election in the future will ever go unchallenged. There's got to be finality to it."

"I'll tell you one thing," Sam said to Bill. "I can't thank Congressman Hewitt enough for putting in the Electoral Commission Act that the Commission's authority is such that 'none can question and whose decision all will accept.'[516] It's unappealable, and that's that."

"Well, our job's not done yet," Bill said, sipping his whiskey. "Louisiana's next, we have to win that one too, and that one is an even bigger mess than Florida."

* * *

In the ornate lobby of the Willard Hotel, I joined George Hoadly and Ashbel Green for their post-mortems amid a round of whiskey and cigars (for which I no longer had any compunctions in imbibing).

Figure 88: George Hoadly (PD)

George was a former law partner of the late Supreme Court Chief Justice Salmon P. Chase. He was a graduate of Harvard Law School, in the same class as Rud Hayes. He practiced in Cincinnati and became a Superior Court Judge there. Originally a Democrat,

Figure 89: Ashbel Green (PD)

he joined the Republican Party during the Civil War because of his opposition to slavery, but returned to the Democrats in recent years.[517]

Ashbel, a fellow New Jerseyan of mine, lived in Tenafly, New Jersey and practiced law in New York City. His grandfather, for whom he was named, was a former

Figure 90: Abram Hewitt

President of Princeton College. He was appointed a Circuit Court Judge in Bergen County, New Jersey, but recently gave up the office due to the press of business.[518]

"Unfortunately, I cannot say that it went well," George confessed.

"When the Commission shut down Raney, I felt doomed," said Ashbel, puffing his cigar.

"It seems that the original sin has been the damning one," George observed. "No matter what we could do at this highest level of government, with all of the princes of the realm before us, it all comes down to an irrational act of theft by the lowest individual in the chain of custody, at the ballot box itself."

"Once the Baker County Judge threw out those precinct ballots, the deed was done," said Ashbel dejectedly. "Nothing that we can do afterward matters."

"It's an unwieldy system that cries to be fixed," I said. "Voting is wholly unprincipled. There are no rules. There are too many steps in the process where things can go wrong and unscrupulous people can get in the way. So much is at stake in counting every vote that hucksters and tyrants will do anything, pay any price, to rig it."

"Perhaps, Abram," Ashbel said to me with a smile, "you can invent a machine that counts votes instead of letting human beings do it?"

"Perhaps one day there will be one," I replied. "One that is infallible, that counts only what the voter wants it to count, and the mechanics of which cannot be tampered with."

"A McCormick Reaper of votes!" George said. We all laughed.

"I found it very strange that the Commission decided not to go behind the certificates, but heard the Humphreys story in its entirety," I commented.

"I have no doubt that Bradley was the holdout on Humphreys," said Ashbel. "Rumor has it that there were many visitors to Bradley's house this past week from Frelinghuysen and other Republican luminaries," he remarked.

"I think that Merrick made a good point at the end about Humphreys' resignation letter and Judge Woods' acceptance," George said, sipping his whiskey. "I have no doubt in my mind that those letters are forgeries. Why would they have never appeared in the Circuit Court's records unless they were forgeries?"

"We could have called a handwriting expert to determine if Judge Woods' signature on the letter was genuine," I suggested.

"No, we could not," Ashbel replied. "This Commission is not a court. If they don't want to take evidence, they need not do so. And they would certainly have turned down a handwriting expert, by a vote of eight to seven!" We all chuckled.

"Well, there are three more chances to rip the one electoral vote that we need out of Republican hands," George said. "And the prospects of doing so in Louisiana, South Carolina, and even Oregon are better than they are in Florida!"

"Let's hope so," I said.

Chapter Thirty-seven – The Final Word on the Florida Electors

ON FRIDAY, FEBRUARY 9, 1877, THE COMMISSION re-convened at ten o'clock for one last hearing on the Florida question.[519]

At the start, there was finally a debate about what the members of the Electoral Commission were to be called in the record. Congressman Garfield noted that Justice Clifford was being called "the Presiding Justice," which he felt was incorrect. "It speaks of you as 'the Presiding Justice.' The query is whether your proper title is not that of 'President.' It seems to me the language employed might carry the implication that we were in some sense a court; that we were all justices, and you the presiding justice."[520]

Another Republican spoke up. Senator Morton said, "It seems to me that the members should not be designated as Justices, or Senators, or Representatives, but simply as commissioners."[521]

It was quite clear to me what the Republicans were doing. They were attempting to discount any similarity that the Commission had to a court of law, in order to preclude it from being accused of failing to adhere to well-recognized rules of evidence.

Clifford was persuaded, of course, and ordered the record corrected to refer to himself as "President" and the other Commission members as "Commissioners." A motion was then granted to close the doors and have the Commission deliberate in private about the electoral vote of the State of Florida.[522]

* * *

Each commissioner had prepared a statement to read to the others that set forth his position on the electoral vote of Florida.

President Clifford reserved his statement to the end. The statements of each of the other commissioners, save one, broke out along expected party lines.

Justice Field, one of the Supreme Court Justices chosen by the Democrats, spoke first. "The returns sent from the several counties to the State Canvassers all disclosed for whom the votes were cast," Field said to his fellow commissioners. "It is not pretended that any of them appeared, or was shown to be either so irregular, false, or fraudulent that the Canvassers were unable to determine the actual votes given for any officer. The pretense is that some of the votes returned were illegally or irregularly given, not that there was any doubt for whom they were intended.

"Under these circumstances," the Justice continued, "the duty of the Canvassers, according to the decision of the [State] Supreme Court, and according to the express language of the statute, was simply to add together the votes and declare, under their certificate, the result as shown by the returns. In so doing they would have carried out the direction of the Legislature. Being added together, the returns would have shown that the Tilden electors were chosen.

"But the Canvassers, instead of discharging the simple ministerial duty devolved upon them, undertook to exercise judicial functions and pass upon the legality of votes cast at various precincts in different counties, hearing evidence and counter-evidence upon the subject, consisting partly of oral testimony, but principally of *ex-parte* affidavits, and in numerous instances, upon one pretense or another, throwing out votes given for the Tilden electors, thereby changing the result. In this way a majority of the canvassers came to the conclusion that the Hayes electors were chosen. In no other way could such a result have been reached.[523]

"After the statement I have made of the character of the returns, and the manner in which they were altered," Field concluded, "there can be no reasonable doubt that the Tilden electors were thus appointed. They received a majority of the votes cast as shown by the returns, and the law of the state declares that parties receiving the highest number of votes for any office shall be elected to such office."[524]

Field did not buy into the argument that the certificate of Governor Stearns was conclusive of the state's choice of electors. "The fact here to be ascertained is, who have been duly appointed electors of the State of Florida, not who have the certificates of appointment. It is the *election* and not the *certificate* which gives the right to the office."[525]

"In the previous day's debate behind closed doors," Field said, "I had put to several Republican commissioners a series of hypotheticals regarding the incontestability of Governor Stearns' certificate. My last one was rather extreme: 'Supposing the Canvassers were coerced by physical force, by pistols presented at their heads, to certify to the election of persons not chosen as electors by the people, and the persons thus declared elected cast the vote of the state at the session of the electoral college; was there no remedy?' And the answer that the Republican commissioners gave me was that for any wrong, mistake, fraud, or coercion in the action of the Canvassers, the remedy must be applied before the electors have voted. The work of the electors is done when they have acted, and there is no power under existing law by which the wrong can be subsequently righted."[526]

"The canvass of the votes in Florida was not completed until the morning of the day of the meeting of the electoral college, and within a few hours afterwards its vote was cast," Field observed. "To have corrected any mistake or fraud during these hours, by any proceeding known to the law, would have been impossible.

"The position of these gentlemen," Field said, "is, therefore, that there is no remedy, however great the mistake or crime committed. If this be sound doctrine, if the representatives in Congress of forty-two millions of people possess no power to protect the country from the installation of a Chief Magistrate through mistake, fraud, or force, we are the only self-governing people in the world held in hopeless bondage at the mercy of political jugglers and tricksters!"[527]

Justice Field concluded his remarks with a plea: "Mr. President, I desire that this Commission should succeed and give by its judgment peace to the country. But such a result can only be attained by disposing of the questions submitted to us on their merits. It cannot be attained by a resort to technical subtleties and ingenious devices to avoid looking at the evidence. It is our duty to ascertain, if possible, the truth, and decide who were in fact duly appointed electors in Florida, not merely who had received certificates of such appointment.

"That state has spoken to us through her courts, through her Legislature, and through her executive," he pointed out, "and has told us in no ambiguous terms what was her will and whom she had appointed to express it. If we shut our ears to her utterances, and closing our eyes to the evidence decide this case upon the mere inspection of the certificates of the governor and Canvassing Board, we shall abdicate our powers, defeat the demands of justice, and disappoint the just expectations of the people. The country may submit to the result, but it will never cease to regard our action as unjust in itself, and as calculated to sap the foundations of public morality."[528]

* * *

The next-to-last statement – the most crucial one, of course – was Justice Bradley's.[529]

"I assume that the powers of the Commission are precisely those, and no other, which the two Houses of Congress possess in the matter submitted to our consideration; and that the extent of that power is one of the questions submitted. This is my interpretation of the act under which we are organized," Bradley began.[530]

"The first question, therefore," Bradley continued, "is, whether, and how far, the two Houses, in the exercise of the special jurisdiction conferred on them in the matter of counting the electoral votes, have power to inquire into the validity of the votes transmitted to the President of the Senate."[531] The President of the Senate, he concluded, performs only a ministerial function; "He is not invested with any authority for making any investigation outside of the joint meeting of the two Houses. He cannot send for persons or papers. He is utterly without the means or the power to do anything more than to inspect the documents sent to him; and he cannot inspect them until he opens them in the presence of the two Houses.[532]

"It would seem to be clear, therefore," Bradley went on, "that if any examination at all is to be gone into, or any judgment is to be exercised in relation to the votes received, it must be performed and exercised by the two Houses. Then arises the question, how far can the two Houses go in questioning the votes received without trenching upon the power reserved to the states themselves?[533]

Bradley answered his own rhetorical question thus: "Each state has a just right to have the entire and exclusive control of its own vote for the Chief Magistrate and head of the Republic, without any interference on the part of any other state, acting either separately or in Congress with others. If there is any state right of which it is and should be more jealous than of any other, it is this."[534]

The Republican commissioners breathed a quiet sigh of relief; the Democrats felt dismayed. Bradley was leaning squarely toward the Hayes camp.

"It seems to me to be clear, therefore," said Bradley, "that Congress cannot institute a scrutiny into the appointment of electors by a state. It would be taking it out of the hands of the state, to which it properly belongs. While the two Houses of Congress are authorized to canvass the electoral votes, no authority is given to them to canvass the election of the electors themselves. To revise the canvass of that election, as made by the state authorities, on the suggestion of fraud, or for any other cause, would be tantamount to a recanvass.[535]

"It is unnecessary to enlarge upon the danger of Congress assuming powers in this behalf that do not clearly belong to it. The appetite for power in that body, if indulged in without great prudence, would have a strong tendency to interfere with that freedom and independence which it was intended the states should enjoy in the choice of the national Chief Magistrate, and to give Congress a control over the subject which it was intended it should not have."[536]

"So much for Joe's liberal view of the Fourteenth Amendment," Commissioner Field turned and whispered to President Clifford sitting next to him. Clifford frowned back, as he voted with the majority against Field's dissent in the *Slaughter-house Cases*.

"And here the inquiry naturally arises, as to the manner in which the electors appointed by a state are to be accredited," Bradley stated. "What are the proper credentials by which it is to be made known who have been appointed?" Citing the 1792 act of Congress on electoral votes, Bradley concluded that "the certificate of the Governor is the proper and regular credential of the appointment and official character of the electors. Certainly it is at least *prima facie* evidence of a very high character."[537]

"It seems to me," Bradley added, "that the two Houses of Congress, in proceeding with the count, are bound to recognize the determination of the state board of canvassers as the act of the state, and as the most authentic evidence of the appointment made by the state; and that while they may go behind the governor s certificate, if necessary, they can only do so for the purpose of ascertaining whether he has truly certified the results to which the board arrived. They cannot sit as a court of appeals on the action of that board."[538]

Next, Justice Bradley set forth a question that he had wrestled with for some time. "I was at one time inclined to think that the proceedings on *quo warranto* in the circuit court of Florida, if still in force and effect, might be sufficient to contradict the finding and determination of the Board of Canvassers supposing that the court had jurisdiction of the case. But the action of the Board involved more than a mere statement of fact. It was a determination, a decision quasi-judicial. The powers of the Board as defined by the statute which created it are expressed in the following terms : 'They shall proceed to canvass the returns of said election and determine and declare who shall have been elected to any office; and 'if any such returns shall be shown or shall appear to be so irregular, false, or fraudulent that the Board shall be unable to determine the true vote for any such officer or member, they shall so certify, and shall not include such return in their determination and declaration.'

"This clearly requires quasi-judicial action," Bradley found. "To controvert the finding of the Board, therefore, would not be to correct mere statement of fact, but to reverse the decision and determination of a tribunal. The judgment on the *quo warranto* was an attempted reversal of this decision and the rendering of another decision." The court could have done so *before* the electoral votes were cast, but not after, Bradley concluded, because the acts of the *de facto* electors are valid and binding until they are ousted from office.Therefore, Bradley concluded, "I am entirely clear that the judicial proceedings in this case were destitute of validity to affect the votes given by the electors."[539]

Bradley dismissed as unconstitutional the *post hoc* attempt by the Florida Legislature to overturn the vote of the Hayes electors. "To allow a State Legislature in any way to change the appointment of electors after they have been elected and given their votes, would be extremely dangerous. It would, in effect, make the Legislature for the time being the electors, and would subvert the design of the Constitution in requiring all the electoral votes to be given on the same day."[540]

To the Democratic Commissioners, Bradley's statement sounded, unlike what they were expecting from rumors emanating from the Democratic National Committee, like a complete capitulation to the Republican point of view and, in light of the party split in the Commission, the end of the Florida case. But almost as an afterthought, Bradley then turned to the matter of Mr. Humphreys.

"It is further objected that Humphreys, one of the Hayes electors, held an office of trust and profit under the Government of the United States at the time of the general election, and at the time of giving his vote. I think the evidence of this fact should be admitted. Such an office is a constitutional disqualification. ...What maybe the effect of the evidence when produced, I am not prepared to say. I should like to hear further argument among us on the subject before deciding the question."[541]

"So, he's leaving the door open a crack," Clifford now whispered to Field.

* * *

From all outside appearances, the closed-door debate was intense.

After three and one-half hours, the commissioners took a half-hour recess. At 2:07 p.m., the recess expired and the secret debate resumed.

It went on for another six hours. At six o'clock, the commissioners took another recess for one hour before resuming debate again.

After another hour, the Commission adjourned. All of the Congressional objectors and lawyers for both sides, as well as I, waited at the main doors of the Supreme Court Chamber for word on the verdict.

The Clerk of the Commission appeared at the doors. "Gentlemen," he said, "the Commission has lifted the secrecy injunction, so I can report to you the outcome in brief. The Commission has decided to accept the Hayes electors as the legal electors for the State of Florida."

"What was the vote?" asked Evarts.

"It was eight to seven," the Clerk replied.

"Eight Republicans and seven Democrats?" asked Merrick.

"Yes, sir," answered the Clerk.

"Were any other votes taken?" asked Green.

"Yes, sir," the Clerk replied. "Debate closed at six p.m. After that, a motion was agreed to that each commissioner would be allowed five minutes to speak finally. After that, Commissioner Thurman offered a motion resolving that Mr. Humphreys was not a United States Shipping Commissioner on November 7, 1876. Subsequent to debate on the motion, Commissioner Thurman withdrew it.

"After that, Commissioner Edmunds offered a motion saying, in effect, that Certificate No. 1 is the proper certification for Florida, and that the four electors for Hayes as President and Wheeler as Vice-President were duly and properly certified.

"Commissioner Hunton then offered a substitute motion stating that Certificate No. 2 is the proper certification for Florida, and that the electors for Tilden as President and Hendricks as Vice-President were duly chosen by the state.

"As the substitute motion took precedence over the main motion, it was voted on first and defeated by a vote of eight to seven."

"Again along party lines?" asked Merrick.

"Yes," the Clerk replied. "But then, Commissioner Edmunds withdrew the main motion.

"Commissioner Garfield then offered a motion," the Clerk continued, "stating that the Hayes electors were duly appointed electors of President and Vice-President for the State of Florida, and that the votes cast by them are the votes provided for by the Constitution of the United States. The motion also resolved that Commissioners Edmunds, Bradley, and Miller would draft a report of the Commission's action. That motion was decided in the affirmative."

"By what vote?" Evarts asked again.

"I have not been given liberty to disclose that vote," the Clerk replied cryptically.

"The Commission then recessed for a half-hour, and after it reconvened Commissioner Edmunds offered a draft report for the President of the Senate that was agreed to by a vote of eight to seven."

It was clear to everyone by now that this vote, too, was along party lines.

"What does the report say about Humphreys?" asked Merrick.

"It states," the Clerk read from his notes, "that the Commission is of opinion that, without reference to the question of the effect of the vote of an ineligible elector, the evidence does not show that he held the office of shipping commissioner on the day when the electors were appointed.

"After that, gentlemen," the Clerk continued, "the transmission letters to the President of the Senate were adopted, the secrecy injunction was lifted, and the Commission adjourned around eight p.m. Upon the motion of Commissioner Bradley, the Commission will reconvene tomorrow at three p.m. That is all that I have to report."[542]

* * *

Back in the Tilden war-room, Judge Black said, "Eight to seven. Eight to seven. Strictly along party lines, including Bradley. Tilden should never have agreed to this!"

We were not arguing to fifteen wise men," Charles O'Conor observed. "We were arguing to fifteen politicians, including the Justices. Party loyalty is all that matters to them. Every one of them wants to run for President or has some other political obsession. Every one of them is totally beholden to his own party because it is the only way that he can advance to his lofty ambition. That cursed Bradley!"

"I'm afraid you're right, Charles," I said glumly.

"Abram, let this be a lesson to you," Ashbel Green warned me. "If, after such a successful career in business, you now plan to launch a career in politics, you will fail. I mean no disrespect to you. I mean that, in the end, all political careers fail!"

"After this, Ashbel, I am not sure now whether I will run for Congress ever again," I replied, depressed about our frustrating experience.

"Well, let's meet tomorrow to prepare the Louisiana case," said Charles, picking up his hat to leave.

* * *

"One down and three to go!" Zach Chandler crowed gleefully in the Hayes war-room. "That was a great job, gentlemen! Thank God for Bradley!"

"We must win each and every one of the sixteen remaining electors, Zach," said Bill Evarts as he poured a Tennessee whiskey into a shot glass. "The dam may not hold."

"Oh, it will hold, all right!" Zach retorted. "All eight of our men have bright futures ahead for themselves, thanks to their work here! So do all of you!" he added.

* * *

"You know, John," Sam Tilden said to his friend John Bigelow, as the two poured drinks and sat in the study of his Gramercy Park home, "I received a visit from a gentleman a few days ago who promised me Justice Bradley's vote for $200,000."

They had just received the telegram from Washington informing Sam of the Florida defeat.

"What an outrageous sum!" exclaimed a surprised Bigelow.

"Oh, I have been approached by others from about three Southern states inviting me to engage in bribery over the last few months," Sam replied as he downed his shot glass. "That seems to be the standard figure down there."[543]

* * *

The House of Representatives voted not to accept the Commission's findings on Florida. The Senate agreed to it. Under the Electoral Commission Act, a disagreement between the houses meant that the Commission's decision would stand.[544]

Chapter Thirty-eight – The Louisiana Swamp

THE FOLLOWING WEEK, IT DID NOT get any better for us. It got far, far worse.

With the Florida controversy behind it, the Joint Session of Congress reconvened on Monday morning, February 12, 1877 to resume the vote count. All went well through the six electoral envelopes from "Georgia" to "Kentucky." When the Senate Teller reached "Louisiana," however, the First House Teller handed President Ferry three sealed envelopes containing competing certificates. Two certificates each named the same eight electors for Hayes and both were signed by Governor William Pitt Kellogg. The third certificate named eight different electors for Tilden and was signed by a Democratic *candidate* for Governor, John McEnery.[545]

This was a bigger unholy mess than Florida, by far.

Off went the letter to the Electoral Commission that afternoon:

HALL OF THE HOUSE OF REPRESENTATIVES

February 12, 1877

To the President of the Commission:

More than one return or paper purporting to be a return or certificate of electoral votes of the State of Louisiana having been received and this day opened in the presence of the two Houses of Congress and read, and objections thereto having been made, the said returns, with all accompanying papers, and also the objections thereto, are herewith submitted to the judgment and decision of the Commission, as provided by law.

T. W. FERRY, President of the Senate

* * *

Governor William Pitt Kellogg was a Northern carpetbagger, a Reconstructionist Republican who was reviled by the white citizens of Louisiana. He had been appointed Customs Collector for the Port of New Orleans by President Lincoln just hours before the President was assassinated on April 14, 1865. After that job, Kellogg served a brief stint as a U.S. Senator from Louisiana. He then ran for governor.[546]

The Louisiana gubernatorial election of 1872 in which Kellogg campaigned was one of the most crooked elections in our republic's history. John McEnery, a Democrat, was Kellogg's rival in the election. The official state election board

Figure 91: Governor William Kellogg of Louisiana (PD)

declared McEnery the winner, but a rival board claimed that Kellogg had won. Things got so ugly that both candidates held inaugurations and inaugural celebrations.[547]

Not only was the governor's race a mess; Louisiana's Presidential election results in 1872 were so corrupted that they were thrown out by Congress as illegitimate. It made no difference in the national election results, however, because President Grant won re-election in a nationwide landslide.

Figure 92: John McEnery of Louisiana (PD)

Louisiana in 1872 was still occupied by Federal troops, whom Grant called upon to install Kellogg in the governor's mansion by force of arms. Kellogg remained in office through the Presidential election of 1876. At the end of that year the Louisiana Legislature appointed him a U.S. Senator, and another carpetbag Republican, Stephen B. Packard, beat Democrat Francis T. Nicholls in another crooked election to replace Kellogg as governor. Packard took office in the beginning of 1877, but already McEnery was making plans to take over as governor.[548]

The machinations of the governor's race spilled over into Louisiana's vote for Presidential electors in 1876. The baseness of the Louisiana State Returning Board was astonishing. There were five seats on the Board, four of which were filled by Republicans. The law required the remaining vacant seat to be filled by a Democrat, but the Republicans on the Board refused to exercise their authority to fill the vacancy, leaving them free to act as they pleased.

There were 83,723 popular votes cast statewide for Tilden. The certificate of the Returning Board, however, counted only 70,508 of them, turning Tilden's majority of more than thirteen thousand into a majority for Hayes.[549] Kellogg, in his waning days as Governor, certified the tally and sent the list of eight electoral votes for Hayes to the President of the U.S. Senate in Washington.

The Returning Board managed to accomplish this magic trick by throwing out more than 13,000 votes for Tilden. More than 10,000 of these votes were thrown out pursuant to a Louisiana statute that gave the Returning Board the power, "after due examination and deliberation," to throw out votes "whenever, from any poll or voting-place, there should be received the statement of any supervisor of registration or commissioner of election, in form as required by section 26 of this Act, on affidavit of three or more citizens, of any riot, tumult, acts of violence, intimidation, armed disturbance, bribery, or corrupt influences, which prevented, or tended to prevent, a fair, free, and peaceable vote of all qualified electors entitled to vote at such poll or voting-place."[550] The Board ordered affidavits and statements alleging intimidation at the polls to be forged in order to justify its trashing of votes.[551]

On top of that, two Hayes electors named in Kellogg's certificates held, at the time of the election, "offices of profit" under the United

States. One was the Surveyor-General for the District of Louisiana, and the other was the Commissioner of the Circuit Court of the United States for that District.[552]

* * *

"Go-getter" that I am, I sprang into action to save the day. Before the Joint Session of Congress resumed, I desperately searched for some political maneuver that could be taken in order to prevent the Electoral Commission from ripping Louisiana's electoral votes out of Tilden's hands as it did with Florida's.

I paid a call to Senator Conkling at his Capitol Hill townhome the Saturday after the Commission had decided Florida in one more attempt to enlist his aid. I believed up to that point that Conkling remained sympathetic to Tilden and that he considered Tilden to be the rightful winner in Louisiana.[553] Conkling was continuing to act as a voice of dissent among Republicans.

"Roscoe," I said to him in his home office, "when the Joint Session of Congress reconvenes on Monday, a speech by you justifying Tilden's right to Louisiana's electoral votes would most likely persuade a great number of Republican members whose votes you control. Will you do it?"

"Abram," said Roscoe, "there is no doubt in my mind as to the election having been in favor of Tilden by a large majority. I think it is disastrous for my party's reputation to take a win for Hayes by deceit. I will make this point on the floor of the Senate on Monday."

"I sincerely appreciate your taking this course," I told him. "The Electoral Commission is turning into a partisan farce. Congress should stop being dilatory and should exercise its Constitutional duty to step in and choose the President- and Vice-President-elect under these circumstances. We have kicked this can down the road long enough."

"I am fully in agreement with you, Abram."

Alas, my plea went unfulfilled. Roscoe did not show up to the Joint Session of Congress on Monday morning. Instead, he boarded a train to Baltimore and missed the continuation of the count.

* * *

In the late afternoon of Monday, February 12, the Commission convened again. The Democratic congressional objectors to the first and third electoral certificates from Louisiana that chose Hayes were Senator Joseph E. McDonald of Indiana and Representative George A. Jenks of Pennsylvania. The Republican objectors to the second certificate for Tilden were Senator Timothy O. Howe of Wisconsin and Representative Stephen A. Hurlbut of Illinois. The same lawyers who served in the Florida case would handle Louisiana as well.[554]

The objectors for each side were assigned two hours to voice their objections. The Commission then adjourned until eleven o'clock the next morning, Tuesday, February 13, to begin the hearing.

* * *

On Tuesday morning, Commissioner Thurman was ill with neuralgia and absented himself from the proceedings. The rest of the Commission voted to continue without him.[555] About a half an hour into the proceeding, he reappeared and took his seat.[556]

Amelia and I resumed our seats in the Chamber. The Louisiana case attracted numerous spectators.

Senator McDonald rose to speak against Governor Kellogg's Certificate Nos. 1 and 3 for Hayes. [557] He objected that the Louisiana Legislature had failed to make rules for appointing the state's electors; that the officers of the State Returning Board had

Figure 93: Senator Joseph E. McDonald of Indiana (PD)

Committed fraud in counting the popular vote; that two of the chosen Hayes electors were constitutionally ineligible to serve as such; that other Hayes electors were ineligible to serve under the State Constitution; and that the State of Louisiana at the time of the electors' appointments "did not have a government republican in form."[558]

The Senator explained in detail the complex status of Louisiana's election laws. Although that law empowered the State Returning Board to throw out ballots only if a formal protest had been filed, it threw out votes with no protests at all.[559] Each of twenty-two parishes gave the Democratic electors "majorities ranging from 5,300 to 8,990" popular votes. But the votes that the supervisors of registration in each parish sent to the Returning Board pared the Democratic majority down by "from 3,459 to 6,405" popular votes. Hence, the Returning Board certified majorities that ranged from 3,437 to 4,800 popular votes *in favor of the Republican electors*.[560]

Senator McDonald recited cases of the Board rejecting sixty-nine polls over twenty-two parishes; rejecting the polls of Grant Parish in their entirety; and refusing to consider 2,914 votes cast for the Democratic electors and 651 votes cast for the Republican electors in the parishes of East Baton Rouge and Orleans."[561] He asserted that the Board "transposed 178 votes from Democratic electors cast in the parish of Vernon to the Republican electors, which transposition has never been corrected. They rejected poll No. 4 in the parish of Iberia, in which were cast 322 votes for the Democratic electors, and 11 votes for the Republican electors, for no other alleged cause than that the commissioner's statement did not show that the word 'voted' had been written or stamped on the certificates of registration presented by the voters."

McDonald claimed that the Board "added over 500 votes to five of the eight Republican electors in the parish of Concordia, and over 500 votes in the parish of Natchitoches, upon no sufficient proof that such votes had been actually cast." [562]

Figure 94: Representative George A. Jenks of Pennsylvania (PD)

"From these and other facts of a like nature," the Senator concluded, "it is charged and claimed that the action of the board of returning officers was so corrupt and fraudulent as to destroy all faith and credit in their canvass and return."[563]

Congressman Jenks followed Senator McDonald with more horror stories from the Pelican State. First, Jenks explained why Kellogg had submitted two certificates instead of just one. Although each member of the Returning Board had sworn that the canvass of votes on which they formulated their result was not final until eight o'clock on the evening of December 5, 1876, a newspaper reporter found out that the formal certificate appointing the Hayes electors as the winners was already prepared by about two or three o'clock in the afternoon of that day. Having been found out, Kellogg decided to submit a second certificate to "verify" the result of the earlier certificate.[564]

Jenks claimed that the popular vote in Louisiana showed a majority of between 6,000 and 9,000 in favor of the Tilden electors. Although the canvass of the Returning Board disappeared after Kellogg's certifications were made, Jenks said, each parish's count was prepared by the parish supervisor of registration in duplicate. One was sent to the Returning Board, but the other was sent to the clerk of the court in each parish. The courts' records were preserved while the Returning Board's records were destroyed. By amassing the records kept by the courts, the Democrats were able to discern that Governor Kellogg's certificates undercounted 13,236 Democratic votes and 2,178 Republican votes, a difference of 11,058. [565]

Jenks reported hundreds Democratic votes being thrown out in Bossier parish and thousands in East Baton Rouge [566] Thousands of Democratic votes and even hundreds of Republican votes were destroyed in West Feliciana parish and East Feliciana parish on grounds of "intimidation" of Republican voters. [567]

Votes in New Orleans, said the Congressman, were thrown out because "it was uncertain on the commissioner's statement whether the number of votes cast was 247 or 249. That is, the figure '7' was not made with sufficient accuracy by the commissioner of election to know certainly whether it was a '7' or a '9.' Because the supervisor of registration could not decipher that figure, he threw out the whole poll." [568]

Then the Congressman detailed the frauds of the Hayes electors themselves. "A. B. Levissee and Mr. Brewster are disqualified under the Constitution of the United States. We will prove that Levissee was a commissioner appointed by a circuit court of the United States ... at the time of the election. We will prove that Mr. Brewster was surveyor of the land office for the land district of Louisiana. He swears himself that three or four days after the election, he wrote a letter resigning and asking that it might take effect as of the 4th of November. This letter was written on the 10th or 11th of November. It was mailed to Washington and received at Washington on the 18th. On the 23rd he received a reply accepting his resignation as of the 4th. Hence on the day of the election he was disqualified from holding this office ...." [569]

Electors violated the Louisiana Constitution as well, Jenks reported. Elector J. H. Burch "was a state senator of the State of Louisiana. By the provisions of the Constitution of the State of Louisiana, it is provided that no person shall hold any two offices under the said state except those of justice of the peace and notary public. Burch was a state senator, we will prove, prior to the election and continues so up to this day."[570]

Another Hayes elector, said the Congressman, "was, prior to the election, district attorney for the district in which the parish of Saint James is located and has continued to hold [that office] to this day. He is disqualified by the State Constitution. We will also show that Oscar Joffrion was supervisor of registration for Pointe Coupée parish. He is disqualified by the Constitution of the State [because] a supervisor of registration is expressly disqualified from being a candidate for any office being voted for during the time of his officiating as supervisor of registration."[571]

Congressman Jenks also added "to many other things that I have not time to recapitulate, that this Board offered by some of its members to sell the result in that state to two different men, one for a consideration of $200,000, to another asking a million."

Sarcastically, Jenks added that "the price was changed in conformity to the probabilities of the purchase."[572]

* * *

By the time Congressman Jenks resumed his seat, the spectators in the Supreme Court Chamber were incredulous at the depth and breadth of corruption that had infested the Louisiana vote. Now it was the Republicans' turn to pillory the Tilden Certificate, No. 2, signed by John McEnery. Congressman Hurlbut rose to perform this task.[573]

Figure 95: Representative Stephen A. Hurlbut of Illinois (PD)

The Congressman attacked the McEnery certificate "in two ways: first, by showing that the certificate itself is not good; second, by showing that McEnery himself is not governor."[574] "William P. Kellogg," Hurlbut said, "was at the time that the certificate was given the only legal and recognized governor in the State of Louisiana."[575] This was established, he continued, not only because he was so elected and installed pursuant to law, but also by the outcome of McEnery's attempt in 1874 to carry out an armed yet unsuccessful *coup d'état* against the state government that President Grant squelched by force.[576]

"Now, if it be true that William P. Kellogg was governor of the State of Louisiana on the 6th day of December 1876," Congressman Hurlbut said, "it is manifestly true that John McEnery was not; and whatever virtue or value in the way of evidence this Commission may attach to the certificate of a governor must be given to the governor who by election, recognition, and all other steps known to the law, was at the time the actual governor, and not to a mere pretender who retired from that contest of his own will in 1874 and has not in any way undertaken to assert or exercise any possible control over the office of governor of that state from that day to this."[577]

The McEnery certificate, said the Republican Congressman, contains no reference "to any source known to the laws from which he derives his information; there is no reference there to any returns appearing on file in his office, because he had no office; he had no returns; he had no secretary of state; he had no man in all Louisiana who would come forward and verify the seal of the state and the signature of the governor by signing 'by the governor, so and so, secretary of state."[578]

Congressman Hurlbut turned to the interpretation of the election statutes of Louisiana that the Tilden side had made, and agreed that "in Louisiana, the election processes instead of beginning from the bottom and coming up, begin from the top;" that is, all power to determine what the true vote is rests with the State Returning Board."[579] But he cast doubt on the Commission's ability, in the short time it had left until the Presidential inauguration, to pour through "several thousand pages of the results of the so-called investigation held by the committee of which I have the honor to be a member .... You cannot read intelligently the mass that is there within the time that lies between now and the 4th of March."[580]

* * *

At that juncture, with the minds of the spectators in the Chamber swirling in bewilderment, Senator Howe rose to offer his objection to the McEnery certificate.[581]

Senator Howe, if nothing else, was blunt.

"We respectfully object that you shall not count the votes for President and Vice-President of the United States tendered here by John McEnery and Robert C. Wickliffe and by their associates, any of them, for this reason, to begin with: You have no evidence before you, none whatever, that either of those was ever appointed as directed by the

Figure 96: Senator Timothy O. Howe of Wisconsin (PD)

Legislature of Louisiana to vote for President and Vice-President of the United States. You ought to have some evidence before you receive those votes, ought you not?"[582]

He declaimed, "We may be ignorant of a great many things in this world, and we are, God knows; but there is one thing of which we are not permitted to be ignorant. We are bound to know who is the governor of a state in this Union; and being bound to know that no state can have more than one governor, when we come to know who that man is, then we know that all the rest of God's beings are not!"[583]

Senator Howe excoriated the reputation of John McEnery, who had sent emissaries to Congress in the past with various schemes to take control of Louisiana. "Do you know, have you heard, of any indication of fraud anywhere or in anybody so bald and palpable as this of John McEnery's attempting to pass himself off, not only upon this high Commission, but upon the nation itself, as governor of Louisiana?

"You would not say that was the effort of a smart knave, would you?"[584]

The Senator, by contrast, lauded the reputation of Governor Kellogg. "I said you have determined that another man was governor of Louisiana, William Pitt Kellogg. For good or for ill, for four years past, William Pitt Kellogg has presided over that state as its governor, recognized as such both by the legislative and judicial departments of that state, recognized expressly as such by the Senate of the United States, ... recognized expressly as such by the House of Representatives .... The President more than once has recognized him.

"Kellogg, I think, will pass here, as elsewhere through creation, as the governor of Louisiana in November last," Howe concluded, "and he tells you who were the constituted electors of that state, in accordance with the directions of the Legislature, to vote for that state in the choice of a President and Vice-President. Do you want more evidence? Will you contradict that?"[585]

Senator Howe finished up by reciting incidents of voter intimidation committed by McEnery and his Democratic cohorts against black voters. Between 1870 and now, Howe claimed, parishes that were predominantly black had flipped from majority Republican to majority Democratic by such intimidation. Armed white men in Ouachita parish had formed "clubs" that intimidated both blacks and whites against joining the Republican Party or voting for Republicans. Republican meetings could be held only with the protection of U.S. Army troops. Others were shot and whipped by armed, disguised white men on horseback.[586]

Senator Howe concluded with this plea to the commissioners: "There is more than one foul stream to be found in the State of Louisiana. That to which you have been pointed may be dirty. Coming right from that State, I know of other and larger streams which are not merely dirty, but are very bloody. ... I want your streams all clean and purified as soon as it can be done. Take the fouler element out, first."[587]

* * *

The same lawyers as before – Messrs. Campbell, Trumbull, Carpenter, Merrick, Hoadly, and Green for the Tilden side; and Messrs. Evarts, Stoughton, Matthews, and Shellabarger for the Hayes side – spent the rest of Tuesday and an exhausting extent of

Wednesday through Thursday, February 14 and 15, fleshing out the legal details underlying the Congressmen's objections.[588]

The lawyers for the Democrats planned to excoriate the all-Republican Returning Board for throwing out thousands of votes. Mr. Campbell recited to the commissioners the Louisiana Returning Board's unjustified repression of 10,000 ballots, both Democratic and Republican, without a single protest of intimidation or harassment being lodged by any citizen that would have given it the statutory authority to do so.[589]

"I appear here for 10,000 legal voters of Louisiana," he argued, "who, without accusation or proof, indictment or trial, notice or hearing, have been disfranchised by four villains, incorporated with perpetual session, whose official title is 'the returning board of Louisiana.'"[590]

Carpenter traced the tortured legislative history of the Louisiana election law, consisting of three inconsistent statutes from 1868, 1870, and 1872, that governed the authority of the Returning Board to canvass votes for electors, fill vacant elector seats, and deal with vote discrepancies.[591]

The confused commissioners asked so many questions that Carpenter exhausted himself trying to answer them all. At last, feeling ill from the smoke of over a dozen candles lighting the darkened room, he requested a suspension of his presentation to the following morning.

* * *

Amelia and I returned to the Supreme Court Chamber on Wednesday morning, February 14. Carpenter finished up his presentation in the early morning, and Mr. Trumbull followed to give the Commission the Tilden side's offers of proof.[592]

Trumbull claimed that the Returning Board did not receive any complaint "of any riot, tumult, acts of violence, intimidation, armed disturbance, bribery, or corrupt influences which prevented or tended to prevent a fair, free, and peaceable vote of all qualified electors entitled to vote at such poll or voting-place," which was required by Louisiana election law for the Board to invalidate popular votes as they did.[593]

He alleged that in many instances, parish supervisors of elections did not report the votes at certain polling places in order to give Kellogg a lead in the vote for elector.[594] The Returning Board reported votes at some polling places for which there was no record that they had ever been cast.[595]

Trumbull urged the commissioners to find that Kellogg and his cohorts had engaged in a conspiracy to certify the election for Hayes despite knowing that he did not win.[596]

* * *

After that, Mr. Stoughton rose to present the Hayes side.[597] They planned to hammer the commissioners with the violence and intimidation that they claimed Black voters had undergone for a long time in Louisiana.

Stoughton gave his own interpretation of the Louisiana election statutes to show that they authorized the Returning Board to canvass the popular vote and eliminate votes in instances of intimidation, as this Board did.[598] He then offered the

Commission his take on why the elimination of votes in some precincts was justified.

"[I] t is said that 10,000 votes were thrown out by the Returning Board, and my learned brother yesterday said he appeared for those men here," Stoughton said. "In forty parishes there was a 6,097 Republican majority. In the remaining seventeen parishes there were 20,323 colored voters registered and 16,253 registered white voters. What do you suppose the problem to be solved was? How to get a majority to overcome the 6,000 Republican majority in the forty parishes. That was the problem!" In other words, Stoughton averred, Democrats in those forty parishes somehow managed to suppress 6,000 Black Republican votes.[599]

"And without even a hint of evidence!" sneered Carpenter at the Tilden end, whispering to Merrick.

* * *

Mr. Shellabarger followed Mr. Stoughton for the Hayes side.[600]

Sam Shellabarger was well-known for his wry wit. He quipped to the commissioners, "One of your body said to me a day or two ago that you had proven to be unanimous on one subject, and that was that this was a great Commission and that the members thereof were all great men."[601]

President Clifford reposted, "There has been no vote on that question."[602] All chuckled at the distinct possibility that he might see fit to call for one!

Shellabarger dwelled on the question of whether certain Hayes electors were ineligible to hold that post because they possessed state offices. Since holding state office was not listed in the

Constitution as cause for ineligibility in an elector, he pointed out, Congress could not make it one.[603] "The two Houses combined have not the power of a *quo warranto* court," he said.[604]

Shellabarger pointed to the injustice that had been visited upon the Negro population of Louisiana by elements intent upon denying them their right to vote. "Why, gentlemen, by actual count made in an official report to the Government of the United States, through the aid of General Sheridan, it is set down as a part of your history that in this blighted and blasted State of Louisiana four thousand and odd citizens have been murdered by plan, murdered by system, by organization, murdered for the purpose of putting down the right of the black man to vote, and that thing has been going on and on and on through these dark and terrible years!"[605]

"I conclude this discussion," Shellabarger dramatically ended, "by saying, gentlemen of America – that is a higher designation than gentlemen of the Commission, gentlemen of America – remember that there is on trial here tonight the question whether those laws made in Louisiana in pursuance of article 103 of her constitution ... enjoining ... the Legislature to make laws for the protection of the right of the freedman to vote can be sustained and enforced. If you fail to execute these laws you will have stabbed your country in that place where ... the life of the country is to be found and is to reside, to wit, in the freedom, the purity of the ballot-box."[606]

Upon Shellabarger's resumption of his seat, Mr. Evarts rose to request an adjournment for the evening before giving his presentation the following morning. The Commission agreed.

* * *

At ten o'clock on Thursday morning, February 15, 1877, the Commission reconvened for Mr. Evarts to make a lengthy final argument for the Hayes side of the Louisiana case.[607] Amelia and I were again in attendance.

Evarts asked who, under the laws of Louisiana, was empowered to count the popular vote – the Governor or the Returning Board. His answer traced that law through a history of confusing enactments and repeals. Evarts concluded that, according to the 1868 law then in force, the Returning Board had that power.[608]

He defended the eligibility of the Hayes electors to fill their positions. He contended that the Constitution does not prohibit state officers from being electors. He defended Governor Kellogg's right to be an elector, pointing to the example of Governor Ingersoll, of Connecticut, who did the same thing.[609]

Evarts defended the actions of the Louisiana Returning Board as consistent with upholding civil rights of the Black citizens of the state. "Now, for these poor people of Louisiana, if the federal power now takes to thwart, to uproot this scheme of energetic law to preserve society there from destruction, and leaves these unbefriended, uneducated, simple black people to the fate from which the state strove hard to save them, I say that you will have made them, by that action, the *victims* of your Constitution, for your Constitution gave them the suffrage, and they are to be slaughtered for having the gift found in their hands."[610]

After Evarts finished, the Commission took a half-hour recess before hearing the rebuttal of the Tilden side.

* * *

The Commission reconvened at one o'clock to hear the rebuttal of Mr. Campbell on behalf of Tilden.[611]

First, Campbell implored the Commission that in its capacity as representative of the Joint Session of Congress, it *did* have the power to do more than just count votes, as did Congress as well. He reminded the Commission of the Congressional resolution, passed during the Civil War, in which the Confederate governments were told in no uncertain terms that they could not send electoral votes to Washington to be counted in the 1864 Presidential election. "And this Government," Campbell said mockingly, "these two Houses speaking in that voice of authority for the whole people of the United States, which was vested in them for that purpose, is now the poor, feeble, paltry imbecile thing that cannot deal with a certificate of a fraudulent returning board?!"[612]

Campbell mocked the Republicans' "states' rights" stance. "But I am told that the action of the Legislature of the state is conclusive; no examination can be made into their authority, no inquiry into the force of their acts; they have the supreme authority to direct on this subject; it is their reserved right, you cannot touch it; you cannot impair it; it belonged to them before you existed; while those states were living you were unborn, and all that you have has been given from them to you; this they never gave and here is a gross usurpation if you venture to inquire into the act of that Legislature."[613]

"Is that true?" he asked rhetorically. "Is that power given to it for the benefit of the state or any gratification of the state, or as a bauble for the state to play with? This joint convention has the power to look into every act of that Legislature; and if that Legislature offends the spirit of the Union, if it contravenes the fundamental principles that lie at the foundation of American liberty, it can reject the votes."[614]

Campbell reminded the Commission what the Congress did with Louisiana's electoral vote in the Presidential election of 1872. "[A]nother exercise of power by the two Houses of Congress, in my judgment a perfectly justifiable and proper exercise of power, was made in the case of Louisiana in 1873, as her vote was rejected in 1865 by the two Houses. The case there was a quarrel in Louisiana between two returning boards. The one returning board, under which the election was made, some ten days after the election was made was annulled by the act of the governor of the state."[615] He did so by having the next legislature pass the 1872 Louisiana election law that repealed the prior law under which the previous returning board had certified the election, and appointed a returning board of his own to choose the electors.[616]

"Regular certificates and regular votes were sent to the Senate," Campbell noted. "But it appeared in proof that [Governor] Warmoth's clerks had done all the canvassing that was done and furnished all the estimates that were made; that the returning board then, if it were a good returning board, had nothing to do with the canvassing and compilation of votes according to the statute."[617] The U.S. Senate refused to receive that certificate in the Joint Session of Congress for that election, even though the electors had been chosen and had voted in a regular manner.[618]

"That case is parallel with the case we make before the Commission," Campbell maintained. "The case we make before you is that the returning board appointed by that act, and required by their oath of office, which defined their powers with perfect precision, to canvass and compile the original returns, never made such a canvass; we say that that compilation never took place; that those original returns were thrown aside and another paper, called by some of the witnesses a 'contabulated statement,' substituted."[619]

Campbell pointed to the precautions that were put in place to ensure that the Louisiana vote would be fair—the appointment of supervisors and aides, constables and deputies, and the U.S. Army were called out to act as "bystanders" at every polling place. "Now is this Commission astonished," he asked, "under that sort of array, that there was not from a single poll, unless, perhaps, one, a protest or report by any commissioner of election that there was riot, tumult, intimidation, confusion, or anything else that the statute speaks of at his box? Nor was there, so far as I have been informed, a single report from any supervisor of registration that there was tumult, riot, or interference, or obstruction in the performance of his duty as registrar." Indeed, Campbell pointed out, Louisiana's voter turnout turned out to be higher than two-thirds of the other states.[620]

Campbell engaged the commissioners for a few more minutes in a discussion of cases and answering hypothetical questions. At last, at 4:30 p.m., the doors were closed for private consultations among the commissioners themselves. The commissioners decided behind closed doors to vote on the Louisiana case by 4 o'clock the following day. At 5:22 p.m, the exhausted commissioners adjourned until ten o'clock on the following morning.[621]

Chapter Thirty-nine – A Look Inside

AFTER THE COMMISSION ADJOURNMENT, A TIRED and depressed U.S. Supreme Court Associate Justice Stephen Johnson Field rode a hansom cab to Ebbitt House for dinner with an old friend who was visiting Washington from San Francisco – Leland Stanford.

Figure 97: Leland Stanford, 1881, Portrait by Jean-Louis-Ernest Meissonier

Figure 98: U.S. Supreme Court Justice Stephen Johnson Field, circa 1895 (PD)

Stanford's many accomplishments are well known to all – President of the Central Pacific Railroad, President of the Southern Pacific Railroad, director of Wells Fargo & Company, one-term governor of California (terms then were two years long), President of Pacific Mutual Life Insurance Company, hammerer of the "Last Spike" of the First Transcontinental Railroad at Promontory, Utah on May 10, 1869, vintner, horse-breeder.[622]

The maître-d' led Field to a curtained table in the back of the restaurant, out of earshot of nosy reporters. He pulled the curtain back. Stanford, already sitting, stood to greet the Justice.

"Stephen," Stanford said, extending both hands to grasp Field's. "It's so good to see you. It's been a long time. You've been so busy!"

"I have been, Leland, and it has been extraordinarily frustrating," Field replied wearily. "I so wish that I were back in San Francisco, listening to mining claim cases!"

Stanford laughed. "Oh, come now, Stephen," he said, "this is important work! The whole country is absolutely riveted on everything you commissioners are doing and thinking! Hayes and Tilden are on tenterhooks!"

Field never had any compunction about discussing his cases with friends like Leland Stanford. Not even Stanford's notorious ties to Republican luminaries like James G. Blaine fazed Field. Nothing on his mind was ever off the dinner table or the bar.

"Leland, we've now heard two cases, and tomorrow we are going to decide on the second one. It is such a farce. We are not fifteen wise men debating difficult issues. We are fifteen old politicians listening quietly and intently to Congressmen and lawyers droning on about hair-splitting topics, and then we close the doors and vote strictly along party lines. We split by party even when we decide whether to adjourn!"

"Well, I cannot say that I am surprised about that, Stephen," Stanford answered as drinks were served. "There are no principles of law here. It's strictly a matter of politics. And politics is strictly a matter of numbers.

"You can argue policy all you want, Stephen," Leland said after sipping his martini. "It's simple arithmetic. Eight is more than seven."

"That's true, Leland, but it is such an utter embarrassment," Field replied. "The fraud at the polls in the Southern states is astounding. There is not one honest man down there, from the bottom to the top.

"And as for the numbers," Field lamented, "there are no numbers, Leland. There are only lies. The carpetbaggers in Louisiana have tossed ten thousand votes out from some eighty thousand registered voters. Not one word of protest was raised to justify throwing out those votes. Ballots were inserted into ballot boxes, but no one knows where they came from. Supervisors and returning boards simply made votes up, certified them to the Governor, he made out his own dishonest certification and sent it on to Congress.

"Congress opened the electoral envelopes," Field said, "and three separate certificates fell out, all by different people claiming to be the 'governor.' Congress had no idea what to do, so they just sent the whole mess to us.

"We are under the gun to decide everything quickly so a President can be inaugurated in less than a month," Field went on. "We sit for days and hours, listening to Congressmen and lawyers spin these complicated webs of legal gobbledygook that nobody can understand or even follow. Occasionally a commissioner wakes up from his slumber and asks a hypothetical question that has nothing whatsoever to do with what the lawyer just said. Then we close the doors, say the usual things, and vote as our party would expect us to vote as if we were marionettes.

"The lawyers offer us evidence," Field said, "and we refuse to take it. Have you ever heard of any court or other tribunal in the world that refuses to take evidence? And the evidence the lawyers offer is damning. Damning!

"The Republican commissioners just sit there and recite that our Commission has no power at all to go behind the falsified certificates of these crooked carpetbag governors to expose the truth. Any Congressional committee ever created has had the power to investigate facts. For some reason, we don't."

"That is terrible, Stephen, terrible," Stanford said, as the waiter and busboy served the steak dinners. "The numbers at the polls don't mean anything, though. It's the numbers in Congress that count. And right now, you commissioners are effectively the Congress, and, like I said before, eight is more than seven."

"As to that, Leland," Field sighed, "I feel especially guilty. Before Congress chose Bradley for the fifth Justice on the Commission, I told Congressman Hewitt that he could count on Bradley to be fair. Hewitt relied on my advice. How stupid I was to give it! Bradley is a died-in-the-wool Republican shill. A few Republican big-shots visited him the night before we voted on Florida and he is toeing the line accordingly."

"You know, Stephen," said Stanford, "there's only one reason for this tragedy. No one in Congress wants to take responsibility for having to choose the President and Vice-President. Every one of them has voters back home whom they have to answer to. That's why an independent body of electors *usually* makes the choice. The electors appear out of nowhere, cast their electoral votes, and disappear.

"The masses remain happy with this state of affairs because they believe that these party hacks are duty-bound to do their bidding. No one in Congress has to take the blame for selecting a bad President this way, so they can rail against the winner during his term all they want.

"But the system is set up by gerrymandering the congressional districts, running 'winner-take-all' votes for electors, and skewing the votes the way the people in power at any given time think will preserve them in office. And it never works forever, Stephen. It always ends up working the same way as rolling the dice in a game of craps.

"That's why they set this Commission up," Stanford said. "The usual, well-oiled machine isn't working this time, and the Constitutional fallback position is unpalatable to the majority party because under that they are guaranteed to lose. So, this puppet show was set up to do what the machine can't do this time and it makes the country think that they are being treated fairly. Of course, they are not."

"You know, Leland, I have infinite respect for the Constitution," Field said sadly. "But I now understand how much of a confusing compromise it was for the Founding Fathers to negotiate back in 1787. The states just didn't trust each other back then. The small states didn't trust the big states, but they thought they were equal sovereign entities to the big states just the same. So the big states had to appease the small states in order to get their agreement to the Constitution. That's why the manner of choosing a President is such a convoluted mess, with an Electoral College and a special mechanism for tie votes and state-delegation voting for President in the House. It was the first of so many twisted compromises that have followed since then."

The waiter brought cigars and each man lit one up. Stanford inhaled a puff. "Out West, as we both know from personal experience, all men are essentially the same," Leland said. "The Chinese are not the same, of course, and they are not treated so. But all others are the same.

"In the South, however, you have two separate peoples occupying the same land and engaging in the same economic endeavor," he said. "They are distinguished from one another only by skin pigmentation. There is no other discernible difference. One deems itself to be superior to the other and perceives no possibility that a person in the lower caste can transfer to the upper caste.

"Suddenly, outsiders come down from the North and nominally set the lower caste free," Stanford continued. "Now both castes are technically equal. Now they may all run the government. In a few instances, the outsiders make people of the lower caste the political masters of the upper caste. That is a recipe for revolution.

Figure 99: "The Freedmen's Bureau," Harper's Weekly, *July 25, 1868 (PD)*

Tapping out a long ash, Stanford continued, "That's what we have now. There is a race war in the South now. The Northerners started it and they won't stop it. And the white business upper caste is winning it because it has former Confederate soldiers and generals and guns and cannon. The lower caste of former slaves has nothing;

the Northerners haven't give them anything with which to defend themselves."

"No matter how this election turns out," Field told Stanford, "the whites in the South will seize all power back and never again let go of it."

Chapter Forty – Again Behind the Closed Doors

ON FRIDAY, FEBRUARY 16, 1877, AT TEN O'CLOCK A.M., the Electoral Commission met again behind the closed doors of the Supreme Court Chamber to decide what to do about Louisiana.[623]

Unlike the Florida case, not every commissioner had something to say about Louisiana. Indeed, many seemed to want to avoid the subject altogether. Only seven of them spoke – three Democrats and four Republicans.

Of all the calamities that befell the Louisiana election, the one topic that most animated some of the Democratic commissioners was the composition and legitimacy of the Returning Board. The Democrats were upset about the Board's vacant Democratic seat that the remaining four Republican members, who were empowered to fill such vacancies, had neglected to fill over the two years prior to the election.

One Commissioner who was particularly aggravated by this fact was Josiah G. Abbott, the Democratic Congressman from Massachusetts. He brought a law

Figure 100: Representative Josiah G. Abbott of Massachusetts (PD)

book to the Commission meeting that contained an 1868 decision by Justice Miller in his capacity as Circuit Judge of the U.S. Circuit Court for the Eastern District of Arkansas. He showed the case, *Schenck v. Peay*,[624] to Democratic Commissioners Bayard and Hunton.

In this case, plaintiff Schenck sued defendants Bliss and Peay over certain real estate in Little Rock, Arkansas. Peay was the original owner of the property. By an act passed by Congress in 1862, assessment boards consisting of three tax commissioners were appointed for each of the states in rebellion against the federal government. The boards accompanied the Union Army into those states for the purpose of collecting property taxes.

Three tax commissioners were appointed to the Arkansas board, but one of the appointees did not qualify and did not act in an official capacity. The other two commissioners proceeded to assess the tax upon lots in Arkansas, and once the time for each lot's tax payment expired, the board offered the delinquent lot for sale at auction.

Bliss purchased Peay's tax-delinquent property at the auction and conveyed an undivided fourth the property to Schenck. Schenck's lawsuit sought from Bliss a partition of the undivided property and a decree to quiet title against Peay.

Justice Miller, in his capacity as Circuit Judge, stated in his decision that the outcome of the lawsuit depended on "the validity of the title conferred by the tax sale," and the only remedy that could be offered by the Court was to have that title nullified, in which case Peay would get the property back.[625]

Schenck, somewhat against his own interest, claimed that "the tax proceedings were accompanied by such positive acts of fraud on the part of Bliss and one of the tax commissioners, that, for these reasons alone, the sale should be held to be void."[626] Miller picked up on this misjudgment, finding that Schenck "disclosed a fatal defect in his own title."[627] The tax board, he held, was not legally constituted because one required member of the board was missing. Said Miller:

> We understand it to be well settled that where authority of this kind is conferred on three or more persons, in order to make its exercise valid, all must be present and participate, or have an opportunity to participate, in the proceedings, although some may dissent from the action determined on. The action of two out of three

commissioners, to all of whom was confided a power to be exercised, cannot be upheld when the third took no part in the transaction, and was ignorant of what was done, gave no implied consent to the action of the others, and was neither consulted by them, nor had any opportunity to exert his legitimate influence in the determination of the course to be pursued.... The law required three commissioners. *A less number was not a board, and could do nothing.* The third commissioner for Arkansas, although nominated and confirmed, did not qualify or enter upon the duties of his office.... *There was therefore no board of commissioners in existence authorized to assess the tax, to receive the money, or to sell the property. If Congress had intended to confide these important functions to two persons, it would not have required the appointment of the third.*[628]

This less-than-a-decade-old decision of Justice Miller, the seniormost Justice of all the other Justices on the Commission save President Clifford himself, torpedoed the position of the one-vote-short Louisiana Returning Board, Abbott and his two Democratic colleagues on the Commission surmised.

During the closed-door session, Congressman Abbott stated that *Schenck v. Peay* "settles the question that the Louisiana returning-board was not a legally constituted board; that it was, in fact, no board at all; and that its acts are not entitled to respect, and are of no force and effect."[629]

"Justice Miller," said Abbott, looking directly at the former across the conference table, "rightfully, I think, and in accordance with principle and the authorities, held that, where the law provides that three shall constitute a board, a lesser number cannot make a legal board at all, and that the law having required three commissioners, there was no board until the three were appointed and qualified. Such is the case with the Louisiana Returning-Board, and its choice of the Hayes electors is therefore null and void."[630]

Commissioner Hunton chimed in too. "This reasoning seems perfectly conclusive," he said, referring to *Schenck*, "and I take it for granted will satisfy the mind of at least one of this Commission [pointing to Miller] that this board of four had no right to canvass the Louisiana returns, and that their determination amounts to nothing – absolutely nothing!"[631]

Commissioner Bayard, referring to the Louisiana statute that required the Board to have five members who represent "all parties," added, "a quorum of the Louisiana Returning-Board is three members, and clearly such a quorum must by law contain 'all parties' in its composition. Without that, its action would be invalid. A Board consisting of four Republicans and no Democrat is defective in an element essential to its lawful existence, as demanded by common decency as well as the law."[632]

This rationale fell on deaf Republican ears. Miller spoke up. "My dear gentlemen," he replied condescendingly, "you are wholly mistaken about the basis for my decision in that case. That judgment, as I said plainly, was that, where three persons are made a board or commission, and two undertake to act without notice to the third, or without the third knowing of or having any opportunity to participate in their doings, the action of the two cannot be sustained. It had nothing to do with the *statutory composition* of the board. It had to do with whether a quorum was present."

"That cannot possibly pass a plain reading of the decision, Mr. Justice Miller," Congressman Abbott testily replied. Your words are crystal clear: 'The law required three commissioners. A less number was not a board, and could do nothing.' Even if what you now say was the main thought in your mind back then, you surely must recognize that lawyers like myself will interpret these words plainly to mean what they say."

"Those words are mere *dicta*," Miller sniffed. "I'm afraid that I cannot enlighten you further on the subject, Congressman."

When it came time to vote, Congressman Hoar offered the lead-off motion for the Republicans. It was to resolve that "the evidence offered" by the Tilden side "should be not received."[633]

Congressman Abbott offered a substitute motion, which takes precedence over the original motion in voting, that "evidence will be received to show that so much of the act of Louisiana establishing a returning board for that state is unconstitutional, and the acts of said returning board are void."[634]

Abbott's substitute motion, voted on first, went down to defeat by a vote of eight to seven.[635]

Abbott then offered another substitute, which also took precedence in voting, that "evidence will be received to show that the returning board of Louisiana, at the time of canvassing and compiling the vote of that state at the last election in that state, was not legally constituted under the law establishing it, in this: that it was composed of four persons all of one political party, instead of five persons of different political parties, as required by the law establishing said board."[636]

That substitute motion was voted upon and went down to defeat too, by another vote of eight to seven.[637]

Abbott tried yet again. He offered as a substitute that "the Commission will receive testimony on the subject of the frauds alleged in the specifications of the counsel for the objectors to certificates Nos. 1 and 3."[638] He was gradually narrowing down the scopes of the substitutes in the hope that one of the Republicans would eventually break off and accept narrower language.

The Republicans stood firm – the substitute went down to defeat by eight to seven.[639]

Changing up the subject a bit, Abbott next offered as a substitute that "testimony tending to show that the so-called returning hoard of Louisiana had no jurisdiction to canvass the votes for electors of President and Vice-President is admissible."[640]

Defeated again, by eight to seven.[641]

Abbott finally pulled his last trick out of his hat, a statement of fraud drawn as closely as possible to the agreed facts that the Republicans would find hard to ignore. He offered as a substitute motion that "evidence is admissible that the statements and affidavits purporting to have been made and forwarded to said returning board in pursuance of the provisions of section 26 of the election law of 1872, alleging riot, tumult, intimidation, and violence at or near certain polls and in certain parishes were falsely fabricated and forged by certain disreputable persons under the direction and with the knowledge of said returning board, and that said returning board knowing said statements and affidavits to be false and forged and that none of the said statements or affidavits were made in the manner or form or within the time required by law, did knowingly, willfully, and fraudulently fail and refuse to canvass or compile more than ten thousand votes lawfully cast, as is shown by the statements of votes of the commissioners of election."[642]

The Republicans did not budge; they defeated the substitute by eight to seven.[643]

Commissioner Hunton then picked up the cudgel laid down by Abbott and offered a substitute that did not breathe the dirty word "fraud." Hunton moved that "evidence be received to prove that the votes cast and given at said election on the 7th of November last for the election of electors as shown by the returns made by the commissioners of election from the several polls or voting-places in said state have never been compiled or canvassed, and that the said returning board never even pretended to compile or canvass the returns made by said commissioners of election, but that the said returning board only pretended to canvass the returns made by said supervisors."[644]

Once again,, defeated by eight to seven.[645]

Next, Commissioner Bayard tried to strike at the two ineligible electors who held federal offices. He offered as a substitute that "no person holding an office of trust or profit under the United States is eligible to be appointed an elector, and that this Commission will receive evidence tending to prove such ineligibility as offered by counsel for objectors to certificates 1 and 3."[646]

Defeated, by eight to seven.[647]

Although Stephen Field was too dejected by the entire course of events to even speak at this meeting, he decided to offer a substitute that would possibly open the minds of the Republicans to an acknowledgment that the evidence presented by the Democrats would be admissible in any other legal forum. He offered as a substitute that "in the opinion of the Commission evidence is admissible upon the several matters which counsel for the objectors to certificates Nos. 1and 3 offered to prove."[648]

Even that went down to defeat, by a vote of eight to seven.[649]

Commissioner Payne, at last, offered the most obvious change: to strike the word "not" from the original motion.[650] That defeat, too, was by a partisan vote of eight to seven.[651]

Finally, Commissioner Hoar's original motion "that the evidence offered be not received" was called for a vote. It passed, as expected, by a vote of eight to seven.[652]

The doors of the chamber were thrown open to the public, and the order against receiving evidence was announced. The Commission began to wrap up the hearing, but Commissioner Strong said, "Allow me to suggest that, before that question is formally passed on, there is the question of the admissibility of the evidence that was offered. We have not passed on the merits of the case, formally at least. I think we ought first to go into deliberation for that purpose."[653]

The suggestion was accepted, and once again the Commission went into confidential session to determine what to do with the Louisiana electoral votes now that none of the evidence of the Tilden side was to be accepted.

The motion dance began once again. Commissioner Morton offered for the Republicans that "the persons named as electors in certificate No. 1 were the lawful electors of the State of Louisiana, and that their votes are the votes provided by the Constitution of the United States, and should be counted for President and Vice-President."[654]

Commissioner Thurman offered a countervailing substitute for the Democrats to throw out the Louisiana electoral vote entirely: that "inasmuch as the votes of the people of Louisiana for electors of President and Vice- President in November last have never been legally canvassed and declared, therefore the votes purporting to be votes of electors of that state for President and Vice-President ought not to be counted, and no electors of President and Vice-President can be regarded as chosen in that state."[655]

Thurman's substitute caused a stir among the Republicans at the Commission conference table. "We have already decided not to receive the Tilden side's evidence," Senator Oliver Hazard Perry Morton of Indiana replied to the motion. "There is nothing to counter the legitimate certificates of Governor Kellogg, which we are not authorized to go behind. Why would we deprive the citizens of Louisiana of their rightful electoral votes?"

Figure 101: Senator Oliver Hazard Perry Morton of Indiana (PD)

"Because they are *not* Louisiana's rightful electoral votes!" Senator Allen G. Thurman, Democrat of Ohio, roared back. The commissioners were stunned at Thurman's display of pique. "That is precisely the problem! The government of the State of Louisiana has so tainted and poisoned the electoral process that its citizens deserve, both black and white, and has done so for a second time, mind you, that throwing eight electoral votes to Hayes by a strict party line vote in this body is nothing short of complicity in a fraud!

Figure 102: Senator Allen G. Thurman of Ohio (PD)

"How can this body ignore all of the evidence that our Congressional committees and investigators have unearthed and consider itself to have done its duty? The Joint Session of Congress is looking to us to apprise them of what the legitimate vote is. How can you call this farce in Louisiana to have been an 'election?' How does this farce do justice to the thousands of men who cast their votes in good faith, expecting all votes to be counted and the winner to be duly announced? How is this not tyranny of the worst sort?"

"My esteemed friend," Senator Morton shot back. "We have spent weeks on two States that have behaved in much the same way. Who is to say that this behavior is unheard of in your State of Ohio, or my State of Indiana? Who is to say that this behavior does not go on in any of the other states of the Union? The State Legislatures appoint the electors, by popular vote or by whatever process they think best. The Constitution does not require them to be chosen by a popular vote at all.

"The legitimate Governor of the State of Louisiana has certified his state's electors and sent their votes to the Senate. Every other Governor has done the same. We must give full faith and credit to the governments of every one of those states, without exception ...."

Justice Field angrily interrupted Senator Morton. "No court in any common-law country would simply disregard evidence proffered to it in this way without weighing its materiality, relevance and probative value! We have been given this evidence by Congress to consider. Why did it give us this evidence in the first place? Because Congress wants us to advise them on its materiality, relevance and probative value. We have considered the cases of two states now, and not once have I heard this Commission breathe a word about whether that standard is met by this evidence!"

"Gentlemen, please!" President Clifford spoke up. "You must maintain the decorum of this body. We must vote, and we must respect the vote of each and every one of us. Let us call the question on Senator Thurman's substitute."

It was defeated by a vote of eight to seven.[656]

Congressman Hunton of Virginia tried one more time for the Democrats. He offered as a substitute simply "[t]hat the votes purporting to be the electoral votes of the State of Louisiana be not counted." This language avoided any suggestion of a reason for the Commission's decision.[657]

It went down to defeat by a vote of eight to seven.[658]

President Clifford then called for a vote on Senator Morton's original motion. It was approved by a vote of eight to seven.The case of Louisiana's eight electoral votes was resolved in favor of Governor Hayes.[659]

At almost nine o'clock at night, after having arranged for the preparation of a report to the President of the Senate, the Commission adjourned and did not conduct another full day of business for five days. Several commissioners left town. That was a wise move.

PART NINE – DENOUEMENT

Chapter Forty-one – The Dealmakers Enter The Ring

BY THE FOLLOWING TUESDAY, FEBRUARY 20, 1877 – George Washington's Birthday – Washington, D.C. was in an uproar. In the House of Representatives, irate Congressmen among the Democratic majority yelled "Fraud!" and "Conspiracy!" on the floor as Speaker Randall banged his immense gavel to demand decorum.

The House rejected the Commission's decision on Louisiana, as it did with the decision on Florida. The Senate accepted the Commission's decision on Louisiana, just as it did with the decision on Florida. With both houses of Congress in disagreement, the Commission's decisions on both Florida and Louisiana stood, as required by the Electoral Commission Act.[660]

Democratic Congressman Samuel Cox of New York rose to read Psalm 94, Verse 20 of the Bible on the floor of the House: "Shall the throne of iniquity have fellowship with thee, which frameth mischief by a law?" Republican Congressman William Kelley of Pennsylvania immediately objected. "So!" said Cox. "The Bible itself must be objectionable to the Republicans!"[661]

In the Senate, all was not serene either, even with a Republican majority. Democratic Senator Samuel Maxey of Texas took to the floor to say that the decision "in effect exalts fraud, degrades justice, and consigns truth to the dungeon!" Republican Senator John Sherman of Ohio angrily replied, "A good deal is said about fraud, fraud, fraud – fraud and perjury, and wrong. Why, sir, if you go behind the returns in Louisiana, the case is stronger for the Republicans than upon the face of the returns.

"What do you find there?" Sherman boomed. "Crime, murder, violence, that is what you find. While there may have been irregularities, while there may have been a non-observance of some directory laws, yet the substantial right was arrived at by the action of the Returning Board!"[662]

Rud Hayes was now only eight electoral votes away from the presidency. Sam Tilden remained one electoral vote short, but the momentum had clearly shifted toward Hayes. The Joint Session of Congress reconvened after the Louisiana decision to continue its electoral vote count. On Wednesday, February 21, 1877, Oregon was found to have submitted two competing certificates. They were submitted to the Commission for resolution. By this time, the Democrats no longer held illusions that the Commission would decide Oregon any other way but for Hayes. They were right.[663]

The Commission's decision on Oregon came on Friday, February 23, at the home of Commissioner Thurman. He had taken ill, and consented to the Commission convening at his home in order to decide the Oregon case. It went for Hayes by a vote of eight to seven, as expected.[664]

I rose in the House on that day to give a speech denouncing the Commission's actions.I also finagled a recess of the House until Monday, February 26, in order to run out the legislative clock on the Joint Session's electoral vote count. As a result, they had only six more working days to complete it.[665]

On the 26th, things began to happen on many fronts. In the Joint Session, the count reached South Carolina, which produced two competing returns that were submitted to the Commission.[666] The Commission declared Commissioner Thurman's seat vacant due to his continuing illness. The Senate voted as his replacement Senator Francis Kernan, a Republican from New York.[667]

That same morning, Edward A. Burke, the chairman of the Louisiana Democratic State Committee, met privately with President Grant. He asked the President if he would support Hayes' dropping his support for the Republican candidate for Governor of Louisiana, Stephen B. Packard, whom white Louisianans considered a carpetbagger. In

Figure 103: Edward A. Burke of Louisiana (New York Public Library)

return, Burke told the President, he could deliver his southern friends in Congress to the Hayes camp. Otherwise, he cautioned, the Southerners would filibuster in the House and prevent Hayes from being inaugurated.[668]

President Grant agreed with Burke's plan. He supported installing Packard's opponent in the gubernatorial race, Democrat Francis R.T. Nicholls, who unlike Packard would not require Federal troops to maintain his control of the governorship. "[T]he sentiment of the country is clearly opposed to the further use of troops in upholding a state government," Grant told Burke.[669]

Burke went immediately from the White House to Capitol Hill to meet with the Ohio Republican leadership. He met with Ohio Senator John Sherman; Hayes' old college friend and war comrade Stanley A. Matthews; and former Ohio Governor Edward

Figure 104: Stanley A. Matthews (PD)

Dennison.[670] They met in one of the many conference rooms that occupy nearly every spare space of the U.S. Capitol that isn't an office, a chamber, or a fireplace.

Figure 105: Senator John Sherman of Ohio (PD)

Figure 106: Governor William Dennison, Jr. of Ohio (PD)

"Ed," said Senator Sherman, "we are certain that the Democrats are going to launch filibusters in the House and Senate to block Governor Hayes from being inaugurated as President. The Southern Senators and Congressmen whom we've talked to would be instrumental to preventing such a national disaster from happening. What can you do to induce them to help us?"

"You all should go see President Grant," Burke replied. "Ask him to remove all remaining Federal troops from Louisiana. I will take care of the rest."

The Senator was shocked. "Are you mad, Ed? Grant would never agree to that. He would sooner send *more* troops into Louisiana than take them out."

"Oh, really?" Burke said, reaching into his inside vest pocket. "Well, maybe you gentlemen might be interested in this document signed by the President himself that I have. He has agreed to do just that."

Burke showed the document, signed by President Grant, to the trio. They read it carefully.

"All right, Ed," said the Senator. He looked to his two colleagues, who nodded their assent. "We will go to the President and ask him to remove the troops from Louisiana. But there is a promise that you must make to me."

"What is that, Senator?" Ed said.

"You Democrats, Sherman replied, "must under no circumstances whatsoever launch the kind of reign of terror that we have seen all over the South against Republicans, no matter whether they are black or white. You also must not challenge Governor Packard's election."

"I believe that I can promise those things," Burke replied without hesitation.[671]

* * *

In the evening of the busy day of Monday, February 26, ten men met at the Wormley Hotel on the corner of 15th and H Streets, Northwest, in the room occupied by William Evarts for the duration of the Commission hearings.[672]

Figure 107: Wormley's Hotel, 1500 H Street, NW, Washington, D.C. (PD)

Among the ten men present were Evarts and Ohio Republicans Matthews, Sherman, Garfield, Congressman Charles S. Foster, and former Ohio Governor Dennison. Also present were Southern

Democrats Edward A. Burke, Congressmen E. John Ellis and William M. Levy of Louisiana, and Congressman Henry Watterson of Kentucky. All four Southern Democrats had served as officers in the Confederate Army.[673]

The purpose of the meeting was to solidify the deal that the Ohio Republicans had made with the Southern Democrats to install Rud Hayes as President, remove all remaining Federal troops from the South, cast off the Reconstructionist Republican governments in the Southern states, and return those states to white rule.

Figure 108: James Wormley (PD)

Ironically, the owner of the Wormley Hotel, James Wormley, was born a free black man. He has been considered as one of the most prominent black businessmen in Washington.[674]

Congressman Garfield left the meeting early, convinced that a political deal should not be made with the former Confederate "southern gentlemen" who were allegedly "resisting anarchy" in the South.[675] The rest remained however, and solidified the details of removing the U.S. Army from Louisiana and South Carolina and precluding a Southern Democratic filibuster in the House.[676]

On Tuesday, February 27, the Commission heard the case of the South Carolina electors in a single day, and decided in favor of the Hayes electors by a vote of eight to seven.[677]

The House rejected but the Senate concurred in the Electoral Commission's decision, making Rutherford B. Hayes the nineteenth President of the United States.[678]

On Friday, March 2, 1877, three days before the President was to be inaugurated (March 4, the traditional Inauguration Day, fell on Sunday, causing the ceremony to be deferred to the following day), the Electoral Commission wrapped up its business and voted to adjourn *sine die*.[679]

.

Chapter Forty-two – A Talk With Mr. Tilden

ON FRIDAY, MARCH 2, AT 4:10 A.M., FOLLOWING an eighteen-hour marathon session, the Joint Session of Congress completed its count of electoral votes with the ten of Wisconsin. Senate President Ferry proclaimed Hayes to be the winner.[680]

I, however, did not witness any of it, even though I was on the floor of the House. I was lying down on my back on that floor, mentally, emotionally, and physically exhausted, having fallen into a coma.[681]

I later learned that members of Congress from both parties surrounded me and tried to revive me. After a time, the Capitol Police brought a stretcher into the House chamber and I was taken out, loaded onto an ambulance, and rushed to the U.S. Naval Hospital nearby. When I regained consciousness three days later, I learned that Rutherford B. Hayes was now President.[682]

* * *

At the start of Congress' Easter recess, Amelia and I returned to our home in Ringwood, near Tuxedo, New Jersey, for a much-needed rest. One afternoon, we invited now-former Governor Tilden out to Ringwood Manor for an outing in the gardens and dinner. He made the trip from Hoboken, a ferry ride across from Manhattan, the 28 miles on the Montclair & Greenwood Lake Railway to Ringwood Junction, a short trip to our home near the New York-New Jersey Line.

Figure 109: Ringwood Manor, Passaic County, New Jersey

"Governor!" I said warmly as he entered my door and he took off his hat and coat. "Happy Easter! Come on in!"

"And the same to you, my boy!" he said, giving me a hug.

We chatted pleasantly as we wandered out to the gardens. Sam always enjoyed the historical artifacts that we kept around the estate, including the old Indian burial ground and the magazine that had stored arms for the Continental Army during the Revolutionary War. Sam's favorite, by far, was the length of immense iron chain, having links three feet wide by nine inches long and weighing 280 pounds each, that had once formed a section of the chain that the Patriots had strung across the Hudson

River to stop British ships – unfortunately, an unsuccessful military endeavor.[683]

Amelia joined us in the gardens at the back of the house, which she had developed and considered her pride and joy. As we sat on chaise lounges on the terrace, a maid poured our drinks and placed them on small tables next to our easy chairs. "Would you like anything to eat?" I asked Sam.

"Oh, no, thank you," he replied. "I know that dinner here will be a filling affair!" I chuckled.

"How are you getting along in Washington?" Sam asked me.

"Oh, fairly well," I replied wearily. "Jimmy O'Brien is still on my tail and will dog me in Tammany Hall in the next Congressional election, you can be sure of that."

O'Brien, the former sheriff of New York County, helped bring down Boss Tweed and his Ring when he turned over to the *New York Times* the City's financial records detailing Tweed's frauds. O'Brien was beloved among New York's Irish community and had come close to beating me for the 10th District Democratic Congressional nomination in the elections of 1874 and 1876.

"How is Roscoe getting along with Hayes?" Sam asked. Senator Conkling, after having been one of the few Republicans to admit that Tilden had won the popular vote in 1876, continued thereafter to be a thorn in Hayes' side.

"Roscoe is very, very unhappy with the President's cabinet picks," I reported to Sam. "You know how jealous he is of controlling the patronage jobs in New York. Well, Rutherford has not consulted with him at all.

"Zach Chandler is also being ignored," I continued. "They both consider it very rash of Hayes to promise to serve only one term as President. They are also very upset with his choice of reform politicians for cabinet posts. He passed over Ben Bristow but made Carl Schurz Secretary of the Interior. I even heard Zach say that 'Hayes has passed the Republican party to its worst enemies!'"[684]

"And I hear that David Key has been named Postmaster General and Bill Evarts will be Secretary of State," said Sam as we sipped our scotches and soda.

"Anyone who appeared for Hayes before the Electoral Commission has a very bright future ahead of them," I replied. "Evarts is a brilliant lawyer, and I can tell you from having attended many Commission sessions that he was the most eloquent litigator there. As for Key, well, he is a protégé of Andrew Kellar, the lobbyist who pushed the Texas and Pacific Railroad scheme that Hayes just scotched. Making Key postmaster is clearly a consolation prize for Kellar."[685]

"Not to mention that Key was a Confederate," Sam interjected.

I had resolved to tread carefully with my friend on the subject of the South. But since he had opened the door, I felt obliged to make a few remarks.

"Well, Sam, you have to admit that Hayes pulled off a remarkable *coup* with the Southern Democrats," I told him. "He reached out to them and promised to pull the Federal troops out of Louisiana and South Carolina. They were waiting for you to say the same thing, but you never did."

"Abram –" Sam said, hesitatingly pulling cigars out of his pocket and offering me one. I took it and lit up.

Sam was surprised. "Oh! You smoke cigars now? I had heard a rumor to that effect."

"Wounds of war," I replied.

"Abram," he resumed what he was going to say, "I'll be honest with you, as I always am. I would never have promised the Southerners that I would pull the troops out. And certainly not this quickly. Not that I care that much for the Republican Reconstructionist carpetbag governments down there. They are as bad as the ex-rebels are. But there is utter chaos in the South now, and the Federal troops are the only force that stands in the way of a total race war."

"President Grant would have certainly agreed with you, Sam," I said, puffing vigorously on the cigar.

After somewhat of a silence, as the cigar smoke wafted across the gardens, I asked Sam, "How are you feeling now about the election?"

"Ah," Sam replied, then silently puffed on his cigar, thinking a bit. "When I woke up the morning after the election, I already knew that something had gone wrong. It was a win, but it wasn't the landslide that everybody was making of it. The popular vote for me was clearly there, but the mathematics of the Electoral College were extraordinarily close. I immediately realized that a protracted political battle would ensue."

He swigged some of his scotch. "When the Louisiana, Florida, and South Carolina votes were delayed right after the election, I got quite depressed. The voting populations of those states are half-black, half-white. Louisiana, in fact, is majority black. And the election machinery of that state is totally in the hands of the Republican carpetbaggers and the Union Army. With a solid phalanx of black voters voting Republican, with whites bitterly divided between the two parties, and with the carpetbaggers and their friends in the Army calling the shots at the polls, I felt strongly even then that I had lost Louisiana."

"Sam," I said quietly, "You and I have been through a lot together. We have had our disagreements. They are all in the past now. But I cannot get over the feeling that if you had fought harder to win the political fight that broke out in Washington afterward, you would have won the electoral vote.

"Do you know what we did in the House after the Electoral Commission decided its last case, Sam?" I said. "We passed a resolution on March third officially declaring that you had been duly elected President of the United States with a total of 196 electoral votes. We counted Florida's four electoral votes and Louisiana's eight electoral votes for you, and Oregon and South Carolina for Hayes.[686] All of us Democrats in the House are convinced that the Electoral Commission was a terrible idea and that the outcome was preordained, especially after Judge Davis dropped out."

"I am a lawyer like you, Abram," Sam replied. "After the election was over, I could think of nothing else to do than to write a brief. And that is what I did. I set to work writing *The Presidential Counts*. I submitted it to the Commission and to every Senator and Representative in Congress.

"We discovered some interesting things about the past Presidential elections, Abram," Sam said. "We found that even as the country moved gradually toward conducting popular votes for President, virtually all of the elections turned out to be decided by the politicians in Washington, not by the voters in the field.

"Now we have a whole new constituency voting in our elections, the black men of the South," Sam continued. "This is a whole new dynamic. The Republicans are taking the credit for giving blacks the vote, and they are going to milk that status for all that it is worth for a long time to come.

"But I am not so sure that that is going to succeed, Abram," Sam said. "Hayes not only made a deal with the Southern Democrats to remove Union troops from the South; he also made a deal with them to recognize their candidates for the governorships of Louisiana and South Carolina rather than his own Republican candidates.[687] That shifts all state power in the South to the whites, and the whites will do everything in their power to restore their priority over their society. It will be very bad for black people, and there is little that can be done to prevent it."

I was very saddened about Sam's prediction for the future. Then I felt compelled to ask him a question that had troubled me from the start of the campaign and had led to many frustrations on my part.

"Sam," I said, "given all this that you see coming, and all that you have gone through to date, I have always been … impressed, shall we say? … by your patience and equanimity with politics. Why is that?"

Sam leaned back in his chaise lounge, puffed his cigar a little, and then recited to me from his amazing memory a passage from Shakespeare's *Macbeth*:

> *Tomorrow, and tomorrow, and tomorrow,*
>
> *Creeps in this petty pace from day to day*
>
> *To the last syllable of recorded time,*

And all our yesterdays have lighted fools

The way to dusty death. Out, out, brief candle!

Life's but a walking shadow, a poor player

That struts and frets his hour upon the stage

And then is heard no more: it is a tale

Told by an idiot, full of sound and fury,

Signifying nothing.[688]

* * *

Amelia, Sam and I had dinner, then Sam Tilden headed back home on the railway to Manhattan. He is an impressive, learned man. I had to admit that I thought his prognostications were right.

And he *was* right.

Not long after the 1876 election, the aspirations of the Fourteenth and Fifteenth Amendments to the Constitution were brought to naught, almost as if there had been no Civil War. White governors and legislators in the Southern states restored the "Black Codes" that had been repealed during Reconstruction, which severely limited the privileges and rights of black people to vote, to hold office, to live anywhere they chose, to use public transportation, and to engage in commerce on an equal footing with whites. Congress and the White House did nothing at all about it.

In 1896, the U.S. Supreme Court decided *Plessy v. Ferguson*, which held that it did not violate the Fourteenth Amendment's "Due Process" and "Equal Protection" Clauses for trains traveling within the State of Louisiana to have "separate but equal" passenger cars for whites and non-whites.[689] John Marshall Harlan, the young lawyer who played an instrumental role in Hayes' successful nomination for the Republican Presidential ticket at their Convention, wrote the only dissent, stating:

> ...[I]n view of the constitution, in the eye of the law, there is in this country no superior, dominant, ruling class of citizens. There is no caste here. Our constitution is color-blind, and neither knows nor tolerates classes among citizens. In respect of civil rights, all citizens are equal before the law. The humblest is the peer of the most powerful. The law regards man as man, and takes no account of his surroundings or of his color when his civil rights as guaranteed by the supreme law of the land are involved. It is therefore to be regretted that this high tribunal, the final expositor of the fundamental law of the land, has reached the conclusion that it is competent for a state to regulate the enjoyment by citizens of their civil rights solely upon the basis of race.[690]

PART TEN – EPILOGUE

Chapter Forty-three – A Final Word About Election Theft

IN RUNNING FOR OFFICE, THE OBJECTIVE is to *win* an election, not to *steal* an election. It is so easy to steal an election. All one has to do is to dump out the ballot boxes and rip up the votes. And, like in Florida, there are plenty of Republican and Democratic hacks with keys to Clerk's Offices who are unscrupulous enough to do just that.

I suppose that one day, there will be machines that will tally votes automatically and be impossible to sabotage. In this golden age of electricity and mechanical genius, I don't suppose that day is far off.

Even so, there is always the human element to worry about. Machines cannot close that loophole. Even with the most accurate counting machines, of which there are many, human beings must be entrusted to communicate the count and transmit it to the appropriate authorities for the purpose of declaring the winner of an election. But human beings are fallible and capable of corruption and misinformation. The electoral system is powerless to stop them from thwarting it. This is why the Hayes-Tilden election faltered.

The Nation confronted this dilemma by choosing fifteen of the wisest men in our government to examine the election and determine which candidate won. But the system was broken; it *could not* report who won. It had been mishandled at its very core, and for that reason no one could trust *any* result that it could spit out. It could not be fixed. No recount could confidently establish which ballot was real, which was a lie, or which ballot was destroyed and didn't even exist anymore.

The Republican members of the Electoral Commission, mistrustful of the popular vote to begin with, reverted to a simple formula – to ignore the vote entirely and rely instead on the mere certifications of men of power. So they ignored all evidence of fraud at the polls and they relied on the word of corrupt governors, not the People. This happened in *America*, "the land of the free and the home of the brave."

In 1876, we were at least fortunate to have two heroic, outstanding gentlemen running for the office of Chief Magistrate of the land. Rutherford B. Hayes has been plagued by charges of illegitimacy in his single term of office. Catcalls of "His Fraudulency" abound in the press. But he has been, at the very least, a decent, honest President. He fulfilled, at least, the prediction of Alexander Hamilton in *Federalist No. 68* that "there will be a constant probability of seeing the station filled by characters pre-eminent for ability and virtue."

But what if probability fails us and we are not so fortunate one day? What if, one day, we are confronted by another Jefferson Davis, or another William Marcy Tweed, or another Napoleon Bonaparte, who has no scruples and is willing to subvert the machinery of government to get his way? Why, we could have a completely honest election, and such a man could destroy it by merely *claiming* that it was rigged.

Our Founding Fathers created a Republic, but they did not create a Democracy. According to our Constitution as originally ratified in 1789, only the House of Representatives was chosen by popular vote. The Senate was chosen by the state legislatures, the Supreme Court Justices were chosen by the President with the advice and consent of the Senate, and the President was chosen by a College of

Electors who were themselves chosen as determined by their state legislatures.

The notion of a "College of Electors" to choose a head of state is an ancient one. The Holy Roman Emperor was chosen by a college of "prince-electors" until the empire was dissolved in 1806. Members of the Prussian House of Representatives are chosen by a College of Electors who are voted into office by the German people. We are not the only nation that chooses its head of state in an indirect way.

Originally, very few American states chose electors by a popular vote. The rest were chosen by state legislators. So the vote for President was determined primarily according to how legislative districts in each state were gerrymandered, either toward Federalists, Whigs, or Democratic-Republicans, and the legislative majority in each state invariably chose electors for its own Presidential candidate.

In this year of 1881, all thirty-eight states hold popular elections for Presidential electors, but it took a long time for all of them to do so. The first popular vote for electors for President was not recorded until 1824. South Carolina did not choose electors by popular vote until 1868. Black men can now vote, but women cannot. Children, of course, are ineligible to vote.

This system is very complicated. A person's choice for President must go through many layers. A person must vote for a slate of electors; or, in some states, for two electors-at-large and an elector representing his congressional district. Then the electors so chosen must meet in their respective state capitals on the same day throughout the United States and vote for their state's choices for President and Vice-President. Then the states must certify the electoral votes and send them to the President of the Senate. Then, in the presence of a joint session of Congress, the electoral votes must be counted and the winners for President and Vice-President announced.

At any layer of this complicated structure, something can go wrong. And in 1876, it went wrong at *every* layer.

If the Founding Fathers' objective for this complicated system were to inject an element of randomness into the process of choosing a President, then that objective has been met. But American Presidents should *not* be chosen at random. The objective of the United States is that "We, the People" rule the land, and therefore the majority of all the People choose our President by electing a body of knowledgeable electors to make a wise choice for them. As Alexander Hamilton said in *The Federalist* No. 68:

> It was desirable that the sense of the people should operate in the choice of the person to whom so important a trust was to be confided. This end will be answered by committing the right of making it, not to any pre-established body, but to men chosen by the people for the special purpose, and at the particular conjuncture.

This constitutional framework, although complex, did not break down in 1876. The College of Electors met in every state capital on the same day and voted, just as it was constitutionally supposed to do. It was the *preliminary mechanics of popular election*, a process not dealt with at all in the Constitution, that broke down. Ballots were miscounted and torn up; voters were intimidated, assaulted, and in some instances, killed; whole precincts of votes were thrown away for no reason; and the agents charged with collecting, counting and certifying the votes acted corruptly and unscrupulously. These agents also appointed as electors men who were ineligible for their jobs.

These mechanisms, operating outside of Constitutional control, broke down in a handful of states; just enough, in a close election such as the one between Governor Hayes and Governor Tilden, to render the entire national endeavor suspect. Not only the four states that were examined by the Electoral Commission, but *every state in the Union* was tainted by these calamities. If these misfortunes can happen in four states, who is to say that they cannot happen in *every* state?

Popular elections are a popular battle, fraught with "sound and fury" as the Bard said. Untrustworthy ballot mechanics lead to suspicion, rumor, falsification, fraud, and controversy, if not outright war. One of our greatest duties as a democratic republic, therefore, is to establish simple, reliable voting processes in every election in every state that assure the widest possible majority that every vote is counted and every count is accurate. Politics is too brutish a game to play any other way.

* * *

I just received word that President Garfield has been shot at the Baltimore & Potomac Railroad Station in Washington. Politics is brutish indeed. I must go.

Abram Stevens Hewitt

Ringwood, New Jersey

July 2, 1881

An Afterword

Abram Stevens Hewitt was defeated in the Congressional election of 1878, but regained his seat for the Tenth District of New York in 1880. He served three more terms in the House of Representatives. In 1886, he ran for Mayor of New York City and won a two-year term of office. He fought Tammany Hall over patronage jobs, however, and Tammany saw to it that he was not renominated for a second term. Ever the "go-getter," Hewitt had a hand in the funding and construction of the future New York City subway system and supervised the construction and running of Cooper Union, his father-in-law's free university in Manhattan. In addition to the Trenton Iron Works, Hewitt formed many other successful businesses. He was a trustee on the boards of a museum and other educational institutions besides Cooper Union: Barnard College, Columbia University, Carnegie Institution of Science, and the Museum of Natural History. Abram Hewitt died in 1903 and is buried in Green-Wood Cemetery in Brooklyn, New York.[691]

Samuel Jones Tilden, the first candidate for President of the United States to win a majority of the popular vote (50.9 percent) but lose the election, left politics after his term of Governor of New York ended on December 31, 1876. He actively courted the Democratic Presidential nomination again in 1880, but declined to run just before the start of the nominating convention because of poor health. Friends courted him for a run for the Presidency again in 1884, but his failing health precluded it. He died in 1886 at the age of 72, and is buried at Cemetery of the Evergreens in New Lebanon, Columbia County, New York. His gravestone bears the words, "I Still Trust The People." He never married.[692]

Rutherford Birchard Hayes served a single term as President, as he had promised, to the consternation of his Republican political colleagues. He was vilified in the press throughout his Presidency with taunts of "His Fraudulency" and "Rutherfraud." He ended Reconstruction by withdrawing Federal troops from the remaining occupied states of Florida, Louisiana, and South Carolina. Their Reconstructionist Republican local governments soon fell into Democratic hands. Hayes faced a Democratic Congress and blocked efforts to weaken or repeal the civil rights acts that had been passed in the 1860s. He was unsuccessful, however, in getting Congress to fund the enforcement of those laws. Hayes made some progress in advancing the cause of civil service reform, but ran into difficulties with Republican supporters of the "spoils system," including Senator Roscoe Conkling. He stopped the Railroad Strike of 1877 by calling on Federal troops to suppress demonstrations and riots, but no Army soldiers died in the process. Unfortunately, however, many strikers and rioters died at the hands of state militias. Rutherford and First Lady Lucy Hayes served wine at their first White House reception, but never did again. After his presidency, Hayes engaged in causes to support education. He died at the age of 70 in 1893, four years after his wife's death. He was buried in Oakwood Cemetery in Fremont, Ohio, but his body was exhumed and reinterred at his home, which is now Spiegel Grove State Park in Fremont. The Park is also home to the Hayes Commemorative Library and Museum, this country's first Presidential library.[693]

* * *

The Electoral Count Act of 1887, Pub. L. 49-90, 24 Stat. 373, codified at 3 United States Code, Chapter 1, was passed by Congress and signed into law by President Grover Cleveland on

February 3, 1887.[694] Enacted over ten years after the Hayes-Tilden election dispute, this law resolved many legal questions that arose for the first time in that election.

The Act places the primary responsibility for resolving election disputes squarely on the states and minimizes the role of Congress in reconciling them. The uncertainty of Congress's role in 1877 was critical to its creation of the Electoral Commission – to create a respected body of experts to advise Congress on what it could and could not do.

The Act creates procedures and deadlines for the states to follow in resolving election disputes, certifying the results, and sending those results to Congress. This is known as the "safe harbor" provision, because if a state follows it and the Governor sends one and only one set of electoral votes to Congress, the Act mandates that this "final" determination "shall govern." In other words, the "safe harbor" provision sets a deadline for sending state electoral determinations to Congress; if the deadline is met, the state faces no uncertainty regarding its popular vote and electoral count. It puts that squarely within the jurisdiction of the states to resolve.

The Act rejects one of Samuel Tilden's key conclusions in *The Presidential Counts* "[t]hat the two Houses may go behind the returns."[695] The "safe harbor" provision effectively codifies the practice that the Electoral Commission developed of not going behind the certification signed by a State Governor of what that state's electoral count is. It is not Congress's role to re-count a state's popular vote on its own. The Act reduces Congress' role to resolving far fewer issues, such as if a governor sends two different slates of electors to the President of the Senate, or if there is ministerial error, or if an elector proves to be ineligible to serve. Broadly speaking, our *federal* union of states governs the mechanics of choosing our Head of State, not a *centralized* body in Washington.

In recognition of the Democrats' dissatisfaction about the cases that were sent to the Electoral Commission in 1877, the Act provides that the making or using of "any false writing or document" in the implementation of the "safe harbor" procedure is a felony punishable by five years' imprisonment. This provision makes it a federal felony to do what Judge Dreiggers and his two cohorts did when they certified a false return to the Florida State Canvassing Board. However, the Act does not specify what is to be done with the fraudulently-counted votes themselves. To this writer's knowledge, it has never happened since. Presumably, that question is also up to the states to resolve.

On December 29, 2022, Congress passed and President Joe Biden signed into law "The Electoral Count Reform and Presidential Transition Improvement Act of 2022," as a part of the Consolidated Appropriations Act of 2023. In the wake of the controversy perpetrated by ex-President Donald Trump over the 2020 election results between him and President Biden, this Act strengthens the Electoral Count Act of 1877.

In particular, the 2022 Act clarifies that the role of the Vice President as President of the Senate in counting electoral votes is "solely ministerial," with no power to "determine, accept, reject, or otherwise adjudicate or resolve disputes over the proper list of electors, the validity of electors, or the votes of electors."[696] This provision puts to rest the theory advanced by Hayes supporters during the 1876 election that the President of the Senate was empowered to resolve disputes arising during the Joint Session of Congress that counts the electoral vote.

Ex-President Trump tried hard to resurrect this theory after his loss in the 2020 election by pressuring Vice President Pence to throw out supposedly "disputed" electoral votes during the January 6, 2021 electoral count of the Joint Session of Congress. Vice President Pence wisely and courageously rejected Trump's attempt, heeding the warning of Samuel Tilden in *The Presidential Counts* that it is "fatal to the public peace" and that it "might enable one man to disfranchise a state, and even elect himself."[697]

* * *

This is a work of historical fiction. Much of the book is fact and much is fiction. Wherever I describe a historical fact, I footnote my source for it. If there is no footnote, I have invented the event. My descriptions of the proceedings of the Electoral Commission of 1877 are accurate but abbreviated. It was necessary to shorten the voluminous record and stentorian speechmaking that went on there. The roles of each character in the book are real, but the interactions among them are not.

As I did in my last book, *The Tenth Seat*, I made extensive use of *www.wikipedia.org*, which I consider to be a remarkable and accurate resource of information. Its authenticity is guaranteed by its practice of open editing, which assures that any misstatement of fact will eventually be corrected by an edit later. Wikipedia.org is a treasure trove of facts as well as a rich source of the many public-domain illustrations that highlight this story.

I am extremely grateful for two excellent resources: *Fraud of the Century – Rutherford B. Hayes, Samuel Tilden, and the Stolen Election of 1876*, by Roy Morris, Jr. (Simon & Schuster, 2003); and *Abram S. Hewitt With Some Account of Peter Cooper*, by Allan Nevins (Harper & Brothers, 1935). I consulted the Morris and

Nevins books for guidance concerning many of the facts that transpired during the controversy, particularly the life and role of Abram Hewitt. I am grateful to HarperCollins Publishers, successor to Harper & Brothers, for their permission to use Nevins' book. Both books are invaluable sources of information about this now obscure but pivotal event in American history.

The people described in this book faced a crisis that is sadly familiar to us today – doubts about the American electoral process of choosing a President of the United States. The men of the nineteenth century who faced this crisis reached across the political aisle, compromised with their opponents, and resolved the dispute imperfectly, but without bloodshed.

The Electoral Commission did not work as perfectly as everyone had hoped. It was still unable to overcome the overwhelming force of factionalism that our Founding Fathers warned against, that the Constitution was designed to repress, and to which human nature often gravitates to its detriment. Today, America's modern leaders have backslid in recognizing the danger of this constitutional impairment. Now we have deranged demagogues who rip insanely at the system in order to seize the prize and satisfy their egos.

Our method of voting is not the only mechanism that we could use to select our leaders. We could resort instead to *coups d'état*, assassinations, coronations, revolutions, wars, and genocides. Every one of these methods has been tried by humanity at one time or another, and none have proved to be better than our own. We should have more faith in our system, as fallible as it may sometimes appear to be.

It is the People, and only the People, who can suppress the nihilists who want to destroy this remarkable system. It is the duty of the People to advance men and women to high office who demonstrate the wisdom of our forebears that up to now has preserved our Constitution and way of life for over two centuries. The Hayes-Tilden electoral dispute is not just an obscure bit of history – it is a lesson for our country's future.

Edgewater, Maryland

Summer 2023

* * *

--

ENDNOTES

--

[1] Wikipedia.org, *John Milton (Florida politician)* (last viewed 1/5/2023).

[2] Wikipedia.org, *Abraham K. Allison* (last viewed 1/5/2023).

[3] Wikipedia.org, *William Marvin* (last viewed 1/5/2023).

[4] Wikipedia.org, *David S. Walker* (last viewed 1/5/2023).

[5] Wikipedia.org, *Harrison Reed (Politician)* (last viewed 1/5/2023).

[6] *Id.*

[7] Wikipedia.org, *History of Louisiana*, (last viewed 1/7/2023) (hereafter *History of Louisiana*).

[8] Wikipedia.org, *1872 United States Presidential election in Florida* (last viewed 1/7/2023).

[9] *Id.*

[10] *History of Louisiana.*

[11] *Id.*

[12] Wikipedia.org, *1868 United States Presidential election* (last viewed 1/7/2023).

[13] Wikipedia.org, *1872 United States Presidential election* (last viewed 1/7/2023).

[14] Wikipedia.org, *Rutherford B. Hayes* (last viewed 1/9/2023).

[15] Wikipedia.org, *Samuel J. Tilden* (last viewed 1/9/2023).

[16] Wikipedia.org, *Rutherford B. Hayes* (last viewed 1/9/2023).

[17] Grant, Ulysses S., *Personal Memoirs* 564 (Barnes & Noble ed. 2003) (1885).

[18] Wikipedia.org, *Abram Hewitt* (last viewed 1/20/2023).

[19] *Id.*

[20] Allan Nevins, *Abram S. Hewitt With Some Account of Peter Cooper* 31-32 (1935) (hereafter *Nevins*).

[21] *Id.*, at 32.

[22] *Id.*

[23] Wikipedia.org, *Abram Hewitt* (last viewed 1/20/ 2023).

[24] *Nevins*, at 32.

[25] *Id.*, at 33.

[26] *Id.*

[27] *Id.*

[28] *Id.*

[29] *Id.*, at 33-34.

[30] *Id.*, at 34.

[31] *Id.*, at 34-35.

[32] *Id.*, at 36.

[33] *Id.*, at 36-37.

[34] *Id.*, at 38.

[35] *Id.*

[36] *Id.*, at 39.

[37] *Id.*

[38] *Id.*

[39] *Id.*, at 40.

[40] *Id.*, at 42.

[41] *Id.*, at 42-43.

[42] *Id.*, at 44.

[43] *Id.*, at 49-55.

[44] *Id.*, at 56.

[45] *Id.*, at 57.

[46] *Id.*, at 57-58.

[47] *Id.*, at 58-59.

[48] *Id.*, at 59-60.

[49] *Id.*, at 64-71.

[50] *Id.*, at 71-72.

[51] *Id.*, at 72.

[52] *Id.*, at 82.

[53] *Id.*, at 142-47.

[54] *Id.*, at 267; Wikipedia.org, *Edward Cooper (mayor)* (last viewed 1/26/2023).

[55] McAllister, Ward, "The Only Four Hundred: Ward M'Allister Gives Out the Official List," *The New York Times* (Feb. 16, 1892); available at Wikipedia.org, *Edward Cooper (mayor)* (last viewed 1/26/2023).

[56] *Nevins*, at 147-49.

[57] *Id.*, at 153.

[58] *Id.*

[59] *Id.*

[60] *Id.*

[61] *Id.*, at 154.

[62] *Id.*, at 156.

[63] *Id.*, at 157.

[64] *Id.*, at 157-58.

[65] *Id.*, at 158-59.

[66] *Id.*, at 159-60.

[67] *Id.*, at 160.

[68] *Id.*, at 162-67.

[69] *Id.*, at 169-72.

[70] *Id.*, at 173.

[71] *Id.*, at 183.

[72] *Id.*, at 191.

[73] *Id.*, at 201.

[74] *Id.*, at 200.

[75] *Id.*, at 199-200.

[76] *Id.*, at 200.

[77] *Id.*, at 202.

[78] *Id.*

[79] *Id.*

[80] *Id.*

[81] *Id.*, at 203.

[82] *Id.*, at 203-04.

[83] *Id.*, at 204.

[84] *Id.*

[85] *Id.*, at 205.

[86] *Id.*

[87] *Id.*, at 206 n.1.

[88] *Id.*, at 205.

[89] *Id.*, at 205-06.

[90] *Id.*, at 206.

[91] *Id.*, at 228.

[92] *Id.*, at 230.

[93] *Id.*, at Fig. 36.

[94] *Id.*, at 294.

[95] *Id.*, at 291.

[96] *Id.*, at 297-98.

[97] U.S. CONST., Amend. XIV, § 2 (1868).

[98] *Nevins*, at Fig. 33.

[99] *Id.*, at 308.

[100] *Id.*, at 309.

[101] Roy Morris, Jr., *Fraud of the Century* 122 (2003) (hereafter *Morris*).

[102] Wikipedia.org, *Fifth Avenue Hotel* (last viewed 2/7/2023).

[103] *Morris*, at 47.

[104] Wikipedia.org, *Liberal Republican Party (United States)* (last viewed 2/7/2023).

[105] *Id.*

[106] *Id.*

[107] *Morris*, at 49.

[108] *Id.*, at 47.

[109] Wikipedia.org, *Ku Klux Klan* (last viewed 2/13/2023).

[110] Wikipedia.org, *Sons of Malta* (last viewed 2/13/2023).

[111] Wikipedia.org, *Ku Klux Klan* (last viewed 2/13/2023).

[112] *Id.*

[113] Wikipedia.org, *Ku Klux Klan*, quoting from Elaine Frantz Parsons. "Midnight Rangers: Costume and Performance in the Reconstruction-Era Ku Klux Klan," *The Journal of American History* 92, 816 (2005), available at Wikipedia.org, *Ku_Klux_Klan* (last viewed 2/13/2023).

[114] *Morris*, at 126.

[115] *Id.*, at 128.

[116] *Id.*

[117] *Id.*, at 129.

[118] *Id.*

[119] *Id.*.

[120] *Id.*, at 130.

[121] *Id.*.

[122] *Id.*, at 131.

[123] *Id.*

[124] Wikipedia.org, *Ku Klux Klan* (last viewed 2/13/2023).

[125] *Political Reformers*, N.Y. Times, May 16, 1876, at 1 (hereafter *5th Ave. Conf.*).

[126] *5th Ave. Conf.*, at 1.

[127] *Id.*

[128] *Id.*

[129] *Id.*

[130] *Id.*

[131] *Id.*

[132] *Morris*, at 48.

[133] *Id.*

[134] *Id.*, at 50.

[135] *5th Ave. Conf.*, at 4.

[136] *Id.*

[137] Wikipedia.org, *1876 United States Presidential Election* (last viewed 2/18/2023).

[138] Wikipedia.org, *1876 Republican National Convention* (last viewed 2/18/2023)

(hereafter *1876 Republican Convention*).

[139] *Morris*, at 51.

[140] *Nevins*, at 299.

[141] *Id.*, at 300.

[142] *Id.*

[143] *Id.*, at 300-01.

[144] *Id.*, at 302.

[145] *1876 Republican Convention.*

[146] *Morris*, at 69.

[147] *1876 Republican Convention.*

[148] *Morris*, at 72.

[149] *Id.*, at 58.

[150] *Id.*, at 59-61.

[151] *Id.*, at 61.

[152] Wikipedia.org, *Thaddeus Stevens* (last viewed 2/19/2023).

[153] *Morris*, at 62.

[154] *Id.*, at 63.

[155] *Id.*

[156] *Id.*, at 64.

[157] *Id.*, at 64-65.

[158] *Id.*, at 66.

[159] *Id.*, at 67.

[160] *Id.*, at 72.

[161] *Id.*, at 71-72.

[162] *Id.*, at 70-71.

[163] *1876 Republican Convention.*

[164] *Morris*, at 78.

[165] *Id.*, at 79.

[166] *Id.*

[167] *Id.*, at 80.

[168] *Id.*

[169] *Id.*

[170] *Id.*

[171] *New York Central Park Total Snowfall, By Season (1869-70 thru 2020-21 Seasons)*, available at https://www.climatestations.com/wp-content/uploads/2021/06/nysnow.gif (last viewed 2/13/2023).

[172] Wikipedia.org, *1876 Democratic National Convention* (last viewed 2/13/2023)

(hereafter *1876 Democratic Convention*).

[173] *1876 Republican Convention.*

[174] *1876 Democratic Convention.*

[175] *Id.*

[176] *Id.*

[177] *Id.*

[178] *Morris*, at 115.

[179] *1876 Democratic Convention.*

[180] *Id.*

[181] *Id.*

[182] *Id.*

[183] *Nevins*, at 309.

[184] *Id.*

[185] *Id.*, at 301-02.

[186] *Id.*

[187] *Id.*, at 309.

[188] *Id.*

[189] *Morris*, at 132.

[190] *Nevins*, at 313.

[191] *Morris*, at 132.

[192] *Id.*, at 133.

[193] *Id.*, at 134.

[194] *Nevins*, at 313.

[195] *Morris*, at 134.

[196] *Id.*

[197] *Id.*

[198] *Id.*, at 134-35.

[199] *Id.*, at 135.

[200] *Id.*

[201] *Id.*

[202] *Nevins*, at 309.

[203] *Id.*

[204] *Id.*, at 310.

[205] *Id.*, at 311.

[206] *Id.*, at 312.

[207] *Id.*

[208] *Morris*, at 136.

[209] "Mr. Tilden's False Oath," *New York Times*, August 26, 1876, at 1.

[210] *Id.*, at 5.

[211] *Morris*, at 138.

[212] *Id.*

[213] *Id.*, at 139.

[214] *Id.*

[215] *Nevins,* at 318.

[216] *Id.*

[217] *Id.,* at 315.

[218] *Id.*

[219] *Id.*

[220] *Id.,* at 313.

[221] *New York Times,* September 2, 1876, at 5.

[222] *Morris,* at 140.

[223] *Id.*

[224] *Morris,* at 141.

[225] *Id.*

[226] *Id.,* at 147.

[227] *Id.,* at 142.

[228] *Id.*

[229] *Id.*

[230] *Id.*

[231] *Nevins*, at 315.

[232] *Id.*, at 313.

[233] *Morris*, at 147.

[234] *Id.*, at 157.

[235] *Id.*, at 162.

[236] *Id.*

[237] *Nevins*, at 319.

[238] *Id.*

[239] *Id.*

[240] Wikipedia.org, *1896 United States Presidential Election* (last viewed 3/7/2023).

[241] *Id.*

[242] *Id.*

[243] *Id.*

[244] *Id.*

[245] *Nevins*, at 319.

[246] *Morris*, at 166.

[247] *Nevins*, at 319.

[248] Wikipedia.org, *Baker County, Florida* (last viewed 3/5/2023).

[249] *Id.*

[250] *Id.*

[251] George G. Gorham, *Some Account of the Work of Stephen J. Field, As a Legislator, State Judge, and Justice of the Supreme Court of the United States*, at 415 (1895) (hereafter *Field Account*).

[252] Wikipedia.org, *MacClenny, Florida* (last viewed 3/5/2023).

[253] *Field Account*, at 415-16.

[254] *Field Account*, at 416. The name of the sheriff is purely fictional. There is no available record of the sheriff's real name.

[255] *Id.*

[256] *Id.*

[257] *Id.*

[258] U.S. Gov't Printing Off., *Proceedings of the Electoral Commission appointed under the act of Congress approved January 29, 1877, entitled "An act to provide for and regulate the counting of votes for President and Vice-President, and the decisions of questions arising thereon, for the term commencing March 4, A. D. 1877"* 5 and 288-90 (1877) (hereafter *Proceedings*); *Field Account*, at 416-17.

[259] *Field Account*, at 416-17.

[260] *Proceedings*, at 290. One account has Tilden's winning margin as 91 votes. *See Morris*, at 175.

[261] *Proceedings*, at 287.

[262] *Id.*, at 288.

[263] *Field Account*, at 417.

[264] *Id.*

[265] *Proceedings*, at 288.

[266] *Field Account*, at 430.

[267] *Morris*, at 176.

[268] *Field Account*, at 430.

[269] *Id.*

[270] *Id.*, at 431.

[271] *Id.*, at 432.

[272] U.S. CONST. Art. II, Section 1, Cl. 2.

[273] *Field Account*, at 439.

[274] Wikipedia.org, *1876 United States Presidential Election in South Carolina* (last viewed 3/12/2023).

[275] Michael F. Holt, *By One Vote* 167, 255 (2008);

Wikipedia.org, *1876 United States Presidential Election* (last viewed 3/12/2023).

[276] *Field Account*, at 439.

[277] *Morris*, at 181.

[278] Nicholas Lemann, *Redemption: The Last Battle of the Civil War* 174 (2007); Wikipedia.org, *1876 United States Presidential Election* (last viewed 3/12/2023).

[279] *Morris*, at 180.

[280] *Id.*, at 181.

[281] *Id.*, at 181-82.

[282] U.S. CONST. Art. II, Section 1, Cl. 2.

[283] Wikipedia.org, *1876 United States Presidential Election* (last viewed 3/11/2023).

[284] *Field Account*, at 432.

[285] Wikipedia.org, *1876 United States Presidential Election* (last viewed 3/11/2023).

[286] *Notes for John Thomas Pickett*, available at https://www-personal.umich.edu/~bobwolfe/gen/pn/p16381.htm (last viewed 3/12/2023).

[287] *Morris*, at 192.

[288] Wikipedia.org, *1876 United States Presidential Election* (last viewed 3/13/2023).

[289] Wikipedia.org, *Electoral Commission (United States)* (last viewed 3/13/2023).

[290] *Morris*, at 197-98.

[291] Wikipedia.org, *Thomas W. Ferry* (last viewed 3/13/2023).

[292] Wikipedia.org, *Old Ebbitt Grill* (last viewed October 11, 2021).

[293] *Morris*, at 201.

[294] *Nevins*, at 345.

[295] *Morris*, at 201; *Nevins*, at 342.

[296] *Morris*, at 201; *Nevins*, at 342.

[297] *Nevins*, at 330.

[298] *Id.*, at 332.

[299] *Id.*, at 335.

[300] Wikipedia.org, *Electoral Commission (United States)* (last viewed on 3/14/2023).

[301] *Nevins*, at 343.

[302] *Id.*, at 343-44.

[303] Electoral Commission Act, 19 Stat. 227 (1877).

[304] Wikipedia.org, *Electoral Commission* (last viewed on 3/14/2023).

[305] *Id.*

[306] *Id.*

[307] *Nevins*, at 365.

[308] *Id.*

[309] *Id.*, at 365-66.

[310] U.S. CONST., Amend. XII (1804).

[311] *Nevins*, at 368.

[312] *Id.*

[313] *Id.*

[314] *Morris*, at 220; Samuel J. Tilden, *The Presidential Counts: A Complete Official Record of the Proceedings of Congress at the Counting of the Electoral Votes in all the Elections of President and Vice-President of the United States, together with all Congressional Debates incident thereto or to Proposed Legislation upon that Subject; with an Analytical Introduction* (D. Appleton & Co., 1877), as reprinted in *The Writings and Speeches of Samuel J. Tilden* 386, 392 (John Bigelow, ed. 1885) (hereafter *The Presidential Counts*).

[315] *Proceedings*, at 18.

[316] Paul L. Haworth, *The Hayes-Tilden Election* 223 (1906) (hereafter "*Haworth*").

[317] *Haworth*, at 223-24.

[318] *Nevins*, at 369.

[319] *Proceedings*, at 2-4.

[320] *Nevins*, at 369.

[321] Supreme Court of the United States, *About the Court*, *Building History*, available at https://www.supremecourt.gov (last viewed June 24, 2023).

[322] *Proceedings*, at 4.

[323] *Id.*

[324] *Id.*

[325] *Haworth*, at 226.

[326] *Proceedings*, at 4.

[327] *Id.*, at 4-5.

[328] *Id.*, at 4-6.

[329] *Id.*.

[330] *Id.*

[331] *Id.*, at 6.

[332] *Id.* (emphasis added).

[333] *Id.*, at 7.

[334] *Id.*

[335] *Id.*, at 7 (emphasis added).

[336] *Id.* (emphasis added).

[337] *Id.*, at 8.

[338] *Id.*

[339] *Id.*, at 9 (internal quotation marks omitted).

[340] *Id.* (emphasis added).

[341] *Id.* (emphasis added).

[342] *Id.*, at 10.

[343] *Id.*, at 10-11.

[344] *Id.*, at 11.

[345] *Id.*

[346] *Id.*

[347] *Id.*, at 13.

[348] *Id.*

[349] *Id.*

[350] *Id.*, at 14.

[351] *Id.*

[352] *Id.*, at 15.

[353] *Id.*

[354] *Id.*, at 16.

[355] *Id.*

[356] *Id.*

[357] *Id.*, at 17.

[358] *Id.*, at 16-17.

[359] Wikipedia.org, *Alva Belmont* (last viewed on 4/21/2023).

[360] Wikipedia.org, *Joseph P. Bradley* (last viewed on 4/21/2023).

[361] *Slaughter-House Cases*, 83 U.S. 36, 122 (1872) (Bradley, J., dissenting).

[362] *Morris*, at 224.

[363] *Slaughter-House Cases*, 83 U.S. 36, 122 (1872) (Bradley, J., dissenting).

[364] *Nevins*, at 369.

[365] *Proceedings*, at 17.

[366] *Id.*, at 18.

[367] *Id.*

[368] *Id.*

[369] *Id.*

[370] *Id.*

[371] *Id.*

[372] *Id.*

[373] *Id.*

[374] *Id.*

[375] *Id.*

[376] *Id.*

[377] *Id.*, at 19.

[378] *Id.*

[379] *Id.*

[380] *Id.*

[381] *Id.*

[382] *Id.*

[383] *Id.*

[384] *Id.*

[385] *Id.*, at 20.

[386] *Id.*

[387] *Id.*

[388] *Id.*

[389] *Id.*, at 21.

[390] *Id.*

[391] *Id.*

[392] *Id.*, at 21-29.

[393] *Morris*, at 223-24.

[394] *Slaughter-house Cases*, 83 U.S. 36, 108 (1872) (Field, J., dissenting).

[395] *The Presidential Counts*, at 386-452.

[396] *Morris*, at 203.

[397] *The Presidential Counts*, at 450.

[398] *Morris*, at 204.

[399] *Id.*, at 205.

[400] *Id.*

[401] *Id.*, at 206.

[402] *Id.*

[403] *Id.*

[404] *Id.*, at 207.

[405] *Id.*, at 207-08.

[406] *Proceedings*, at 29.

[407] *Id.*

[408] *Id.*

[409] *Id.*, at 30.

[410] *Id.*

[411] *Id.*

[412] *Id.*

[413] *Id.*

[414] *Id.*

[415] *Id.*

[416] *Id.*, at 31.

[417] *Id.*

[418] *Id.*

[419] *Id.*

[420] *Id.*, at 32.

[421] *Id.*, at 33.

[422] *Id.*

[423] *Id.*, at 34.

[424] *Id.*

[425] *Id.*

[426] *Id.*

[427] *Id.*, at 35 (emphasis added).

[428] *Id.*, at 35.

[429] *Id.*

[430] *Id.*, at 37.

[431] *Id.*

[432] *Id.*

[433] *Id.*

[434] *Id.*

[435] *Id.*

[436] *Id.*

[437] *Id.*

[438] *Id.*, at 38.

[439] *Id.*

[440] *Id.*

[441] *Id.*

[442] *Id.*

[443] *Id.*

[444] *Id.*

[445] *Id.*, at 38-39.

[446] *Id.*, at 39.

[447] *Id.*, at 40.

[448] *Id.*, at 40.

[449] *Id.*, at 40.

[450] *Id.*, at 40.

[451] *Id.*, at 40.

[452] *Id.*, at 40.

[453] *Id.*, at 41.

[454] *Id.*, at 41.

[455] *Id.*, at 42.

[456] *Id.*, at 42.

[457] *Id.*, at 43.

[458] *Id.*, at 43.

[459] *Id.*, at 43-44.

[460] *Id.*, at 44.

[461] *Id.*, at 45.

[462] *Id.*, at 45.

[463] *Id.*, at 45.

[464] *Id.*, at 45.

[465] *Id.*, at 46.

[466] *Id.*, at 46.

[467] *Id.*, at 46.

[468] *Id.*, at 46 (internal quotes omitted; italics added).

[469] *Id.*, at 46-47.

[470] *Id.*, at 47.

[471] *Id.*, at 47.

[472] *Id.*, at 47 (italics in original).

[473] *Id.*, at 47.

[474] *Id.*, at 47.

[475] *Id.*, at 47 (italics added).

[476] *Id.*, at 48.

[477] *Id.*, at 49.

[478] *Id.*, at 49.

[479] *Id.*, at 49.

[480] *Id.*, at 50.

[481] *Id.*, at 50.

[482] *Id.*, at 50.

[483] *Id.*, at 50-51.

[484] *Id.*, at 51.

[485] *Id.*, at 51.

[486] *Id.*, at 52.

[487] *Id.*, at 52.

[488] *Id.*, at 52.

[489] *Id.*, at 52.

[490] *Id.*, at 52.

[491] *Id.*, at 52.

[492] *Id.*, at 52-53.

[493] *Id.*, at 53.

[494] *Id.*, at 53.

[495] *Id.*, at 53.

[496] *Id.*, at 53.

[497] *Id.*, at 53.

[498] *Id.*, at 53.

[499] *Id.*, at 53.

[500] *Id.*, at 53.

[501] *Id.*, at 53.

[502] *Id.*, at 53.

[503] *Id.*, at 53.

[504] *Id.*, at 53.

[505] *Id.*, at 53.

[506] *Id.*, at 53.

[507] *Id.*, at 53.

[508] *Id.*, at 53.

[509] *Id.*, at 53-54.

[510] *Id.*, at 54.

[511] *Id.*, at 54.

[512] *Id.*, at 54.

[513] *Id.*, at 55.

[514] Wikipedia.org, *William M. Evarts* (last viewed May 12, 2023).

[515] Wikipedia.org, *Samuel Shellabarger (Ohio politician)* (last viewed May 12, 2023).

[516] *Nevins*, at 343.

[517] Wikipedia.org, *George Hoadly* (last viewed May 12, 2023).

[518] *"Judge Ashbel Green"* https://www.findagrave.com/memorial/197801693 (last viewed May 12, 2023).

[519] *Proceedings*, at 56.

[520] *Id.*

[521] *Id.*

[522] *Id.*

[523] *Id.*, at 246.

[524] *Id.*

[525] *Id.*, at 247.

[526] *Id.*

[527] *Id.*

[528] *Id.*, at 249.

[529] *Id.*, at 259-61.

[530] *Id.*, at 259-60.

[531] *Id.*, at 260.

[532] *Id.*

[533] *Id.*

[534] *Id.*

[535] *Id.*

[536] *Id.*

[537] *Id.*

[538] *Id.*, at 261.

[539] *Id.*

[540] *Id.*

[541] *Id.*

[542] *Id.*, at 56-57.

[543] *Morris*, at 225.

[544] *Id.*

[545] *Morris*, at 226.

[546] Wikipedia.org, *William Pitt Kellogg* (last viewed on May 16, 2023).

[547] *Id.*

[548] *Id.*

[549] *Field Account*, at 430.

[550] *Id.*, at 430-31.

[551] *Id.*, at 431.

[552] *Id.*, at 431-32.

[553] *Morris*, at 225-26.

[554] *Proceedings*, at 57.

[555] *Id.*, at 57-58.

[556] *Id.*, at 58.

[557] *Id.*

[558] *Id.*

[559] *Id.*, at 59-60.

[560] *Id.*, at 60.

[561] *Id.*

[562] *Id.*

[563] *Id.*

[564] *Id.*, at 62-63.

[565] *Id.*, at 63.

[566] *Id.*

[567] *Id.*

[568] *Id.*, at 63-64.

[569] *Id.*, at 64-65.

[570] *Id.*, at 65.

[571] *Id.*

[572] *Id.*

[573] *Id.*

[574] *Id.*

[575] *Id.*

[576] *Id.*, at 66.

[577] *Id.*

[578] *Id.*

[579] *Id.*, at 67.

[580] *Id.*

[581] *Id.*, at 68.

[582] *Id.*

[583] *Id.*

[584] *Id.*, at 68-69.

[585] *Id.*, at 69.

[586] *Id.*, at 70-71.

[587] *Id.*, at 71.

[588] *Id.*, at 71-117.

[589] *Id.*, at 72-80.

[590] *Id.*, at 72.

[591] *Id.*, at 74-77.

[592] *Id.*, at 77-80.

[593] *Id.*, at 81.

[594] *Id.*

[595] *Id.*

[596] *Id.*, at 81-84.

[597] *Id.*, at 93.

[598] *Id.*, at 95.

[599] *Id.*, at 97.

[600] *Id.*

[601] *Id.*

[602] *Id.*

[603] *Id.*, at 99.

[604] *Id.*, at 101.

[605] *Id.*, at 102.

[606] *Id.*, at 103.

[607] *Id.*

[608] *Id.*, at 105-07.

[609] *Id.*, at 108.

[610] *Id.*, at 110.

[611] *Id.*

[612] *Id.*

[613] *Id.*

[614] *Id.*, at 111.

[615] *Id.*

[616] *Id.*

[617] *Id.*

[618] *Id.*

[619] *Id.*

[620] *Id.*, at 113.

[621] *Id.*, at 117.

[622] Wikipedia.org, *Leland Stanford* (last viewed August 2, 2021).

[623] *Proceedings*, at 117.

[624] *Schenck v. Peay*, 1 Woolw. 175, 21 F.Cas. 667, 2 Am. Law T. Rep. U.S. Cts. 111 (C.C.E.D. Ark. 1868) (hereafter *Schenck*).

[625] *Schenck*, 21 F.Cas. at 669.

[626] *Id.* at 670.

[627] *Id.* at 670.

[628] *Id.* at 670-71 (emphasis added).

[629] *Proceedings*, at 234.

[630] *Id.*, at 234.

[631] *Id.*, at 228.

[632] *Id.*, at 215.

[633] *Id.*, at 117.

[634] *Id.*

[635] *Id.*

[636] *Id.*

[637] *Id.*

[638] *Id.*

[639] *Id.*

[640] *Id.*

[641] *Id.*

[642] *Id.*

[643] *Id.*

[644] *Id.*

[645] *Id.*

[646] *Id.*

[647] *Id.*

[648] *Id.*

[649] *Id.*

[650] *Id.*, at 118.

[651] *Id.*

[652] *Id.*

[653] *Id.*

[654] *Id.*

[655] *Id.*

[656] *Id.*

[657] *Id.*

[658] *Id.*

[659] *Id.*

[660] *Morris*, at 228.

[661] *Id.*, at 227.

[662] *Id.*, at 228.

[663] *Id.*, at 229.

[664] *Proceedings*, at 178-79.

[665] *Morris*, at 231-32.

[666] *Id.*, at 233.

[667] *Proceedings*, at 179.

[668] *Morris*, at 232.

[669] *Id.*

[670] *Id.*

[671] *Id.*, at 232-33.

[672] *Id.*, at 233.

[673] *Id.*

[674] Wikipedia.org, *James Wormley* (last viewed June 3, 2023).

[675] *Morris*, at 233.

[676] *Id.*, at 233-34.

[677] *Proceedings*, at 192.

[678] *Morris*, at 234.

[679] *Proceedings*, at 193.

[680] *Morris*, at 237.

[681] *Id.*, at 238.

[682] *Id.*

[683] *Nevins*, at 148.

[684] *Morris*, at 243.

[685] *Id.*, at 243, 253.

[686] *Id.*, at 242.

[687] *Id.*, at 253.

[688] William Shakespeare, *Macbeth*, Act V, Scene 5.

[689] *Plessy v. Ferguson*, 163 U.S. 537 (1896).

[690] *Plessy v. Ferguson*, 163 U.S. at 559 (Harlan, J., dissenting).

[691] Wikipedia.org, *Abram Hewitt* (last viewed June 13, 2023).

[692] Wikipedia.org, *Samuel J. Tilden* (last viewed June 13, 2023).

[693] Wikipedia.org, *Rutherford B. Hayes* (last viewed June 13, 2023).

[694] Wikipedia.org, *Electoral* Count *Act* (last viewed June 23, 2023).

[695] *The Presidential Counts*, at 450.

[696] Wikipedia.org, *Electoral Count Reform*

and Presidential Transition Improvement Act of 2022 (last viewed June 23, 2023).

[697] *The Presidential Counts*, at 450.

Did you love *To The Victor*? Then you should read *The Tenth Seat: A Novel*[1] by Steven Glazer!

THE TENTH SEAT

A Novel

By STEVEN A. GLAZER [2]

Much has been said in political news lately about "packing" the U.S. Supreme Court with additional Justices besides the present nine. This is nothing new in the history of the Court. Congress has changed the number to as few as six and as many as ten. This novel is based on the life story of Stephen Johnson Field, the only tenth Justice to have ever served on the Supreme Court, who served from his 1863 appointment by President Abraham Lincoln until 1897.

Field is the second longest-serving Justice on the Court (William O. Douglas served the longest). He left his legal practice in New York City for the California Gold Rush of 1849 and practiced law in California during the wild early days of the Golden

---

1. https://books2read.com/u/49LBW8

2. https://books2read.com/u/49LBW8

State. He became its Chief Justice only ten years after starting his law practice there, and was elevated to the U.S. Supreme Court by President Abraham Lincoln only eight years later.

===

Winner of Honorable Mention for Fiction at the Hollywood Book Festival, 2023

"Having been a judge himself, Glazer, in his first novel, explores the life of Field, his judicial mindset, and how some of the decisions in which he took part shaped the course of American history."

-- Hon. John Dring, senior counsel in energy regulation at Vinson & Elkins LLP and former Administrative Law Judge, writing in **Washington Lawyer Magazine**

"Fist-fights, brandished pistols, and a fatal second duel all enliven the Field saga. In a nice counterpoint to the novel, those events are completely factual. Glazer, obviously a lawyer and almost as obviously a judge, unearths historical facts and animates them through fictitious dialogue that draws the reader in."

--Robert M. Snider, administrative hearing officer in Southern California and retired California Deputy Attorney General, writing in **Los Angeles Lawyer Magazine**

About the Author

Steven A. Glazer is a retired lawyer and Administrative Law Judge who practiced in Washington, D.C. for 46 years. He now lives outside of Annapolis and writes historical fiction novels.